Charles 1

SHADOWS OF FIRE

Memoirs of a Life in Transition

Shadows of Fire
Memoirs of a Life in Transition
All Rights Reserved
Copyright © 2021

This is a work of fiction. Names, characters, businesses, places, events, and incidents are either the product of the author's imagination or used in a fictitious manner. Any resemblance to actual persons, living or dead, or actual events is purely coincidental.

The opinions expressed in this manuscript are solely the opinions of the author and do not represent the opinions or thoughts of the publisher. The author has represented and warranted full ownership and/or legal right to publish all material in this book.

This book may not be reproduced, transmitted, or stored in whole or in part by any means, including graphic, electronic, or mechanical without the express written consent of the publisher except in the case of brief quotations embodied in critical articles and reviews.

ISBN: 978-1-7369000-1-7

Cover Photo © 2021 Charles Firecat Burnell. All rights reserved – used with permission.

Dedication

This is dedicated to my children, for seeing value in me when I could not see it in myself. You truly saved my life in more ways than perhaps you will ever understand. Thank you for giving me light when I could not otherwise see the way. You both are truly a blessing.

A special dedication also to all those who struggle with the trauma of abusive relationships. Please remember that you are more valuable than you feel. You deserve dignity. You are worthy of respect. You are worth loving and deserve to be happy. Never forget that you are not alone, and when you are ready for help, there is a wide world of support and opportunity awaiting you.

Prologue

When Cat brought her new husband to meet Katie, she was really more interested in visiting with her old friend. Jim was exhausted and Katie was full of energy. So, Jim rested while Katie and Cat went out for coffee. The two young women were gushing with stories and an overwhelming desire to share them with one another. Jim didn't seem to mind an opportunity to rest and wasn't terribly interested in listening to the young women catch up.

Jim laid down on the couch. His long legs propped up at south end of the couch made everything in the room look just a little bit too small. Pulling a lap blanket over his head, he closed his eyes. As he nodded off to sleep, he could hear his wife and her best friend talking. As they moved down the hall, their voices became more faint and eventually quiet overcame him.

"You're going to love this cafe!" Katie exclaimed, as she turned the key to lock the apartment door. She turned to face Cat. "We don't even have to drive! It's a beautiful day, and a short walk." She paused to take Cat by the arm. "And we have so much to catch up on!"

Cat smiled wide, as she let Katie lead her down the hall of the apartment building. "Yes! We do! So much has happened! And I am married now! All grown up and married to a man in the Army! Who would have guessed it?" Cat kept up with Katie's quick pace and soon they were on the sidewalk in the sunshine.

Once the two old friends were alone with each other, Katie stopped and turned to look Cat. Without letting go of her friend's arm, Katie asked, "Are you pregnant? Is that why you got married?"

Cat pulled her arms loose to smooth the fabric of her blouse down. She insisted that wasn't the case while showcasing her trim figure. Katie seemed relieved. "Well, you do look good. But you're hiding under those baggy clothes! Maybe we need to go clothes shopping?"

"Sorry honey. We don't have time for that today." Cat responded, as she continued to follow Katie up the sunny block. "I've only really got time for a coffee. I wish I had more."

"I know. I know. A woman can wish though, can't she?" Katie stopped walking and reached into her purse. She pulled out a pack of ultralights and a lighter. "I only really have a little while too."

Katie lit her cigarette and pointed to the small courtyard before them. Cobblestone anchored wrought iron tables and chairs. The tabletops covered with marble glistened through the trellis filtered sunlight. They made their way to a secluded table after placing their orders at the counter.

The two gossiped over coffee about what had happened in their lives since they had last spent time together regularly. *It's been almost two years! How could so much have happened? I can't let this much time pass between us again!* Their cups sat empty while the two held hands intermittently as they talked. After a couple hours, Katie got nervous about all the things she was expected to have accomplished by the time her husband returned from work. Returning to the apartment, Cat roused her new husband from slumber. As they were leaving the women hugged one more time. Warning Jim to "take good care of her." She wished them safe travels and hurried them out the door.

Next, they headed to Dad's house. Cat was very nervous. *I was in pretty bad shape the last time Dad saw me!* She had been traveling, going to demonstrations and concerts, and not been taking good care of her health. Now she was showing up married to a man in the Army! *I wonder what he is going to say! Maybe now he will stop worrying about me.* She wanted Dad to see that she was becoming a 'responsible adult.' She still wasn't sure what a responsible adult was supposed to look like.

Dad was very surprised to get a call from her. Since they had to leave Katie's place before her husband returned home from work, they had a few hours to kill before Dad would be home. Jim spent the rest of the afternoon driving around Contra Costa County. Cat showed Jim where she had gone to school. She showed him her favorite place on the bike trail. She shared with him, places that held memories for her, and the memories that accompanied them. In the evening, landing at the house she grew up in, they joined Dad for dinner.

Dad was a surprise. He briefly inquired whether there was a baby on the way but didn't press it further when Cat assured him that there was not. Once his initial fears were put to rest, Dad was welcoming and showed his approval. She felt good about Dad's acceptance of her new husband. He had been in the Army as well and had respect for the self-discipline that being in the service afforded. When he once more, expressed concern about her being pregnant. She assured him that there was no baby on the way and he gave them his blessing. He also presented her with a couple of savings bonds that her grandfather's sister had left Cat when she passed away.

That night Cat shared the same bed with Jim that she had shared with Annie the previous Summer. Lying in bed next to her new husband, she wondered if she had made the right decision. *Am I really going to be happy being married to a man?* She was ashamed of herself for asking these questions. *It shouldn't matter. It's time to grow up.*

The next day, Jim and Cat headed to Berkeley. Again, they toured places that held memories for her. She showed him the view at Inspiration Point. She took him to Telegraph Avenue. Visiting the Cafe' Med, they got coffee and hung out for a while. She hoped to run into people that she knew from her past. She wanted to visit as many people that she missed as she could. She had no idea when she would be able to make it out to California again, and this felt more like home than Oklahoma did. Getting anxious about making it back to Ft. Sill on time, Jim insisted that they would have to head back to Oklahoma soon.

Jim decided they would take the southern route back and headed out towards Stockton. Taking turns driving, they drove almost non-stop heading back to Lawton. When they arrived back, they crashed on Rick and Mary's couch. After getting a good night's sleep, they returned to Mama's house. By this time, she had gotten a call from Dad, and was well aware of the new marriage.

Upon arrival, the couple got a brief congratulation, and a full ration of shit from Mama for "denying her the opportunity of seeing her daughter get married". Mama and Will insisted that they have a "proper gypsy wedding". So, the newlyweds agreed on a second ceremony in a couple of months.

Despite the fact that Mama had not married Will, his mother had treated Cat like one of her grandchildren as soon as she met her. Cat didn't argue with her. She tried to be respectful of elders. Although there were plenty of things about the old woman that she disagreed with, she chose not to voice her opinion. She firmly rejected the concept of being related to Will and was glad that Mama had not actually married him. Still, Cat made a point to visit the 'grandmother' regularly.

Will's mother smoked two packs of cigarettes a day. She was pleased that Cat had married an Army man. "Now you can go to the post commissary to buy my cigarettes by the carton tax-free!" Sitting in a cloud of smoke, with the television as a backdrop, Cat would sit and listen to the old woman explain about politics and current events. Listening and nodding her head, Cat's empty responses led the old woman to believe that she agreed with her.

The more she visited the shorter Cat made her visits. The old woman thought Central America was Kansas and truly believed the reason why there was a hole in the ozone layer was because "those damn commies keep shooting missiles up in the air." There was only so much Cat could handle.

Author's Note

My teachers always complained that I was a daydreamer. Lost in thought, I seemed to have a difficult time staying grounded in the moment, in the present. While it may have posed a challenge to the educators who were trying to help homogenize me, it has proven to be a useful tool in processing the challenges and stressors that I face as an adult. Writing has played an integral part in this processing. Creative writing has enabled me to tap into memories that were so well buried, hidden deep within me, and pull them to the surface. While I have been daydreaming for decades of writing stories based on my adventures, I never imagined how much I would learn and grow from the experience of working through the rough draft that was my own personal timeline. I began writing my memoirs and once I had a couple hundred pages of memories in chronological order, I began filling in the blanks. At first, I ignorantly thought I would be writing one book. I soon came to realize that I would have to break the story apart. Again, I underestimated the number of pages it takes to truly tell a story. So now, I offer you the second book in what will be a series. I cannot promise how many books it will take to tell the story. Perhaps there will be one more. Perhaps there will be two. Perhaps I will continue to write more. While these stories are fictionalized, the inspiration continues.

I feel compelled to warn you, that you are embarking on a story that contains content that you may find triggering. The story line includes accounts of physical, emotional, and sexual abuse. I included these elements in the story because they had a direct impact on the way I interacted with my dysphoria. While I have taken artistic liberties in my effort to fictionalize events, I have also taken special care not to glamorize violence. My goal is simply to help people understand what these situations may look like through a lens of dysphoria.

I hope very much that you benefit from hearing my stories. I have written them for the sake of sharing, for the benefit of empowering other community members. If you know someone who will benefit from this book, please help them find it.

You are strong. You are worthy of love. You are beautiful.

SHADOWS OF FIRE
Part One

Chapter 1
Newlyweds

Cat and Jim were eager to settle into their new home together. Jim was looking forward to getting out of the barracks. Cat was overjoyed at the prospect of their potential privacy. After spending the last couple of years feeling constantly insecure about her safety, she was eager to thoroughly saturate herself with the joys of nesting. Jim was supportive of anything that appeared to make his new little wife happy.

When Jim returned to Ft. Sill, he was quick to submit all the necessary paperwork documenting his marital status. Informing the appropriate persons that he would be moving off-post into a rental house with his new wife, he gathered up his belongings. Cat spent the better part of the day visiting with her mother and little brother and gathering up her own belongings. Next, they got back in touch with the landlord of the house they would be moving into. Within the week they had moved into their own place.

Nearly a foot taller than his perky little Firecat, Jim enjoyed standing behind his wife, placing his large chin on the top of her head, and wrapping his long arms around her. Her soft hair would glisten just below his eyes, reflecting the sun with its bright hue. He was amused at his ability to so fully envelope her and delighted when she would loosen her muscles and fall back into his arms. Often, she would get worked up about something that seemed insignificant to him. All he had to do was wrap her up in his long lanky limbs, and she calmed right down.

Immediately upon their return from eloping, Cat began driving Jim to work on post in the morning, so that she could use his truck during the day to run errands. Her first order of business was to fill up their newly acquired, empty, three-bedroom house. She drove around perusing thrift stores and alleys. Within a weeks' time, she had populated the house with enough furniture to have a housewarming party. The couple were excited to invite as many people as they could think of together. Soon invitations had been extended to people that Cat had never met.

Jim had been a regular fixture in Rick's living room for long enough that he felt the loss of his friend, when the newlyweds returned from their road trip. The two young men had been best friends. Now, Cat threatened that connection on which Rick had grown to depend. Blind to his friend's jealousy, Rick's name was first on Jim's list to invite to their housewarming.

The day of their housewarming party, Cat was nervous. She knew she would be meeting several people that were in the Army with her new husband. She felt awkward and uneasy welcoming so many military people into her home but contemplated how to best present as a wife that Jim could brag about. *I will be in the kitchen when our guests arrive. I will have a full spread of food on the dining room table. They won't even see me at first.* She fantasized as she washed dishes by hand in their new kitchen. *They will walk into the living room and marvel at the beautiful wood floors and tall ceiling. Then, they'll see the spread, with the nice tablecloth. And then I will step out of the kitchen, with my apron on, and ask them all what they'd like to drink. And bring it to them. And disappear into the kitchen to clean up some more and work on refilling the trays in the dining room.*

As the evening unfolded, the scene did not play out as Cat had imagined. Rick arrived with his wife, 30 minutes before guests had been invited to arrive. He announced his presence robustly. As he burst through the doorway, he dismissed his wife, by letting go of her arm and walking away from her. The quiet wife hesitated, as if briefly contemplating protest before continuing to the kitchen to lend a hand. Upon hearing Rick's voice at the door, Cat resigned herself to remaining in the kitchen until someone more interesting arrived.

Rick was a short stalky man. His wife, Mary, was strong and slender, with long, straight, blond hair. Thick shoulders carried Rick's ego high above the rest of the room. He always made sure to muscle his way into the center ring of any social gathering, and often left Mary behind in the process. Fading into the background, she embraced the role of his wife. Cat was in awe of how effortlessly Mary was able to ensure that every time they received guests, their house was beautiful.

Before Jim and Cat got married, they had been a consistent fixture at Rick's place. Rick always had a buddy nearby to side with him in an argument. He had also enjoyed having Cat around to flirt with. His efforts had proven unsuccessful, but Rick didn't accept failure. He simply pressed on. A true American soldier, the Army loved him, his wife loved him, he certainly loved himself, and Cat detested him. She had been glad to be able to stop going over there so often and thereby avoid Rick. Still, she was eager to show off their new home to Mary.

Despite the rocky start, the event was a success. Guests arrived in a slow steady flow until the peak of the evening. About midnight, the slow steady flow reversed, and the numbers began to thin. By two in the morning, the few that remained had settled into various positions on one of the many couches or chairs that lined the living and dining rooms. Cat and Jim retired to their room, closing the double french doors and the thin white curtains that separated them from their guests. Delighted in their success, they two relished each other with drunken ferocity before passing out.

Both Cat and Jim were quick to take advantage of the privacy of their new home. The honeymoon period did not last long. Despite their best efforts to ignore the outside world, daily routines and social lives intervened. Soon the two settled into admiring each other from across the room and teasing each other in passing. Watching the tall strong man from across the room made Cat feel safe. *I am taken care of now. He will protect me. He will make my father proud.*

At first their house was quiet during the week, and only filled up with Jim's Army buddies on the weekends. It didn't take long for folks to start coming around during the week as well. Folks began coming to Cat and Jim's house for social time as if it were a place of business, like the night club, or the cafe. During their road trip, the night club had gone bankrupt and closed its doors for good. With the closure of the club, their place quickly turned into a replacement hang out. Every night they had cases of Miller's Light and card games until the wee hours of the morning.

As the bar had closed so close to Cat and Jim's move into the big house, it was a natural transition for friends to begin gathering at their place in the evenings. The first couple of weeks, friends began arriving around the same time they would have arrived at the bar, when it was still in business. By the beginning of May, people being at the house had become somewhat of a constant. Many hours of the day, Cat's company would consist of only one or two people. When Jim was home the crowd was much larger.

Rick began coming over frequently and "moved himself into" their second bedroom. This gave him a home away from home when he didn't want to be around his wife. Cat protested some but felt powerless to do anything about it. He began coming over, even when Jim was not there. Still Rick continued to hit on her. He even got so bold as to ask her one day, "Why haven't you slept with me yet?" She was appalled.

Cat reminded him," What's wrong with you? You have a wife!"

He responded, "Everyone else has slept with me at least once, so why won't you?"

Cat told him that she would rather sleep with his wife, Mary, than him. This didn't deter him from making advances. The more Rick came around, the more they butted heads. He was pushy and talked Jim into doing things that Cat did not approve of. It didn't take long for Cat to begin fighting with Jim about his best friend. She suggested to Jim that he marry Rick instead, since he stood up for his best friend, but not for his own wife.

When Cat was especially grumpy, Jim would go over to Rick's place to hang out, leaving her alone in the house. Being alone never lasted very long though. There were almost always people at the house. It got so busy that Cat put a marquis sign in the front window. It was an old open and closed sign that Will had pulled out of a dumpster. It still had some of the little while peg-back letters for spelling out messages. She giggled as she changed up the peg-back lettering with catchy phrases to suit her mood.

Friends arriving would see the sign first thing. If the couple were not home, folks hung out on the front porch couch until someone arrived. She began switching the sign to "closed" when she really wanted alone time. Instead of going away, they would simply hang out on the front porch until she came out or switched the sign to "open".

Folks didn't go to breakfast at IHOP very often anymore. Instead, they came to the house. Cat cooked for everyone. She made coffee for anyone who wanted it. She made breakfast for anyone who crashed at their place. She spent time every day fighting the cockroaches in the house, and cleaning. Every day she cleaned. Still, when Mama came to visit, she always accused Cat of being filthy and lazy. "Your house is not clean enough." *I clean every single day! Nothing is good enough for you!*

Evenings began with beers and snacks. Their core crew of friends were basically Jim's friends who had gone to the bar to escape the barracks. Many of them had been going to Rick and Mary's place a lot. Now Rick had a place to go hang out to get away from his wife. Most nights the house was full by midnight.

Two couches lined the walls in the front room, keeping the stereo system company. There were often a couple of people hanging out playing DJ. A large table, perfect for games, sat in the middle of the dining room. Chairs all the way around, the table was littered with cards and drink glasses. Drinking games lasted until there was nothing left to drink. People slowly stepped out of the game until there was just a few of them playing rummy.

Eventually Cat would either go crawl into bed with Jim or lay down on the yellow love seat in the dining room. Getting very little sleep, she continued to run on a thin line between coffee and exhaustion. The early quiet became her favorite time of day. With only her new cat Frederick to keep her company, Cat used the quiet to try and spend time with herself. It never lasted very long. Still, every second was worth it.

Cat had to get up extra early to drive Jim into work because he had to be on post before eight. When she awoke early enough, she liked making coffee and breakfast while Jim ironed his uniform. Paying careful attention to starching his collar, Jim listened to his wife bubbling at him from the kitchen. After breakfast together, Cat would drive Jim into work, and then continue on her way running errands and watching for help wanted signs.

Despite her best efforts, some mornings fell flat. Getting up before dawn was not Cat's favorite thing to do when she had been up late the night before. Still, she was glad to have transportation and would drive Jim to work in sweats, only to return directly home. *Now that I don't have to worry about income, and I have a supportive Army husband, I really ought to be using these resources to better myself.* Cat felt guilty lying around the house all day doing nothing but spend his money. She told herself that she needed to do more than just clean the house and play hostess. *I should really get at least a part time job so that I am making my own spending money.* She resolved to begin trying to get things accomplished.

Every day that Cat got up early enough to drive Jim into work, she watched for help wanted signs as she made her way through town to Ft. Sill. She meandered through the different neighborhoods, varying her routes on the way home to watch for more signs. She stopped at the neighborhood corner store and picked up a paper. Sitting at home, she read through the help wanted while drinking coffee. Most jobs required skills, experience, or education she did not possess. *How am I supposed to get experience if nobody will hire me? None of these jobs will work for me.* She'd get frustrated and abandon the newspaper, returning to the kitchen for another cup of coffee.

Cat tried going into the mall to look for help wanted signs. As she entered the brightly lit mausoleum of manufacturing, she winced. *This place feels unnatural. Everyone in here is staring at me. I can't believe I ever actually wanted to go hang out at the mall when I was a kid.* She walked past open storefronts and island kiosks, searching for the store names she recognized from the want ads. By the time she found businesses advertising "help wanted", she'd be too nervous to make a good impression. Shifting in her skin, she'd approach the counter, ask for a job application, and then scurry for the door. As soon as one application had been achieved, she would escape through the nearest exit and spend the next twenty minutes looking for their truck in the parking lot.

Cat's version of searching for a real adult's job had not procured any lucrative results. She resigned herself to believing that lack of experience and education were going to keep her from being successful, so she stopped looking for signs. Instead, she began looking for programs that would help her develop her skills and help her get a job. She located the nearest adult school and signed up to take her GED. She also discovered a training center on post, for military wives. She began attending a skills class where they talked about how to write a resume and properly prepare for a job interview.

Some mornings Cat would lay in bed, without the energy to move quickly, and she would forgo the opportunity to use her husband's truck. Lying in bed until long after the truck had pulled out of the driveway, she'd lay on top of the blankets, eyes closed. Eventually her bladder and urge for regular routine would move her from their small square bedroom, and into the belly of the house.

Easing into a slow morning routine, Cat made coffee and breakfast for whomever was still around or showing up. The civilian friends who slept late on one of the many couches had not awoken and people coming from elsewhere had not yet arrived. Fred followed her around, with wide ears. He was quick to learn the sound of her empty coffee cup as it hit the table. She told him, "Wait until I've had a cup of coffee, please." Fred respectfully listened. Once he heard the empty cup hit the table, he immediately began gently attacking her ankle. He loved to play in the quiet morning.

Sitting on the floor of the dining room, Cat felt the pure love from this animal that was learning to fight from her. He was a good listener and took care to lay near her and keep her company when she was not feeling well. On the good mornings, they played for a while before he would ask to go out. Once out the door, he was off roaming and hunting. Gallivanting around with his gang of cat friends and foes, he spent most of the day gone.

Fred always came home by sunset, often a little scratched up. He knew Cat would love him no matter what kind of trouble he got into during the day, as long as he was home early enough.

Some days the previous owners of the now-shut-down-night-club would come to visit with Cat. Not together though. Their marriage had gotten worse. He came to Cat for emotional support. His estranged wife came to visit Cat with her new boyfriend, when she was hiding out from her husband. Their open marriage was backfiring with a rampant lack of fidelity. Jim and Cat shook their heads witnessing this dynamic pattern of unhappiness unfolding within their social circle. Still, Cat tried to not take sides and simply let them make their own mistakes. Eventually they stopped coming around. Cat was too busy drowning in her own misery to really be of any help.

During the days, Cat began rotating crowds of people throughout her activities the same way she had done when she was sleeping in the laundry room. The patterns in which she interacted with different folks differed from her road friendships. Now she was the home base that others moved through, instead of her moving through other homes. Cat was glad to have so much space to offer and welcomed the activity more of the time than she was willing to admit to herself. Though she complained of the lack of privacy.

Some days, Cat would visit Mary while the guys were at work. She knew that Mary would likely be alone in the evening, and Cat would have to deal with Rick and the rest of the gang. *I can't understand why Rick is so happy to be away from her. Mary seems like such a nice gal! She is always nice to me!* Cat liked talking with Mary and checking out whatever furniture project she had going. Their house was full of beautiful colors and intricate patterns. *She is so nice and so smart. How did she end up married to such an asshole?*

Chapter 2
Ceremonies

In May, Jim and Cat took another road trip. This time they drove up to Iowa to visit Jim's family. His little sister was graduating High School and it was essential that they were present. They had to explain to everyone multiple times, that all had to leave, as the couple were packing up the truck. Even after locking up the house, a couple of people lingered on the front porch, insisting they were waiting for a ride.

This time Jim only took a couple of days off, planning for a short trip. They agreed to take turns driving. Stopping only for gas and bathroom breaks, they were determined to make it to Jim's hometown in less than two days' time. Driving through Missouri, Cat was amazed at the devastation she witnessed through the moving window. They drove through several little towns that looked like they'd be really cool, except, they were virtually empty.

Cat asked her husband what the deal was with all the 'ghost towns.' "What had happened to these towns?"

His answer was short. "Walmart."

Jim explained that the small-town economy had fallen apart when independent business owners had lost their customers to Walmart. She decided that she would try to refrain from shopping at Walmart in the future. It was a little challenging to put this decision into action with few alternatives in Lawton for grocery shopping. She vowed to do as much of her shopping at the commissary as possible when they returned to Oklahoma.

Arriving at the house Jim grew up in was an awkward experience for Cat. She knew very little about his family. He had only described his mother as 'an alcoholic'. Jim had explained that he had enlisted in the military to get money for college, and, among other reasons, 'to get out of this small Iowa town'. Now here, she seemed to feel his dislike for the place. The family members already gathered seemed excited to accept Cat into the family and made sure to include her in preparatory activities.

The house was a perfect box. It had been a mail-order home from Sears & Roebuck. Back in the old days, when you could buy a house from Sears, they would deliver all the materials and instructions. It would be up to the buyer to put it all together. Cat was amazed at the idea. *I feel like I'm in an old movie.*

The bottom floor was reserved for the kitchen and common areas. The second and third floors were bedrooms. The bedrooms were small, rectangular, and all exactly the same. Cat felt strange sleeping in Jim's childhood bedroom. She wondered how such a large man could have been comfortable in such a small room.

The next day was the graduation ceremony. Cat was not excited about all the commotion. While she understood that graduating High School was an accomplishment worth celebrating, she had not been actively involved in High School, so it was not something that she naturally related to. To make matters worse, her sister-in law was only a year younger than her. Tall and beautiful, with long legs and long beautiful hair, Cat was enamored with her. Feeling ashamed by how attractive she found her new sister-in-law, Cat made no effort to get to know her.

As the day progressed, the small box house got more and more crowded. The more people arrived, the easier it was for the young couple to remove themselves from the obligations of family activities. A couple of Jim's old high school buddies showed up to show their support for his little sister. They too had younger siblings in the graduating class and were pleased to escape the awkward celebration passing the time with Jim and Cat.

Late afternoon ripened into the sticky auburn sky as the old friends visited in the front yard. Tan metal folding chairs sank slowly into the dry grass, while Cat nervously gathered empty beer bottles and stacked them by the front porch. Sunset welcomed fireflies, and friends began to leave. After Jim had said his last goodbye, he turned to his sleepy wife.

"Let's get the hell out of here." Jim smiled at his sleepy wife. "It's not all bad here. The sunsets are gorgeous, and the stars are even better when we get away from town."

Exhausted from the day, Cat had been fighting to stay awake for at least thirty minutes. Craning her head back, she screwed up her eyes and looked up at the sky. "The sky is big here too. Just like in Oklahoma."

Jim tugged at Cat's hand, coaxing her up from the tan metal folding chair. "This is nothing. Wait til we get out of town!" She shut her eyelids gently, and she slumped a little in the chair, as if asleep. She remained limp for a moment, allowing him to lift her out of the chair with her arms dangling. "I've been looking forward to sharing this with you." Holding her in his arms securely, he kissed her forehead.

Cat wrapped her arms around Jim's neck. Her muscles came to life as she opened her eyes to look into her husband's face. His bright blue eyes sparkled, illuminating his wide grin. She smiled back and kissed him as she lowered her legs, reaching for the ground with her feet. Jim lifted her higher and she tightened her grip around his neck. The two played briefly in the twilight before allowing her feet to balance firmly in the sparse grass.

"It has been nice meeting your family and high school friends." Cat pulled back from her tall husband, reclaiming her arms and hands, she began to fidget with her hair. "But I have to say, it has all been really exhausting." She looked up at Jim apologetically.

"What do you mean? You don't have to sugar coat things for me!" Jim shook his head, laughing heartily. "This weekend has been hell!" He stepped towards Cat with his arms outstretched. "Of course, you are exhausted!" He wrapped his long arms around the sleepy young woman before him. "No babe. I want to show you where I always went to think, when I wanted to get away from my mom."

Cat closed her eyes, breathing in the moment. The sticky summer air pressed her yellow sundress against her back, while a gentle breeze played with the bottom hem. *This place does not feel safe, but he smells like safety. I know everything is going to be okay. If we can just hurry up and get home.* Jim nuzzled her hair behind her ear, making a path through the silky fibers with his nose. Electricity shot through her body as his lips met the cool skin behind her left ear.

"I love you." Jim's hot breath amplified the feeling running down Cat's spine as he spoke. "Let's get our stuff and get out of here." He released his hold and continued in a normal tone. "I'm just gonna fold up these chairs and go check on my mom. Why don't you go up to my room and get our stuff packed up?"

Cat responded in kind, folding up the tan metal chair she had been sitting in. "And then you are going to show me your special place?" Her thoughts briefly lingered on the old pathways along the bike trail where she had brought Saxophone boy years before. She inquired while they continued folding metal chairs and stacking them against a nearby tree. "You have to show me first. I want to see! Then we can go home."

Jim grinned in response, as he tucked his left hand into a stack of three chairs. Cat reached for the other three chairs, and Jim protested. "No babe. I just need you to get the door for me." He folded his right hand into a hook, lifting up the second stack of chairs. "Alright now. Quickly would be great."

"Yes dear." Cat hastened up to the screen door. She opened the screen, and then knocked on the front door briefly before opening the heavy front door. *He probably thinks it's silly I knocked.* She shrugged her shoulders as she pushed to door open and got out of his way.

"Thank you." Jim puffed, as he moved quickly to set the chairs down. Leaning them up against the back of the couch made a loud clanking noise, alerting Jim's mother they had come back into the house. Cat heard Jim, begin their goodbyes as she slipped quietly up the stairs towards the bedroom. Once in the room, she was pleasantly surprised to find that her husband had already packed up their bags and laid them neatly on the bed. *I wonder when he snuck in and did this? He must really want to leave! I don't blame him. I don't feel comfortable here either. Probably not for the same reasons, but it will be nice to be home.*

Cat picked up the large, carpeted suitcase and turned around to find Jim walking through the doorway. "I'll take that." He announced, as he moved forward into the room. He took the large suitcase out of her hand. "Why don't you just make double check around the room to make sure I didn't miss anything?" He continued talking as he started back downstairs. "I will take this to the truck."

Cat glanced around the room. Jim had been very thorough. He had even dusted the shelves, wiped down the desk, and made the bed. *Wow. He really cleaned up. Jim must really hate this place. I can understand while he felt trapped here. There is something stifling about this little box.* The quick glance was enough for her to determine the only thing left to carry was the oversized patchwork knapsack that she had taken to using as a purse. *I carried so much with me for so long. It feels strange to have so little to carry.*

The couple exchanged one last round of "Congratulations!", "Thank you", "Love you", and "Don't wait so long to visit", before escaping the old mail order house. Jim was enthusiastic about sharing his favorite star gazing spot with Cat but did not insist on lingering long. By the time they reached the first truck stop, Jim was ready for coffee and Cat was fast asleep.

> Jim took me to his special place. He wanted to be romantic. The stars were beautiful, amazing, so clear. Like nothing I'd ever seen before. I smiled. I thanked him. I gave him a kiss. And yet I felt guilty. I should have been more present. When I took Saxophone boy to my special place, I was upset that he wasn't more present. But it was all wrong. Jim is all right. He is smart and funny, romantic and yet, all I could do was try not to flirt with his sister. I'm sure nobody noticed. I feel really bad. I should be happy to be with Jim. Maybe there is something wrong with me? I am happy to be with him. Of course, I am happy to be with him. We get along great. I am going to be happy. Everything is going to be great.

Will was the youngest of five brothers. His mother kept in touch with all her sons. She often shared stories about the great success and accomplishments of her middle boys. Living far away in a land not Oklahoma, they were free from the daily barrage of overflowing ashtrays and maintenance requests. Between her youngest and oldest sons, the honey-do list was taken care of while still taking special care not to cross paths with one another.

When the grandmother spoke of her eldest son, it was often with ill regard. Bob doted on his mother and she milked it. However, she was not blind to his improprieties. Bob was a grizzled old carpet layer who drank entirely too much. When Will approached his mother's block, he always slowed down to quiet the engine. Cruising by the house, he would refrain from stopping when Bob's truck was in the driveway.

In early Summer, one of the other grandchildren arrived in Lawton. Cat first learned of Doug and his family through smoky stories of Bob's failures, while playing the role of the doting granddaughter. Doug had not been in contact with his father for several years, and upon turning 18 years old, had ventured out to Oklahoma to find his father. When he arrived, Doug found that his father was unstable and unhealthy. Doug spent a great deal of time visiting with his grandmother when he did not feel safe in his father's home. During one of Cat's visits to the grandmother's home, she introduced Cat to "her cousin Doug."

Seeing Doug reminded her of the extreme contrast she was currently living in. A year before Cat had been participating in demonstrations, hitchhiking in search of her soul's true home, and verbally rejecting the concept of the governmental and social systems that it seemed they were "supposed to grow up and fit into." She didn't know what was true for her, but she knew that the example that had been provided to her thus far did not feel healthy to her. Doug's brilliant rainbow burst tie-dye brought memories of Dead Tour flashing through her mind. *Now I'm living in Lawton, Oklahoma, the burnished back side of the buckle of the bible belt.*

A year ago, she had been running in and out, around and through crowds of deadheads, hippies, beatniks, gypsies, and punks. Now she was in this culturally benign location married to a man in the Army. Jim was entertaining enough. They had enough socially in common to get along well, but they were already fighting. After a brief period of honeymoon bliss, Cat was again unhappy. *I'm still not any closer to understanding why I'm so miserable.* Developing a new pattern of daily habits, she had settled into the misery of a marriage that was in no way right for her. Meeting Doug reminded Cat of all the things she had loved about the west coast, and it briefly distracted her from her own self-inquiry.

Cat wasn't sure exactly what it was supposed to feel like being an adult. She thought that getting married would help her along the path of growing up. She thought that perhaps the next step was to have a child and start a family. *Kids are cute but they are loud and demanding. Isn't having a cat enough? Who makes these rules? Maybe it's what I am supposed to do?* Lost in thought, she laid on the front couch, petting her happily sleeping cat. She knew that something didn't feel right, and she really wanted to feel better.

Cat shifted her thoughts to focus on the upcoming hand-fasting ceremony. Soon after returning from their whirlwind road trip wedding and honeymoon, Mama had informed Jim and Cat that they would have a proper hand-fasting at Summer Solstice. They were taking this really seriously and for some reason, it seemed a lot more intimidating that the courthouse had been in Colorado. *I wish it wasn't so important for everyone else that we do this. It seems like an awful lot to prove to the world that I am capable of making my own decisions. Funny, when it comes down to it, I get very little say in the matter.*

Cat resigned herself to participating to make her mother happy, because something inside her liked the theatrics of ritual, but mostly in the hopes that something in the ritual would trigger some divine message. She was looking for a sign that would tell her what direction to go next. She pushed forward smiling as the plans developed around her. She didn't have to do much to make it all happen.

Cat felt bad for Jim because he was a really nice guy. He was obviously enamored enough with her that he chose to marry her. *That has to mean something. So, why am I unhappy already? Shouldn't I be out of my skin excited?* She felt guilty for not being happy. Petting her cat, her thoughts continued to drift. *Jim is a great guy. We get along great. We're like pals, buddies, like one of the guys. Most of the time anyway.* She felt like her husband treated her like an equal, like he recognized her worth. That was important. Something still wasn't right.

Doug's face popped in her mind and she was reminded of the stark contrasting turn her life had taken. Cat was presented with a new person reminding her of the freedom that she missed from the road. *I wonder if we ever met each other at any shows. I've been so messed up that I don't even remember most of the last couple years. It shouldn't matter anyway. I have a different life now.* Occasionally she would still go with Will to help on small projects. When she did, Doug was there to ride along as well. Doug and Cat made small talk while they worked, getting to know each other sober and on equal ground.

Bob began showing up at the big house. Arriving when her husband was not home, with a case of cheap beer, he tried to conduct himself in a manner that Cat was not comfortable with. During one of these visits, he brought Doug with him. Not long after Doug's arrival in Lawton, he was told 'he was no longer welcome in his father's home.' He spent some time staying with Mama and Will. Soon after, Cat offered him space in the house. There was plenty of room to share.

Mama got the second wedding, just as she had insisted. She had been engulfed in planning for a couple of months. It was set to take place in the Wichita Mountains on the Wildlife Refuge as close to Summer Solstice as they could manage. Jim's family drove down from Iowa. Many friends attended from Lawton. Dad flew out from California. Jasper and his best friend road tripped out to

Oklahoma and attended the wedding as well. The house was noisier than it had yet been. Dad bought a dozen pizzas and a whole lot of good beer for the "night before the wedding" dinner.

Mama made the wedding dress, and a gypsy dress shirt for Jim. Will made the wedding cake. Everyone was involved. Cat just wanted it to be all over. *I know it's a really big deal. But this is too stressful. And there are too many people in our house.* Mama had planned the majority of the ceremony. Cat wasn't exactly sure how it would all unfold. *I feel like I'm just along for the ride. Nobody understands how miserable I am. They just don't know.* Cat had already spent hours sitting on their front porch, crying, inner turmoil wrenching at every inch of her being. Writing violently emotional poetry and praying for some kind of sign to steer her in the right direction, had thus far been hidden while Jim was away at work. Now she had no privacy with all the people around. Now she had to hold it all in and pretend she had never been happier.

It felt good to have Dad there. His approval meant a lot to Cat. She wanted him to be pleased with her. What Dad thought about her was more important to her than she could begin to describe. Still, Jim and Cat had already begun fighting. She was nervous that someone in their family would notice that they were already having problems in their marriage. She was glad when all the commotion was over, and people were leaving. The memory of Dad walking her to the altar almost meant more to Cat than the actual wedding. His acceptance seemed to her, to make all the commotion worth it in the moment.

In addition to participating in the second wedding for her first marriage, Cat managed to obtain her GED that June. She had been practicing with a study guide for several months, and finally registered with the local Adult School for testing. Two days of testing flew by and soon she was waiting for a letter that would confirm or deny whether she had passed. Cat was pretty sure about the four bubble tests. She was not as confident about her ability to compose an effective essay on the spot.

Cat received her GED certificate in the mail in time for her nineteenth birthday. Much celebration followed. Now, when she was job hunting Cat could honestly say she had a diploma. Before, she had simply been lying. Afraid that nobody would hire her without a high school diploma, she had listed the Mendocino High School Annex as the school that she graduated from. It hadn't made a difference though. After a few months of irregularly job-hunting, she had not gotten one interview. She felt only a little more confident from the class with the other military wives. *One more step forward. I just have to keep taking steps forward.*

Chapter 3
Poetry and Pills

With the closure of the bar, more people began going to the little Cafe' on the other side of town. The cafe began staying open later for Open Mic evenings. Jim and Cat went with many of their friends. Cat participated, reading some of her 'Notes From Coffee' and some of her more abstract poetry. She read a poem that described the emotional state she had experienced as a result of being raped. As the words came out of her mouth, she felt eyes through the window watching her. She glanced sideways towards the window as she spoke, unwavering in her recitation. She saw nothing out of the ordinary and dismissed the feeling as she bowed to the small room.

Shards of glass and shadows of blood filtered through the imagery. Some people understood what she talked about. Others simply applauded the intricate darkness of rhythmic pictures that poured from her face as she stood before the microphone. Cat fell in love with the experience of the poetry readings. She enjoyed listening to other people's art. The openly artistic sharing drew her attention, and she began to feel like she was on the right track.

In preparation for Cat's birthday, she made a point to invite all the friends from poetry. She invited all her old friends from the club. When her birthday arrived, Jim's crew of military buddies all showed up as well. It was a loud party. Too much alcohol and too much drama, it started out slow and quiet, gradually increased and then eventually died down with people puking over the front porch railing and all the couches full. *It doesn't seem much different than any other night. I guess when you're an adult, birthdays just don't really matter anymore anyway right?* Despite the success of the evening, Cat did not feel festive. With the evening winding down, she slid the front sign to 'Closed' before opening the screen door and stepping onto the front porch.

Cat sat on the edge of the porch, head spinning. The hot summer night ensured that she was not too cold and laid down on one of the great couches. She gazed into the bushes that lined their porch. She had been spending a lot of time on their porch lately. It was her favorite part of the house. Dark shadows rustled in the bushes below. *Why do I always feel like someone is in there watching me? There's nothing there. It's probably the cat.*

Cat got up off the couch, wavering for a moment, she attempted to steady herself. She quickly gave up standing and sat down on the edge of the porch. Letting her legs dangle, she kicked the bushes. *Why are you always watching me? Who are you?*

"Fred? You in there?" She mumbled, as she pulled her legs back up from the scratchy branches. "Of course not. You're probably asleep on my bed hiding from all the people."

Cat shuddered and suddenly felt extremely exposed. Her heart began to race as she glanced around the neighborhood. *Everything is quiet. Everyone is asleep. Its *three in the morning. What the hell is your problem Firecat?* Using the pillar that held up the roof, Cat steadied herself, as she brought herself to her feet. *Too much drinking. That's what it is. I should just go to bed.* She stumbled through the front door, angled into the bedroom, and crawled onto the bed next to a big sweaty, sleeping Jim.

Cat decided that she was not too old for birthday presents. As a gift to herself, she purchased some painting supplies and canvas boards and began composing her first abstract paintings. She had drawn doodles and patterns and sold them for change when she was traveling. She had played with paints in her mother's studio as a younger child. This was different. She tried to let her brushes move across the canvas the same way she let her pen move across her notebook paper when she was writing. *It feels like magic. Maybe this is what I have been looking for?*

Mama came to visit occasionally with Little Brother. He played around the house and in the yard, while Mama had tea with her daughter. Cat was proud to show her mother the new paintings. Mama pointed out flaws in Cat's technique. "Your lines are too sloppy. If you want your paintings to look good, you need crisp lines." *First, she criticized my ability to clean house. Now she is criticizing my ability to paint.* Cat was disheartened. *Other friends like my art. Why does she have to be so mean?*

Sometimes Little Brother got dropped off at their place for several hours. Mom needed a break and of course Cat was expected to oblige. Some of her friends had young children. When Little Brother would get dropped off, she immediately began calling friends with kids. Having them over made babysitting a little easier. *There is only so long I can entertain a 2 ½ year old with a stereo.* Rick suggested that she simply let him watch Ren & Stimpy in the big TV room.

I don't think that The Ren & Stimpy Show provides a very wholesome example for a little kid. I don't want my little brother learning that it's normal to put people down, call them stupid and crazy, and act so violently. Of course, she got flack for her opinion and the guys inevitably stuck him in front of the television whenever Cat turned her back.

By the end of the Summer, Will began coming over to the house to use their dining room as an office for business. He never asked permission. He just moved himself in. He left papers behind with phone numbers on them. His mess of paperwork, notepads, and files added an extra challenge to Cat's housecleaning efforts. She would shuffle it all together and tuck the stack away. Then, when Will returned, he would bitch at her for moving his stuff.

Will was having trouble getting jobs. He seemed concerned that the longer he stayed at home, the more Mama would be aware of his lack of work. Money was tight and their stress was high. He tried to make work plans that included Cat, without asking her permission.

Irritated, she attempted to solve the dilemma by hooking him up with other jobless friends that were hanging around the house.

Summer rolled by with wild parties, tearful arguments, and plenty of hangovers. In the midst of the chaos, Cat sat pulling her hair out. *I don't feel like myself. When I look in the mirror, I don't like what I see. Everyone says I'm a pretty girl. I don't see it.* She thought she had a mannish face and tried to improve it with make-up.

Cat craved emotional bonding and affection. She enjoyed spending time with the girls, like she had enjoyed watching The Facts of Life as a kid. She wasn't really interested in clothes and make-up, but she sure liked playing dress up with them. After spending time with the girls, she could go to bed with her husband and secretly fantasize about the girls from the afternoon.

Jim liked hanging out with the guys. Rick was still Jim's best friend and made a point of letting Cat know that he wasn't going anywhere. Between Rick showing up unannounced at the big house, and Jim disappearing with Rick, Cat started to blame their arguments on him. *I'm married to a man who shows more dedication to his best friend than to his own wife. This is not how a marriage is supposed to work.*

She didn't know exactly what her expectations were, but she felt like Jim was falling short. *This marriage thing was supposed to be my path to adulthood. Why am I not feeling fulfilled by this experience? Did I pick the wrong person? Maybe I am just being emotional because something is wrong with me? Maybe it's just PMS.*

Cat's periods became irregular, and something felt strange inside her. Her health began to react to her emotional state. She couldn't clearly explain what was happening. *My insides are all wrong. Maybe I'm pregnant? God, I hope not. But maybe that would be wonderful? Maybe this feeling that I'm missing is a baby?* Doctors' visits provided different information. She was not pregnant, and the doctors couldn't find anything wrong. She questioned whether they were even trying.

After several visits with no apparent progress, the doctor explained that Cat's female reproductive system seemed to be shutting down, like it wanted to go into menopause. "At nineteen years old," the doctor explained, "there is no logical reason for this. So, I'm just going to put you on birth control." He handed Cat a prescription paper that she dutifully accepted. *My female parts don't want to have anything to do with me. Why is my system shutting down? Am I dying? He doesn't care. Just take these pills and don't call me ever.*

The pills would "force her girl parts into action" and could, he warned, potentially make it difficult for her to have children later. Taking the medicine forced Cat's body into patterns of blood loss that made her feel more like an alien than she had before. The more she looked in the mirror, the more unhappy she became. *What am I missing?* She spent long hours discussing the philosophies of life with Doug after everyone else had passed out or gone home. The more Cat talked with Doug, the more she longed for the freedom of the road. *I'm never going to find myself as long as I am stuck here in this house.*

Battling the ups and downs of being young in the military provided enough emotional instability, that their medicine cabinet accumulated a veritable candy shops worth of anti-psychotics, antidepressants, and mood stabilizers. Several of Jim's Army friends made frequent visits to the doctor. They would be prescribed something, take it for a few days, and bring it over to share with others. A frequent visitor had left behind a large bottle of Lithium.

Cat secretly tried taking some Lithium, in small amounts. *Maybe it will help me*. She didn't want anyone to know how much she felt tormented and quietly hoped that one of the abandoned prescriptions might alleviate some of her sadness. The lithium seemed to have no effect on her at all.

Cat was overwhelmed by her misery. She decided that if she could not find happiness here in this life, that she was ready to leave for another life. *If a couple don't help me, maybe I should just eat them all*. Crying in the bathroom, she poured a handful of the little pills into her palm. Two by two, she gulped down thirty little Lithium pills with water. Finally done, half gagging and stained from hours of tears, she retired to the love seat in the dining room. The night was especially quiet, something that had slowly become more frequent as the days got shorter. Pulling the blanket over her head, she prayed that sleep would overtake her forever.

Sometime later, in the middle of the night, Cat awoke nauseous and spinning. Half running, she stumbled to the bathroom just in time to empty her stomach violently into the toilet. Searing pains of fire tore at the inside of her throat and stomach. Again, she threw up into the toilet. Half gagging, and crying, this continued for about ten minutes. She barely had time to flush the toilet between eruptions.

Blood came out of her mouth as fluid continued to pour out of her. Jim lay asleep in the bedroom next door. *Doesn't he hear me? How can he not? Why isn't he coming to help me? I just want someone to love me. He is my husband. He is supposed to love me and even he doesn't care.* The fluids ran out and Cat had to continue to drink water, just to put something into her stomach.

Doug emerged from his back bedroom. He brought her water and held back her hair. He didn't ask her what this was wrong, or why was happening. He didn't judge her. He just held her hair, wrapped his arms around her, and comforted her when she needed it so badly. Crying, gagging, vomiting, and passing out in between this series of actions, the night dragged on. Hours went by. She prayed for death. Death never came, only severe stomach pain. Sometime in the wee hours of the morning, Cat was able to return to the little yellow love seat where she remained for the better part of 24 hours.

Jim never asked his wife about the night of sickness. When the morning came and Cat was not up making coffee, Jim acted as if it was a normal day, like any other. "Are you going to get up?" Jim asked the lumpy blankets in the dining room.

"I'm not feeling well." Cat responded from under the blankets. "Leave me alone." Jim walked away without questioning his wife further. *I don't want you to leave me alone. I want you to sit by my side and ask me questions. I want you to care.* Cat wanted someone to ask the questions that she had been seeking for so long. As had happened so many times before, her prayers were not answered.

Within 48 hours, she was back off the couch. Doug was gentler around Cat but did not bring it up in conversation. Within a week, it was ancient history, buried in the past. Jim did make a point to ask Cat to come to bed in their room, rather than sleep on the couch. Quietly, he worried, but kept his concern to himself. He didn't know what to say, or how to bring it up.

By Halloween, Cat was grasping at straws. She made a plan to dress in drag for the Holiday. She would dress in a man's suit, and she convinced Jim to dress up as a woman to match with her. Binding her breasts with an ace bandage, she remembered trying to bind her breasts with a scarf to panhandle in the Castro. *This is so much easier with an ace bandage! It would be even easier if my tits weren't so big!* She looked at her image in the mirror. *It's hard to feel festive. This doesn't feel festive at all.* Her image looked normal. Completely normal. It struck her as odd, that she didn't feel like she was in a costume. She dismissed the thought and focused on Jim instead.

Cat expected that it would take some convincing to get her husband to dress up as a woman. She was surprised when he not only agreed but proceeded to actively participate in the costume planning. He even shaved his face, chest, and legs for a more authentic effect. Tall and shaved with a red sweater skirt and matching red beret, Jim was full of spirit for Halloween. *He is an ugly woman. But he is so enthusiastic! He is much better looking as a man. Strange. I am much better looking as a man too.*

The chaotic partying of their motley crew was in raucous form for the event. A culmination of months of gradually increasing debauchery, Cat hit a peak of misery and couldn't take it anymore. *Everything feels fake. None of this is really happening. Or at least, not the way it should be.* She muddled through the days and nights on autopilot, coffee and breakfast, chores and errands, dinner and guests, bedtime and sex. It all looked the same, and as long as she kept filling the cupboards and dinner table with food, Jim kept giving her money to do it.

Will's behavior continued to make Cat uncomfortable. His morning arrival "for work" in the "office" that he had claimed in her dining room had gone too far. She was witnessing too many suspicious details for her to feel like she could trust him anymore. Cat was starting to become truly concerned about his ability and intent when it came to taking care of her mother's needs.

Mama and Will had been trying to find a way to escape Lawton but could not afford to leave. Cat began actively trying to find a way to leave. She decided that she wanted to run back to Oregon. She devised a plan to get the whole family out there. Jim would be finishing up his enlistment period within a year's time. If he had an address established in Oregon, and agreed to enlist in the Oregon National Guard, the Army would pay to move his entire household.

Cat decided that she should leave early to establish the family address. She could bring one of everything she needed to start a small household. She suggested that if Mama packed up her stuff in their house, Jim could claim it as his, and get the military to move their stuff as well. It was a long thought-out plan, whether it was well thought out was debatable. Will helped Cat weld a frame onto the back of Jim's little Ford Ranger, and the packing of a small household began.

The day before Cat was set to leave town, she went to Mama. She wanted to warn her mother of the lack of integrity with which Will had been conducting himself. "I'm concerned about your wellbeing. I am going to do everything I can to try and make a home base in Oregon." She knew Mama felt trapped in Lawton and desperately wanted to escape. "I want you to be alright." Cat thought that somehow, she could save her mother. Mama's response cut deeply.

"You are lying about Will! He doesn't do that. He works hard." Cat stood stunned. *Is she just scared of the truth? Or does he really have her fooled?* "You are manipulative and toxic." *How can she be saying this?* "You are just running away from your problems! As long as you keep running away from your problems, you will continue to be a poisonous person." Tears welled up in Cat's eyes, and her stomach rose in her chest as her mother continued. "You are never going to find happiness. You deserve all the misery you find."

Cat's pain sat like a big pile of lithium in her heart, and she wanted to vomit all the feelings out. She left her mother's house feeling hated by the person who had been the most important to her only one-hour prior. November 16th Cat left Oklahoma with the intent of never returning. She asked Doug if he too, wanted to get out of Lawton.

"I need someone to help me with driving, and I'm not really looking forward to the loneliness of traveling alone. Two people can accomplish so much more than one alone." Doug was easy to convince. As they headed out of town, they both took off their shoes and rejoiced in the freedom that lay ahead of them. When they reached the border of Oklahoma and Texas, Doug asked Cat to pull over. He got out and left his shoes on the Oklahoma state side of the line. A token of his intent to not bring his Oklahoma experiences with him. Pulling back onto the highway, they turned up the music and looked forward to the future.

Chapter 4
Grown Up Shoes

Doug and Cat were committed to driving all night. Windows down, hair flying in the wind, both friends felt the excitement of a new beginning. The two had been relatively quiet until they hit the Oklahoma border. After crossing the border into Texas, they both felt liberated and fell into deep conversation. Doug shared stories about his childhood. It felt good getting to know him better and it raised questions she wasn't expecting. *Why can't I remember much from my childhood? I should be able to. It wasn't really that long ago.*

The cool evening breeze got colder as they made their way up the mountainside into the night. Striving to put as much ground between them and the recent past from which they fled, the road felt too long. Exhaustion made the night impassable. Finally, they conceded and pulled off the road in the early morning hours. Parked on a snow-covered hillside, the lights of Albuquerque, New Mexico shone brightly below the little truck.

Weary from the road, and excited about what may lie ahead, Doug and Cat crawled into the covered back. With all the bare essentials tucked neatly along the sides of the truck bed, the center was reserved for sleeping. With barely enough space for one person to lay comfortable, the two travelers nestled under heavy layers of blankets to try and stay warm. In the dark, their limited visibility heightened their remaining senses. It didn't take long before the intimate closeness of the two bodies led to physical affection.

Doug and Cat took turns stopping each other to talk quietly with tense voices. As if someone might be listening, they whispered in one another's ears. The two friends enjoyed the intimacy of their connection. *It seems a natural consequence. After spending so much time getting to know each other. Of course, we would be physically attracted to one another.* Cat ran her fingers through Doug's long dark hair and fireworks shot down through her belly. *I don't feel this kind of electricity when I am with Jim.* She tried to dismiss feelings of guilt with her mother's words. *What is between the worlds does not concern the world.*

Cat breathed deeply, taking in the heavy scent of Doug hair. *Doug understands my need to be free. And this is where I am right now. Be present. In the moment. Breathe in. It will be okay.* Both travelers shared with each other a great fear that being physically intimate would forever change the dynamic of a friendship. *What we've had up to this point has been a wonderful thing. I don't want to lose such a good friend. But how could this ruin anything? It will only bring us closer, right?* Eventually they rationalized their way through hours of lovemaking, falling asleep warm and comforted in each other's arms.

First light of dawn opened Cat's eyes as it reflected in the back window of the camper shell. Dizzy from a whirlpool of emotions, she wiped the sleep from her eyes. Crawling out from under the warm blankets, she climbed out and made her way to the cabin of the truck. In pajamas and untied shoes, she started up the truck, and turned the heater on. Snow glistened along the side of the highway. Bright stars bounced along the ground, creating a glare that reminded her she needed coffee.

Pulling back onto the road, Doug continued to lay asleep in the back for a few miles. Soon, he awoke, staying under the blankets until he was ready to climb in the front. A tapping on the connecting window alerted Cat to his consciousness. She looked for a convenient place to pull in. The next gas station stop gave them a place to use the bathroom, refuel, and most importantly, get coffee.

Driving west into the morning, the two travelers remained quiet. Cat fumbled through the radio dial, searching for a signal as she drove. *Mostly country and static.* With her left hand on the steering wheel, she blindly chose a cassette from the console. She pushed Pearl Jam into the stereo with a 'click' and the silence was broken. Doug sipped his coffee silently from the passenger seat.

The tape automatically continued to the other side, and then began to repeat side one. This time, Doug pulled a larger cassette carrier out from underneath the passenger seat. He pushed the eject button, and the loud click signaled the end of Pearl Jam. Silence gave way to the echo of the motor and the wind as it whistled across the hood of the truck. Cat said nothing, hands firmly gripped to the steering wheel. *I don't know what to say. Did I make a big mistake last night? Am I making a big mistake right now? Please say something.*

Sound filled the cab of the truck once more, as Led Zeppelin brought in the morning. Cat relaxed a little. Houses of the Holy brought back a good feeling of friendship from high school. *I never dated any of those guys though. That was different. I was just one of the guys. It's okay.* Song filled her chest, and her shoulders dropped a little. She smiled as she reached out her right hand to turn up the volume. Still Doug said nothing.

One hundred and fifty miles more and the small house truck was pulling in for gas and a bathroom. A half dozen cars in the large gravel parking lot suggested they were not busy. Cat pulled up to the pump and turned off the truck. The silence was immediate. No music, no motor, just a quiet echo of the highway nearby.

Cat opened the driver door and turned to Doug. "I'm gonna go pay for some gas." She climbed out of the truck and paused. "I'm gonna use the bathroom too, maybe get some coffee." The steel echoed in the cold wind as she closed the door. She turned to look at the gas pump. "Number seven. Number seven." She thrust her hands in her pocket and pulled out the keys to make sure she had them. She looked at them, put them back in her pocket. "Yes, I have the keys." *Shit. What was that number?*

Cat then looked up at the pump number and repeated it aloud twice more. Then she repeated the process with her keys once more before turning and walking toward the shabby red building. *Pump number seven. Pump number seven. Pump number seven.* She grasped the keys in her pocket with her right hand, while checking her left pocket for her wallet. When she reached the building, she pushed a big glass door open in search of the cashier.

A small mud room shielded the outside wind from the patrons of the diner. Cat welcomed the warmth, as she opened the second glass door. She paused to glance around the room and locate the cashier and the restroom signs. She immediately felt eyes on her. *I've got this. I've traveled plenty. Y'all can't scare me.* She turned to her right and approached the cashier's desk. An older woman stood behind the counter, pensive and ready.

"Twenty dollars on..." Cat hesitated and turned around to peer out the window in the direction of the gas pumps. She saw Doug getting out of the truck and turned back to the cashier. "Pump number seven please." She put a twenty-dollar bill on the counter and picked up one of the plastic covered menus. She scanned the menu quickly before putting it back. She looked up at the apprehensive woman and smiled. "Thank you. "She pointed in the direction of the restroom signs as Doug came in through the door behind her. "And your restrooms?"

The older woman nodded with a quiet grunt and tried to smile back at the young woman. Doug walked past her as the two women exchanged words, and Cat completed the conversation by following him. They each entered their respective restrooms without a word. As she was washing her hands, Cat asked her reflection if Doug was ever going to talk to her again, but the reflection said nothing.

Cat walked back through the dining room and nodded at the cashier before leaving the cafe. "We'll be back. I'm hungry!" She smiled at the older woman. "Just gotta pump my gas, and re-park the truck." Cat pulled the heavy glass door into the mud room, and then the second door to the outside. *She can't scare me. But those doors are something! Have I lost my strength since I haven't been working with Will? I thought I had built up some muscle.* She dismissed the thought as she approached the gas pumps.

Doug returned to the truck as Cat topped off the tank. He hastily got into the truck and closed the door, rubbing his hands together to emphasize his feeling about the temperature. She put the pump back into its receiver and replaced the gas cap. Cat was quick to turn the truck back on, when she got back in the cab. With the motor, the radio came on full blast. She turned down the radio and turned up the heater, before turning to face Doug.

"I think I should just re-park the truck over there." Cat pointed to the small row of cars that lined the sidewalk leading up to the entrance of the diner. "I looked at the menu. We could get breakfast for pretty cheap here."

Doug nodded in agreement. Cat put on her seat belt before putting the truck in gear. She turned the wheel and slowly moved the truck away from the gas pump towards the parking area. Ice crackled under the tires as they pulled into the parking place. She turned off the truck and removed the keys. "Let's eat!" She exclaimed and then paused to watch her hand put her keys into her own pocket. She opened the truck door and climbed out. Doug followed her example. The two truck doors closing in unison echoed more fiercely that she had expected, and she thrust her hands in her pockets. *Keys? Check. Wallet? Check. Okay. Here we go.*

Silently, the two travelers approached the diner for the second time. This time, Doug held the door open for Cat, smiling softly at her as she passed. She returned the favor at the second door and smiled back at him. *Does this mean everything is okay?*

First through the entrance, Doug took the opportunity to approach the older woman behind the counter. "Two menus please." She picked up two menus from the counter that stood between them and handed them to Doug with disdain. He ignored her demeanor, as he took the menus from her hand. "Thank you. And two cups of coffee. And two cups of water. Please."

Doug turned away from the counter to face Cat who was standing behind him. He handed her a menu and motioned towards an empty booth by the window. "Come on. Let's sit down."

The two travelers sat down at the booth with the table between them and immediately began removing layers. They each piled their extra jackets and hats on the seat beside them. Cat had just finished neatly tucking her extra layers into a tidy bundle when the older woman brought them their coffee. Cat was quick to thank her and smiled very intentionally up at the woman. *Okay lady, now go away.* The woman responded accordingly, indicating to simply let her know when they were ready to order.

Doug and Cat sat silently. Doug put down the menu and picked up his coffee cup. He took a sip and glanced around the room. The roadside gas and diner was small, with dusty, black and white checkerboard floors. Thick glass tabletops held down red and white picnic style table clothes stapled gunned underneath the table, along the edges. Doug was glad to see the only other customers in the diner were seated at the counter. Their loud conversation suggested to him that either, they had a hearing problem, or they wanted to make sure that he could hear what they were saying.

Either way, Doug thought that their current environment gave him, yet again, another perfect opportunity. He knew that Cat had been waiting for him to speak. He knew that she was not prepared to hear what he had to say. In the safety of this public place, he could discreetly speak with full confidence that she would keep her cool, and not overreact. He took another sip of his coffee and put the half empty mug carefully down on the table.

Cat continued to hold her menu up, moving it back and forth until it was just the right distance not to be blurry. She felt Doug's breathing, carefully timed and rhythmic. *He is trying to think of how to say something to me. Isn't he? I can feel it.* She held the menu up, continuing to read the same eight items over and over. *Two Egg Breakfast with toast and your choice of ham or bacon.*

Rancher's Omelet with your choice of hash browns or grits. French Toast with apples or a banana...

Doug reached out and took the menu from Cat. "Do you know what you want yet? He held the menu in his hand briefly, expecting a response. 'Because I'm hungry and I want to order."

Cat nodded in agreement. She did not protest when he placed the two menus together, at the edge of the table. She did not protest when he raised his hand and got the servers attention. *A little more abrupt than I would say is necessary. They certainly won't forget us here.* She smiled gingerly, covering it by tilting her head down, and putting her hand over her mouth. Cat blushed when the older woman approached, and Doug turned his gaze to Cat and spoke. "And the lady will have?"

"Breakfast sandwich with egg, ham, and cheese. Please! Cat responded, grinning wide at the woman taking her order.

The woman turned back to Doug, took his order, refilled their coffee cups and then disappeared with the menus in her hand. She placed the menus back on the counter as she passed into the kitchen with their ticket. Doug watched her as she returned from the kitchen and walked directly back to hide behind the safety of the loud customers at the counter. Doug turned his attention back to Cat, waiting patiently across the table from him.

Doug spoke quietly and clearly. "Don't freak out. Keep your cool." Looking directly at Cat, so she would know he was serious, he continued. "I have a gun." He could see panic in her face, but she continued to smile. "Not here. It's in the truck." He took a deep breath and picked up his coffee cup. He took a sip as if they were having a perfectly normal conversation and returned it to the table.

A noise came from the kitchen and soon the older woman was bringing them their plates. Doug paused briefly as he saw her approach, picking up his cup to empty it for another refill. Cat thanked her with a smile when she placed their food on the table. The server was quick to evacuate the travelers' conversation. Doug revealed to Cat that Will had given him a handgun before they left town. Cat was mortified. *I hate guns. I can't believe I was sleeping in a bed with a gun! What if it had gone off?* He told her he would show her the gun later and explained how Will had made him promise to take care of her, "no matter what". *What the hell is that supposed to mean? Do they really think I am that incompetent?* Cat made it clear that she was not okay with the whole scenario. Doug didn't appear to feel much better about it.

After leaving the Diner, Cat returned to the driver's seat. Doug returned to the passenger seat. Neither turned on the radio. Neither spoke. The two traveled silently for hours until one of them finally mentioned needing to stop for a bathroom. They both agreed it would be nice to stretch their legs, and the gas tank seemed to agree. At the next truck stop they only lingered long enough to gas up, get coffee, and smoke a cigarette. By the late afternoon, they both felt they had covered enough distance that somehow it might be safe to talk again.

Driving and talking, they discussed some finer details of their plan. They would make a pit stop in Sacramento along the way. This would give them a chance to rest. Also, Doug was concerned about his younger sister who was pregnant. He wanted to be able to stop in and check on her. Concerned about questions that might come up, they discussed how he would present her. They decided that they didn't really want his family to know who she was, or what they were up to. *They can think I'm just some hippie chick. They will never know the difference and it won't matter in the long run anyway.*

Doug didn't seem to focus on anything long term, but rather stayed primarily in the moment. He talked about his family only after Cat prodded him. Naming off his siblings, he shared stories of his childhood sparingly. He didn't talk about his parents much. He warned Cat not to be too concerned about his family. They would make a quick obligatory visit to his little sister's. Then, they would go visit his mother for a longer rest.

Cat carried a lot of painful emotions, as a result of her last conversation with her own mother. *I'm not sure I even want to help them now. My mother hates me. And I certainly have no desire to help Will. But my little brother is stuck in Lawton with them. And I did take Jim's truck.* Cat wasn't sure that she was still motivated to follow through with the original plan of setting up house in Oregon. Still, she knew that she loved Oregon. They had all the things and all the intent. It seemed logical to at least attempt to follow through with the plan for now.

Not wanting to allude his family to her true identity, Doug agreed he would introduce her as Rabbit. She had been fond of this nickname when she was traveling. She had defaulted back to 'Cat' when she was in Lawton because that's what her mother called her. Doug's family wouldn't question him showing up with a crazy hippie girl named 'Rabbit'. Unknown to the travelers, rumor of their escape from Lawton preceded them. When the two arrived in Sacramento, his mother already knew who Rabbit really was, and had been warned of their arrival.

Chapter 5
Conspiracies

After hours of peaceful paths of easy flowing cars, passing occasionally between wheat fields, the cars began furiously crossing paths in an effort to win some secret race. Panic filled Rabbit's chest. She swerved to avoid collision twice, then a third time. "I don't think I can do this!" She gripped the wheel with tight knuckles. Doug helped Rabbit navigate rush hour traffic long enough to get them off the freeway.

"We can take the back roads to my mother's house from here." Doug announced, and Rabbit veered down the off-ramp. The setting sun painted the evening sky in amber and burgundy hues. Shadows jutted out from behind large trees lining the road. Large trees gave way to small trees. Just as suddenly, the small trees disappeared to be replaced only with dark shadows under an indigo blanket. "Ya. Ya. Turn right at this intersection."

Winding through the levy roads, Rabbit went over her story one more time. "I was just traveling and picked you up hitchhiking. We don't have to go into detail." She kept hearing the Lawton Grandmother introducing her to "her cousin". She pictured Jim's grimaced face standing over her. *You are just going to keep running. What are you running from?* Mama's voice echoed in her head.

Doug agreed that less information was better. "I just need to stop in and let my mom know I am in town. She'll kill me if I don't. Then we can go to my sister's. My sister and her husband are chill. We can kick it there for a while."

The couple arrived holding hands. Hiding her secret, Doug's mother was courteous to her son and the girl. She asked a couple of prying questions, but given the hour of arrival, was glad to have them move on. Heading back out into the night, Doug directed Rabbit back out onto the dark levy roads. Whistling, the wind cut through sparse oaks, rooted fiercely in the wet soil. Twinkling gems lit the indigo blanket above, reminding the couple that the world was immense and their moment seemingly insignificant. Rabbit breathed deeply. Silence cradled the space between them in the cab of the truck.

Rabbit cut the headlight, pulling gently into the gravel driveway next to the oncoming duplex. A petite young woman with long straight brown hair and the protruding bulge of an embryonic parasite emerged from the entryway of the cream-colored building. Sharp neat cuts framed the doorway and windows. *That must be his sister. She looks just like him!* Without a word to his driver, Doug opened the door of the truck before Rabbit had a chance to turn off the engine.

Rabbit hesitated in the truck. Rolling down the window, she lit another cigarette and turned off the engine. She watched the two speaking first quietly, and then boisterously laughing. The laughing was cut short with a brief exchange of silence as Doug motioned for Rabbit to get out of the truck. The pregnant woman's eyes darted to the truck and followed Rabbit as she quietly ambled towards the building. Wind blew her hair in her face as she walked, reminding her that she was not dressed for a winter night.

"You must be Rabbit!" The woman smiled broadly, glanced at Doug and then attacked Rabbit with a quick shoulder hug. She stepped backed, looked around and shivered. "It's fuckin' cold out here guys. Let's go inside!" She continued as they made their way into the brightly lit living room. "You'll never guess what I heard about you!" Doug's sister was quick to fill them in with the details of the family rumor mill.

Rabbit spoke as little as possible and tried not to interact much. She was mortified to hear the story. Animated in her story, the woman didn't notice Rabbit quietly curling up in a ball in the corner of the overstuffed velvet couch. The deeper the story got, the farther into the crushed velvet she sank. Invisible, Rabbit learned Doug's family had been warned she had stolen a truck and he had stolen a gun. The two of them had been described as "on the run and unpredictable."

Oh, my gods! What is she thinking while she's telling us this story? She can't really believe it, can she? Rabbit's thoughts were interrupted by something shiny. The storytelling host paused briefly, cocked her head to the side, tilting slightly, so that her straight brown hair fell past her shoulders. Landing softly on her belly, her hair landed across her chest. A momentary glimmer of tension in Rabbit's chest sharply caught her attention. She caught her breath as a grin spread across the pregnant woman's face.

Invisible, and absolutely still, Rabbit held her breath as words tumbled out of the woman's mouth. Chuckling, she chided her brother. "So what kind is it? Do I get to see it brah? Show me your piece Doug." Panic shot down Rabbit's spine. Landing in her stomach, panic quickly became nausea. Rabbit tried to remember to breath slowly and quietly. *So, does that mean she believes the story? That didn't really happen. This can't be happening. We're gonna go to jail. My life is over.*

Rabbit rolled over into the couch, burying her face in the crushed velvet. *I am invisible. I am invisible. I am invisible. I don't matter. I don't exist. You can't see me because I'm not here. I'm not real. This isn't real. This isn't really me.*

Doug sat in the kitchen with his sister, as they caught up on the last year of each other's adventures. Doug's shoulder's spread across the width of a small kitchen table. Hunched over a piece of paper, his pencil moved gracefully over the sheet. Hunched over, his long black hair sheltered his drawing from view. His sister's voice cackled in the background. "Are you sleeping brah? I'm in here making food for you and your little criminal friend over there and talking to you. And you're not even listening!" He lifted his head in response and showed her what he'd been working on. "Shut the hell up. I'm not sleeping. I'm making art!" He motioned to his traveling companion in the living room. "She's got the right idea. I should be sleeping, but I was listening to you."

Speaking with her hands, and by extension, a large plastic spoon, Doug's sister instructed him. Like a conductor in an orchestra, she was able to get him to make a bed on the floor for the two to sleep. Next, he took out the trash. Then on to the next task. Her instructions and his actions moved harmoniously until, the sonnet concluded with, "Now go wake her up. Dinner is ready." Without question, or perhaps too tired to argue, he obeyed without hesitation. Doug descended on the sleeping girl, who for the last couple hours had moved in and out of sleep. She had come to believe that she was invisible. That if she was able to fall asleep, that this nightmare would end, and she would be able to return to the collective unconscious.

Sister hollered good night noises as she went down the hallway to bed. Doug sat watching the beautiful sleeping girl. In the moment, he was enamored with the treasure he brought back from Oklahoma. Eventually, he gave into the soft sounds of her breathing. "There's food. You gotta wake up to eat." Doug pulled the hair out of Rabbit's face, exposing her eyelids to the light overhead. Neatly tucking her hair behind her ear, he brushed her cheek with the back of his hand. She squinted, looking up to see an aura of light with his face in the center. *God, I love the way he smells!* She smiled and put her arm over her eyes. "Five more minutes."

"There's almost nothing left." Throwing words over his shoulder, Doug sauntered into the kitchen. Rabbit lifted her head. *My body is made of stone. There's no feeling.* Blood began rushing through her extremities, and Rabbit tried to get up from the couch. She could hear the sounds of Doug fixing her a plate in the kitchen. Attempting not to make a sound, she slowly dragged her tingling legs across the living room carpet. Holding onto the arm of the couch, she grimaced and grit her teeth while lightly tapping her feet.

Doug popped his head around the corner. "What are you doing?" Grasping the back of sofa, Rabbit was standing on one leg. Shaking the other leg and whimpering, she looked miserable. He put the prepared plate down on the kitchen table and went in for the rescue. "What's wrong Baby? Why are you crying?" The girl looked miserable and ridiculous. He struggled not to laugh as he moved toward her.

Rabbit lunged into Doug's arms, wrapping her arms around his shoulders. She let all her weight fall on him. *He doesn't even falter. So strong.* Small pearls of teardrops glistened on her cheeks, but she was clearly no longer crying. She smiled weakly up at him and replied. "My legs had fallen asleep, and they are waking up. It hurts to stand up. But I was trying to wake them up!" Holding onto his waist, she returned to balancing on one leg while shaking out the other. Trading off, she did both twice, for good measure, despite the fact that the tingling had since subsided.

After confirming that she was going to live, Doug guided Rabbit into the kitchen. He instructed her to sit down and eat dinner. "My sister is a good cook. She's already gone to bed." He sat down at the table opposite her. "We get some sleep. In the morning we can take a shower and then…" He hesitated, returning to a drawing that he'd apparently been working on for a while. She looked down at his hands. *That's my sketchbook. Hah. That means I get to keep that Sun.*

The mashed potatoes disappeared first. Rabbit picked at the meatloaf. *I don't really like meat. Why does everyone always expect me to eat it? You have to have protein. You should be thankful for the free food. We don't have unlimited money.* Doug sensed her discomfort. "I know you don't like this whole gun thing. I just have to go see someone." *I don't want to meet any more new people. Not after last night's story! Who knows what people think of me?* She blinked at him and took a bite of meatloaf. "You don't have to worry about it. I will take care of it. It'll be fine. Everything will be fine." *Better not ask any questions unless I really want an answer. And I really don't want to know. I just don't.*

The two exchanged few words before heading to bed. Climbing onto a pallet of blankets on the floor, the young travelers quickly fell asleep. Arms and legs intertwined; the long road anchored their bodies firmly under the blankets. Their spirits lifted. His sat under a tree, playing a guitar. Hers wandered lost in an empty house, searching for a crying child. When the two awoke, the sun was blaring into the window, heating up an already warm living room.

Driving the back roads from sister's house, Doug seemed irritable. Getting lost was easier than he liked to admit. So much construction had happened since he'd been down these old back roads. All the landmarks were different now, and even some of the streets. His short temper and guesswork navigation made Rabbit feel three feet tall. By the time they reached the little Chinese market, she was practically in tears. *Can't let him see it. Can't let him see it. Gotta be cool. I'm cool. No, you're not. You're ugly and stupid. Shut up!*

"You don't have to come in. In fact, it's probably better that you don't." Doug faced straight ahead as he spoke to his driver. Rabbit removed her hands from the steering wheel, placing them carefully into her lap. He turned to face her, leaning in to kiss her cheek. "I promise I won't be very long. Just relax. I got this." As he got out of the truck, he instructed her to lock the doors and not go anywhere. "And don't open the truck for anyone but me." Then he walked beyond the market gates, around a corner, and out of sight.

Waiting in the truck, Rabbit examined her surroundings. Iron bars protected the glass entry door to the market. A pull-down screen blocked anyone walking by from being able to see inside. The windows were small, about shoulder high, and plastered with opaque advertisements for products captioned with text in a language that she couldn't identify. *I wonder what delicious snacks they might have hiding on their shelves. Exploring Asian markets is always like a treasure hunt for new things!*

The sidewalk in front of the market was dingy and chewed up. *We could be in West Oakland right now. Only this is prettier. More trees. I like trees.* She looked across the street. The street was lined with trees as far as she could see. The late afternoon sun dappled the leaves. Yellow, red, green, and amber leaves rustled their autumn rainbow, occasionally releasing a few more straws into the wind. Rabbit closed her eyes. She suddenly felt very alone. *What if he doesn't come back? What if he just ditched me here with the gun in the back of the truck somewhere? What if he sells it and takes off with the money?*

Rabbit noticed her bladder pushing on a nerve somewhere. She squeezed her thighs together. *He told me not to go anywhere. Where would I go? I have no idea where I am? Not to unlock the truck for anyone but him. What an asshole. And the way he talked to you! No. I screwed up. Of course, he would get upset. Nobody deserves to be talked to that way. No. Its fine. Everything is fine. Of course, he's coming back. I sure hope its soon. It's been over an hour. I really gotta piss. Where would I go? I'd go find a fuckin' bathroom! That's what I'd do.* Clenching her thighs tightly with her hands tucked neatly between, her body waited like a statue. Arguing shadows failed to notice the silent stirring of a silhouette growing behind the veil.

Doug's face appeared accompanied by the daydream shattering echo of knuckles on glass. Rabbit jumped, wetting herself slightly. She quickly clenched her muscles tightly as she leaned over to unlock the passenger door of the truck. He got into the truck, slamming the door shut. "I don't want to talk about it." He announced curtly. Placing his left hand on the dashboard, he turned to his driver. "Where are we going from here?" She started up the truck, checked the mirrors, and pulled out onto the street.

Facing forward, Rabbit drove south on the tree lined street, whose name she did not know. "I don't know. Some where I can take a piss would be great! You took over an hour and I have been waiting." He tried to make a joke and she scolded him. Poor timing. The sun had set while he had been absent. The sky was darkening as she drove, and she had a hard time seeing signs well enough to read them. He tried to direct her, and despite his confusion and a few road detours, managed to eventually navigate them to a Truck Stop.

Hitchhiking had provided plenty of practice holding it for way too long. Still, it didn't make the experience any less unpleasant. Rabbit was glad to be able to use the bathroom. She was also thankful to be able to stretch her legs. She was disappointed to discover blood in her underwear when she was sitting in the bathroom stall. She flushed the toilet but remained sitting, skirt pulled up to her waist and underwear around her knees. *Gross. This feels so alien. It's like a curse. This is not for me. Why does this have to keep happening. Mom told us all about this, stupid. You know why it's happening. Aren't you proud to be a woman right now? Shut up! All of you!*

She grabbed a handful of toilet paper, trying to scrub the fabric. *Of course. I could go out to the truck and dig through clothes, come back in, and change my clothes. But I really don't want to draw that much attention.* The paper frayed pink but made little impact. She flushed the frayed paper down the toilet, using the fresh water to rinse off the inside of her thighs. She dried off with more toilet paper. Then, pulling 6 squares of toilet paper off the roll, she carefully folded them. Fold over fold, she kept working with the paper until she held a small rectangle. She tightly rolled it until she had what looked like a small tampon. *I hate doing this. I hate my body. I swear, someone made a mistake somewhere.*

The two travelers only spent a short time in Sacramento. Now it was nighttime, and they were headed back out on the road for Oregon. Rabbit was tired, and anxious. *I'm so much happier when we're traveling! I don't know how long I can drive tonight though.* Something was poking at her, but she was focused on the getting to Oregon. She wanted to believe that everything would work out exactly as planned. *If we can just get away from this city, I'm sure I'll feel better.* Streams of light yellow and white appeared rhythmically against the black of the window. The night winds pushed the truck, reminding her of the weight of her eyelids. "I'm gonna pull over at the next off ramp. I'm too tired to drive anymore." She looked over to see Doug already asleep against the passenger side window.

Rabbit parked the truck discreetly in the back of a lot clearly used by big trucks. She turned on the cab light and noticed the gas gauge. *I hope we don't run out of gas money before we get settled somewhere!* She sighed and spoke to the truck as if responding to a child asking for another glass of water past bedtime. "We'll get more gas in the morning. I'm not dealing with it right now. I'm exhausted." She nudged Doug. "Hey. Wake up!

So, you can go back to sleep. You will be much more comfortable in the bed!" He muttered something and opened the door.

Rabbit locked the passenger door. She gathered her wallet, keys and smokes, before climbing out of the cab. Standing in the dark, she double checked to make sure she had the key before pushing the button to lock the driver door. Then, just before closing the door, she stopped and checked her pockets again. Pulling the key out, she looked at it, then put it back in her pocket. "Good." Then she closed the door.

She walked to the back of the truck. Doug sat on the tailgate of the truck smoking a cigarette. "What took you so long?" He asked, half-teasing, half-flirting. She stumbled and regained her footing. "Graceful." She blushed. *I'm so glad it's dark. If it was light out, I would look like even more of an idiot.* Sharp pains shot through Rabbit's abdomen. Fire pulsed between her legs, and she strained to hide her discomfort. She pulled a cigarette out of the pack sitting on the tailgate next to Doug.

"I just had to make sure I had everything." He raised his eyebrows at the response. "Mainly, the keys. It would suck if I locked us out of the truck." He added that it would also be stupid. She shrank just a little. Glowing amber in the darkness, something hid behind Doug, just beyond her perception. Sleepy, the girl finished her smoke before climbing into their makeshift bedroom. He stood up to close the tailgate before climbing in. Soon they were both tucked in and fast asleep.

Morning came quickly. Then the gas station. The road followed. Midday delivered leg stretching stops with peanut butter sandwiches. They had already spent several days doing this and thinning pockets had arrived before Doug and Rabbit had reached their destination. The two began soliciting for gas change when they stopped. They used the most effective tools they had. Doug played his guitar and Rabbit sat next to him, trying her best to look humble and pretty.

By the time Doug and Rabbit made it Eugene, they were near broke. Their arrival brought her a brief period of refreshed hope. *If we can get jobs, then we can get a place. It will all work out.* Rabbit called Jim to let him know they arrived safely in Eugene. "Why didn't you call me sooner?" They argued on the telephone some. Then Will got on the phone and began railing into her about upsetting her mother. "What were you thinking, talking to your mother like that?" *If these guys want me to stick to a plan, this lack of encouragement certainly isn't helping.*

Chapter 6
Angel

Thanksgiving was almost upon them and Rabbit was feeling completely rejected by her family. She attempted to look for a job their second day in town. She walked around looking for signs, but clerks seemed more interested in getting her out of their stores than giving her an application. She was disappointed, even more so when Doug didn't seem as driven to try and find work.

Doug spent a few days playing guitar on the street for whatever change he could drum up. It wasn't much, but it paid for cigarettes, and a little food. Cold and damp, Rabbit sat drawing next to him as he played. *My throat hurts. I can't get sick. Why does everything happen at once? What is going to happen next? What if nobody will hire me?* Going to bed for the evening, they moved the truck only as much as necessary, trying to conserve gas. "We just have to move it to a different neighborhood." Doug suggested. "Or at least a different street. And make sure not to park in front of someone who's gonna call the cops on us." She nodded in agreement while she drove.

They repeated this pattern for a couple of days. Doug exhibited no interest in actually getting a job, or an apartment in Eugene. He made it clear that he really just wanted to get back to the West Coast. Enamored with her strong connection to Doug, she nodded, listening.

You knew this all along, didn't you? He isn't really interested in me. He was just using you. No! He wasn't. Doug is my friend. We have a special connection. You just shut up. All of you.

Rabbit told Doug that she wanted to do 'something special' for the holiday. "I want to see the ocean again. I miss it so much." He agreed and on Thanksgiving Day, they drove out to the coast. They spent the night in the back of the truck listening to the wind over the Pacific Ocean. Too cold to go out and enjoy it, the cliffs too high to provide easy access, she accepted the view of the water as her Thanksgiving feast.

Hours of warm affectionate intimacy led to solid sleep under heavy blankets. When the early morning sun woke Rabbit, her empty stomach reminded her of their lack of food. She decided that she would start the drive back to Eugene early. *A free meal is only a couple hours away if I can make progress early.* Climbing in the cab of the truck, she started the drive while Doug continued to sleep in the back.

Winding around the empty misty road, Rabbit turned the radio up. Driving in the early morning with the sun behind her and Edie Brickell's voice in her ears, she felt a hint of freedom. *There is happiness around one of these corners. I just need to figure out how to recognize it.* Then, the world began to spin uncontrollably. Panic shot through her nervous system at light speed.

Rabbit had been driving the posted speed limit. An inexperienced driver, she did not recognize the dangers of black ice on the road. Hitting a patch of icy slickness, she lost control of the truck. As she tried to compensate for the fishtailing, she found herself rolling into trees and brush. It happened so fast, that in a moments time, she was pinned on her side.

The front windshield was half gone. Tree branches pushed their way into the cab. Stuck on her side, pinned by the steering wheel, Rabbit looked down to see a small amount of blood trickling from her left hand. The tiny shard of windshield was easy to remove. She didn't see any other signs of bleeding. Her heart raced. She couldn't move. She looked up to her right to see the passenger window facing the sky. The back window was full of tree brush and she could not see anything else.

Terrified, she began screaming and crying. *Someone has to help me. I'm stuck!* She didn't know if she could move, or if she could move, how she was going to get out. She didn't know where Doug was, or even if he had survived. Time stood still as terror ran through her chest and she prayed for life and death at the same time. Confused and overwhelmed the next few moments passed before her in slow motion, over and over again.

Rabbit heard voices that she didn't recognize and then Doug's voice was searching for her. She called for help again. Hands reached down into the cab of the truck and fished her out. Shaking and sore, she climbed off the hull of a vehicle to witness all of their belongings strewn across the side of the road. Like Easter eggs in a chaotic mess of brush and broken trees, there was no use trying to save it all. Moments flashed before her in stop frame motion as an angel emerged with a blanket.

Being reborn. The butt of so many jokes. As if you can become something entirely new. Yesterday is gone. So far into the past that it never happened. Like a virgin. Fresh and clean. What does a shower get me? What if I use anti-bacterial soap? There's a new life hiding at the bottom of that pump bottle. Refreshing. Clean. Pure. For only 99¢ you too can be reborn!

Do I have to die to be reborn? If I don't die first, means I have two lives. Dual lives, like dual citizenship. I can be good AND bad. Why not? That WOULD be more balanced. In theory. I will never be balanced. Because I died, before I was reborn. I've died several times. And there was that angel...

A fine layer of hair. Like Sinead O'Connor. Thin Beautiful. Cool and quiet. From nowhere. No puff of smoke. No fairy dust. I didn't even have time to make a wish. And with the blanket. Around me. Amazing.

Cool blue pools. Eyes so deep and pure. A reflection of heaven. I was reborn in her arms. And she was gone. Nobody saw her. She was never there. Like magic. Fabric. Material. Materialized. Magically. From nowhere. Gone. Not here.

But it's here in my arms. It has to be real. She was HERE in my arms. She HAD to be real. So quick and light. Without breath or thought. I died before her and was reborn in her arms with only the tall pines as witness.

He said I was crazy. Making it all up. He should have died. Who saved him? I'll never know. Pure stroke of luck. He must be the bad for my good. My enabler. My justification. Justify. Mystify. It's all a lie. Story. Tell them a story and they'll shut up. Buy in. Pay up. 99¢ Rebirth in a bottle. Sanitizer.

She was smooth though. Silky. Not sterile. Not like soap or alcohol. More like a sea breeze. Salt air breathes life into the dusty corpse. Suddenly the beach is flooded. Thick white foam rises. Coating.

This doesn't feel clean. Or alive. There's enough salt here to kill anything. Little death becomes a big death. Rebirth transforms into afterlife. Does that mean I don't get another chance? Is this all that's left over? I wanted more. My greedy little soul wanted her to save me again. One more chance to feel her angelic arms around me. To feel her wings lift up. My soul.

To crush the ice, lift the bag high. Thrust it hard. Powerfully. Towards the earth. Shatter all the bricks into splinters of rebirth. Fill a glass and offer her a drink. It's the least you can do after she saved your life.

Shaken by the shock of their sudden loss of home and overwhelmed by what she would come to view as a truly spiritual experience, Rabbit reflected blankly on the circumstances. *The best thing to do would be to ride with the tow truck driver into the closest town. Otherwise, we might be stuck on this quiet road for days waiting for a potential ride.* The driver had better things to do than to wait around while they picked through the brush trying to identify the most important items to save.

Doug had not been hit by flying butcher knives, the coffee pot, or any other potentially hazardous items. The two travelers grabbed their back packs stuffing them with as much clothes and blankets as they could fit. Rabbit grabbed her paintings and some art supplies. The driver agreed to take them as far as the shop where he would drop the mangled truck frame. He also agreed to give them $50 cash for what automotive tools they were able to salvage from the wreckage.

They grumbled about how much potential money they were being ripped off for, as the tow truck driver pulled away with a few hundred dollars' worth of their tools. Still, it was better than walking away empty handed. They rode back to Eugene silently, sitting tightly, side-by-side in the front of the tow truck. Their bags piled on their feet and across their laps made for an uncomfortable ride. Wind moved through the truck and Rabbit was reminded of the frightening ride so many years ago, in the logging truck from Booneville to Cloverdale. By the time they arrived back in Eugene, they were cold, bitter, and terribly hungry. The day that was supposed to have been wonderful had turned into a nightmare.

When they reached town, the driver was reluctant to take them too far in. He was cold and tired, and he knew these kids weren't paying. He pulled into the first shopping center they encountered. He stood quietly while the young couple pulled what remained of their stuff out of the cab of the tow truck. The driver said nothing and tried to hide his impatience. He had been expected home hours ago. He would be able to justify his tardiness with a fantastic story and the knowledge that he had just doubled his tools.

What remained of the broken camper truck lay mangled on the flatbed trailer of the tow truck. The frame was bent so badly that only two wheels touched the flatbed. Doug stacked up all their remaining possessions against the brick fronting of a grocery store while Rabbit wept openly at the loss of their home. Doug showed no signs of trying to hide his irritation, and Rabbit quickly quieted down and wiped her face.

The parking lot lights revealed a light dusting of snow starting as the store signed flickered above the commercial awning. Standing in front of a grocery store, the two shocked travelers watched the tow truck drive away and with it, their only source of shelter from the cold. They had nowhere to go, and no idea what to do next. Rabbit sat down on the ground and laid her back against their gear. She closed her eyes and imagined that for just a moment, everything would be alright. *This is just another adventure. I am free. I am alive. Life is good.* She opened her eyes and looked up at Doug who was leaning quietly against the wall beside her.

"How about we walk downtown and get a coffee?" She smiled at him. "If this is an adventure, then I guess it just got exciting."

The next day, Rabbit called Jim to inform him about the death of his truck. Again, he fired angrily into the phone at his estranged wife. He was disappointed that she had not called more frequently. Why had she waited so long to call? Why had she only called after she wrecked his truck?

She responded indignantly. "I have been driving a long time. And it hasn't been easy. And it all costs a lot more than what I expected. And I am doing the best that I can!" She began to cry into the phone for a moment, and then choked back the tears. She returned to the initial plan that had been discussed and agreed upon prior to her departure. "I brought everything to start a house so you could move here too! And now it's all lost somewhere in a hill side." She began to cry again into the phone, choking and hyperventilating. "I could have died. But I didn't. And I'm glad I didn't. But now I don't know what to do."

Will jumped onto the line to emphasize his displeasure of the situation. "Don't play stupid with me missy. I know all about you and Doug and the gun." Rabbit held her breath. Will's voice was stern. She was not sure what she was going to say or do, but she knew that he couldn't be trusted. "While you have been out gallivanting around the country with your 'cousin,' I have been here trying to take care of your mother and your little brother. But that doesn't matter right now."

Unable to hold her breath any longer, Rabbit gasped. "What are you talking about!"

He began scheming about what to tell the insurance company. "We have to figure out what to tell the insurance company so we can get the most money. But you have to cooperate."

I cannot trust this man! How could I have left my mother in his care. This man is insane! The voice at the other end of the receiver faded in and out while Rabbit attempted to tether herself somewhere near enough her body to maintain control without actually having to be present. Doug walked up and sat down next to Rabbit, holding two coffees. Silent, he motioned for her to take one. She felt herself dragged back down into her body as the arm reached out and accepted the warm cup. Doug sat pensively waiting for Rabbit to finish the call and turn her attention to him. She glanced at him, nodding in thanks, and returned her attention to the telephone.

"Why not just tell the truth?" Her question was dismissed with indistinguishable ranting, so she hung up the phone.

Their lack of faith and severe disappointment provided no comfort. She looked at Doug solemnly.

"They are going to be no help." Rabbit answered Doug's silent gaze, then took a sip of the coffee. It had already begun to cool, and the creamy richness did little to warm her. "We are on our own here and I don't know what to do."

Chapter 7
The Yellow Foot

Rabbit decided that there was no reason to call Oklahoma back. *If they aren't going to help me, I have no way to help them. There's no reason why I should have to put up with abuse.* She didn't have anything to say to Jim. She didn't really love him anymore. *But Doug is amazing. That man is going to give me children someday.* A small silhouette froze. A single tear appeared and disappeared back into the darkness.

Doug and Rabbit soon found themselves struggling to stay warm. Snow on the ground, sniffling and sneezing, their efforts to find warmth and sustenance yielded meager results. Worried that the wet environment would ruin her paintings, Rabbit took them to the local community center. "They are very important to me. I don't want them to be destroyed by the weather. Would you please take care of them? You can hang them on the wall! I will come back for my artwork as soon as I can find housing for myself!" The administrators received the paintings responding with non-answers. She shuffled out the door, embarrassed and feeling hopeless.

Bickering with discomfort, Doug and Rabbit spent the nights napping at the laundromat, and days begging for change just a block away from the University campus. People shuffled past them quickly, looking the other way. Nobody was in the mood to help. Finally, the couple gave up on Oregon and headed out to the highway.

Hitchhiking back to California felt like an immense failure. *Now I'm proving my mother correct. I am a failure. I'm worthless. Helpless and broken, I'm just following Doug, expecting him to save me.* In this shamed and broken state, they made their way back to Sacramento.

At first, they stayed with some of Doug's friends in the secret apartment. Rabbit found herself looking down a familiar line of trees. *Now I get to finally see what kind of goodies they have in the little market!* This time when Doug headed around the corner from the market, he brought his traveling partner with him. Behind the market, into the alley, and up the fire escape to a hidden apartment they descended in the night.

Sleeping in the living room, the nightly parties were smaller than the ones she had experienced at their big house in Lawton. These were people she didn't know, and she felt no comfort in getting to know them. Rabbit suspected that they thought very little of her. More arguing followed, soon, she was waiting for Doug's instruction before doing anything. She would not leave to go any farther than the little corner store downstairs. She was afraid that if she went farther, she would return to find him gone without her.

Rabbit felt entirely too lost and dependent. She felt unsafe and unwanted, and clung to a shameful hope that somehow, he was going to save her and help her find happiness. The desperate feeling of limbo dangled the girl by the ankles. When Doug's friends were forced to move, roommates went in different directions, and the two found themselves again without a warm place to sleep. They began spending nights at his mother's place on the north side of the metro area. Something was not clicking between them. Rabbit felt rejected.

I am just a burden. I'm terrified and I don't know what to do with myself. She felt ugly and crazy. *It's my fault that everything has gone wrong. It's my responsibility to fix it. If I can figure out how to fix it, then he will love me again. Then I will feel beautiful again.* Rabbit spent too much time waiting for Doug to pay attention to her. As she became less important to him, she became more depressed, and thereby less attractive to him. Grasping at straws, she strained to gain the approval of his family.

It was a long walk down the railroad tracks into town. Without much money for transit, they simply followed the transit lines on foot, until they could get to the part of town where the light-rail was only a quarter. Sometimes, they attempted to sneak on without paying. Rabbit was always afraid of getting caught. Still, trying to get spare change from passersby required being in a place with foot traffic. This meant heading downtown.

Rabbit wasn't making any progress. She felt just as trapped as she had been in Lawton. She sat quietly in thought on a wooden bench by a bronze sculpture. Occasionally Rabbit drummed up the courage to ask a passerby for spare change. Watching the pretty women in clean looking miniskirts with button up blouses, knee high boots and long trench coats, her thoughts wandered. *What would it take to get these pretty ladies to talk to me? Will I ever have my act together enough?*

What am I thinking? Why would they want to have anything to do with me?

Stumbling through the days with short money-making shenanigans didn't get Doug and Rabbit very far. It was getting old fast, and Rabbit knew that something would have to change, or she would simply leave again. She was terrified of what to do next. *I am still married to a man in Lawton. My mother was waiting for me to fail miserably. What legal obligations do I have to this man anyway? What can I do to win back my mother's faith?*

The best thing that Doug's mother could have done for her was to kick them out. Rabbit had been waiting for something. Not sure what exactly she was waiting for. Perhaps she was waiting for Doug to save her. Regardless, when it was down to the wire, Rabbit took the steps to save herself. Meeting with a landlord, she talked their way into a midtown apartment. Doug got a job at a little Deli, and she immediately began working very hard to find a job of her own.

Rabbit was nervous going into her interview for a position at Java City. Her self-esteem was boosted when she was hired on the spot. She went home to their apartment giddy with self-confidence. She immediately began projecting necessary income, budgeting, and trying to determine how she was going to make it all work. When Doug arrived home, she babbled on excitedly about the turn of events. She tried to explain to him how she had all the numbers, and everything was going to be fine. He showed little enthusiasm and made vague listening noises. Oblivious at first, Rabbit began to trail off and wandered in the kitchen, when she realized that he couldn't care less.

Rabbit got three to four shifts a week. Some shifts were opening shifts. She had to be up and out the door early enough to walk twenty minutes to work. In school, it was sufficient to simply arrive on time. Other "jobs" she had in the past had also been relatively loose. *This is a different scene. I want to do a good job. I want to be taken seriously.* Rabbit wanted to finally succeed at something.

Rabbit spent time focusing on crunching numbers after each paycheck. She wanted to make sure the bills would always be paid on time. She wanted to prove to her parents and herself that she wasn't a failure. *I want to be able to save and get ahead.* She included in her budget, small amounts to feed her urge to paint. Rabbit even began paying attention to her own personal health. She began trying to eat healthier and party less. The toll that her unhealthy lifestyle choices had taken on her daily wellbeing was becoming more apparent to her. Something was driving her to take better care of herself.

Doug seemed disinterested in these new habits. Instead of nesting in their new home, he frequently left his girlfriend behind to go to party with his friends. She stayed at home alone. When she did accompany him, she felt like she was a burden. People interacted with her as "his girlfriend". Nobody seemed to notice that Rabbit was a person with her own identity. This started to bother her, and she began to get jealous of his personal time. Of course, his reaction was defensive, and they argued more.

Voices in Rabbit's head notified her whenever an attractive woman would come into her work. Her desire to be intimate with women nagged at her. *Doug doesn't even know I exist anymore.* She began looking at ads in the paper, trying to find a friend that she could be herself around. Although she still didn't know exactly who that was. *Maybe I just need to make some new friends. Maybe I will find a girl I can be close with?* The few encounters that followed her interest in the newspaper ads did not answer any questions for her. Instead, they amplified her personal insecurities.

Rabbit had been plagued with a recurring dream for a while, but the frequency was increasing, and she was not sleeping well. Wandering through an empty house, she could hear a baby crying. Or was it two babies? She searched each room, looking in every closet. Opening every door, the crying always sounded like it was just on the other side of the wall. Something told Rabbit that it was her baby crying. She felt sorrow, fear, and loss. Waking up in a cold sweat, tears reminded her of scars she held inside her heart for the unborn children.

Rabbit felt ugly and alone and she believed she was on the verge of breaking up with Doug. She was sad to think that they had lost such a close friendship by becoming physically intimate. She promised herself she would not pursue a relationship like that with a man again. Not sure exactly how to end it, and terrified of her family finding out that she had failed again, she continued to go through the motions.

Rabbit tried to let go of expectations associated with what Doug was doing with his time. She spent time hanging out in Capital Park, drawing and writing. She tried to make friends with people that looked like the type of people that she had gotten along with in the past. Nobody really seemed interested in anything more than a party acquaintance. When she was clearly not looking for a party, her loneliness followed her from the park to their apartment, and into her paintings.

Feeling like she was wandering blind in a mist, Rabbit prayed for some kind of a sign to steer her in the right direction. Walking home from work one afternoon, she found a toy in the dirt by the light-rail tracks. *A yellow rubber what?* Remembering her mother's fondness for collecting orphans, she picked up the toy in the dirt. She couldn't tell exactly what it was, but it looked to have been attached to a keychain at one time. It was really dirty, and she rubbed it with her thumb and shirtsleeve as she walked. As it got a little cleaner, she began to realize it was a teething toy. *It's a foot!*

How funny. Why would I find a foot? Is this a sign that it's time to keep moving on? Doug and Rabbit's arguments were also getting more frequent. Emotional. She was dissatisfied. She wanted to be with girls. He wasn't so fond of the idea. Though she had convinced him that a threesome might be fun. They tried that and it went terribly sour. He made it clear that he did not want to do that again. It had been all her idea and really had taken some coaxing. She wasn't happy about the way it had turned out either. *Maybe I should just leave and try to find a girlfriend instead?* Rabbit was jealous when Doug spent time with other people. *I must really just need a break.*

Rabbit dismissed the brief thought that a teething toy might be a sign of a coming child. Laughing and shuddering at the idea of what she might have to deal with if that were true, she moved on to other thoughts. More comfortable thoughts. Springtime thoughts. Spring brought so many colors; she was inspired to distract herself with painting.

Chapter 8
Father's Day

In May, Rabbit purchased tickets for an upcoming concert, with the intention of taking her dad for Father's Day. As spring progressed, she got more excited about the show. Dad is going to come to Sacramento to visit me! *We'll get to spend a whole day together!* The Grateful Dead were coming to the amphitheater and it felt like a family reunion was coming to town. *Its extra special that I get to take Dad to a show! Now I have an opportunity to show Dad that I am not a failure!*

Midweek before the show, the deadheads began showing up. Wednesday afternoon, Rabbit was finishing up her shift at the Cafe'. A truck with a cab-over camper pulled into a parking space a half block up the street from the Cafe'. Dirty patchwork travelers moved in and out of their traveling wagon, as Rabbit listened to the manager complain about them. "I hate those dirty freaks. I can't wait until they come in! It's going to make my day, calling the police and having them removed!"

Counting the minutes until her shift was over, Rabbit prayed that the deadheads would not come into the Cafe'. As soon as she clocked out, she grabbed her backpack and headed across the street to warn them. She felt no fear in approaching them right away. "Hey Now! I'm glad to see you made it safely into town for the show, but I have to warn you to stay away from that Cafe'." She pointed across the street to the Java City.

Even though they didn't know her, they recognized the familial camaraderie of a fellow deadhead. They appreciated the warning and asked where a better place would be. Rabbit gave them a little run down of the midtown options, and after a short time, offered that they could stay at the apartment for a day or two. It didn't take long for her new friends to liven up the quiet sadness of the apartment. By the time Doug got home from work, there were a handful of hippies cooking dinner in the kitchen and libations were bountifully circulating. He didn't seem at all upset by the circus taking over their home.

Rabbit loved the smell and sound of an apartment full of hippies. It reminded her of the way The Oasis had been whenever the Dead came to the Bay Area. *Partying is okay sometimes. I have been good. And Jerry coming to town is cause to celebrate!* Part of her longed to go with them when they traveled on past Sacramento. But Rabbit was trying to be a responsible adult. *Dad will be arriving in a day or so, to visit and I really want him to see how I am finally not failing.* Rabbit warned her new friends that they all had to be gone by the time Dad arrived. They were appreciative of the hospitality. "No problem sister! I understand about parents! We're just happy to be here now!"

Doug and Rabbit went to the Friday night show with their new friends. Tripping through the magic mist of music, they spent a wonderful evening dancing. After the show, they rode back to midtown with their new friends, and proceeded to continue the evening's festivities.

Sometime in the early hours of morning, Doug and Rabbit retreated to their bedroom in search of privacy. Colors touched senses that she could not describe adequately with words. Emotions and passion intertwined sparking a closeness that she had not experienced with him in a while. A strange feeling overtook her. *We have just made a child.* She shuddered and looked at the clock. 4:25 am.

Rabbit was quick to dismiss this intuitive feeling as simple paranoia. She tucked the brief moment of clarity away in the back of her mind. It was an unnecessary fear that she didn't want to carry with her. Tucking her arms around Doug, she closed her eyes as they snuggled into a colorful dream state. Ribbons of lights danced under her eyelids as she fell asleep listening to the sound of Doug's breath in the darkness.

First light inspired Rabbit to rise quietly, leaving Doug in the bedroom still sleeping. She made coffee and began cleaning the kitchen up. She began quietly making morning noises, and the house guests seemed to take the gentle cue. Once the first batch of coffee had brewed, she filled 2 cups and brought them back into the bedroom. She placed one of the cups on the floor near the closet and brought the other to the corner where Doug lay sleeping on their makeshift bed, a thick pallet of blankets stacked on the floor. She placed his coffee on their milk crate side table and kissed him on the forehead.

Rabbit returned silently to her own coffee. She picked up the cup, took a sip, and left the room nervously. *Did that really happen last night? I was just imagining that wasn't I?* Shaking her head, she grabbed a pack of smokes off the counter, and thrust them into her pocket. Feeling around in her pocket, she made sure she had a lighter before tiptoeing through the bleary people slowly gaining consciousness on her living room floor.

Outside the apartment, Rabbit sat down on the sidewalk. She placed her coffee cup on the ground and pulled out her smokes and lighter. She removed a cigarette and placed the pack next to her coffee cup. After lighting her cigarette, she placed the lighter neatly on top of the pack. She took a drag, exhaled, and picked up the coffee cup. *Coffee and cigarettes. The perfect way to start the day. I hope today is a good day.*

Rabbit sat quietly enjoying the sound of the morning breeze. She heard noises coming from inside that informed her Doug had gotten up. His voice was not often loud but had a quality that was rich and distinct. It carried through the window and out onto the street. Something about it frightened her and she dismissed the thought. Something moved in the bushes nearby, startling her out of her thoughts. *What was that?* She stared at the hostas shining in the morning sun. *There's nothing there.* She looked down into her cup. *And there is nothing there either. Time for a refill.*

Rabbit got up from sitting cross-legged. Her legs tingled and she had to lean against the wall to keep from falling. *Dammit. My legs fell asleep again. I hate it when this happens!* She waited a moment, steadied herself, and then stamped her feet in an attempt to get the blood flowing. She reached down, grabbed her smokes & lighter, and stuffed them in her pocket. With the empty cup, she opened the door to be greeted by a circle of smiling faces in a cloudy room that smelled of coffee, cigarettes and pot.

By 11 am, all of the new friends had cleared out, taking Doug with them. Rabbit paced around the small apartment, nervously awaiting Dad's arrival. She opened all the windows in an effort to air out the stale smell of smoke. Dad wouldn't arrive until later in the afternoon, so she would have plenty of time. She spent the next few hours pacing around the apartment making sure every last little mess had been addressed. When Dad got there, Rabbit was able to show him a clean apartment.

The apartment appeared to be meagerly furnished with only the small amount of furniture and belongings that were sensible to have. Rabbit knew that most of their stuff had been procured from various garbage piles. She had no plans of sharing this detail. She wanted him to be proud of her. He seemed impressed. She began to feel a little more confident with the potential of a good visit ahead. He drove them to the amphitheater where the concert was scheduled.

Walking through Dead Lot, Rabbit shared a few stories of traveling with her dad. He listened and seemed to like being there. He seemed to enjoy the colorful and friendly atmosphere but commented, "I just don't understand how people can make a life of it." He added,

"Eventually, people just have to grow up and get jobs." She winced. *I am trying my very best to be what he wants me to be. Today, we can just enjoy ourselves.*

Fireworks exploded in Rabbit's chest as they made their way through the ticket gates. She had spent more concerts outside than inside. The excitement of "actually making it in" never seemed to get old. They moved through the river of people past concessions and merchandise stands towards the amphitheater greens. "We'll figure out where we're gonna be and then I can go get drinks." Dad proclaimed as they moved onto the grass.

The pair claimed a patch of grass, laying a small blanket out on the ground. Rabbit set down her bag on the blanket as her father headed back out towards the concession stands. She took off her jacket and sat down on the blanket beside her bag. As the crowd moved around her, she stretched out her legs and let her thoughts wander.

I wonder if I will see anyone I know. I wonder if they will think I am a cop when they see me hanging out with my dad. They won't know it's my dad. They'll think he's an undercover. Or maybe I won't see anyone I know at all. I almost never actually run into anyone. But everyone says they've been to the same place. What are the odds that it's an accident? Or do people just avoid me? Or am I avoiding them? Maybe I am invisible? Why do I feel hollow? She looked up to see her father walking toward the blanket smiling broadly with a drink in each hand. *No. This is going to be a good day. I am here with my dad and we are going to have a nice time. I need to stop trying to ruin everything.*

Dad arrived at the blanket, handing Rabbit a large plastic cup of lemonade. "Hold this too," he said, extending the second beverage to his daughter before sitting down on the blanket next to her. "Now I can do this!" He exclaimed, as he reached in his pockets. Both hands emerged holding large silver paper wrapped packages. "Now I'll trade you. You give me my drink back and you get a hot dog!"

More people had crowded into the patchwork of blankets onto the grass since they had arrived on the green. Rabbit and her father sat listening to the music and enjoying their lunch. Smiling, Dad announced, "they had onions AND kraut," as he unwrapped a hot dog smothered in onions, mustard, and sauerkraut. "I didn't know if you'd want kraut, but if you do, you can have some of mine." She shook her head as she unwrapped a silver paper packet. "Okay More for me!" he replied before shoving the mountainous dog in his mouth.

Rabbit opened her packet to find a polish sausage with onions and lots of mustard. *Just like I used to order when we went to baseball games.* She smiled and looked over at her father. He was smiling and eating and watching the people. *I don't see him happy like this very often.* She slowly ate her sausage while the band started the first set. People moving through the crowd snaked through a winding series of patches of uncovered grass. Occasionally someone would dead end at their blanket, apologizing while hopping across the blanket to continue on their way.

The live music was, as always, moving and melodious, filling Rabbit's heart in a way incomparable to anything else in her life. By halfway through the first set they were both standing, and the crowd had filled in all the empty spaces that could possibly be filled. Dad started by simply tapping his foot. Over the course of several songs, he slowly began moving more and more of his body. By the end of the evening, he was dancing with his whole body.

Rabbit found it endearing to watch her father. Normally, she would have spent the concert wandering around, reaching out to strangers, with the hopes of making new friends while searching for old ones. This time, she stuck with Dad for the whole show. As the last song started, he quickly gathered up his stuff, urging his daughter to follow his example.

"Traffic is going to be horrendous getting out of here. We should get a head start." Dad explained as they moved briskly through the crowd. "It looks like we're not the only ones with this idea." He added, as they joined the crowd pouring out of the exit gates into the warm night. Rabbit remained silent, focused only on keeping up with her father.

Cars moved slowly through the parking lot toward the exit. Dad tried to make simple conversation. He asked about her job. Did she like it? Was she thinking about going to school at some point? She was distant, answering briefly without commitment. She apologized, indicating she was tired, and leaned her head against the window.

Rabbit closed her eyes, allowing herself to drift away while the truck waited in queue to return to the roadway. *This is our day together and I don't want to ruin it. He moved me out on Father's Day when I moved to Berkeley. I never even bothered to tell him 'thank you'. Maybe this will make up for it. I really do love my dad. I want him to be proud of me.*

Rabbit fell into her body as the truck turned onto her street. She opened her eyes, yawned, and ran her fingers through her hair. Dad pulled up to the curb in front of her apartment. She told him Happy Father's Day one last time as she pressed the door handle firmly and opened the door. "Thanks! I had a good time! I can't stick around though. I have an hour drive to get back home again."

The following week, Jim arrived. Rabbit was courteous with an intentional distance. Still, she was curious. She brought a clean towel out for him. "I expect that after sleeping in a van, you'll be glad to get a shower and spend an evening sleeping in an apartment." She suggested, handing him a clean towel. She paused awkwardly, not wanting to share details of her adventures after leaving Oklahoma, and still wanting to know his story. *It's not really my business. I am the one who left him behind.*

The void was quickly filled as Jim began answering her unasked questions. Jim was living out of a VW bus and had been staying in the Bay Area with Jasper. After getting kicked out of the Army, he had left Lawton with Mama and Will. He said that he had traveled with them for a little while, and then moved along on his own. They seemed to get along with each other in a relatively matter of fact manner.

Rabbit had warned Doug that Jim would be coming to visit. Doug simply replied that he wasn't going to make any changes in his daily life just because her ex-husband was coming to visit. When he arrived home from work that evening, Rabbit and Jim were talking. When they heard the doorknob turn, they both stopped and looked at the door. As Doug walked through the living room he nodded at Jim. No words were exchanged, and the two men made no attempt to engage further. Doug grabbed something from the fridge, took it into the bedroom, and closed the door.

Jim and Rabbit sat silent for a moment. She broke the silence by stating, "He probably won't come back out tonight. "Jim nodded as if to say that he understood. They sat silent for a moment more, and Rabbit got up. She got two glasses of water from the kitchen and returned handing Jim one. The two sat chatting for a little while longer as they slowly nursed the glasses of water.

The sun had set in the window behind Jim. Shadows fell across the living room, and Rabbit began feel herself fading. After listening to the short summary of Jim's last seven months, she politely excused herself from the conversation. She asked if he needed any more blankets or pillows before disappearing into the bedroom where

Doug had been practicing guitar. Settling in for the evening, she was distinctly aware of an awkward feeling, sleeping in the bedroom with her boyfriend, knowing that her estranged husband was sleeping in the living room. *Strange small world.*

The next day, Doug got up early and headed across town to go to work. Rabbit had the day off and an agreement with Jim that they would attempt to take care of their divorce while he was there. Of course, Rabbit would be paying for the divorce. *I suppose he only followed me looking for some kind of closure. He already knew that our relationship was over. I am looking forward to the end. I'm not really sure where I am going or what is going to happen next. But I know now that I was way too young to get married. It was ridiculous for me to expect that getting married was going to somehow give my life meaning.*

Rabbit came to the conclusion that if she had met Jim somewhere in the punk scene in California, their relationship probably wouldn't have lasted much longer than a three-week fling. The circumstances in Lawton had been different. Unfortunately, the location had not made up for the lack of substance necessary to ensure longevity in their relationship with one another.

Rabbit answered an advertisement for "quick & easy divorce". A couple hours later Rabbit and Jim walked into the office of a local divorce attorney. They anticipated a quick process but learned the truth of the process upon arrival. The attorney had advertised a low rate. It turned out that a quick divorce would be pretty easy to do, since they didn't have any community property. There were no children, houses, joint credit cards. There was nothing outstanding that they would have to divide.

As they sat in the office, waiting for the attorney to draw up the paperwork, Rabbit and Jim bickered about small details. He began to smile when she became irritated. She didn't like arguing. He made a comment about how sexy she was when she was angry. That really pissed her off. "That is why we are getting divorced. I don't like being angry." Of course, there was so much more to it than that. Without words, they agreed not to discuss the really deep reasons, and deferred to the easy responses. After it was all over, Jim left town. Rabbit returned to her now normal routine.

Chapter 9
Unsolicited

It had only been a few short months since Doug and Rabbit had gotten settled into the midtown apartment. Time seemed to move quickly, and a great deal changed in those short months. Rabbit had clearly started nesting, while Doug seemed more interested in flying the coop. Now that she didn't have to spend all day on the corner, bumming change, or trying to hustle a safe place to stay, she was able spend time doing things she actually wanted to! She spent her free time amusing herself painting, walking, singing, writing, and observing the world in between her shifts. She tried to talk to Doug about her days. He showed little interest unless it had to do with sex or food or drugs. She wanted him to see her accomplishments, to praise her, to love her. More than anything, she wanted to be loved.

Early summer was Rabbit's favorite time of year. The weather was beautiful, and it made her antsy. *I feel like it's the season to travel. But we're not doing that now. Everyone has to grow up and get a job eventually.* She decided to walk to the Deli where Doug worked. When she arrived, she decided she was craving pickles. She bought one of the giant kosher dills out of the Deli jar. The ladies that worked with Doug teased her about being pregnant. She scoffed at the concept. Walking back home, she ate about half the pickle and decided that she had eaten quite enough. She didn't feel well at all and went to bed soon after she got home.

The week leading up to her birthday, Rabbit felt uneasy. She zombied through her opening shifts. She did not go to Capital Park after work. She did not go downtown, or to the pier. Rabbit went directly home and was in bed by noon for three days in a row. Napping away the afternoon, she waited after work for Doug. Of course, he had other plans, and returned home later than she expected. By the end of the week, she was in shambles.

Walking to work, the day before her birthday, Rabbit struggled to wake up as she moved forward down the sidewalk. Rubbing her eyes, she dodged roots and lifted cement protruding in her path. *I'll be awake enough to make coffee by the time I get there. Let's hope I don't bust my face in the process.* She lifted her left leg higher to step over an especially large root that had pushed its way through the old sidewalk. *It's amazing how strong they are. Streets and sidewalks are paved over its roots. It's grown-up drinking toxic rain. And still it persists. I can be that strong. I am doing it now. I feel like shit. And I am going to work anyway. On time. And not hung over.*

Rabbit paused as she reached the edge of the cafe parking lot. She knocked back the hood of her sweatshirt while pulling a comb out of her right back pocket. It took her less than a minute to run the comb through her hair and weave a neat braid down her back. Tying the end of her braid, she brushed her hands against the front of her jacket and headed for the back door.

Rabbit had managed to not get scheduled for work on her birthday. Working opening shift, followed by a day off usually meant that she would do something after work and spend her day off recuperating, but she didn't feel very festive. *Some luck. I'd rather work on my birthday and have the day after off. But I'm not saying a word. The manager is a prick. The less I have to talk to him, the better.* As her co-workers arrived, Rabbit took refuge in the regular routine at work.

Barreling through the opening checklist, it wasn't long before it was opening time. Standing at the register, Rabbit turned on the auto pilot function and left her body. Smiling robot girl took drink orders and lined up paper cups. For the next five hours the line of customers grew and shrank and grew and shrank, until eventually it fizzled out altogether.

In a dark room, deep inside the robot, a huddled human sat on the ground sobbing. *Why do I feel like shit? I always feel like shit, but this feels different.* The figure rocked, pulling a soft blanket tightly around their shoulders. *No, I don't always feel this way. I was getting better.* Hands warm up rubbing against the soft blanket. *I was trying to be healthy. I haven't been partying with Doug. I have been staying home. Something else is wrong.*

Rabbit glanced up at the clock. *Five more minutes.* Her focused shifted as she snapped back into her body. The edges of the room seemed to waver slightly, and she got a little dizzy. *Deep breath kid. You can do this. It's almost your day off.* The manager seemed to appear out of nowhere at just the right time, to change out the drawers for the shift change. Rabbit disappeared as quickly as the manager had appeared for the new shift. *That guy is creepy! I hate how he just appears, and he stands way too close.*

Rabbit hastened to make her way down the block. Exhaling when she crossed the next street as if she had been holding her breath for the last ten minutes. A weight lifted off her chest and she found herself smiling a little. *Tomorrow is my birthday and I have the day off!* The world tilted slightly, and she stopped walking. Dizzy, she took a moment to catch her breath. *Just a few more blocks and I can sit down and relax.* Her vision stabilized and she returned to walking, but slower than her normal gait.

Rabbit felt eyes on the back of her neck. She stiffened slightly, sped up just a little, and paid close attention to make sure her pace was steady and her path unwavering. The faint clicking of bicycle spokes whispered in her left ear. "Hey girl, where you off to in such a hurry?" She heard a guy's voice coming up behind her. Rabbit glanced over her shoulder to see a young guy following alongside her on his bike. The half-zipped hoodie hanging loosely off his shoulders, showed only a plain T-Shirt beneath. His sweatpants were as plain and generic looking as the 10-speed he was riding.

Rabbit tried to ignore the man on the bike. Staying focused on the path in front of her, she hoped he would just move on. She could see her block rapidly approaching. "Come on baby. Don't be a bitch. Why don't you talk to me?" The voice sounded like he was right in her ear.

She stayed focused ahead and responded curtly. "I'm just going home from work. I want to get home."

Panic shot through Rabbit's chest. The moment was frozen. The figure sat rocking in the dark cold room. *Oh my god. Oh my god. He's touching me. He's on a bike and I am walking. Why is he touching me? Is he going to rape me? It's the middle of the day. We are in public. I travel all over this country and this is where I get accosted?* She looked down to see the guy on his bike frozen next to her, with his arm outstretched, his hand on her breast.

The moment passed. Rabbit swung her arms out as he ran. *I'm almost there. I'm almost home.* She could hear the guy cursing her. *Did I knock him over? Is he going to follow me? What if he sees where I live?* She turned a hard right, cutting down the alley behind her apartment building. Ducking behind the dumpster, she froze, listening. *Is he coming? Did I lose him?* She heard no bicycle clicking and decided it was safe enough to come out. She moved quickly down the pathway past the pool and through the courtyard until she made it to the apartment door. She fumbled for the key, and once inside, locked the door behind her and pulled her curtains closed.

Sinking down into her bean bag chair, Rabbit breathed deeply. *That just happened. That really just happened.*

Happy Birthday to me. Today is my last day of being a teenager and this is how the day starts. She grabbed a blanket that lay in a pile on the floor nearby. Kicking off her shoes, Rabbit pulled the blanket over her head to hide from the sunlight. A single tear escaped as she closed her eyes.

The light was dim when Rabbit awoke abruptly. "What time is it?" She said aloud in the darkening room. *Nobody else is here. Who are you talking to? Myself, of course. Because I'm crazy. What's new? But seriously, what time is it? Did I sleep all day?* She got up and turned on a light to check the time and confirm that she was indeed alone in the apartment. *Almost six o'clock. I wonder if I will even see Doug today. He is always gone.*

Rabbit went into the kitchen to make a peanut butter sandwich. She noticed the little rubber foot. *A baby toy.* She recalled the deli girls teasing her the previous week. *I'm not pregnant. I had my period on time.* Rabbit's periods were pretty easy. The first day was always rough, but they usually only lasted three days. Her last period had been on time and had even been unusually light and easy. Her eyes moved back to the little rubber toy. "There's no need to stress myself out over this. I will just go to the store, buy a pregnancy test, and take it. Then I will see there is nothing to worry about." She spoke out loud, with only herself to hear. The words reassured her, and her logic seemed reasonable.

Rabbit grabbed her backpack and rifled through it, disposing of trash and making sure she had her wallet and keys. *It's warm, but there is a breeze. You never know.* She stuffed her hoodie into her backpack and glanced around the room to locate her sandals. *Right by the door where I left them. I'm good.* She threw her backpack half on, one strap secured loosely on her left shoulder as the right strap quietly pressed into her back. She slipped on her sandals and headed out the door.

Rabbit headed out of the apartment courtyard and towards the corner. Halfway down the block, she stopped. *Did I lock the door?* She turned around and returned to check the door of her apartment. *Yes. Its locked. Okay. Good.* She paused briefly in front of the door to double check everything in her backpack. *Keys? Check. Wallet. Check. Jacket? Check. Walkman? Check. Do I have any good tapes? Eric Clapton. Okay. That will do. Notebook and pens? Check. You never know. Maybe I will find adventure along the way?* She double checked all the zippers on the backpack one more time, and then threw the strap back over her left shoulder before heading out of the courtyard toward the sidewalk.

The warm summer breeze did not require a jacket. Rabbit stumbled as her sandals moved loosely on her feet. She stopped under a big oak tree, pulling off her backpack as she knocked her shoes off. She bent down, picked up her sandals and dropped them into her the backpack. This time, she put the backpack all the way on. She secured the straps by pulling them a little tighter, paying extra attention to make sure that her load was evenly balance.

Rabbit stopped again at the next shady corner and exclaimed aloud. "Wait! What am I doing?" She pulled her backpack off once more. Balancing on one leg, she bent her right knee up as a makeshift table. Holding the pack on her knee, Rabbit rifled through her belongings until she located headphones and the Walkman. With headphones, Walkman, and cassette precariously balanced in her right hand she flipped the pack back onto her left shoulder. Switching the handful to put her right arm into the strap, freed her hands to put the headphones on.

Headphones secured over her ears; Rabbit slipped Eric Clapton Unplugged into the cassette player. She adjusted the volume, adjusted the straps to her backpack, and then proceeded along the path. Hopping quickly across the sunny pavement, she dawdled in shady patches. Clapton's smooth voice captivated her as she danced on the bumpy sidewalk beneath the trees.

Only about a half mile walk to the drug store. *Nothing better to do. I will pick up a test. Just to put my mind at ease. But I'm sure I'm just being stupid.* Her thoughts wandered as her legs moved deftly along a well-trodden path. Around roots, over buckled cement, and across busy streets, autopilot followed the rhythm guitar. She rocked and nodded as she bounced west towards the blaring sun awaiting the edge of midtown.

Rabbit continued walking while retrieving her sandals from the bouncing satchel. She paused at the busy corner, dropping the sandals onto the ground at her feet. She slid her feet into them and turned to press the walk button on the pole to her left. A click echoed in her ears as the tape came to an end and brought her quickly to the present. Gravity hit hard and the girl almost lost her balance. Leaning on the pole to her left, she surveyed her surroundings. *How did I get here?*

Suddenly distinctly aware of how much sweat was dripping down her face, Rabbit was overwhelmed by a sensation of being watched. Cars in all four lanes of the busy thoroughfare slowed as drivers turned to stare directly at her. In slow motion, frame by frame, she took in her surroundings. Somewhere in a hot shadowy alley, a bewildered boy smells the stench of piss and asphalt, cars, and pizza. It hung in the air like incense. He blinked searching the shadows for the source of the smell.

A half block up, Rabbit took note of a bus stop bench occupied by three people. Green paint peeling revealed old splintering wood. A couple sat on the bench while the third sat up on the back of the bench, feet planted firmly on the seat between the couple. She watched him wrap his shirt around his head. She listened as beads of sweat shone on his shoulders reflected the echoing madness of the music blaring out of the boombox on his lap. The light in the crosswalk changed to the little white man, and Rabbit stepped off the curb.

Chapter 10
Blue Girl

Pane by pane the row of stores flashed closer and closer. Time sped up as she approached Tower Records. Opening the door, Rabbit was immediately brought back to the present by the rush of canned air pushing against her wet forehead. "You gotta check that. Hey! You gotta check that bag chickee." Rabbit turned her head, realizing someone was actually talking to her. Blue hair and blue eyes gleamed fiercely at Rabbit. A blue plaid baby doll dress clung to the curves of her small perky breasts.

Rabbit's thoughts got hot and shadowy. Somewhere a lonely boy groaned. The clerk looked ready to jump over the counter if necessary. Rabbit flushed with embarrassment. *I'd love it if she jumped my bones. So cute!* She removed the backpack, pausing to put her Walkman and headphones in the bag. "Sorry about that. Wait a sec." She located her wallet and keys, shoving them in her pocket. Making sure all the zippers and strings were secure before handing over the pack gave her a chance to make conversation. She opened her mouth, and all that came out was "Thank you."

I am such an idiot. What did I think I was going to say? Hi. Do you have a boyfriend? That's okay. So do I. Wanna mess around sometime? Can I have your number. Ya right. Never gonna happen. I'd probably get punched in the face. Man, she was cute. Rabbit quietly talked to herself as she browsed the cassettes on the back wall. She finally settled on one from the discount rack, and one new one. Ultravox and The Beastie Boys. *I can justify this. I work hard. I put up with a lot of bullshit. I should be able to buy myself a birthday present.*

Rabbit was disappointed to discover a different clerk behind the counter when she went to check out. She paid for her new tapes, retrieved her satchel, and headed out the door. Exiting the air-conditioned building, she was pleased to notice that the summer evening had already begun to cool a bit. *I bet it dropped down to at least ninety. At least there's a breeze.* Hot wind dusted her hair with a light layer of grit from road construction down the road. She ran her fingers through her hair, pausing to tie it in a knot on the top of her head. *The breeze would help more if it wasn't hot wind. But the sun will be setting soon. It may even drop another five degrees!*

Walking north towards the pizza joint, Rabbit noticed the blue haired girl from the record shop. She was sitting, legs crossed, smoking a cigarette. Red Mad Dogs perched on her perfect nose; she took no notice of Rabbit as she approached the outdoor seating. Rabbit took a seat at a table not far from the girl in plaid. She nodded her head toward the blue girl, as she placed her backpack on the black patio table in front of her. *Now's my chance to not be stupid.* "Hey. How's it going?"

The blue girl flicked her cigarette butt into the gutter as she got up out of the black metal patio chair. Without looking at Rabbit, she responded "It's fucking hot."

Without indicating any desire for a response, she headed back towards the record shop. Rabbit pulled her cigarettes out of her backpack. *What did I think was going to happen? You are so stupid. Get over it. She means nothing. She's just some random girl. She's probably too old for you. And what are you doing looking at girls anyway? You have a boyfriend. But he doesn't want me anymore. There's something wrong with me.* Tears began to form behind her eyelids, and she squeezed them tight behind her sunglasses.

The moment paused as Cat tried to pull away from her body. Across the street, standing just out of sight, the shadow of a boy observed the conflict. "If I don't do something soon, I may never get the chance." Pensive, he struggled to move into view, but something held him back. Like a magnet the two were drawn toward each other. Only the magnet was somehow flipped, and Rabbit was pushing against him. "This doesn't make sense. I want her to see me. I just want to be seen."

Something pushed and pulled, twisted and repelled within the confines of Rabbits personhood. The pause ceased, time continued, and change in motion caused a brief dizzy spell. She decided she was finished with her cigarette and flicked the butt into the gutter. Shoving her newly purchased cassettes into her backpack, she took inventory. *Wallet, check, keys, check, Walkman., check. What else am I supposed to get before I go home?*

She looked up the street to see the evening light come on at the Rexall up the block. *Oh ya. I was going to go to the drug store.* Hesitating for a moment, she looked up and down the block for someone familiar. *Why does it matter? Who are you expecting to see? Nobody, I guess. It doesn't matter. I guess. What is wrong with me?*

The shadows stank of sweat and piss and pizza. The boy remained against the alley wall; eyes shut tight. He was afraid to open them and see what else was in the room. *Pizza. I smell pizza. That's right! Pizza! I can't take it in Rexall with me though. So, I will get that on the way back! I deserve pizza.* The thought of a big slice of pizza lifted her mood. She tried to keep her thoughts light and shallow as she browsed the aisles. Uneasy, she looked up to see the cashier eyeing her and her backpack. *Oh shit! He probably thinks I'm gonna steal something! I better hurry up.* She grabbed a cheap bottle of shampoo, holding it clearly in front of her. A couple aisles down, she located a pregnancy test. Pressing it up against the back of the shampoo bottle, she tried to hide what she intended on purchasing. She approached the cashier and quietly put them on the counter with a twenty.

Rabbit ignored the dirty look she swore the clerk was giving her. She shoved her change in her pocket. "Thanks." Grabbing the white plastic bag off the counter, she turned toward the door. Again, she was fluid and graceful, pulling the satchel half off as she walked. She quickly buried the drug store bag into her pack before reaching the door to the pizza shop. Suddenly the smell of pizza soured her stomach. *On second thought, pizza does not sound as good as I thought it did.*

The setting sun strengthened the shadows as Rabbit headed back into the tree lined neighborhood. *I wonder whether I will even see Doug today. I bet he will forget my birthday. Doesn't matter. I don't matter. I'm not even real. This isn't really me. This is all just a dream, a fantasy, somebody else's life. Whoever is directing this movie should give me a raise because I don't think anyone could play me quite like I do. If someone made a movie about my life, who would be cast to play me?*

The dark apartment was musty. Rabbit unlocked the door leaving it wide open as she entered. She dropped her bag onto the floor against the wall. She bent down to pull her cigarettes out of the bag. She pulled a lighter out of her pocket and sat down in the doorway of the apartment. Lighting her smoke, she gazed out into the courtyard. The hostas and ferns were comforting. *I really do like it here. Why am I so unhappy?* The boy in the shadows lay sleeping soundlessly. She looked past him, blind to the shell in the shadows.

Rabbit sat silently. The breeze guided the smoke from the burning cigarette. She watched it disintegrate into the evening air. "I have to move past this." She spoke to no one, to the empty courtyard. "I have to be more than this. I am more than this. I will paint." She put the cigarette out on the sidewalk and picked up the butt. Standing up, she glanced past the courtyard out onto the street. *I wonder if he will come home.* "Shut up. That doesn't matter. Tonight. We get to paint."

Somewhere in the shadows, the boy shifted in his sleep. Turning from one side to the other. No position was comfortable. But sleeping is always more comfortable than the alternative. She paused briefly in the door sensing the presence of the sleeping boy. She glanced into the courtyard once more. "There is no one there. You're crazy." She held her breath as she closed the door. She latched the two locks and exhaled.

Rabbit got her paints set up and found herself too sleepy to actually paint. Getting up early and staying up late was alerting her to another necessary point in taking better care of herself. *Yes. I deserve to sleep. I did a lot today. I am not lazy. I went to work. I took a nap... I got exercise. But you spent money. I shouldn't have done that.* "Shut up! Y'all need to shut up already. How many are there of you in my fucking head?" Rabbit chuckled forcibly, shaking her head and hissing through her teeth as she got up. Grabbing her smokes off the table, she announced to the seemingly empty room, "One more smoke, then I'll go to bed. I can leave all this set up and it'll be ready for me tomorrow!"

Sitting in the doorway, Rabbit sensed the presence of someone unseen. She shifted uneasily and got up to pace on the sidewalk while she smoked. "Is there someone there?" Only the sounds of passing cars, the light rail in the distance, and a faint echo of far-off sirens answered. *I'm just crazy. Doug always says I'm crazy. Everyone always says that. Maybe it's true. I might as well make the best of it.* Putting out the short end of the smoke on the sidewalk, she headed into the apartment. Closing the door behind her, she hesitated at the locks. "I guess I better leave the deadbolt unlocked in case Doug comes home."

In the bathroom, Rabbit emptied all the cigarette butts from her pockets into the waste basket. Removing her clothes, she climbed into the shower. Adjusting the water temperature so a cool, but not too cool, refreshing rain removed the top layer of the day, she let it pour over her head. Eyes closed, she imagined standing in the woods. A waterfall washed over her as she took in the ferns dappled in sunlight and shadow. Someone is there in the woods. The blue girl appears in a blue plaid bikini.

Rabbit feels her mound swelling, her clitoris hardening. Rubbing soap between hot legs, cool water steamed down the waterfall as the girl in plaid approached. Hearts race. Muscles tense as they reach out to kiss. She turns up the heat, plugs the tub, and lays down. Thighs pulsing, Rabbit closes her eyes to find the blue girl laying in the moss beside the waterfall. The bikini top is off.

Clutching at her swollen sex, Rabbit groans. The waterfall grows to a pool and Rabbit turned off the faucet. She lay in the tub, dozing in a pool, surrounded by ferns. Listening to the birds, she wondered where the blue girl had gone. It didn't seem that urgent though. Maybe just a passing thought. Then no thoughts. The blue girl moved quietly past, rounding a corner, and disappeared into the shadows. Somewhere in a dark alley, a sleeping boy shifts to the side, unconsciously lifting his leg to make room for an erection. The boy looks up to find himself deep in a forest. Nestled between ferns, he looks through the mist to glimpse a girl with long blue pig tails walking towards him.

"Hey Babe. Come to bed. You know you can drown that way?" Doug's voice startled Rabbit out of a cool misty redwood forest. "Get out of the bathtub and come to bed." She lifted herself out of a tub full of cold water. Doug stood in the doorway, extending a hand and a towel. "You really gotta be careful. You think I'm joking? I don't want to come home to find you dead in the bathroom." Half-asleep, she steadied herself with Doug's steady muscular arm. Something hot pulsed between her legs. "You look like a giant raisin." She blushed and grabbed the towel out of his hand.

"Thanks. Thanks for that." Rabbit responded as she dried off her arms and legs. Doug retreated to the bedroom and began getting undressed. Hanging her head upside down, Rabbit twisted the towel around her hair, and then flipped it back to hold it in place. She walked into the bedroom rubbing the towel on her wet hair.

"You might as well give up and come to bed." Doug said, "That towel is as wet as your hair." She smiled at him as she pulled the towel off her hair. "Oh, that's sexy. And tonight, for dinner we're having cold raisins."

Rabbit laughed and threw the wet towel at Doug. "Shut up! You know you love me." She climbed under the thin summer blanket that covered their makeshift bed on the bedroom floor. *Doug is home! He's home and he's being nice to me. Maybe my birthday will be okay after all.* Snuggling up against his long torso, Rabbit nuzzled his coarse dark hair. The smells of his day filled her lungs as she closed her eyes and returned to the woods where she searched for an answer, or a question. *What was I searching for? Where was I going?*

Chapter 11
The Test

Mid-morning was announced by the sound of the apartment door closing. Rabbit opened one eye to see the bed empty next to her. She opened the other eye and peered around the room. *No note. No obvious gifts left behind. I'm not ready.* She closed her eyes and rolled over, pulling the blanket over her head. When sweat dripping in her eyes forced her to open them again, the blankets were in a pile at her feet.

Rabbit sat up. Long legs outstretched, she bent in half, extending her fingers towards her toes. She held the position for the duration of three deep breaths before sitting up. Spreading her legs wide, she repeated the stretching pattern three times. Once aiming for the left foot, once between her legs, and once aiming for her right foot, she stretched, counting slow deep breaths. Drawing her feet in towards each other, she pressed the bottom of her feet together.

"Today is my birthday." Rabbit announced to the seemingly empty room. "I am now officially twenty years old. I really didn't believe I would live this long." Lifting the naked body up from the nest of bedding, the young woman stretched her arms out like tree branches. She took one more long deep breath. "And today I will celebrate this victory by spending the day painting!"

A small overflowing laundry basket was stationed against the south wall of the bedroom. One long stride landed

Rabbit directly in front of the basket and she squatted down to dig through the clothes. Two knees cracked beneath her. "Geez. Happy Birthday! You're old now. This is what it feels like." Grabbing a purple gauze sundress from the pile, she stood up to the sound of more crackling. Small twinges of pain shot from behind her knees down her calves, and up the back of her thighs.

Ignoring these nerve signals was easy. Rabbit ignored warnings all the time. Pulling the dress over her head, she headed into kitchen. *Time to make coffee! No. You should go buy yourself a coffee. No, I spent money yesterday. I can't afford to do that every day. You should totally go buy yourself a good coffee for your birthday.* Standing in the kitchen, Rabbit swung around and placed her hands on the edge of the counter. "Look. Y'all can shut up. I am not going into work on my day off." Silently, she rinsed and filled the decanter for the coffee machine, she had picked up at Goodwill. She poured coffee grounds into the filter basket, swung the basket closed, and pushed the red power button.

The little coffee machine that could, slowly woke up while Rabbit sat in the doorway of the apartment. Peering out into the midday courtyard, she tapped her cigarette. Smoke clung to the space next to her door. She looked up and took note. *No wind. A day of no change. Everything is still.* She looked to the left, inhaling once more. Exhaling she stared into the strategically placed ferns. *It still feels like there's someone watching me.*

Rabbit smashed the short cigarette into the ground and got up. Sweat made her dress stick to the middle of her back. Turning to enter the apartment, she left the door wide open. After retrieving a cup of coffee, doctoring it up with just the right combination of milk and sugar, she returned to her perch on the front porch. After another cigarette, the coffee cup was empty. She returned to the kitchen for a refill and headed for the art supplies awaiting her return.

Rabbit spent the better part of the day painting. Music played. Occasionally, she put the paintbrush down to dance until the end of a song. Then she'd refill her coffee cup and take a smoke break perching in the shadows of the front door. After each break she returned to her creations. She spent the rest of the week painting after work. She talked to Doug very little. When she tried to talk to him about her paintings, he showed little interest.

Several days passed. Rabbit needed to make the trek across town to the grocery store. This usually took a couple of bags and a few hours. Doug agreed to help, which of course should make things easier. *We don't actually get to spend the day together much anymore. I know it's just groceries, but at least I don't have to do it alone.* Doug sat, leaned over, tying his shoes. Rabbit sat on the floor and dumped out the contents of her backpack. She started to push it all into a pile against the wall. "What is that? When did you go up to Rexall?" Doug questioned the contents of her pack.

"Oh ya. I forgot. I was out running around last week." Rabbit tried to dismiss the questioning, piquing Doug's interest. He leaned over and grabbed the plastic bag, expecting to find condoms, knowing that they never used them. If he caught his girlfriend with condoms, it would give him an excuse to leave. The young woman protested as his large hands ripped open the bag she had so neatly tied shut. "A pregnancy test?" His face went white, then flushed. "Were you even going to tell me about this?"

Rabbit hesitated. The big scary man grew an inch with each word that bellowed out of his mouth. Meanwhile, she felt herself shrinking, shaking more and more with each echoing syllable. "I forgot. I... I bought it because I was being paranoid. But then I stopped being paranoid and forgot about it." She blinked back tears, clutching at her hands. *Why does he have to be so scary? What did I do wrong? I always screw things up. Everything would be better if I didn't always screw things up.* "I... I haven't even taken the test. See? The package is still closed." She pointed at the blue and white box dampening in Doug's sweaty grip.

"Well. Why'd you waste the money if you weren't gonna take the test?" Doug's face screwed up as his thoughts began to race. "You were going to tell me, were you?" Rabbit started to reach out to grab the slowly crumpling box. She hesitated, fearing he would lash out. She started to speak. He sensed her bravery and attacked. "You're fuckin' someone else, aren't you? You're fuckin' someone else, and you got pregnant, and you wanted to make sure and take care of it without me ever finding out!"

Shadows painted the room in dingy gray and olive tones. Antique sconces reflected the echo of a sleeping body. Silently, the outline glimmered against the surrounding dusty floor. Tongue and groove exposed footsteps of smeared dusty patterns searching for a hiding place. Behind a shuttered cabinet, a figure is contorted into the small space, arms and legs folded into each other. In the center of the room, hiding in the middle of the hidden echo, Cat rocked back and forth.

The young woman curled into a fetal position, rocked fiercely, as muddy waterfalls splashed down hot cheeks. "No!" She protested. "No! There's nobody else! I love you!" Sharp pains shot up folded calves, and she cried out. The tall young man grew three inches taller. The woman uncurled her limbs, watching legs grow longer. The room around her suddenly seemed so much taller. Emotions fell out of carnival mirrors and the scary man approached.

"What the hell is wrong with you?" Doug unclenched his fist, dropping the blue and white box on Rabbit's belly. Pane by pane, the box moved through twelve miles of emotions, gently bouncing off her belly and landing on the floor beside her. She turned her head and looked up at her boyfriend. "Well... Are you going to take the test, or not?" Anger had given way to fear. A life of misery flashed before his eyes. He wondered what happened to the brave free spirit he'd met in Lawton, and where did this sniveling pitiful crazy woman come from? "Take the fuckin' test already. Let's get this over with."

Rabbit wiped her face with the bottom of her sun dress. She tried to suck the snot back in her running nose, consequently making a noise not unlike a small pig with a sinus infection. Doug made a snide comment that she ignored. Wordlessly, small fingers grasped a crumpled blue and white box as long elastic legs shrunk, bent, and moved towards the bathroom. Muscles, ligaments, and bones communicated at micro sonic frequencies, directing a hand to push the bathroom door closed. Confident that autopilot was sufficiently in control, the brain began sending spurts of emotion triggering chemicals straight to the young woman's solar plexus.

Brain, eyes, and hands worked together to unfold the paper directions. One side in Spanish, the other in English, provided step by step illustrated instructions. *Do they really think I need instructions on how to piss on a plastic stick?* The waxy paper fluttered to the floor. The front of her dress draped across her lap. Fingers fumbled, tearing at the plastic sleeve that contained the magic stick of doom.

The door opened into the bedroom. Doug lifted his arm to cover his eyes from the bathroom light on their bed. Rabbit emerged hysterical. Flinging herself down beside him, she curled up into a fetal position. Large tears formed rivulets down her face, as she clutched her knees. Uneasy, Doug attempted to comfort her, petting her hair silently. Tears began dripping in her nose and she choked. She began coughing and he supported her as she sat up.

"I just don't want to have to do that awful thing again!" She sat leaning into Doug's chest. His earthy smell calmed her slightly. She sniffled and choked, wiping her nose on her dress as she spoke. "You don't understand how awful it was. There were girls in there who thought it was just a joke! Like a form of birth control. They didn't seem to care!" She burst out giving way to a fresh waterfall of tears. Doug just kept petting her hair. Staring at the poster on the wall, he knew there was nothing he could say in that moment that would have made any difference. Women just get emotional, if you want to be with them, you have to be able to put up with this.

Rabbit took another deep breath. It felt good to be in Doug's arms. She could feel him petting her hair. "I just can't handle this right now. I just don't want this to be happening. Can we just wait to deal with this? I'm scared, and I'm tired. And I just want to lay down in your arms." Doug smiled, patting himself on the back for his diligence and patience. He responded by supporting her back and head with his arm and lowering her down to the pillow. When she landed there, his hair fell all around her face as he kissed her.

A week passed with little conversation between the two young lovers. Doug made a point to be at home by midnight. Rabbit paid close attention to what she said and how she said it. Terrified by the decision she was facing, she was desperate to talk to Doug, but afraid of what might be said, and of breaking down. *If I get emotional, he will shut down. He'll just stop listening. Then he'll start yelling. I can't stand the yelling. But this is the rest of my life. I can't do it alone. He doesn't really want to stay. He's just going to break up with me.*

Alone with her thoughts, Rabbit turned over, trying to find a more a comfortable position. It wasn't late, but she had to work an opening shift. *It's always so hard to fall asleep while the sun is still up.* Totally exhausted, and yet unable to sleep, she lay loosely in her body. Digging up memories of Psychology class in High School, she tried to remember the relaxation methods that her Psych teacher had taught them. Starting with her feet she slowly tensed the muscles in her body, moving gradually up her legs. Breathing with slow intention, she followed the instructor's directions.

For over a year, Rabbit had been haunted by recurring nightmares of a crying child. Always it was somewhere alone and frightened. She could hear it and would go searching through every room in the house. It was always a different house. She was always alone, searching for the crying infant in the dark.

Now, the nightmares about the crying child seemed to have stopped. They had been replaced with a young boy. Or at least the shadow of young boy. *Maybe not too young. Maybe a teenager. But he's scrawny. In the shadows. Behind a fire, in a campground somewhere. Maybe it's not a boy. It's only a shadow. Is someone following me?* Rabbit's legs began to cramp up. Her thoughts had wandered too far, and she forgot to let go. *Let go. Let it go. Let it all go. Remember. You can remember, and then let it go. Nobody is following you.*

Rabbit tried to maintain some control as she gradually released her muscles. First from her head and neck, then across her shoulders and down her back. Deep breathes burrowed into darkness and with it she was delivered into the dreamscape. The girl with blue pig tails appeared from the mist and took her hand. "Before you make any decisions, there's someone you really ought to meet." Together the two disappeared into the woods. The breeze sang softly in the branches of the redwoods as their footsteps faded.

The relationship between Doug and Rabbit had been on the verge of complete disintegration since they had first arrived in Sacramento. He felt burdened by this woman. He felt a connection, and the sex was good. But she was crazy! Still there was something about her that kept him coming home. Maybe it was just convenience? He hadn't been sure he cared. Now this was happening, and he was confused by feelings he didn't expect.

If there was a child coming, there was a serious decision to make. Rabbit knew that ultimately it was her decision to make. The plague of nightmares had initially become more frequent when the two first moved into their apartment. And then, sometime in the last few weeks they had actually stopped! She hadn't noticed at first. Now, looking back, the discovery brought with it a great sadness. Something in the shadows tugged at her heartstrings as she considered her inability to care for a child. She couldn't bring herself to go through that kind of procedure again.

Doug and Rabbit walked through midtown. The evening breeze was warm, and movement made it easier to talk. They both knew they had a serious discussion necessary and felt trapped by circumstances. Walking in the summer evening helped ease the feelings of confinement and made it easier to talk about uncomfortable subjects. Rabbit mentioning the option of putting the child up for adoption triggered a response from Doug that she was not expecting.

"We will not give our baby away to some stranger!" He grew hot with emotion. Reaching out for Rabbit's hand, as they walked, he continued. "I couldn't live with that. And what if they grew up thinking that their parents didn't love them, didn't want them?" He squeezed her hand. "I couldn't bear it." Rivers of emotion crashed like waves against each other. Hope and fear, joy and sorrow, the thrill of adventure, and misery of loss, all churned in her chest when he squeezed her hand. *He really loves me?*

Doug insisted that he wanted the child in his life. "But if you really want this child, then you've got to do this with me." Rabbit explained, her long voice pleading with him to understand. "You've got to actually be around to help. Like, you can't be staying out until midnight, or one or two. You need to actually keep a job, and then come home when you're not working." He nodded as she spoke. *I wonder if he really gets it. He can't just keep partying. If we have a child that becomes the center of our life.*

"Yes. Yes. I know all these things." Doug responded to her pleas. The couple continued to hold hands as they walked in the hot summer night. He made all the listening noises acknowledging that he'd have to live a different life as a parent that they had been doing. He made it clear he'd do whatever it took to make the necessary life changes. He stopped walking and turned to his lover. "I will prepare myself to be a father. I am afraid and excited. But I am sure this is a blessing." Rabbit clung to his words like they were made of gold. She agreed to keep the child, and promptly quit smoking cigarettes.

Chapter 12
Ashland

More conversations continued daily, as the couple discussed what steps they ought to take to prepare for the coming of a child. Rabbit expressed her distrust for the California welfare system. "I have seen way too many hippies get their children taken away." She convinced Doug that they should leave the state. She did not want to have a child in California. They decided to return to Oregon, agreeing that it would be a better place to raise a family.

Rabbit began preparing for the move by visiting the public Library. Sorting through the phone books, she found the correct phone book for Ashland, Oregon. She compiled a mailing list of cafes and restaurants. She prepared a resume and drafted a cover letter introducing herself. She stated in the letter that she would be moving to the area and was interested in any potential job openings that might be available. She closed the letter stating that she would follow up on the letter with a personal visit to their business in August.

Doug and Rabbit got rid of a lot of their stuff. She figured it would be easier to simply replace stuff than to try and move it all, especially when they really didn't know where they would be going. She didn't want all the money to go too fast. She was also concerned about being robbed or somehow losing their stuff. She went to the bank and purchased as many travelers checks as she could afford. *This way, we can budget our money.*

Doug and Rabbit wanted to rent a one-way moving truck. The rental of the truck came with a month's free rent in a storage locker. It seemed like a great deal, except they wouldn't rent to Rabbit because she was under twenty-five and didn't have a credit card. Doug's cousin Nina offered to help. They had grown up together like siblings and she felt a compulsion to look after Doug. They packed up the bare essential clothing and personal belongings into the moving truck, opting to get rid of easily replaceable items. With everything packed up, they left the empty apartment to go spend the night at Nina's house. The next morning the fleeing couple escaped Sacramento before sunrise, with the intention of driving straight through to their destination.

Hitting the road in the truck, Rabbit was anxious and excited. *It always feels good to travel. Heading back to Oregon again!* Leaving in the early morning meant they wouldn't have to pull over to sleep. But she got nervous towards the end of the drive because they were cutting it so close. They arrived in Ashland late in the afternoon. Less than 30 minutes before the office closed, they managed to sign the papers and get assigned a storage locker. They hastily emptied the truck into the storage locker and returned the truck. Leaving most of their stuff in the storage locker, they left carrying with them only bare necessities.

When Doug and Rabbit arrived in downtown Ashland, they found the park where everyone seemed to hang out. Parking themselves on the grass, they laid out a blanket. He wandered a bit while she rested. Then she wandered a bit while he rested. When Rabbit walked down the main street, she looked for businesses on her follow-up list. The first business that she recognized from her list was a little bakery called Manna From Heaven.

Taking a deep breath, Rabbit walked in the door with good posture and an air of self-confidence. She introduced herself to the man behind the counter, explaining, "I sent my resume in the mail. I just wanted to follow up." He responded that he had not received her resume. She was not deterred. "I've just moved to town and I am looking for a job. Do you have any openings?" Rabbit handed him a fresh copy of her resume. He looked her up and down. He responded again that he had never received her letter, following it up with "But if you would like to wait a little while, I will be happy to talk with you."

She sat down at a table looking around at the decor. The bakery smelled good. *I wouldn't mind working here. Not going to tell him I'm pregnant though. He will never hire me if he knows I'm pregnant.* She straightened up when he came around from behind the counter. He held her resume in his hand. The interview was brief. He seemed to have already decided to hire her and was more interested in her potential schedule. Rabbit tried to remain calm. She could work any shift. It was all fine. He told her to come back for her first day of training the following Monday. She never followed up with any of the other businesses. She didn't need to. She had gotten hired the first place she walked into!

Returning to the park, Rabbit was excited to tell Doug the news. She sat down on the blanket and she kicked off her little purple mary-janes. Wiggling her toes in the sunny grassy, Rabbit shared the news with her boyfriend. He congratulated her. Still, she felt like he was irritated that she had been successful so quickly. *I'm not going to let that get me down. Everything is going to be great!*

Rabbit grabbed her large purse with one of everything in it. Crossing the street in her bare feet, she went to the payphone in the main square. Standing across the street from the park, in a small courtyard, she pulled change out of her purse and began putting quarters in a public phone. Calling Dad made her nervous. She knew that he would be disappointed with her for leaving without telling him. *But I have a job already! Maybe he will be proud of me for taking initiative and getting a job so quickly?*

Pushing her purse around with her feet while she stood at the phone booth, Rabbit heard her father's voice pick up on the other end. He was glad to hear from her and concerned. Of course, he wanted to know why they had left. She told him that she was pregnant. She bragged to him about how prepared they were. "We have money to move into a place. I already have a job here." *Everything is going to be great!* He cautioned his daughter that no matter how prepared she thought she was, nothing could truly prepare her for having a child.

She was disappointed in his lack of faith but promised to call again soon. She hung up the receiver and glanced once more around the courtyard.

Not far from the phone booth Rabbit noticed an interesting fountain, like a small waterfall. The day was warm, and she felt invigorated by the pace in which everything was happening. With no concern about who was watching, or whether it was even legal, Rabbit decided she would wash her hair in the fountain. She pulled soap and a rolled-up towel out of her large purse. Taking her shirt off, she was stripped down to a sports bra and her loose skirt.

Kneeling down, Rabbit turned her head upside down and let the water run down her scalp. Twisting her body around, she made sure all of her hair was thoroughly wet before using the soap. Scrubbing her scalp and around her ears, Rabbit laughed at people taking notice of her ritual. Again, she dunked her head into the falling water of the fountain. Rinsing until she was sure she had gotten all the soap out took a little time. When she lifted her head up, flipping her wet hair back, water dripped down the front of her sports bra.

Grabbing the edge of her rolled towel, it unrolled in mid-air. Turning her head upside down again, Rabbit briefly towel-dried her long hair. She wiped water out of her ears and glanced around the main square. She got a few interested looks, but nobody was coming to arrest her for acting inappropriately in public. Rabbit pulled her shirt back on. She wore the towel on her shoulders to keep her wet hair from soaking her shirt.

Rabbit put the soap into a plastic bag, stuffed it into her purse and crossed the street back to the park. She sat back down on their blanket. She laid the damp towel in the sunny grass next to their blanket to dry and tied her hair up in a messy bun-knot. *I've accomplished enough for the day. Now I'm hungry. I want fresh strawberries!* Doug was hanging out making friends with the hippies in the park. Playing hacky sack with a few other guys not far away, she looked for something she might have on hand to curb her appetite. Rabbit dug through her purse and pulled out some crackers and a bottle of water. She nibbled a little. *This is not what I want.*

Nervous about approaching new people, Rabbit remained on the blanket. Looking around the park to see who might be friendly, she resigned herself to solitary entertainment. Picking through her bag, she pulled out various items. Crystals, tarot cards, and various trinkets lay in front of her. Like a dragon counting her treasure, she took inventory. She rearranged her trinkets for a while. Then, pushing them aside, she proceeded to shuffle her tarot cards. Pulling different cards, Rabbit placed a great deal of faith in the signs before her. Everything going forward was going to be a learning experience. She felt like she was on the path of a great journey and she was really excited.

After a little while, Rabbit began to grow impatient. She was really hungry. *I could eat two whole baskets of strawberries.* Things moved in slow motion around Rabbit as she waited for Doug's return. *Will he abandon me here? Surely, he'll come back. His bag is here. Why wouldn't he come back? Why would you think that?* People played hacky sack nearby, but Rabbit didn't see them. Children ran by trailing their parents, but she didn't see them. Lost in thought, her heart began to race. A gray shadow of sadness began to creep into her legs. Pain shot through her calves, and she tried to stretch out her tingling legs.

Rabbit looked up to see Doug turning the corner that spilled into the town square before her. Sitting on the lawn in the mouth of the park provided for a broad view of three different streets that fed into the town square. The little courtyard in the center completed the picture-perfect setting. Rabbit sighed. *Of course, he's coming back. I told you everything is going to be great!* Doug arrived at their blanket accompanied by a few new friends. Introductions were shared all around as they made themselves comfortable. Their seating positions created a circle of which Rabbit seemed just a little removed from. Her presence next to Doug anchored her to the group, while enforcing the image of his ownership of her. Sitting on the blanket with the rest of their stuff, Doug briefly presented his girlfriend, as if she had been the culmination of an abbreviated "tour of the house."

He loves me! Then why is he in front of you instead of beside you? Shut up! Rabbit reached out and scratched at Doug's back in affection. She scooted closer to him and reached out silently to hold his hand. He obliged for a few moments until pulling away to grab his guitar.

Doug loved playing guitar and even more, he loved being the center of attention. He had managed in short time to gather a group, and as he played more people joined their circle. Soon Rabbit was immersed in a large group of people hanging out with them. *Does this mean that we will make friends right away? I hope so! I need friends. I need someone to talk to other than Doug.* She looked around the circle to try and figure out who felt safe. She made little attempt to start conversations while Doug was playing though. His biggest groupie, she sat enraptured with the way his fingers moved across the fret board.

Doug put his guitar down to take a break. People began to chat among each other. Rabbit's stomach made a sound that only she could hear, reminding her of the importance of strawberries. She announced to the whole crowd that she was starving! Inquiring about a grocery store, she was given walking directions to the local natural grocery store. Soon, she convinced Doug that they ought to pack up their encampment and take off in search said grocery store.

Doug agreed that food sounded good and moved slowly to help. Rabbit packed up what she had strewn out across the blanket. Carefully she rolled up the towel, so that it would take up as little space as possible in her purse. She had years of practice packing a variety of things for carrying with her. She tried to always be prepared for any necessity. Rabbit's purse was large, with a long enough strap to carry it long wise from her right shoulder to her left hip. Patchwork, and bulging, she had packed up everything she had previously unloaded. They stood up and shook out the blanket.

Walking through town with a couple of their new friends, Doug and Rabbit got a little tour. The local couple pointed out places of interest and possible future necessity. When the party of four reached the natural grocery, the new friends gave Doug their address. They pointed up the street including some vague instructions. Rabbit didn't pay attention. As soon as the couple left them at the store, she focused on Doug. Her cravings were strong. She wanted soft french bread, soft cheese, and fresh strawberries. Stopping in front of the store, she dug one of the travelers checks out of her bag.

Rabbit was overwhelmed by how many people she saw going in and coming out of the store. *There are so many people! I'm so tired and hungry.* She convinced Doug to go in the store with a list and let her stay outside with all of their bags. Knots in her stomach twisted and churned. Their bags sat in a pile at the foot of a patio table. Metal chairs sat around tables half shaded by brightly colored umbrellas. Relaxing at one of the tables, feet up and eyes closed, she did not look out of place in the seating area.

Emerging from the grocery store, arms full, Doug walked towards her. He seemed glad to be done with the inside of the store. Next time, she would have to force herself to go into the store. She pulled out a pocketknife, to spread the cheese. Tearing at the loaf, she buttered the soft bread with cheese and handed a large piece to him. Together, they devoured most of the bread pretty quickly. She munched on the strawberries while he played guitar.

Hanging out in front of the grocery store for a while, they noticed the air getting cooler. The sun made its way toward the horizon and Doug was reminded that they had not yet set up camp anywhere for the evening. Packing up their stuff, they prepared themselves for walking again. Heading east along the road, leaving the grocery store behind them, the couple crossed the railroad tracks. Warehouses lined the streets for a couple of blocks. Venturing into the fields that bordered the warehouse district, they aimed for a tree sheltered by tall grass.

When they reached the tree, Rabbit decided that they had walked far enough. Dropping her bag in the grass at the base of the tree, she sat down to view the path they had just made through the grass. The tops of the cars parked next to the nearest warehouses peeked up over the grass, barely in their line of sight. It was reasonable to believe that if they had a hard time seeing people on the street, then people would likely have a difficult time seeing their camp. Trampling the grass under the tree, they created a space large enough to pitch a tent.

Once the tent was up, they made their bed, lining the inside of the tent with the rest of their belongings. The color of the tent would blend into the shadows of the grass and trees nicely once the sun had completely set. Rabbit felt safe. As they crawled into the tent for the evening, she was excited to snuggle into bed with Doug and review the events of the day. They had found the center of town, discovered the best place to get food, and found a safe place to camp. She had gotten a job and they made some new friends. She was excited about the prospect of what tomorrow might bring and happy to finally be alone and relaxing.

Over the next couple of weeks, Doug and Rabbit continued to stay in the field. While working at the bakery, she was able to snack on little bits of bread and soup, lowering their overall food costs. Still, the money was going fast, and she knew the cold weather would soon be upon them. When she was not at work, she spent most of her extra time hanging out in the park with new friends. She knew they would not be able to find a place to live until he was also working. Rabbit started getting worried that Doug seemed to spend quite a bit of time hanging out, and not very much time looking for work.

Cooler temperatures signaled the arrival of another evening. Doug and Rabbit headed to the grocery store for her favorite dinner of french bread, cream cheese, and strawberries. Doug sat outside the store playing his guitar while he waited for Rabbit to return from inside. He knew she wouldn't be in there long, but it was better than doing nothing, and perhaps he could make a coupe bucks while she was spending money. Rabbit pushed her way through the aisles, trying to remember to breath and not focus on the everything around her. Laser focused on her short list, she was quick to navigate the store and make her way to the register. She had not been feeling well and needed food that would calm her stomach.

Rabbit emerged from store slightly green but victorious. She held the french bread up high as if it were the Sword of Excalibur before taking a seat at the table adjacent to Doug. He kept playing music while she prepared a bit of bread and cheese. She did not wait for him and immediately began eating. She had been so hungry that feeding herself felt like an urgent matter. At first, the food was comforting.

Suddenly, Rabbit felt awful. Frozen, she was too nauseous to move quickly. She turned around and threw up on the sidewalk behind her seat. Mortified by her public display of vulnerability, she apologized profusely to Doug for embarrassing him. He was disgusted by the mess, and immediately began packing up to leave. Leaving the area quickly, she continued apologizing as they made their way back to camp. Doug moved hastily, almost as if he was trying to lose Rabbit far behind. After that night, she began getting sick frequently.

Chapter 13
Moving In and Moving On

Rabbit kept a notebook in her bag where she wrote all the important phone numbers and appointments. She kept track of budgeting, goals, and notes of resources and progress made. Methodically, she made her way through the checklist of necessities. She had gotten them a message phone, mailing address, medical coverage, food stamps, and had begun seeing a regular doctor for prenatal care. Visiting the doctor, she inquired about the sickness. The doctor indicated that morning sickness was absolutely normal, and she had nothing to worry about.

Morning sickness quickly began affecting Rabbit's ability to work. It was so hot in the bakery that fighting off her nausea became almost unmanageable. She kept the doors open, trying to create a breeze. Then the flies would come in and bother customers. She was nauseous everywhere, and the heat of the bakery made things so much worse! As it got colder outside, the dizziness began to wane. Rabbit's stomach started to settle a little more easily. She would think that everything was going to be fine. Then, soon after arriving at work, it would return. She was having a real problem handling the heat of the bakery kitchen. Ovens and coolers all warmed the back room with insufficient air circulation as she pushed to get her food prep done in little batches of five minutes.

Thankful for the slow days, long breaks in customers allowed Rabbit to spend more time hanging her head out the door. She explained to her boss that she was trying her best, but she had to take a lot of breaks. No longer able to hide the pregnancy, she was thankful that he was sympathetic. He suggested that she take as many breaks as she needed and not worry so much about how long it took her to get her prep tasks done. He assured her that she would in fact complete them all, as long as she kept going back to her task until completion. While she was only able to maintain the job four months, the money she earned while working made a difference for them. The employment experience she gained was helpful. Her bosses' earnest attempt at being sympathetic to a pregnant woman, secretly imprinted itself somewhere in the shadows of her soul.

> Set goals that are reachable and organize your tools in a manner that does not strain you. Stay focused on the task at hand only as long it is not unhealthy. Take short breaks often. Snack when necessary. Always return to your task, until you've reached completion. It doesn't matter how long it takes to accomplish your goals as long as you keep going back. Recognize when you've accomplished your goal, but don't get too distracted. It's time to start setting up for the next task on your list.

When Rabbit got sick so frequently at work that it became a sanitation issue, she felt it was time to respectfully resign. Her boss was understanding. She was thankful for the help he had given her, and he wished her the best of luck. She had been hounding Doug to try harder to get a job. They couldn't continue being homeless. The belly was growing, the days were shrinking, and the nights were getting colder. They would need to find a place to live soon, and she was getting nervous. He managed to get a job working for Taco Bell. It was on the other side of town and so they began to explore options for places to live closer to his work.

Doug found a gal who had a VW Bus in her driveway. She said it didn't run, but they could stay in it for a while. Rabbit was happy about it at first. They attempted to get it running, with the hope that they talk her into selling it to them. The only female in the group, her pregnant belly confused their friends, as she showed interest in the workings of the project. The guys were trying to rebuild the motor.

Rabbit wanted to be a part of the project and they didn't know what to think of it. She got to help when they handed her a carburetor and a rebuild kit. Like an intricate puzzle, she worked on it until she had to finish the project by flashlight. She never got to find out whether she did it correctly, because they failed to get it running. Doug did, however, talk their host into giving them the bus.

Rabbit stayed in the bus by herself when Doug went to work graveyard shifts. During the day, he slept in the VW, while she took the city bus downtown to be social. A few weeks of the couple living in the driveway and already it became "a problem". "You can take the VW with you, but you are going to have to move on." Finding someone to tow the van took a little time, but they managed to get it dropped off in the Taco Bell parking lot. To keep from being towed by the city, they had to move the van every couple of days. So, every couple of days, they pushed it through the parking lot to another space.

This lasted a few more weeks. It was frightfully cold at night. Rabbit hung out in the freezer of a Volkswagen while Doug worked the graveyard shift. During the day, she had to continue heading uptown, so that he could sleep. She talked to everyone she could and through their new network of friends, scored them a room to rent.

Moving into a house already shared by several others gave Rabbit hope. Memories of the community feeling she experienced at The Oasis echoed through her as she began making plans with their new house family. One of the new house mates was a sweet little hippie gal named Brooke. Together they talked about the prospects of raising their children in close proximity. "Will our children grow up as best friends? Or would they grow to hate each other? Perhaps someday they will marry?" They agreed that anything could happen, and the future would reveal itself in due time.

The house was older, in a neighborhood around the corner and up the hill from the library. The walk down the hill was not bad but walking up was a bit of a chore. There was a nice view of the neighborhood from atop their hill. Gardens with little fences lined people's yards. Rabbit had been freezing in the bus at night. Now she could sit in the warmth of the house and look out the window at the cold. It was beautiful and she was thankful for simple blessings.

Once they got settled into the new place, Rabbit felt secure enough to bring up leaving. She was getting itchy feet for travel. Knowing that travel would be a thing of the past once the baby was born, she convinced Doug to let her take off for one last trip. *I will never be free again. I am making this choice. I will never again be able to backtrack on this choice, so one for the road. Just one more goodbye to the life I am choosing to leave behind.* He wasn't thrilled about her getting to travel while he had to work. Still, he didn't seem to be at all worried about whether she would come back.

Hitchhiking down to California alone, the taste of freedom was melancholy. Rabbit relived the good feelings she associated with having no ties, no boundaries. She briefly entertained the idea of taking off by herself and disappearing into the sunset. *That wouldn't be responsible though. I would miss Doug. I'd be alone and afraid with a new baby. I'm not being rational.* She forced herself to focus on the transition of becoming a responsible adult. *This is like a going away present for me. Things will never be the same again.* Thoughts and feelings filled her chest as the baby inside her kicked and squirmed.

It only took a couple of days to make it down to Sacramento. Rabbit visited Doug's family, then headed to the Bay Area. Visiting with Dad was nice. Dad had gotten back together with her little sister's mom. This time they had actually moved into together. Sister was in Middle School and was not particularly happy about the new living arrangements. Focused on the job of parenting a young teen distracted Dad from hounding Rabbit about details. When the pregnant young woman talked, her father listened, and seemed to give her the benefit of the doubt. She was an adult now and these were her mistakes to make. He no longer seemed concerned about sheltering Rabbit from herself.

One day during her visit, Rabbit took BART out to Berkeley. Walking down Telegraph Avenue, she saw people she recognized from her drug days. She looked blankly ahead as she walked slow and steady. *I'm not really sure I want them to talk to me. Maybe if I ran into someone that really was a good friend? Or one of my mom's friends from The Oasis?* Sadness was the only meaningful relic of a strained childhood that Rabbit could salvage in the moment. Struck by the desperation of her surroundings, her choice to move forward with her life away was reaffirmed. *I definitely do not want to raise a child in this environment.* Heading back to Contra Costa County, she began to miss Doug. *I'm ready to go home. I'm ready to go back to Oregon.*

Packed into the truck, Dad drove Rabbit back up to Ashland. With little sister squeezed in the middle of the bench seat, they made their way North. It was a long drive, still the trip was much quicker than hitchhiking had been. Ten hours later, they were walking in the front door of her home. Doug exchanged greetings and then politely excused himself for work. The housemates present exchanged pleasantries with Rabbit's family. Dad sat to rest for only a short time before announcing that he needed to hit the road. Within an hour he was taking her little sister and heading back to California.

As the weeks progressed, the winter holidays quickly approached. In an effort to keep herself busy, Rabbit began gathering with a group of their new friends during the day in a nearby church. They were using a room in the building to dip natural beeswax candles for a fundraiser. Paid per candle, the money she brought home was a tiny amount compared to their cost of living. Still, it gave her something to do. She wasn't locked in the house pining away the time, but instead was able to stay social and receive social support while actively participating in a positive community project. She liked the friends they were making in Ashland.

In California, members of her peer group had judged her as being conservative. Here, the very same attitude towards things was being perceived as liberal. Some of the folks within their social group were vegan. They convinced her that eating meat was bad for the baby. She didn't really eat meat very often anyway. She enjoyed vegetarian foods and acknowledged that healthy eating was essential for good health. This took things a step further. They convinced her that it was immoral to drink mothers' milk from another species. Furthermore, eggs were immoral for eating when pregnant because they were the unborn children of another species. She could understand the rationale and conformed her eating habits accordingly.

When Thanksgiving arrived, Doug and Rabbit were invited to a vegan holiday dinner complete with a gluten roast in place of a turkey. All the men hung out together and the women were expected to flock together. Doug seemed to get along well with their new friends. Rabbit was not welcome in the men's circle and did not feel a strong connection to the other women. They were all nice enough, but she liked it better when they were not separated by gender, but rather focused on common interest. Feeling out of place, she stayed quiet by herself most of the time.

Sitting in the front room, her peripheral vision played tricks on her. Although her back was facing the door, Rabbit seemed to be able to sense when people were passing by the front windows. *Growing eyes in the back of my head? I'm going to be a parent. Oh my god.* She felt that uneasy feeling of being watched. She spun around to peer through the box windows that framed in the front door. The streetlights shone through the stained glass inlaid in the top half of the carved wooden door.

Rabbit made sure to move quickly, spinning while advancing towards the windows in one fluid movement. Without curtains, it was easy to see there was nobody outside the house. *I did that way too fast!* Rabbit tried to catch her breath as she landed on the windowsill seat.

"Damn this body." Movement under her blouse reminded her there was more than one body affected. *I keep forgetting. This affects everything! I mean, I guess it makes sense. I am making another human. But geez, why can't I just function properly?* She rubbed her belly, talking to her growing person. "I'm sorry. I wasn't talking to you. I love you. You are wonderful. Just have a little patience with me. I'm still learning about this stuff."

Sitting in the window box, Rabbit could hear men talking in the living room. She could hear women talking in the kitchen. She didn't feel like she belonged in either place. *I don't really want to be in either place. Why do the men get to talk about philosophy and history and politics while the women are expected to be cooking and cleaning the kitchen? What if I want to talk about philosophy? Why am I being too conservative or too liberal simply because I have strong political views? If I were a man, it wouldn't be too much! It would be well received, debated, discussed. And if even if it were eventually shot down, I would at least be taken seriously. If this is what being an adult is about, then I understand why it's called getting old, because this shit is getting old fast.* Her thoughts were cut short by a shadow in the yard.

Flickering shadows of blue and yellow dart out of a barrel. Two silhouettes disappear and reappear from behind the flames. Blue pig tails contrast against a red flannel jacket. Red flannel arms wrap around a boy's shoulders. "I tried to show her. She couldn't see you yet." His silhouette is empty. There is shape but no form, outlines and shadows, but no details. Only the glistening of the tear as it falls. *I know I saw something.* Rabbit peered intently through the glass, studying every detail within her line of sight.

Again, there was a glisten, a tiny shimmering tear, appeared briefly. Rabbit started to get up quickly and stalled for a moment. "No, I don't want to get dizzy. She opened the door, using the door handle to steady herself as she got up. Stepping out into the cold evening, she looked around the yard. *Nothing.* She paused for a moment, allowing the cold winter air to give her relief from the hot flashes she had been plagued with. *Pregnancy in winter means I never get cold!* She smiled and looked around at the frosty crystals clinging to nearby plants.

She saw the glimmer again between two trees. Rabbit looked, blinking, trying to see more closely. The light went away. *A firefly? In winter? In Oregon. I am just crazy. Forget about it.* She turned around slowly and made her way back into the house. "I'm just growing eyes in the back of my head. That's all. Guess what? You're pregnant. And you're going to have to spend the rest of your life dedicated to someone else. But guess what? Bonus! You get eyes in the back of your head! But trade-off. You get to feel like shit a lot of the time." She closed the door behind her and place her shoes in line with the other shoes in the entry room, before returning to the kitchen.

The week after Thanksgiving snow began to fall and Rabbit finally began to cool off. Walking around with a heater inside her, she was quick to get dizzy and tired. Being overheated often led to nausea. *I am sick and tired of feeling sick and tired!* Walking out in the snow flurry, she was overjoyed at the beauty of it all. If Rabbit had been too cold, perhaps she would not have enjoyed it as much. In her current state, she had found 25 degrees to be the perfect temperature for walking downtown. Walking back up the hill became a slippery challenge that resulted in much laughing. Glad to be back inside after trekking through the snow, Doug did not share her amusement.

Soon Doug was no longer employed at Taco Bell. He refused to share the details with his girlfriend. The burden of their financial situation rested heavily on Rabbit. Doug was not as dedicated to job hunting as she believed was necessary. As her anxiety increased, so did the tension between the young couple. The holidays added stress to the already uncomfortable arrangement. Midst their arguments, the couple had begun discussing escape plans. "I don't want to be homeless when I give birth to my child, Doug!" She pressed him for a solution to their problems. *He wanted me to keep this baby. He told me he understood. Now, he has to take care of me and the baby. That's all there is to it.*

Christmas was stressful. Doug and Rabbit were arguing often and loudly. There was little privacy in the crowded house, and their housemates were clearly uncomfortable. Men took sides with Doug, while women took sides with Rabbit. Rational discussion did not occur in any way that would provide a pathway to resolution. By New Year's Eve, their relationship had taken a turn for the worse.

In addition to their financial stress, confusion surrounding Rabbit's sexuality was posing problems in her relationship with Doug. She believed that she had to share her heart and soul with Doug if they were going to be together always. Instead of appreciating her honesty, Doug was appalled at what he saw as abnormalities, dis-ease, and dis-function. She was still attracted to women and being honest with Doug about it was only making things worse. On New Year's Eve, Rabbit tried her best to make herself beautiful despite her growing belly. She wanted desperately for him to think she was beautiful. She wanted him to be happy to be with her.

They went to a local party, where several of their friends were supposed to be attending. She asked Doug whose house they were going to. He just shushed her. "Don't worry. You're beautiful. It doesn't matter. Its New Year's Eve. Can we just have one night without the nagging?" Rabbit responded with silence. Her silenced continued longer than she had originally intended. He announced that he would not be refraining from sobriety, despite the fact that she was unable to participate. "Why should we both have to suffer?"

As Doug became intoxicated, his behavior gradually became more unkind towards her. By midnight, Rabbit found herself feeling very alone in a house full of drunk people. A boom box in the kitchen had been playing the same song by 4 Non-Blondes for at least 45 minutes. Singing along at the top of their lungs, a group of drunk young women gathered in the kitchen around a radio. "No! No! Play it again! Play it again!" *Here we go again. I wish I had somewhere else to go. I actually liked this song before. Now, I don't think I ever want to hear this song again. Ever.*

It was too loud and smoky inside. Rabbit wanted to go outside. She stepped out the front door, if only for a breath of fresh air. *Jeezuz! It really is fuckin' cold out here! Freezing even for a pregnant woman! Universe, you have won!* She threw her arms up in the air, cursing at some unseen deity and then turned back around and went into the smoky party. She wandered through the rooms looking for someone that she could just sit and talk with. She found Doug in the living room. There was a girl on the coach with him that the couple had only just started to befriend.

Now, when Rabbit needed him most, Doug was betraying her. *Who am I to judge? I know I was just talking earlier this week about how I wanted us to be more open. But it's New Year's Eve. I wish someone wanted to be close to me. I wish I weren't surrounded by drunk idiots.* She walked out of the room without saying a word. Putting all her layers back on, she prepared for the cold winter night. As she left the house, the midnight wind cut into her face. Crying about her misery and loneliness, she wandered the neighborhood in the dark. Eventually, she made her way back to their house and went to bed. Later, Doug got mad at her for leaving the party without saying anything to him. This, of course, led to another fight.

Chapter 14
I Want My Baby

With the new year upon them, Rabbit's house mates were beyond agitated with all of the fighting. They were concerned about Rabbit and Doug's ability to continue paying their fair share. Discussing their options, the couple agreed that being homeless with a baby just a couple of months away was not an acceptable option. They needed a safe place to be and had run out of luck in Ashland. With tails between their legs, they returned to Sacramento to stay with Doug's cousin Nina and her husband. They didn't have any children, and both worked a lot. They assured Doug that it would not be a problem, they would not "be in the way."

Upon arriving in Sacramento, Rabbit moved quickly to obtain medical insurance to cover labor and delivery. It was difficult to find a doctor's clinic willing to take a new patient so far along in her pregnancy. When she was able to locate a clinic, she was pleased to learn it was an all-women's clinic. They were listed as a local clinic. Getting directions for public transit decreased her enthusiasm. The clinic was on the far opposite end of the metro area from where they were staying. *If I were driving, it would take close to an hour to get there! This is considered local? But guess what! I have to take the bus!*

One bus to the light rail, then taking the train to another bus, the trip took her about 2 & ½ hours one way. Sitting in the waiting room at the clinic, Rabbit rested, exhausted from the trip across town. The welfare clinics were packed and slow moving. The visit easily took an hour. She was informed that she would need to come into the clinic once a week because she was so close to her due date. This would give her an opportunity to meet every doctor on staff at the clinic. Which doctor actually delivered her baby would depend entirely on who happened to be on shift when she was in labor. Taking public transit to see the doctor was a whole day of travel for her. She dreaded having to make this long trip every single week.

Rabbit had tried to keep everything natural during her pregnancy and wanted to have a natural delivery. During her first visit to the women's clinic, a nurse described the way it would work at the hospital and encouraged her to visit the facility prior to going into labor. Rabbit was unhappy that she would be stuck having her baby in a regular hospital. *I wanted to have a natural birth at home. I was hoping we would have our own home by now. But nothing is working out right.* When she inquired about painkillers during labor, the nurse informed her that their clinic did not work with epidurals or heavy-duty painkillers, so that would not be an option. It made her feel a little better knowing that she could at least be assured of not being drugged during labor. The doctor she met with the first time seemed nice enough.

The idea of another long transit trip weighed heavily on her mind. It was so exhausting! Sitting on the sidewalk, Rabbit snacked while she waited for the bus. *Another 2 & 1/2 hours and I get to take a nap!* A weekly trip to the doctor's office on public transit would be exhausting. Still, she could see the benefit of being able to meet all the different doctors in the clinic. After several weeks passed, she had met them all, and decided she was comfortable with all but one of the doctors.

By February, Rabbit began getting intermittent contractions. Anxious and unsure she called the hospital and the advice nurse told them to come in just in case. Laying in the hospital bed, she was nervous. *I just want to get this over with. I hope that everything is okay. I hope they tell me this is the real thing. I am so done being pregnant.* They turned out to be false starts and she was disappointed when she was sent back home. The nurses at the hospital assured her that "first babies are often late." They showed her how to time the contractions. "You don't need to come back until your contractions have maintained five-minute intervals for at least 2 to 3 hours consistently."

Rabbit slept very little during the first week of March. Contractions frequently woke her up. Lying awake in bed next to Doug, she stared at the clock. Keeping track of her abdominal pains, she'd get excited after the first hour of regularity. By the second hour, she would be so exhausted that she'd fall back asleep. Within a couple of hours, she would awaken and repeat the process. When her restlessness disrupted Doug, she moved to the couch and continued watching the clock.

Rabbit tried calling the advice nurse a couple of times and the woman on the other line insisted that it would be a waste of time to come into the hospital this early.

Unfortunately, the pains never became regular. Instead, they just sort of merged together. The pain was constant, spiking and fading with intervals that did not seem to care about the nurses' instructions. The pain was not concerned with the clock, or anything else. When her pain levels were lower, Rabbit worked on packing the hospital bags. When the contractions spiked, she just laid down on the floor and waited for them to pass. Within these small intervals, she managed to pack a bag with clothes for herself and the new baby.

While Rabbit was hidden away in the apartment watching the clock, the weather outside grew more and more extreme. Laying on the couch, she watched the news. Rain had been falling non-stop for several days. Much of Sacramento County was underwater. Miles of homes were being evacuated due to flooding. From the warmth of the living room, she could not feel the impact of the severe storms. When her pain became so great that she could not stop crying and could not walk without help, she called the advice nurse again.

"How long have your contractions been regular?" the voice on the other line inquired.

"There is no consistency. The pain just gets worse, and then less, and then worse." Rabbit bawled. "I can't get up! It won't stop hurting!"

Again, the phone spoke to her, "That doesn't sound normal. Perhaps you should come in? How long has this been happening?"

Frustrated, Rabbit responded in between tears. "I know this is not regular! I keep calling and you guys keep telling me to wait! But it has never gotten normal! It just keeps getting worse! It hurts so bad! Can I please come in now??" The voice on the other end of the phone assured Rabbit that they would be ready for her when she arrived, and she hung up the telephone.

Doug walked into the room and found her laying on the floor crying. With the phone receiver still in her hand, she looked up through the flood of tears and saw his irritation. "It's time to go now. I have to get everything together. Please help me." He grumbled something about how it was 'about damn time' and went into the other room to wake his sister up. She instructed him to gather the hospital bags.

Nina and her husband helped the couple to their Rodeo. Floods poured down out of the midnight sky. Nauseous and screaming when the sharp pains shot through her, Rabbit felt terrible about distracting the driver. Much of the roads were flooded and the freeway was clearly unsafe for anyone to be driving. The scene pictured in the windshield frightened her. *Now is not the time to be in a moving vehicle. If I didn't need to be heading to the hospital right now, I don't think I'd agree to a car ride anywhere in this weather!* Rabbit tried to stay focused, praying under her breath.

Arriving safely at the hospital without getting into an accident was a miracle in itself. Still the rain was pouring down. Once checked into the labor room, Rabbit called Dad from the hospital phone. He answered the phone hazily. "It's time Dad." She heard him wake up quickly at the sound of her voice. He asked her what hospital she was in. She gave him the info and he responded that he would be there soon. Click. Dial tone. Exactly one hour later, he walked into the hospital room.

Rabbit did not ask him how he had gotten there so fast. She knew that the storms were not safe to drive in at much higher that 40 to 45 miles per hour. Mathematically, it did not work out. He would have had to been driving at 100 miles per hour or more to make it that quickly from Walnut Creek. She was astonished and thankful that he had made it there without an accident. The numbers in her brain were quickly pushed out of the way by more sharp stabbing pains. She called out ferociously and this time, she did not bother to try and keep quiet. *I'm in the hospital now. There is no reason to try keeping quiet.*

When a doctor finally came in to check on her, Rabbit was relieved to see it was one of the 'nice doctors' from her clinic. The doctor was kind and gentle, inquiring, "What can we do to make you more comfortable?" Rabbit described the pain in her back. She heard the nurse say something about 'back labor' to the doctor, as the woman scribbled something on a clipboard.

"She has not dilated very much. She will need to dilate a whole lot more before she will be able to give birth." The nurse encouraged Rabbit to get up, suggesting that she 'walk the halls. "Walking should help you dilate faster."

Carefully, Nina helped Rabbit climb off the hospital bed. The two women walked slowly together. They made it as far as the doorway before Rabbit was hit with another sharp pain. She crumpled down on the ground and screamed out. As it passed, she was again helped up off the floor and they made their way into the hall. Walking the halls didn't last very long. Rabbit was so tired, that she didn't have the energy to keep walking.

Back in the hospital room, Rabbit decided that she needed to get in the shower. *Perhaps hot water on my back will help?* Stripping off her clothes, she needed someone to hold onto while she stood under the water. Another stabbing pain ran through her abdomen and her back. Disgusted, she quickly changed her mind about the shower. Trying to put clothes back on, she was hit with another pain.

Over and over, the pregnant woman kept changing positions. She tried the bathroom again. Then she tried laying down on the bed. Then she was sitting on the bed. Then she was sitting on the chair. Then she was pacing in the room. Moving from one position to another, Rabbit continued to search for a place that did not include the pain. Nothing was comfortable. With each passing hour, she became more frightened and exhausted. By morning light, she was so tired that she was passing out completely between contractions. Three minutes of sleep interrupted by such extreme pains convinced her that she was going to die.

Laying in the bed, holding on to Dad's hand, Rabbit poured her trust deep into his eyes. In her mind, voices told her that she was going to die. *I'm going to die in labor. My daughter will grow up with someone else raising her. I'm not gonna make it. I don't want to die in pain.* She prayed between contractions. *Please just show me mercy. I don't want to die in such extreme pain. I want to live to hold my baby in my arms. I want to be able to look into her eyes.* The love that Rabbit felt coming from Dad was so strong, she wanted to believe he was there to save her. *If I do die today, at least my Daddy is here with me.*

Doug was exhausted as well. Sleeping on the chair, he seemed irritated by the noise his girlfriend was making. He just wanted to be able to sleep and she was not helping matters. Everyone was tired, but he seemed to be the least supportive. He had suffered interrupted sleep for several days already and his patience had long since evacuated just like all the people in shelters waiting for the storm waters to recede. Thankful for Nina and Dad, Rabbit tried to ignore Doug. Looking out the window above the chair in which he slept, she observed the ever-falling sky. Rivers filled the air and she felt like the world was coming to an end.

It was almost 11 am when the nurses told them all that 'the mother' would have to start pushing soon. They also warned her that the shift change would be occurring soon. It would take a little while for the new shift of staff to make it back in to check on her. "Not to worry, everything is going to be fine. The nurses will continue to check on you, and the doctor will be in as soon as the nurses have confirmed you are dilated enough." Then at noon, Rabbit saw the sun.

Looking out the window above the sleeping Doug, Rabbit saw the clouds part. The rain ceased, and the sun peeked out making the moisture on the window glimmer like jewels. The new shift of nurses came in and informed the group that they 'would be sending the doctor in as soon as possible'. They instructed Dad to coach her on pushing through the strongest contractions. Drowning in a haze of exhaustion and pain, Rabbit stayed focused on Dads eyes. Every time the pain was strong, she squeezed his hand tightly.

Then the new shift doctor entered the room. *No! Not her! Of course, it had to be the one doctor that I am not comfortable with!* Rabbit was mortified to see her walking in with long fingernails. Even with gloves on, the young woman could feel the doctor's sharp nails cutting into her soft vulnerable places. She had already been traumatized by the child birthing experience thus far. The doctor was cold and matter of fact. Her bedside manner left the young mother feeling jagged and sore like the flesh between her legs.

Within thirty minutes of the sun coming out, her Jule was born. As the nurses took the baby and placed her on the scale, Rabbit could hear her crying. *I'm still in pain. I have to keep pushing? Why??* The nurses tried to explain 'the afterbirth' and assured Rabbit that she could take something for pain now. "It won't hurt the baby because she's already been born." She succumbed to the advice and took the medicine they offered.

"I want my baby." Rabbit said in a strained and tearful voice. "I want to see her."

They placed the baby on her mother's chest and Rabbit tried to nurse her right away. Jule wasn't interested, and the new mother felt rejected. Still, she held the new baby in her arms. "I love you! I love you so much!" Looking up at the window, the light had disappeared. The clouds had again closed in on the world, and the rainstorm had returned.

They took the infant out of Rabbit's arms, assuring her that "she will be taken care of. It's your time to rest." She protested a little. Dad told her that she didn't need to worry, and she believed him. She let them move her to a recovery room and quickly fell asleep. When Rabbit awoke, she again asked for her baby. They brought Jule to her, placing her in a clear plastic bed next to Rabbit's hospital bed. Trying again to nurse her, the young mother fell asleep with her daughter in her arms.

Together the two slept peacefully, until a nurse came in and removed the baby from Rabbit's arms. The nurse insisted that it wasn't safe to sleep with the baby. "You could roll over on her and kill her in her sleep." *Preposterous! I would never do that!* Rabbit was angry. She didn't want them to take her. They insisted they would bring her back whenever she wanted and wheeled the sleeping baby back to the nursery.

Every time Rabbit woke up, she asked for her baby. Every time she tried to nurse her, they would fall asleep together. The nurses became irritated with her. She was not following the rules. The next morning, a doctor came in and informed her that she would be signing her release papers and they would be sending her home later that day. "We get to go home?"

"No," the doctor responded, "You get to go home. We will be keeping the baby for a few more days for observation. She is not eating normally, and we need to make sure she is healthy before you can take her home."

Rabbit asked, "How is Jule supposed to nurse if I'm not here to feed her?" She was informed that they intended on bottle feeding the baby sugar water to get her to start eating regularly. Rabbit was livid. She lost her temper and insisted that she was not going anywhere without her baby. Period. "I do not want you giving her bottles of anything! If she gets used to a bottle nipple then I will have an even more difficult time nursing her! The hell if I'm going to let some hospital staff undermine my parenting before I've even begun! You do NOT have my permission to give my daughter bottles!" The doctor was not pleased. She repeated that she would be discharging Rabbit, but not the baby. "I am not leaving. Even if I have to stay in the waiting room. If that is what I have to do, I will do it. I refuse to leave the hospital without my baby!"

The nurses reminded Rabbit that upon discharge, she would no longer get food from the hospital. She would not have any assistance when she needed to go to the restroom. She would not be receiving any painkillers, or any other help. Rabbit didn't care. She posted herself in the waiting room closest to the nursery and continued to bother the nurses regularly. "Anytime at all you want Jule to try and eat", she insisted, "you have to let me nurse her."

Upon further inquiry, Rabbit found out that they expected her to nurse for thirty minutes on each breast, every three hours. When she tried to feed her baby, Jule nursed for about 10 minutes on one side and promptly fell asleep. Then an hour later, she would wake up hungry. Rabbit would nurse her on the other side for about ten minutes and Jule would fall asleep again.

The nursery staff was dissatisfied. Rabbit was appalled. *How can they expect such a small newborn to eat so much?!* Still, she held her ground and stayed camped in the waiting room. Eventually after a day of this, the staff gave up and agreed to let Rabbit take her home. Still, there was another roadblock. Nina was not available to come pick them up. Doug and Rabbit would be taking public transit home with the newborn. The idea was exhausting! *At least we can go home now.*

The staff insisted that they would not be allowed to leave the hospital with their baby unless she was in a car seat. "Why do we need a car seat? We don't have a car! We are riding on a bus! I am carrying my baby in my arms!" Still, the staff would not budge, insisting it was state law. Rabbit argued with them about it for a while and then she sent Doug away to retrieve the car seat. Five hours later, he returned sopping wet from the trip on the buses and light-rail in the rain. He had the car seat and no patience left at all. He was short tempered all the way home. Finally, two and half hours later, bickering and exhausted, they arrived at the apartment with the baby and all of the hospital stuff.

Chapter 15
Smoke

In the days following the return from the hospital, Rabbit focused all of her attention on caring for the new baby. Entrusting their livelihood in Doug's ability to provide, she hounded him about the necessity of getting a job. He didn't seem motivated to find a job. She bombarded him with her anxieties. Soon, the arguing became too much for Nina and her husband to handle. All parties felt trapped by the circumstances, so after Nina gave him a stern lecture, Doug began taking active steps. Within a week of trying, he managed to get a part-time job working in food service. Between his sleep patterns, work schedule, and social time with friends, caring for the baby continued to be her full-time responsibility.

Soon after Jule was born, Nina found out that she too was pregnant. The crying baby at night and all the hustle and bustle began to be too much and it was time for Doug and Rabbit to move on. Doug came home announcing that he had found a room for rent with a co-worker. "It'll be cheap, and I can commute with them." Nina's husband helped the young couple deliver all their newly acquired possessions to the midtown apartment, while Nina stayed behind napping.

At first thought, moving into the apartment in Midtown with Doug's friends seemed like it was going to be great for them. *If we're living with Doug's friends, maybe he won't be absent as often?* Doug emphasized that the location would be closer to downtown, so she could get out and about more frequently, without having to wait around for him. *Why would I want to go anywhere without you and Jule? He doesn't want you around. Shut up!* Rabbit was hoping that the move would help them both feel less isolated. Instead, she ended up isolating herself even more.

When they arrived, Rabbit discovered that they were walking into an upstairs apartment full of smoke. She was dismayed. *Did they not understand that we're bring a baby with us?* Rabbit insisted that if they were going to be paying an equal share of rent, they needed to be respectful and not smoke inside. It was not healthy for a baby to be sleeping in an apartment full of smoke. They made listening noises and put out their cigarettes. When she went into the bedroom, she could hear them bitching about her and her demands.

They seemed to think that she was being unreasonable. Convinced that they could simply tell her what she wanted to hear, and then do whatever they liked, she was not shown any respect. Rabbit tried to talk with Doug about the situation, and he seemed to treat her the same way his friends had. After a week or so of politely requesting clean air in the common areas, she simply stopped trying to be social. Rabbit proceeded to spend the better part of the next month locked in their bedroom, hiding the baby from the smoke.

Rabbit was appalled and felt like she was the only one who cared. Mood swings tore her from one end to the other. She spent the first couple of weeks sleeping with the baby. When Jule woke up, Rabbit would wake up and care for her. When the baby fell asleep nursing, Rabbit would nap with Jule cradled in her arms. The new mother was filled with the fear that she would not be able to properly care for her beautiful Jule. Pure love poured out of her into the tiny new face. She was very protective of Jule. *She's a fragile miracle, counting on me to bring her the whole world.*

Rabbit used cloth diapers. Nina had thrown a small baby shower for them. One of the gifts was a large box of cloth diapers containing various sizes. This proved to be a priceless gift. Money was scarce, so Rabbit washed the diapers in the bathtub by hand and hung them to dry. Unfortunately, being winter, it was challenging to get them to dry before they froze. Carrying a frame pack of wet diapers and pushing a stroller, she splurged on dryers at the laundromat a few times.

Sleeping when the baby slept, Rabbit allowed her schedule to be dictated by Jule's needs. Waking only to feed and care for the baby, she continued to further isolate herself. Doug maintained his job for a month or so. When he wasn't working or sleeping, he spent the majority of his waking hours hanging out in the smoky living room. The guys got high and played video games and took turns complaining about the inconvenience of living with Rabbit and the baby. She pretended to be asleep more than she actually slept, as she didn't want to face the scrutiny of their house mates.

Postpartum depression was rough, and her anxiety increased. The fights increased. Rabbit's feelings of being trapped grew and she began to feel as if Doug hated her and the baby. She wanted to feel loved and cared for. Instead of listening to her and trying to be supportive, Doug blamed their problems on her mental instability. Telling her that he was 'avoiding her because she was hard to deal with' sent her into fierce emotional seizures.

One day, Rabbit got so upset that emotions took over her body and sent her flailing on the floor in convulsions. She hit her head too hard, and her neck swelled up. The experience left her in so much pain, that Rabbit begged Doug to accompany her and the baby on a trip to the free clinic. Through tears of frustration and pain, she tried to explain that she needed him to help care for their daughter so that she could seek medical care. Though the request seemed reasonable in her head, he clearly thought otherwise. "Please. I don't ask you to take of her much. I understand that you have a job. But I am hurting so bad. Please help me." The smoky front room full of guys began to egg him on, after the continued to cry and repeated requests. Once pushed by his peer group the reluctant father agreed.

After sitting for what felt like hours in the clinic waiting room, Rabbit was finally able to see a nurse. The nurse told Rabbit that she 'needed counseling' and suggested she 'take ibuprofen for the pain'. Rabbit was disgusted. *This has not been helpful at all. Now Doug will just say that I'm crazy every time I am in pain.* She silently slumped into the waiting room chair for a moment. Doug puffed out his chest, pulled an 'I told you so', and turned toward the door.

Walking out the clinic door, he strode to the end of the block before stopping to look back. Rabbit was not behind him. He stood motionless, pausing for a moment in indecision. Inside, Rabbit double checked to make sure that nothing was being left behind in the clinic. She straightened out her sweater, with the diaper bag hanging across her chest. She leaned down and kissed Jule on the forehead. "It's okay baby, I love you." Then, without another word, Rabbit pushed the stroller out the front door of the clinic to the Sacramento evening air.

Doug stood at the corner, leaning against the stop sign. Halfway through a cigarette, he spun round on his heel when he saw Rabbit push the stroller out of the clinic door. Facing towards home, he began walking without waiting for her to catch up. His long legs offered a quick pace, even with his ever-casual gait. She tried to catch up with him without running. By the end of the second block, she had reached his side with the stroller. She tried to speak to him casually, to hide her frustration and just be coy. It was quickly met with blunt disdain. He bitched at her the rest of their way home for wasting his afternoon. When they got back to the apartment, Rabbit crawled back into bed with the baby and cried herself to sleep. Doug returned to the smoky living room.

The new parents only lived in the Midtown apartment for a few months. Things got pretty tough for them. Rabbit had been staying home taking care of the baby. Doug's part-time job was short-lived. He got fired or quit. She never learned the details of the story as he was not interested in providing them. It was gray area that triggered defensive responses when she tried to inquire further. *I know better. He will start yelling and get mean. I just have to wait and let him decide what we do next.* Ultimately, they ended up leaving the Midtown apartment and going to stay with Sister and her boyfriend in West Sacramento.

Sister and her boyfriend had an apartment in a low-income area of West Sacramento. The neighborhood was rough and dirty. Doug tried finding work and managed to get on with a property management company taking care of clean-outs and maintenance throughout the metro area. The hot Summer mixed with hard labor resulted in a grumpy young man with little compassion for whatever internal trauma Rabbit was trying to heal from. Doug enjoyed the baby when it was convenient and took no shame in pawning duties off onto her when he was tired. Still, he seemed to be determined to at least attempt to be a father and a provider.

Doug's little sister was also pregnant again. There was no child around from the previous pregnancy, so Rabbit decided against asking any questions. It was none of her business. *Something awful could have happened. I don't want to open any wounds.* The two young women spent days hanging out, slowly cleaning up, and eventually planning dinner while the men were at work. Rabbit took care of Jule while Sister watched daytime television talk shows. She became especially excited by the shows with arguments and drama. Rabbit quickly lost interest in the television and focused her attention instead on the wonders of her new child. *At least, they understand the importance of not smoking around the baby.*

Sister obtained a walker for the baby and presented it to Rabbit as a gift. Jule wasn't old enough to walk, but she seemed to like being social. Putting her in the walker not only kept Jule from reaching things that were more than 8 inches away; it also kept her upright in the middle of everything. Rabbit put toys on the tray for the baby to play with. She put books on the tray. They used it as a makeshift highchair. Sitting on a milk crate, with one foot lodged underneath the walker, Rabbit could keep the baby from rolling away while she attempted to teach Jule about wonders of eating rice cereal.

Doug's labor job enabled him to disappear all day on most days. When he came home from work, Rabbit would tell him about whatever Jule had done that day. She unloaded all of her hopes for a future on Doug. She put pressure on him to help them get out of his sister's place and into a place of their own. He argued with her a lot. By the end of June, she was exhausted from the arguing. Stress had become her coffee and she was wired to the point of anxiety. She ran away from the uncertainty of West Sacramento and went to visit the house she grew up in.

Somewhere in the process of returning to California from Ashland, the true identity of the expecting mother was uncovered. Once it was revealed that all of Doug's family was 'in the know,' Doug's mother brushed off familial rumors as unimportant. She instead focused on the new person that she had been 'blessed to get to know.' She made a point of accepting Rabbit into the family. "Regardless of what your legal name is, I met you as Rabbit, so that's what I will call you. The rest doesn't matter to me." Sister, Cousin Nina, and the rest of Doug's family followed the matriarchal lead.

She had continued to live as Rabbit. She was introduced as Rabbit sometimes, but usually as 'Doug's Girlfriend' or 'The Old Lady.' She felt invisible, without an identity, she was simply a tool. A servant there to take care of the child, without needs, wants, rights, without dignity, she sat quietly in the corner of her existence questioning who she really was. *This Rabbit person is a pitiful human. Here I am but no one sees me.*

Any confusion seemed to be cleared up when the baby's birth certificate had listed Firecat as the child's mother. She began to remember how unpleasant it had been when she was a child enrolled in elementary school as 'Cathy.' At first, the disguised identity had seemed like a valid way to protect her from the abuse of her peers. Over time, it had made her feel like she was hiding her true self, and thereby unable to make real friends. It had been a confusing and isolating experience for an eight-year-old.

The present situation brought the memory to the surface, and Cat shook it off. *This is different. Everyone knows who I am. Rabbit is just a nickname. You should be able to handle this. Are you just stupid? I am not stupid. No. You're crazy. Plenty of people have nicknames. What are you so freaked out about?* Dad and all of the family in his world still referred to her by the childhood name 'Cat'. She would get to spend a week being Cat. She was pleased when she realized that the name Rabbit would not be spoken for seven days. *Visiting the house I grew up in, once again. Such a strange blend of happy and sad. I am happy to be welcomed back, but the minute I walk in the door, I am reminded of how much pain I've experienced in this house.* The trip to Dad's world reminded Cat how out of place she felt in the suburbs.

Chapter 16
Twenty-One

Dad arrived in West Sacramento to pick up his daughter and granddaughter on a hot muggy afternoon. Driving Big Red back to the Bay Area, he spoke very little to his daughter. Dad loved his truck almost as much as he loved his daughter. Big Red was the first vehicle he had purchased brand new. He had put so many miles on the engine, and with it, there were so many memories. There were all the conversations he had with Cat to and from baseball games, taking her to see the horses, saving her from her mistakes, and introducing her to new ways of seeing the world. *My daughter has grown up in this truck. Now here she is a mother and I'm bringing my granddaughter home in Big Red.* He smiled to himself.

The young mother sat, strapped in, leaning her head against the half open window. Keenly aware of her sleeping daughter strapped in the car seat beside her, she remained silent. *Cat is a child. A memory. A figment of a depressing imaginary story. A shadow of a past that was somehow supposed to mold me, to prepare me for this future, this present in which I am totally lost. I don't know who I am. Everyone else seems to think they know who I am.* Jule stirred. Cat placed her hand strategically on the baby's lap, allowing sleeping fingers to wrap instinctively around her index finger. *Who am I kidding? I don't have to have an identity; I have a purpose.* She smiled half-heartedly with a growing love for her daughter.

Visiting the old stomping grounds, Cat still felt like everyone stared at her when she was walking down the street. *I'm turning 21 now. I'm not a kid anymore. I still don't feel like a responsible adult.* She was floundering, out of water her gills didn't do her any good. Clarity in the moment brought attention to the fact that she was unhappy with her circumstances. *I feel powerless to make things change. I'm not even sure what would really make me happy.*

In evening, Cat sat at the dinner table with what felt like a new family in her old home. Little sister and her mother, Dad and Cat were seated around a nicely set table. Within Cat's line of sight, in the living room, in the fantastic convertible stroller lay the sleeping Baby Jule. *Dad's life has changed so much. While I have been off destroying my life, he's been rebuilding his.* She peered over the scene at the dinner table to watch her sleeping babe, while slowly picking at her food.

Cat refrained from speaking unless spoken to, a habit she had developed with Doug. The contrast to her previous talkative self was alarming to Dad. "Hey, you still know how to ride a bike, right?" Cat looked up from her plate.

"Well, technically, in theory yes. But I have the kid now." She pointed to the big blue stroller. He suggested that they could get a trailer or a bike seat. She added that a basket for groceries would be very helpful. By the end of the conversation, he proclaimed that he would be taking his daughter to a bicycle shop the following day.

The end of her meal was announced by the sound of a crying baby. Cat excused herself to the living room to attend to Jule. Dad smiled to himself as he cleared up the dishes.

Cat was nervous leaving the baby with her new Grammy. *I trust them. I mean, I know that she will be okay. But what if she gets hungry? She will be fine. You are worrying too much. It's good for her to get to experience the love of family from the very start. You never got to spend much time with your extended family. You know you want this for her. Jeezus man. It's only a trip to the bike shop.* She took a deep breath and put her seat belt on.

As Dad drove Big Red to the bike shop, he explained to his daughter "I know you don't have a car, and that would really help. But I can't afford to buy you a car, so a bicycle is the next best thing." She nodded wordlessly. Fingers grasping at hands, she nervously twitched in her seat as they crossed town. She remembered this bike shop as the place where she had picked out the bike for her bike route as a kid. The unpleasant bits of the memory seemed less important, offering a warm fondness for the shop.

Cat looked at mountain bikes, street bikes, and cruisers. She liked the style of the cruiser the best. "I don't need anything too fancy. Just comfortable and practical." Stretching her hands out to grip the handlebars, she flipped her leg over the side of a shiny blue cruiser. Aluminum flecks glittered in the sun as she tried the bike out in the parking lot. It was a little awkward, but the clerk insisted everything could be adjusted. The clerk took measurements with Cat on the bike.

Next, they browsed baskets, seats and helmets. The clerk informed the shoppers that the shop would be able to make all the appropriate adjustments and installments if they didn't mind coming back to pick up the bike. Dad immediately agreed. He turned to Cat who marveled at all the choices in the shop. "It is the prudent thing to do. Time is money. Besides. This is what they do for a living."

Cat took BART out to Berkeley with Jule in the big blue stroller. Struggling with the stroller, she managed to get up the escalator leaving the Berkeley subway station. Walking up to Telegraph Avenue, pushing the stroller, she wondered if she would see anyone that she knew from her past. Walking past street people sitting on their packs and bedrolls, it dawned on her how far she had come in the last couple of years. *I might be wandering around in a daze, but at least I have a purpose.* She looked down at Jule who was watching the light change colors as they passed under a canopy of trees.

The freedom from responsibility to which she had once clung so desperately, had been lost forever when she agreed to have this baby. Now, Jule stared up at her, eyes wide taking in all the color as they walked. Cat sang to her baby and talked to her. *You are my whole world now and I have a duty to provide you with the best world I can. I have no idea how I am going to accomplish this great task, but I will never give up trying.* Her beautiful daughter was the center of the universe and living proof of the divine miracle of life.

Walking through the UC Berkeley campus, Cat stopped for the Drum Circle. Lifting Jule out of the stroller, Cat wrapped the baby in her arms and danced with her. Remembering being a young girl, going to drum circles with her mother, she danced without shame. She recalled dancing as a child in front of the drummers, while her mother had sat nearby with her sketchbook. Her daughter cooed and laughed in the Summer sunshine until she became tired and hungry.

As Cat put the baby back in the stroller, Jule protested by crying. Eager to remove the sound of a crying baby from the pleasant rhythm of the drum circle, she pushed on to a quiet shady place on campus. Stopping again, Cat laid a blanket out on the grass. Changing her diaper and resting to nurse for a little while improved both of their moods tremendously. Once she packed everything back up and began walking, Jule fell asleep quickly in the stroller.

Walking up the Avenue, Cat recalled memories associated with different places she passed by. *It's odd to see how much has changed in such a short period of time.* Some businesses had changed. Bottega had become a Schlotky's deli. The place where the Berkeley Inn had once stood was now an empty lot full of trash, surrounded by a tall chain link fence. The street seemed dirtier, and somehow more desolate.

Cat wandered all the way down to the Cafe' Med, half hoping to find someone who would be happy to see her. Of all the people that she could possibly happen to run into, she was surprised that is happened to be Maureen.

They had not spoken in years. Neither of them even lived in the Bay Area. They both happened to be in town visiting and had gone up to the Avenue for a very short period of time. Maureen was glad to see her old friend. She had cleaned up her life and gotten a job working as a prison guard somewhere. Cat was astonished. It reminded her that she still had a very long way to grow in her own life.

After a few hours of wandering around Berkeley, Cat headed back through the hills on the subway. Returning to Walnut Creek, she tried looking up friends she had known from school. The only person she was still in contact with was Carrie. Carrie was excited to hear from her old friend. They made plans to go out and have a drink her on her birthday.

When Dad brought Cat back to the bike shop on her birthday, the shop had outfitted the new bike with a back seat for carrying Jule. They equipped the front with a big basket and the back rack had additional wire folding baskets. *Now I can get around with Jule much more quickly. I can visit people and go grocery shopping. I can do things without Doug's help!* She expressed her gratitude for the thoughtful birthday gift as they drove back to Dad's house with Cat's new 'Mercedes' in the back of Big Red.

Leaving Jule with her family once more, Cat went to Dallimonti's to meet up with Carrie. *It feels odd meeting an old friend from elementary school in a bar.* Cat recalled them being kids together, stealing cheap cans of beer from the mother's boyfriend and sneaking them into Carrie's bedroom. Now, the two young women were both twenty-one and meeting in an actual bar. Cat arrived first and awkwardly battled the uncomfortable feeling of not knowing what to with herself. Fidgeting in her seat, she waited for Carrie to arrive. When Carrie walked through the door, Cat got up to greet her old friend.

The two hugged briefly and then sat down to visit. A waitress came around to the table and took their drink orders. Cat requested a spiked "Root Beer Float". Carried teased her for ordering a "froofy" drink. The pair giggled when asked to show their identification cards. Cat was excited being able to use her ID for the first time in a bar. They laughed together. They talked about old times. When the drinks arrived, Cat sipped the float. *Way too syrupy!* Strong and sweet, she left almost half the glass full when their visit ended.

Checking the time, Cat apologized, "I wish we could hang out longer, but I still have a family dinner to attend." Carrie responded that she had to go to work anyway. She teased Cat one last time about the Root Beer Float. They got up from the table and headed to the door together. Standing on the sidewalk they hugged and said their goodbyes. They exchanged promises about trying to keep in better touch with each other and walked their separate ways.

Dad let Cat choose the restaurant for the birthday dinner. "Pacific Fresh, because I love fish and it's a special treat!" Piling into the family car, Cat stayed relatively quiet. As they entered the restaurant, she felt strange. *This doesn't feel any different than any other family dinner. It could be a birthday for any one of us and it would be exactly the same. What makes today different from any other day?* The hostess approached the group and addressed Dad, confirming the number in their party. Cat followed silently at the end of the line.

Once seated with menus, the waitress approached the family and suggested that they place their drink orders. Dad reminded his eldest daughter, "Now you can order anything you want. It's your 21st birthday, so you *have* to order something with alcohol in it!" She didn't really know what to order. Still a little queasy from the extraordinarily sweet concoction at Dallimonti's, she opted for a Sierra Nevada Pale Ale. Sipping it slowly over the course of the dinner, Cat didn't pay much attention to finishing the beer. More interested in the red snapper, she tried hard to evade personal conversation.

Sensing her uneasiness, the new grand parents did not deliver the expected 'So what are you going to do with your life' line of questioning. Instead, they asked about Jule and Doug. Hoping to hear some funny tales of their grandchild, they shifted in their seats. Cat attempted to sidestep the questions with vague answers. Occasionally, she'd find something to get animated about. Once the short story would end, Cat would return to her cave.

Sensing her uneasiness, the grandparents instead turned the conversation onto more exciting topics. Dad's soon to be wife reviewed the agenda of items already completed, and what still remained, as she prepared for their wedding the following month. Her energy plenty made of for Cat's lack thereof. She was thankful for the opportunity to hide in plain sight. Her thoughts wandered up the skirt of a passing waitress. *If I was a man. Oh, the things I would do to her. I am so glad nobody can read my mind. What is wrong with you? Shut up.* Her eyes shot down to the bottle of beer in her hand and she took another small, slow sip.

Sitting under a tree in the parking lot, a shadow scratched at the dirt with a small branch. Unseen by passing drivers, as details evaded the naked eye, the small smoky form seemed determined not to disappear. A squirrel ran up the tree, paying no attention to the letters appearing in the loose soil below. I. AM. REAL. The message failed to transmit. The signal was broken by the sound of a crying child, buffered by the clucking of her family as they moved through the parking lot.

The next night, Cat again left her daughter with the 'New Grammy.' This time Dad took her out to the bar he liked to frequent. They had nice staff and televisions for watching sports. Dad explained, "Your birthday dinner didn't really count as going out to a bar for your birthday." Cat ordered vodka and amaretto. Dad laughed at her. "Vodka is what you drink when you don't want people to smell alcohol on you! You can drink legally now! Don't you want something better." He teased her.

She defended her choice, responding, "I like Amaretto! And the two go nicely together."

They talked a little. He wanted to know what she was going to do now. She didn't know. *I guess I will have to go back to Doug and try and make things work.* Absent-mindedly, she played with the damp cocktail napkin. *I have no idea what is going to happen, or how I am going to handle it. Life would be so much easier if I could look into the future. I know that I will never be able to live up to Dad's expectations. I wish he didn't expect so much of me.* They didn't stay long or connect very well, but Cat appreciated her father's attempt.

Cat thought it was funny, that after spending almost a decade hiding from herself with intoxicants, she didn't really have much of a desire for them. *Now that I'm 21 years old, I can get into a bar without bribing the door man. I don't need a fake ID. I could simply walk in without any problems, but I'm so nervous going into places where I don't know anyone.*

Chapter 17
Mourning Music

After spending a week or so visiting the Bay Area, Rabbit returned to West Sacramento. Feeling trapped in her circumstances, and still very much in love with Doug, she maintained a state of disequilibrium. Focusing only on the tasks at hand, she took care of her lovely daughter. She indulged in the unfolding of her life. She was there to observe every first laugh, step, and word. Relying on her partner to provide food and shelter was something that she chose to accept temporarily. The price for being able to spend the first year with her daughter seemed like a reasonable trade-off. Undetected, the shadow of a fire within her began to protest as she slowly began to shatter.

As Rabbit focused on creating a sustainable schedule of rituals as a new parent, she worked to let go of previous patterns she perceived to be unhealthy. She did nothing to hold on to the memories of the past. All memories of the past were pushed back. *I will reinvent myself as a responsible parent. I will be the whole world to my daughter for years to come. It is of the utmost importance that I take this responsibility very seriously.* She expected Doug to do the same thing, and his difference in opinion and actions triggered a great deal of civil unrest between them.

Spending so much time focusing on her daughter, Cat began to forget how to focus on herself. The parts of her that still felt alive were directly connected to Rabbit's love relationship with Doug. The growing gap between them contributed to her fear of instability. She felt unstable within herself and looked outside of herself for answers, as she had done for so many years already. She decided that everything would be better if they had their own apartment. She began to put pressure on Doug to do more to find them a place of their own to live. Rabbit tried to sleep when her daughter slept. While Doug sat up drinking and smoking with Sister's boyfriend, the lost new mother laid under blankets pretending to sleep.

Trying to remember what it felt like to be herself, Cat despaired in a dark void of memories. Combing through shadows that seemed almost forgotten, her feelings of disorientation were amplified. She felt cold deep in her bones. Something in her searched for a firelight in the void. Alone in the darkness, she laid in her bed, wrapping her arms around her sleeping Jule. Crying silently over the baby, Rabbit tried to remind herself, "My love for her is all I need to get through this long night."

It was a typical hot August day in West Sacramento. Jule was five months old now and spending more time awake between naps. In the kitchen, Cat turned the radio on while she did chores. The walker rattled as her exploratory driver navigated around the room. Listening to music, the young mother talked to her baby as she danced across the kitchen. Cleaning dishes and putting them away was more fun with music. Today they seemed to be playing a lot of Grateful Dead music which had put her in a good mood as soon as she turned on the radio dial.

Then, the DJ started talking. He announced that Jerry Garcia had died. Cat stopped in the middle of the room. Tears welled up in her eyes and she felt her heart sink down to her feet. Suddenly feeling sick to her stomach, she sat down in a chair at the kitchen table. The walker rattled nearby, and she remembered that her daughter could see everything she did. For a moment she struggled to hold back her tears.

Sitting at the table, Rabbit listened to the DJ talk briefly about the legacy of Jerry Garcia. Born in 1942, he had been playing music with the Grateful Dead for thirty years. Cat had grown up listening to the Dead. Going to concerts as a child with her mother had been a prominent part of her childhood. Interacting with the Rainbow family had an immense impact on her as a child and a young adult. Rabbit had been given her name as a direct result of interacting in a world she never would have discovered if not for the magical music of Jerry Garcia.

The interconnected flow of energies present at Grateful Dead shows had been something like a spiritual experience for her. She knew that she had to be a house person. She had to provide some kind of consistency for the new person she was raising. Nevertheless, the idea that Jerry Garcia was never going to play another show brought her great sadness. She would never have the chance to let go and feel free at a Dead Show. Ever again. Her god had died.

Grasping the edge of the table, Cat could hold it in no longer. Tears rolled down her face in a constant stream, dripping onto her blouse. Her heart sank even deeper, recognizing that her anguish was affecting Jule. She picked up her baby and danced, hiding her face from Jule's soft gaze. Jerry Garcia and David Grisman piped out of the little speakers of the kitchen radio and she let memories of happy moments at concerts pour into her. She felt an overwhelming urge to pack everything up and run away with her daughter.

After an hour or so of listening to beautiful heart wrenching radio, the DJ announced that a gathering was already starting at Capitol Park in downtown Sacramento. *The child has been fed. All the dishes are done. I have nothing that I have to do except take care of my daughter. I can do that just about anywhere.* She decided that she had to go to the wake. *I will never have the opportunity to take her to a Grateful Dead show, but I am going to take her to this.*

Gathering up all the necessities for a long day trip, Rabbit packed her bag. *Cloth diapers, diaper covers, plastic bags and wipes. Extra clothes, blankets, snacks and drinks for the both of us.* Leaving a message for Doug explaining where she had gone, she loaded her daughter into a frame backpack and left, pushing a smartly organized stroller. *She will be happier if she can see everything.* The stroller worked to carry all the stuff and doubled as a bed when the baby was sleeping.

Heading across town, Rabbit walked north until she crossed the river between the cities. Crossing over into Sacramento, the difference in economics was visibly apparent. The buildings were kept in better condition in Sacramento. The tree lined streets leading up to the State Capitol were packed with cars. The streets were cleaner, and there were visibly more police. *West Sacramento is shabby compared to the Capitol City.*

As they reached the park, a gathering of people could be seen from the street. The local radio station had towers of speakers set up from which they were broadcasting the music for everyone to enjoy together. They played a live recording of a Grateful Dead show from beginning to end. She recalled the feeling at the Soccer Fields next to the Greek Theater when she had first fallen in love with the music and the people. Here, a melancholy feeling moved fluidly through the crowd with the music.

They are all happy to be sharing this together. They were all sad about the loss of such an important person in their lives. Rabbit searched for a little while, hoping to find other people she knew. She saw only a few familiar faces. Parking the stroller next to a tree, she laid out a blanket and removed the frame pack. Taking Jule out, she sat her daughter down on the blanket next to her. She allowed herself to let go of expectations and simply enjoy her surroundings with her daughter.

Picnicking in the middle of the crowd, Cat played with her baby. They got up and danced a while. Itchy feet wanted her to keep moving. Again, she felt the urge to run away. Instead, they walked around through the crowd acknowledging shared feelings of loss with strangers passing. At one point the weeping dancing mother realized that she had just shared a moment with another famous musician. She was stunned. *I just exchanged meaningful sorrow with a living artist who's impacted my life. But it doesn't matter. He is simply another person in mourning.* They had paid their respects to one another as equals. Nothing more and nothing less.

Rabbit returned to the blanket with her daughter. The baby was tired and overwhelmed. The young mother's energy level was also waning a bit. Resting against the tree, she snuggled with Jule, nursing her underneath a soft yellow blanket. Beautiful music moved through her body. She closed her eyes, sensing the people as they walked and danced around her. Moving in and out of consciousness, she relaxed, and half napped with her daughter.

Doug arrived later in the afternoon. Music had been happening for hours. News reporters were there taking pictures. Police were roaming around, but not really hassling anyone. It felt like Dead Lot, one last time. Doug roamed around some before settling on the blanket. The sun was setting, transforming the air into a cool indigo river wind. As wind blew through the trees, the baby began to get fussy. *This outing has lasted long enough. We are all tired and the radio station is beginning to pack up. I guess it's time to head home. I only wish it wasn't such a long walk back.*

Walking home, Doug carried the frame pack with a fussy Jule. A bonnet head bobbed up and down, peaking over the top of the frame pack. Falling asleep as he walked, Jule was quick to silence. Pushing the stroller beside him, Rabbit attempted to talk to Doug about her unhappiness. She wanted to be happy. He said he wanted her to be happy. *I really believe that we will be happier when we aren't sharing a home with other people.*

Their conversation was tense. It was important to Cat to feel heard, to feel supported, to feel loved. Doug was quick to get defensive, to which Rabbit responded with tears. He'd squeeze her hand tight and slow his voice until she calmed down enough to stop crying. Then, with deep breaths and good intentions, they try to continue talking rationally. They repeated the cycle a few times before eventually reaching to Sister's apartment.

Before walking up to the door, Doug turned to his little girlfriend. He reached down and wiped tears from Rabbit's eyes, bent down, and kissed her deeply. "I agree that we need our space to be a family and promise to try harder to support us." He paused, took a deep breath, and finished. "I will find us a home soon. Please don't worry." Then he turned around and walked through the door into a dark and slumbering room.

In late August, the unstable family returned to the Bay Area together. Dad was finally remarrying. After fifteen years of dating off and on, Cat's little sister and her mother were finally there to stay. The wedding was going to be huge and there would be family coming from all over the country to help them celebrate. Even Cat's grandmother was going to be there. *I wonder how this will go. I haven't seen her since I was eight years old when she tried to tell me my mother was going to Hell.* She winced.

Stress levels were high getting ready for the wedding.

Cat was getting nervous about seeing people that she had not seen for several years. Doug proclaimed he didn't like being included in the chaotic mix of people. When the wedding day arrived, they packed up the baby and all the necessary accouterments and shuttled up to the horse club on Mt Diablo. They arrived several hours before the wedding was set to start. Helping with some of the set up took less time that simply keeping Jule occupied.

The horse club was a beautiful place to get married. The great hall was lined with big windows providing a scenic view of the surrounding valley. The ceremony was set to take place outside, and the reception would be in the great hall. Late August meant that they were all sweating in the shade waiting for the ceremony to happen. A large wedding party, all the children from previous marriages stood in line to honor their parents as they prepared to ceremoniously join lives. Standing awkwardly in a hand sewn pink calico dress and creme colored flats, Cat fidgeted with her hands behind her back. She felt terribly uncomfortable. *I really just want to sit in the back row somewhere. I can't wait to be out of this tiny little dress.*

A catered dinner followed by live music furnished a festive scene for all. Cat's Godmother found her comfort zone, taking on the role as bartender for the event. Long tables lined three edges of the banquet hall, leaving room for a small stage. While everyone ate, the band set up. Once the music started, some guests lingered at the tables while others got up and danced. Of course, Dad insisted that Cat dance for at least one song with him. A few drinks in them already, they stumbled on the dance floor stepping on each other's toes. He kept reminding his daughter, "You're not supposed to lead. You're supposed to follow."

Cat and Doug were glad when the evening was over. Returning to the old ranch house, they relished the opportunity for sleep and looked forward to returning to the quiet sanctity of their own world. By the end of the month, they would be moving out of West Sacramento. The property management company that Doug had been working for would be renting an apartment to them. *We get to move back to Midtown!* Rabbit was excited. *The neighborhood is not terrible. We'll be closer to the light rail. I can get around easier. We'll have privacy. This will be marvelous!*

Chapter 18
Cause to Celebrate

The new apartment had built in shelves in the living room. Rabbit set Jule up in the bedroom, organizing it to meet the needs of her daughter. Doug didn't protest much. He didn't seem to care one way or the other. As long as she was happy, he was satisfied. She relished the opportunity to really start nesting. She began making a baby quilt in the patchwork style that she had once made hats and bags. While Rabbit continued to focus her attention on the care of her daughter, Cat dared to begin making allowances for personal time.

Doug brought a very large painting home that he had found behind a dumpster. He suggested that she could paint over it and she was excited to do so. Five feet long, it would prove to provide her with several months of relaxation and prayer. Trying to paint while the baby was sleeping did not always work out very well. When Jule awoke, she was mobile enough that Rabbit could not keep her out of the painting supplies. Doug was gone more than he was home. Occasionally, with much negotiation, she would convince him to agree to an afternoon of babysitting. Rearranging his schedule to give her a break, Doug made allowances to watch the baby while she painted but was quick to leave for band practice as soon as Jule was solidly asleep.

Colors swirled on the canvas. As music filled her ears and heart, Cat let her emotions flow through the brush, capturing all her yearning for travel and movement.

Dragons flew across the canvas, slowly emerging as the picture grew over time. A pathway in the center of the picture led the viewer into the distance towards a place that she could no longer see. She missed the feeling of kindness and open acceptance. As if remembering the very best parts of a fairy tale, she pictured herself dancing in the middle of the rainbow family. Surrounded by fire and incense, darkness and light, the shadows called out to her. Familiar shapes moved toward her from a distance. She saw a glimmer of blue. *Yes. The painting needs more blue.*

Drawn back to the canvas, Cat looked down at the plate covered in the remnants of past blending. *What did I just see? Where was that?* She searched the canvas for the place the blue called out to her, but it wasn't there. She looked down at her tubes of pigment. *I don't have that color. I could mix it. But where did you want it?* She scanned the canvas again. *No. It's not here. It wasn't here.*

Rabbit felt a chill run down the back of her neck. She carefully leaned the canvas against the protruding countertop before attempting to stand up. Blood rushed into her legs and she stumbled to feel the floor. "Dammit. I hate it when that happens." She heard Jule making sounds of waking up and glanced around the room. *Yup. It's just me again. I guess my painting is done for the day.* She pushed herself off the wall and took long slow steps as she gained feeling in her legs. "I hear you honey. Mommy's coming."

Spending long nights alone on the couch in the living room, the baby slept in her crib in the bedroom. Doug was off at band practice and Rabbit was at home with the baby. This occurred frequently, giving her ample time with nothing but her thoughts to consume her. She cried, listening to Cheryl Crow's *Strong Enough* piping out of their little radio. "Lie to me" the little radio wailed. *I know he's lying to me. I know he doesn't really love me anymore. He is just going through the motions, but he is not invested in being a parent the way I am. I can feel it.* She wanted desperately to run away and rejoin the rainbow family. Still, she was convinced that if she did, she would be subjecting her baby to an inconsistent lifestyle. *I don't want to be homeless with a child.* She was terrified of what would happen if she were completely on her own. So, she continued to push through each day, as weeks and months passed without change.

Thanksgiving morning started out slow and sleepy until the telephone rang. Nina was in the hospital, in labor. Instead of attending a Thanksgiving feast, they would be spending the day in the hospital. Rabbit proceeded to pack up a long days' worth of stuff to take care of Jule, while Doug shuffled around distracted. He hadn't really been looking forward to another holiday filled with family arguments. Still, compared to spending a day in the hospital, the holiday arguments sounded pretty good. Before long, the young family was headed for the hospital.

A couple hours of public transit, walking, and arguing with each other about the importance of being present and supportive for Nina, the young parents arrived at the hospital. Rabbit utilized the bottom of a utility closet to make a nest for the baby. Sitting in an overstuffed chair, she nursed the baby to sleep. She felt empowered, after accomplishing this seemingly minor task, and smugly tucked the baby into the closet bottom bed. Leaving the baby sleeping, Rabbit pulled up a chair to sit by the bed and offer Nina support.

Nina was with me when I was in labor. She brought me to the hospital and stuck around to be supportive when Doug was busy sleeping in a chair. Now I get to be here for her. Doug had little patience for very many people. He didn't want to have anything to do with this labor. As soon as Jule began to stir, he resigned himself to caring for the baby while Rabbit assisted his cousin. Nina's mother was getting on Nina's nerves. She made a big fuss trying to banish her from the room. After most of the room had cleared out, Nina turned to Rabbit and asked her to stay.

The day was long and exhausting. Everyone was hungry. Doug wasn't thrilled about spending the day this way. Still, he was excited when the baby was born, making a point to get a glimpse of the new family member. He was the most thankful when the day was over, and they were able to return home. Once they were safely home, Doug was free from the prying eyes of family and strangers. He let his exhaustion pour out on his girlfriend. Soon she was crying. She opted for the safety of sleep and crawled under blankets with her baby. *Another night. Just another miserable night. What's Thanksgiving? There are no holidays here. Tonight is no different from any other night.*

Doug and Rabbit argued a lot. She was miserable and tried very hard to keep her unhappiness to herself. When her feelings finally emerged, they were explosive and messy which fueled his emotionally abusive behavior. With the holidays in full swing, she recognized that Jule would not remember her first Christmas. She wanted to do something meaningful. She needed something uplifting. Rabbit wanted to do something that would help her to feel better, when much of her life felt terrible. She remembered how many people had been happy receiving gifts from strangers, when she was homeless in Berkeley. She gathered up clothing and toys that her daughter no longer used or would never use. Wrapping each gift, she marked the outside of the gift with an age and gender.

Christmas arrived and they planned to spend Christmas Eve and Christmas Day at Doug's mother's house. The visit was wrought with family arguments. Most of them were on edge. Rabbit questioned why they all argued so much. "Y'all are lucky to have each other. I grew up with no siblings. I begged the universe to bring me someone to talk to, to play with, and of course it never happened. I don't understand why y'all are so hateful towards each other." Holidays had been quiet growing up without brothers or sisters. Rabbit had always wished that holidays could be more eventful. Now, the fighting made her rather uncomfortable, and she searched for a way to escape. *That's right! I brought the bag of recycled gifts!*

Rabbit convinced Doug's mother to drive her down to Loaves & Fishes where the Christmas Free meal was happening. Both women seemed relieved to be able to get away from the arguments and chattered excitedly in the car about the importance of giving back to the community. Parking down the street from the community center, they had a short walk to get to the people. Rabbit carried Jule while her companion carried the bag of gifts. Approaching people accompanied by young children, hand outstretched with a gift, Rabbit wished each of them a Merry Christmas. Many of recipients looked confused. Some of them were openly appreciative. As soon as they had run out of gifts, they headed back to the car and left.

Doug and Cat went to visit her parents in the Bay Area the following weekend for a 'Second Christmas.' Dad came to pick them up in his wife's car. Doug sat in the front seat so Cat could sit next to Jule. After an hour and a half of virtual silence, they arrived to the loud and boisterous commotion of a big family. *Christmas was never like this growing up. I always wanted a big family like this when I was a kid. Now that I'm in the middle of it, I just want to run and hide.* Here, there was a lot less fighting than there had been with Doug's family. Doug and Rabbit seemed to make up for it by fighting among themselves. As she had been uncomfortable at his family's celebration, it was clear that he was also equally uncomfortable with her family.

Doug, Rabbit and Jule returned back to the Midtown apartment at the end of the weekend. Everyone seemed glad to get away from the commotion of the newly acquired family. Doug had to return to work and Rabbit was not feeling well. She had been extra tired lately. The stress of their current living situation was taking its toll. Money was extraordinarily tight. Fighting occurred frequently in their relationship. To make matters worse,

Jule had begun weaning herself from nursing. The rejection Rabbit was receiving from her partner, and then from her own baby was adding up and seemed to magnify her depression.

Rabbit spent hours regularly traveling across town to gather up free groceries from various food pantries. She was malnourished. She had been subsisting on a poor diet mainly consisting of fried batter. Making a batter of water and flour, she added seasonings when she could. Sometimes, she would get vegetables from a food pantry and incorporate them into the mix. Filtering the used oil, and storing it in a can, she tried to stretch the oil as long as she could.

With Jule weaning herself off of breast milk, the need for obtaining food that she could eat was taking its toll financially. Groceries were expensive. They were receiving WIC benefits and food stamps, but that only went so far. There was little room for anything fancy. Getting cheese was a special treat. Anytime that Doug spent money on anything other than a necessity, it led to some kind of argument.

When New Year's Eve arrived, Rabbit desperately wanted to spend the evening with Doug. She wanted a nice evening of romance and affirmation. She needed to feel loved, appreciated, needed. Instead of spending the evening with her, Doug went out for a gig with his band. *My feelings are hurt. He wants to hang out with the guys more than he wants to hang out with me.* He briefly suggested that she could come too, knowing that she would decline. She insisted that it was too much with the baby, and that it would be much more prudent for her to stay home with Jule. He shrugged it off and promptly left.

Rabbit locked the door of the apartment. Listening to the radio, she laid on the couch trying to get her baby to nurse and snuggle with her. Jule refused, fussing and rejecting the breast. Finally, she gave up and gave in, offering her baby a bottle of formula mixed with rice cereal. Jule gladly accepted the bottle and fell into a heavy slumber. Getting up without waking her was not as awkward as it had been when she was a newborn. With fluid movements, Rabbit was able deliver her to the bedroom and tuck her into the crib.

Returning to the living room, Rabbit laid down on the couch and cried. *My partner doesn't want me. My baby doesn't want me. I'm completely useless. If I died tonight, nobody would miss me.* She got up and paced the living room floor. The desire to pack everything up and run away pulsed in her veins. Quietly creeping through the bedroom, she went into the bathroom and shut the door.

As the young woman showered, she examined her body. *What is wrong with me?* Cat felt out of balance and didn't know why. Getting out of the shower, Rabbit gazed at her reflection in the mirror. She saw an ugly unhappy young woman. She saw someone that didn't look like her. She was confused by the internal conflict. She scoured every detail of her face. *What exactly am I looking for?*

Rabbit returned to the living room. She heard gun shots, or possibly fireworks, going off in the neighborhood nearby. She looked at the time. *Doug won't be home for several hours. There is no point in trying to wait up for him.* Rabbit tucked herself into the blankets on the couch and allowed herself to cry until she could no longer feel her own body. Floating above the scene, she felt her spirit leave in search of a happier place.

Chapter 19
The New Year Arrives

Doug arrived after the sun rose. He had been up all night and was still intoxicated from New Year's Eve festivities. His girlfriend was angry that he had been out all night. She wanted him to be happy to see her, and all he was really interested in doing was sleeping. Closing the blinds, he tried to block out the light. As the baby awakened, he gruffly suggested that it would be best for her, to care for Jule in the bedroom. The crying aggravated his mood. Trying her best to feed and change the baby, she avoided the living room. When she needed to go into the kitchen, she crept quickly and quietly, rushing to return to the bedroom.

Sometime mid-morning, Rabbit began cramping badly. She went to the bathroom and found that she was bleeding. She had not menstruated since before she had gotten pregnant. She had been told that as long as she was breastfeeding her baby, her cycle would not return. The onset of the menstruation made her cry. Reminded of the rejection she had experienced the night before, she cried in the bathroom. Doubled over in pain on the toilet, she tried to clean herself up, so that she could return to the bedroom. She knew that her baby needed her. Angry that Doug was not helping, her thoughts reviewed every way that he had let her down recently.

Rabbit tried returning to the bedroom to play with Jule. The baby had been crying in her crib for attention. She needed to be changed and fed. She needed interaction and activity. Doug barked about the severity of the noise and she closed the door to the bedroom. As she picked Jule up, cramps tore into her gut so fiercely that Rabbit was afraid she would drop her baby.

Rabbit laid the baby down on the floor to change her diaper. Jule was busy being her mischievous self, trying to roll over and crawl away while Rabbit attempted to clean her up. "Please go easy on me honey. I am in so much pain. Please." The baby continued to act her age, not understanding what her mother was asking of her. She wanted to play! Rabbit just laid on the floor crying while Jule climbed on her, trying to get her mother to play with her.

Her face stained with tears, Rabbit could feel blood seeping from inside her, staining her thighs. Placing her daughter back in the crib with toys, she returned to the bathroom, closing the door halfway. Sitting on the toilet, the cramps continued to worsen. Unlike a regular period, the bleeding did not slow down after going to the bathroom. Sharp pains shot through her and she cried out. *What is happening to me?* Memories of having a miscarriage at fifteen shot through her mind as painfully as the cramps shooting through her abdomen.

Jule was getting fussy in the bed. She wanted to get out of her crib. She wanted to eat and play. Rabbit worried that Jule could hear her crying and tried to hold her tears quietly inside. She tried to get up from the toilet and spilled blood on the floor. Leaning over to clean up her mess, she felt hot lightening pulsing through her back. Unable to hold back the tears, she sat on her hands and knees on the bathroom floor.

Still on all fours, Rabbit pushed the bathroom door closed until she heard the click of the latch. With one hand on the sink and the other on the edge of the bathtub, the young woman struggled to stand up. She stripped off her clothes and climbed into the shower. Carefully balanced against the shower wall, she closed the plastic curtain and turned the water on. Hoping that the sound of running water would be louder than her, she allowed herself to cry. With each sharp pain, she cried out, just as she had done in labor. The warm water running down her back provided only a very small amount of relief. *This must be a miscarriage. It has to be. No regular period would be this painful.* She watched as the blood flowed freely at her feet.

Cat could hear her baby crying in the other room. She felt powerless to help her. She could hear Doug yelling at her from the living room to take care of the baby. He had a headache and was trying to sleep. *I'm supposed to be taking care of the baby and keeping her quiet. Now he's mad at her for being loud.* In spite of the noise of the shower, Rabbit could still hear Doug yelling at her from other room to keep it down. His profanity shot through her body like great knives, tearing at her insides as blood ran down the drain.

Similar to the back labor, the pain never really went away. Instead, it maintained a hot crampy ache in her abdomen and back, interrupted every couple of minutes by severe shooting pains. Another knife of lightening shot down her back and she cried out. Cat looked down to see more than just blood. Pieces of fleshy matter were mixed in the flow. Her heart wrenched. *That had been a baby inside me! There was a baby. And its dead.*

Rabbit could hear her partner yelling in the living room. Instinctively, she responded, "I can't leave the shower!" Fragments of words shot out of her teary face. "You don't understand. It was a baby! It hurts so bad!" He never came into the bathroom to check on her. *Why is he so mean to me?* Her head pounded and her whole body hurt. She stayed in the shower for almost three hours until the blood flow slowed enough to get dressed again.

Finally emerging from the bathroom, Rabbit retrieved her flustered daughter. Taking care to address her needs as quickly as possible, she made snide remarks to Doug as she passed through the living room to the kitchen. "What's your fucking problem today?" he asked roughly. "Nothing that matters. I was just busy having a miscarriage in the shower. I've got it covered now." She responded shortly.

Rabbit gathered snacks and bottles from the kitchen and returned to the bedroom. She closed the door to the bathroom, as well as the door to the living room. She laid a blanket on the floor. Placing toys on the blanket, she propped herself up on with a pillow. Jule sat on the blanket, happy to finally be free from her crib. She handed Jule snacks, one at a time, until she seemed satisfied. Exhausted, the young mother allowed herself to nod off while her baby played next to her.

After a while, Jule started fussing again. Rabbit changed her diaper one more time. Then, with a bottle of formula, she snuggled up on the floor with her. Finally, they fell asleep together on the bedroom floor. When Rabbit awoke, the sun had set. Carefully putting her baby girl back in her crib, she returned to the bathroom. After cleaning herself up, she crept through the bedroom into the living room. The living room was empty. They were alone in the apartment again.

Stress and pain rooted itself in Cat's reality as normal. In fleeting moments, she strained to reach through the thin veil of dysphoria that enveloped her. Rabbit put on a show for the humans she was forced to interact with, while Cat silently wept in the dark. In the hot darkness, a shadow began whispering in her ear. In the darkness, she reached out, trying to find the source and in the void, she found only herself.

The year progressed with passionate arguments and passionate sex separated by long periods of isolation. Rabbit developed and maintained a pattern of survival that relied less on Doug and more on a series of rituals that ultimately centered around her growing Jule. Mornings were a series of rituals. As Jule's needs gradually changed, Rabbit slightly adapted her routines. The consistency made Rabbit feel like she was starting to gain a little control in her own life. This cycle usually shifted and pivoted backwards when Doug appeared after several days of absence.

After an evening of arguments, and disturbingly abrupt make-up sex, the mood in the midtown apartment was solemn and still. Rabbit paused in the doorway that separated the bedroom from the living room. Doug lay on the living room floor casually handing a plastic book to Jule who kept putting it down again between them.

He hasn't been unkind this morning. He hasn't said much. But then he doesn't usually. Except when he's being mean. I hope that he isn't mean today. She walked around the pair on the floor and rounded into the kitchen.

Rabbit turned on the radio, taking care to keep the volume low. She refilled her coffee cup and went to the fridge for some milk. *If Doug is going to hang around for a while and play with Jule, I could actually make us some breakfast!* She peered into the refrigerator as she returned the milk carton to the rack. *What do we actually have that he will be impressed by? If I make a nice breakfast, maybe he will stay longer? Maybe we can take Jule to the park together? As a family!* Searching for very best ingredients she could procure; she'd checked all the cupboards. She moved jars in the fridge, making sure not to overlook any possibility for a more impressive meal. Then, with intention and determination, she thought about how her mother had once cooked long ago. *When I was a kid, she could make a meal out of anything. Before she retreated to her cave.*

Rabbit was able to come up with a few different things, but not very much of any particular ingredients. They only had one egg. There wasn't enough pancake mix for pancakes and the milk was almost gone. She checked the dairy drawer. *Nothing. Not even butter.* She checked the produce drawer. *One tiny apple. Some carrots. No. I am not making carrots for breakfast. I need those for Jule later.* A few minutes of rummaging and she had her chosen ingredients lined up on the counter. About a half *cup of flour, equal parts pancake mix and instant potatoes. Add some water and oil. That will make a batter.* She smiled to herself. *I've got this.*

Rabbit diced up the apple and tossed them in her skillet with a little oil. She added a spoonful of sugar and sprinkled in two seconds of cinnamon. The oil crackled and popped, signaling her to reduce the heat. *I hope I don't mess this up.* She put the lid on the apples and turned to address her mixing bowl. In the bowl she combined the three dry ingredients, blending them together thoroughly. In her measuring cup, she mixed the last egg and 3 seconds of oil. She topped of the cup with water before adding it to her dry mixture.

Smoke began to fill up the little apartment. "What the hell are you doing in there?" Doug snapped, from the living room floor. Jule began to fuss.

"Making breakfast!" Rabbit whipped around to remove the lid from the apples and a loud crackling noise filled the kitchen. She turned the burner off, pulled the pan off the stove and put it in the sink. Steam lifted up around the pan as the cool damp surface of the sink collided with the irritation of the hot skillet. The fire alarm began screaming and Doug jumped up to open the front door. Rabbit whipped around the counter to pick up the screaming baby. *I can't even make breakfast. I can't do anything right.*

"Please just make it stop!" Rabbit bellowed to Doug over the sound of the wailing alarm. She retreated to the bedroom with Jule, in an effort to soothe the startled child. She closed the door, muffling the sound of Doug cursing the smoke and the noise. *I will do what I always* do. *I will take care of the baby. It seems like it's the only thing I'm good at.*

Rabbit danced to a silent song as she patted Jule on the back until the alarm ceased its battle cry. Both mother and daughter were still rattled from the commotion. So, Cat kept dancing. She hummed and bobbed around the room, hugging the child until they were both humming and dancing together. When they emerged from the bedroom, Doug had gone. The radio was off. The front door was closed. It was silent and they were again alone in the apartment. *I knew it wouldn't last. I wonder if he'll come back this time.*

The young woman sat down on the living room floor with her daughter. Her thoughts wandered as the child, restless, began picking up and throwing each toy that sat within reach. Cat pulled back into the shadows, rocking, and let Rabbit step forward into the moment. Autopilot kicked in and Jule was soon saddled in her walker with snacks.

Rabbit turned the radio back on. This time, she turned the volume up a little and began to sing along. She looked at Jule, pausing her warbling to explain that "now it was time for Mommy to clean." Picking at the burnt apples in the skillet, she ventured to taste one. Crisp and slightly sticky, it actually tasted good. Chewing up the little morsels reminded her that she was still hungry. Everything was where she had left is. *I bet these pancakes are still going to be good.*

Rabbit finished making the batter, without the apples. She added a little cinnamon and sugar to the batter. She washed out her skillet and placed it back on the burner.

Steam rose as the burner warmed up against the wet pan. *Mental note. Dry the pan next time.* Before long, the steam had passed, and the batter was cooking evenly in the skillet. She cooked all the batter, stacking the potato pancakes on a plate. After eating a few, she wrapped up the rest and put them in the fridge for later. *I can eat those for a couple days. Everything is going to be alright.* And so, the cycle of rituals began again until the next time Doug showed up.

Chapter 20
My Daughter

Late at night, Rabbit tossed and turned. Uncomfortable in her waking life, she sought to escape in sleep. Depression brought exhaustion and she was disappointed when Jule showed less interest in napping. In the twilight space between sleep and awake, Cat searched for clues. Every few weeks the excess burden of the accumulating stresses got to be too much. Cat called her Dad and asked to come for another visit. Dad's wife would drive to Sacramento and pick up Cat and Jule on Thursday. They would spend the weekend, and Dad could drive them back home on Sunday evening. The two left only a note at the apartment, indicating where they had gone, and when they would return. She repeated this, disappearing a few weeks later with the baby in February.

Visiting her family helped Cat to feel loved. They seemed truly interested in her, what she needed, and what would make her happy. *If only I knew what I needed. If only I could understand why I'm not happy. I have a beautiful child. I am not homeless. My boyfriend doesn't beat me. I have no reason to complain.*

Dad's new wife enjoyed spoiling the grand kids. She took pleasure in taking Cat shopping for 'anything you or the baby might need.' Once in the car, her new stepmother asked more personal questions. She asked questions that Cat was scared to answer. *She wants to know whether I am happy with Doug. I'm not happy. But it's not his fault.*

There's something wrong with me. That's all. But I don't want to tell her that. She wouldn't understand.

Two visits in a row, Rabbit returned to Sacramento with more stuff than before. They loaded her up with more clothes and toys for Jule. The second time, her family also sent her home with several bags of groceries. She was thankful. *I probably could have gotten more, but I didn't want to be greedy. They insisted this was nothing, but this is so much more than I ever get from the food bank. Doug will be so happy with all the food! Maybe he will come home for dinner?*

This time, Doug was waiting at the apartment when Rabbit arrived home Sunday evening. The blinds were tilted in the living room window just right, so that she could see Doug pacing in the living room as Big Red pulled up to the curb. She took a deep breath as she opened the door to the truck. Diving into the crisp evening breeze, she made her way to the apartment door with Jule asleep in the car seat under her arm. The door opened as she approached revealing her partner fuming. "Where have you been?"

In response, Rabbit pushed the car seat into his hands. "Great! You're home! You can take Jule while I unload the truck." She turned to head back to the curb. *Don't you say another word. Not in front of my dad.* She could hear Doug stiffen up as her father began walking up the sidewalk with a handful of grocery bags. Rabbit passed him, heading to the truck for their overnight bags.

Rabbit entered the apartment with an armload of overnight bags. She dropped a knapsack and the diaper bag off her left shoulder onto the couch. Her purse and backpack fell off her right shoulder missing the pile and tumbling onto the floor. The contents of her purse falling in a pile in front of the couch extinguished the silence. "Well. I think I got all our stuff out of the truck."

"Good." Dad replied as he emerged from her little fridge. "I put your milk and cheese away. The rest is still on the counter." He motioned to the mound of plastic bags separating them. "I better get going. I've still got to drive home." He walked around the rounded counter to stop in the living room to hug his daughter. "Don't forget to call if you need anything."

Rabbit nodded in agreement and followed her Dad to the door. She watched him walk up the sidewalk to the curb and disappear around the back of the truck. She heard the truck door open and shut and waited for the sound of the motor to fade before closing the apartment door. She turned around to see Doug standing in the doorway to the bedroom holding Jule.

"So, you think it's okay to just leave town without saying anything to me?" Doug scowled. "You can't just take my daughter like that!"

Cat paused at the door. *Your daughter? You are never around! I do all the work.* Doug seemed to grow taller. Cat shrunk down and Rabbit stepped forward, moving toward the kitchen. "I left you a note. I didn't know what else to do." *Don't look him in the face. Just focus on what you're doing. He won't do anything bad. He loves us. I know he does.* She couldn't look him in the eyes. She couldn't let him see her fear.

"My stepmother bought more jumpers for Jule." Rabbit emptied grocery bags onto the counter as she spoke.

"And my dad took me grocery shopping." She stacked cans in the cupboard as she spoke. "They decided that it would be best to have Jule's birthday party in Walnut Creek. Our apartment is too small, and March is too unpredictable for planning an outdoor party." She rambled, pretending like she could not tell he was angry. "They have a nice big house. Big enough for all the cousins."

Rabbit continued to ramble on, providing details for the birthday party while she finished putting away food. Without pause for his input, she began preparing dinner. Jule tugged on Doug's hair as he bounced her on his hip. Rabbit continued rambling. By the time the whole plan for the big birthday number one had been completed, she was placing a plate on the counter for Doug. "There. Dinner for you!" She turned to him offering a big smile and her arms outstretched.

Doug grimaced. "It sounds like I don't really have a say in the matter." He loosened his grip on the child, allowing Rabbit to take Jule out of his arms.

"Well, ya. I know. My stepmother got excited with the planning. But less work for us!" Rabbit placed Jule in the walker on her way back into the kitchen. 'Why don't you just enjoy the fact that I came home with groceries and stop worrying?" She grabbed a bowl of food for herself and pulled the walker over to the couch. She shared her dinner with Jule by handing her one noodle at a time.

"Noodle." Jule stated firmly, with an outstretched hand. Rabbit smiled and responded by handing her another noodle coated with cheese sauce. Little orange blotches quickly stained the toddler's face, like squirts of pigment waiting to be mixed.

Rabbit turned, to look over at Doug silently emptying his plate. "Did you hear that? She asked for another noodle." He showed little response. "She does that now. You know?" She handed Jule another noodle as she continued. "Our daughter is really smart."

"Yes. Of course, my daughter is smart." Doug put his empty plate down on the counter. "And yes, I said, "my daughter". She is MY daughter, and you have no right to take her away from me." He stood up, glowering at his girlfriend. "You don't have any reason to leave here anyway."

Rabbit kept her focus on Jule. Distinctly aware of her daughter's presence, watching and taking it all in, she forced herself to continue to smile. She picked a piece of broccoli out of the bowl and handed it to Jule before responding. "Well, sometimes I need to go get groceries, or simply need to take the baby for a walk. We all need our exercise." She picked up the half-eaten broccoli off the floor and place it on the walker tray before handing Jule another cheesy noodle. "And there is absolutely nothing wrong with going to visit family. I think it's important that Jule know her family. Besides, we couldn't afford to throw a birthday party like this. My dad is making that possible, and I, for one am thankful for the help."

Rabbit tried to focus on regular routine, self-care and caring for her daughter, as a tool to block out Doug's anger. *He can't be mad at me for living while he is gone. He is gone all the time.* She could feel him steaming across the room. *It makes him even angrier when I don't take the bait. But I know better. I didn't do anything wrong. I deserve to be treated with respect. Maybe he was just worried about me.* She resigned herself to brushing past his anger with sweetness. *Maybe if he likes what he gets when he's home, he'll come home more?* She smiled at him from her station on the couch.

Doug grunted as he turned into the bedroom. He closed the door firmly behind him. Soon Rabbit heard the sound of him practicing guitar in the bedroom. Child and mother silently smiled and danced in their seats while they listened to the melody and finished the bowl of pasta. Jule began to fuss a little as Rabbit returned to the kitchen to deposit the empty bowl in the sink. She rinsed a washcloth and wrung it out before returning to Jule. Moving better in the walker, Jule met her mother halfway.

"Mom-mom." Jule stretched out her arms to be rescued from the walker. Rabbit instead responded by wiping her daughter's face and hands with the washcloth. The toddler protested, but the process was quick. Soon she was at the hip, helping put the washcloth back in the sink. Then she helped mom make a bottle. *I don't hear the guitar anymore. I wonder if he's coming back out. I hope not.* Jule grabbed the bottle out of her mother's hand and immediately began suckling the warm thick fluid.

Rabbit heard the sound of the bathroom door close. A quiet click reverberated through the walls. *Why does he feel the need to lock the bathroom door? What is he hiding?* She walked slowly about the living room, gently bouncing Jule. The silent toddler laid her head against her mother's chest. Cradled in her mother's arms, her eyelids fluttered as she nursed herself to sleep. *Does he even care about me? He says he cares about Jule, but he never sticks around long enough to really spend time with her. He should be happy that his daughter is well taken care of, instead of being mad that someone else is doing it. I'm doing all the work!*

Jule had transitioned directly from rolling to trying to walk. There had been very little crawling. Since she had discovered bookshelves, she had posed a much greater challenge to keep up with for her mother. Not only did she make a point to empty all the shelves every day, but she also subsequently used the empty shelves to steer herself around the room. When the extra support ended, Jule simply latched onto her mother's legs. Rabbit had been excited about the built-in shelves when they had first moved in. With a growing toddler, the shelves had proven to be less useful. Everything within reach had to be age appropriate and infant safe.

Rabbit stared out the front window. Pieces of the sidewalk moved in slices in front of her eyes. Wind moved random leaves along the empty sidewalk. *Nobody wants to go out walking at night when it's this cold.* She shivered, remembering being homeless in the winter. The cold had soaked into her bones and remained deep inside her joints, chilling her for months after. *I'm so glad I'm here where its warm. Are you really? Are you really glad you're here? You have a miserable life. You have nothing but stress. Nobody cares about you. Nothing matters now.* She moved her gaze from the front window to the toddler in her arms.

Jule lay asleep in Rabbit's arms. With the babe nestled in her left arm, she used her right hand to gently remove the half empty bottle from the tiny fingers. With slow graceful movement, she glided across the room and placed the bottle on the counter. She looked back down into her arms, placing her hand within reach of the tiny fingers. Small lips pursed as she slept and grasped onto her mother's hand, where the bottle had once been.

"You matter to me." Rabbit whispered. "I love you so much honey." She smiled at the tiny sleeping person in her arms. *You are my daughter. I won't ever let him take you from me.* "Sounds like I better hurry up and get the bed ready. Daddy will be out of the shower soon." She timidly opened the door to the bedroom, glancing to make sure that Doug was indeed still in the bathroom. She entered the bedroom and placed Jule into her crib.

The sun had long since set by the time Rabbit was able to get Jule to sleep in her crib. Rabbit cleaned up what mess remained from their simple dinner. She quickly refreshed their pallet of blankets on the bedroom floor before Doug emerged from bathroom in only a towel. As soon as he sat down with a towel to work on his hair, she made her way into the bathroom with her own towel.

"My turn!" Rabbit announced as she closed the door to the bathroom. She paused before turning the knob to lock the door from inside. *He doesn't trust me. Why should I trust him?* The warm water was more important than actually cleaning. Pouring down her back and through her hair, she felt, if only for a few minutes, that she could actually breathe.

Doug heard the shower turn off. He threw the damp towel on the floor above their pillows and quickly situated himself under the blankets. He listened to his girlfriend dry off and brush her teeth. With his eyes closed, he metered his breathe and pretended to be asleep. Once she crawled into bed with him, he revealed his true interest with firm and rough attention. *At least he still thinks I'm beautiful. He still wants me.* She silently succumbed to his advances.

Lying beside Doug as he fell asleep, Rabbit felt used. Something about her felt like an empty shell. Tears rolled silently down her face. She dared not move. *He can't hear me cry. It would only make him mad.* Angry Doug frightened Rabbit. It was as if he became someone else, someone detached and much darker. She inhaled slowly, holding her breath, and then metering her exhalation. *If he hears me crying, but thinks I'm asleep, he won't wake me.* Nestled beneath the blankets, laying on her side, back to Doug, she fell asleep focusing on her own breath and the sound of her daughter's breathing in the crib nearby.

Chapter 21
This is All for You

Rare moments of happy silence offered Cat an opportunity to sit silently in Rabbit's belly. The young woman stood in her kitchen with a cup of coffee, a notepad, and a pen. She was pleased to see so many tasks had already been crossed off the list. Jule was asleep. Doug was gone. *Supposedly he will be here. We'll see. He's been nice this week. Only because he knows that I will be taking Jule to the Bay Area this weekend, whether or not he's around. I don't understand why he gets so weird. Hopefully, he won't be mean to me around my family.* She refilled her coffee cup with the usual regiment of cream and sugar. *He knows my stepmother is supposed to be here at Noon. If this is really important to him, he will show up.*

She peered across the room out the front window sipping her coffee. *I hope he doesn't show up too soon. I kind of like when he's not around.* She felt a pang of guilt but was quick to dismiss it. She picked up the notepad and pen, accompanied by her steaming mug, and moved into the living room. She sat on the floor with her back against the couch. *Much Better.* She sat cross-legged with her coffee mug situated southeast of her right knee. She pulled her knees up together and them stretched her legs out in front of her to make her lap flat enough to hold the notebook. She glanced one more time at the to-do list for the upcoming weekend.

Most of the things had already been taking care of by

her new stepmother. *I've given invitations to all of Doug's family. All I really need to do is pack. My family has pretty much taken care of everything else.* She flipped the pages past the list to an empty space within the notebook.

> Something inside me is trying to hide
> Something inside me is hiding
> I want to reach out, to ask them why
> But I don't know where to find them
> Something is hiding in the man who sits beside me
> Someone scary and frightened
> I smell them coming, I feel their breath
> My heart races, anxiety heightened

Upon waking, Jule was immediately dissatisfied with her current arrangement. Her diaper was wet. The room was cold and silent. She wanted to feel better and made her feelings known to her mother. Cat put down the notepad and pen, carefully sidestepping the mug of quickly cooling coffee. Swiftly, the child was whisked out of the crib and placed on the floor of blankets. Mother cooed at her daughter smiling wide. "Of course, you want your diaper changed! I don't blame you. That looks uncomfortable."

Rabbit handed Jule an extra cloth diaper to examine while she skillfully removed the wet diaper. She warned Jule, "Sorry, honey, this is going to be cold, but quick." She lifted up the toddler's legs to tuck a new folded diaper and wrap under Jule's hips. "There you go." Jule had little time to protest as Rabbit had become quite proficient in the cloth diapering process. *Those fancy*

Velcro diaper wraps that I got at the baby shower have really been a life saver! She had also managed to sell her family on the idea of the more natural approach. *Hopefully, I will get more at the birthday party this weekend.* "Do you want have some pants?"

Dad's wife had suggested they celebrate Jule's first birthday at their house, since it was big enough for the whole family. Cat had agreed without consulting Doug. She knew this would lead to arguments but decided it was worth the sacrifice. There was no way she would have been able to give Jule a birthday party. She didn't have any way buy birthday presents. She wouldn't have been able to buy all the food. *Dad always bought the bare minimum for me. Now his wife is spending so much. At least I know Jule will never go without!*

Rabbit was distinctly aware of her financial limitations and was trying to get better at asking for help. Still, she felt especially uncomfortable engaging with Doug's mother any more than necessary. If she had been forced to ask Doug's family for help, the birthday party would have just turned into another day of family feuding. *I hate the way they argue when they all get together. Doug doesn't usually start arguments around my dad. Hopefully, it will work the same way with his family.* Rabbit had notified all the Sacramento family. Doug's mother would be coming with his younger siblings. His cousin Nina promised that she would coming with her new baby.

There was a little bit left to pack. Cat's stepmother would be there to pick them all up at noon. She had made the point that by picking them up midday, she could avoid both morning and afternoon rush hour. If she didn't get out of Sacramento before 2 o'clock on a Friday, it could take twice as long to get home. Rabbit was determined to hide any problems that might be occurring between herself and Doug. She was afraid of being judged as a failure. She knew that her Dad had high expectations for her, and she was terrified of falling short.

Jule rolled over, pulling herself up on her mother. "Mom-mom-mom."

"I'm sorry honey." Rabbit responded, hugging her daughter. "Mommy just gets lost sometimes." She smiled big at the little girl, pulling her away and holding her under the arms, enabling Jule to teeter on her small unstable feet. "You need some more clothes. Its cold outside! And Grammy is coming to pick us up today!"

Rabbit sat Jule back down on the blankets before crossing the room to their laundry baskets. Jule made her way across the room, fussing over the challenge. She failed to reach her mother before Rabbit turned around with a handful of clothes. She picked up the little girl with one arm and returned them both to the blankets. Helping Jule to get dressed took some time. *She seems to think its a game. Please just let me put these damn close on you.*

"Please be nice for Mommy." Rabbit struggled to get Jule's little fingers through the sleeves of her jumpsuit. "Please cooperate. I'm just trying to get your clothes on you baby." She took a deep breath and forced a big grin for the little girl. "We want today to be a good day. Daddy should be home soon. Grammy will be here in a couple hours." She released the clothed toddler who had decided it was time for a new activity. "It's going to be an exciting weekend!"

Jule began heading for the small brick and board shelf that sat below the bedroom window. Rabbit followed her daughter, scooping her up on her way to the living room. The toddler protested briefly, until the change of scenery distracted her from her dissatisfaction. "I think I need to have more than coffee. You want some breakfast honey? I bet you are hungry!"

On their way to the kitchen, Rabbit deposited the toddler into the walker. Jule immediately began scooting after her mother and the two were soon in the kitchen. Jule wanted to be close to her mother all the time. The air smelled of danger and she knew that her mother would keep her safe. Rabbit reached down and handed her daughter a graham cracker. "Here you go honey. That will get us started."

Rabbit moved through the morning with ease. Jule was mostly satisfied, as long as she was close to her mother, and had something to put in her mouth. Mother kept small fingers of graham crackers at the ready, as she proceeded to line up their weekend bags on the couch. She examined the checklist as she wiped her daughter's face clean. *Everything is ready. Now all we need is Doug to arrive before my stepmother does.* Jule began to fuss.

Rabbit pulled the toddler out of the walker that kept everything in the apartment safe and just out of reach. "No wonder you are unhappy. You are soaking wet." She carried the crying toddler to the bedroom before stripping off her clothes. "Don't worry. I know you don't like this, but I promise you will feel better in clean dry clothes."

Rabbit heard the sound of the front door as she cleaned up the soiled child on the floor in front of her. She heard Doug grumble about the line of bags on the couch. Jule tried to roll out of reach while Rabbit wrestled to clean her bottom and legs. Soon a pile of soiled diaper and clothes lay just out of the child's reach, and she was being strapped into a fresh clean diaper and wrap.

"I know its chilly in here honey." Rabbit chatted with the little girl as she completed the task at hand. "Now we need to get you some clean clothes!" She pulled a long-sleeved tie-dyed onesie over the little bald head, and gently moved to guide the little arms through the sleeves. She lifted the little hips to pull the fabric down her back and affix the snaps over the bloated diaper wrap. "You are definitely bottom heavy." She chuckled. She layered sweatpants, a little hoodie and tiny little socks on the toddler before letting her loose on the floor.

Rabbit scooped up the pile of soiled material and headed to the bathroom. Doug opened the door as she was standing up. Hands full, she paused to address him immediately. "Oh good! You got home before our ride got here! I have everything ready for me and Jule." She moved into the bathroom kneeling by the toilet. She continued to talk to Doug while she rinsed the soiled material in the toilet. "I didn't pack anything for you because I didn't know what you'd want to bring. There's time though. She isn't supposed to be here for another 45 minutes."

Rabbit flushed the toilet and tossed the wet clothes, diaper and wrap into the hamper under the sink. She turned on the faucet and proceeded to wash her hands with soap and hot water. *Please be nice this weekend. Please be nice this weekend.* The steaming water bit her hands and she pulled away quickly, splashing water on her belly. *Dammit. Why am I so clumsy?*

She looked up at her reflection above the sink. Steaming water rushed out of the faucet, clouding the image before her. She reached out to turn off the faucet. The water stopped rushing leaving only her breath to echo in the small, tiled bathroom. She wiped the mirror with the edge of her towel and examined herself in the mirror. *Why doesn't he love me? Is it because I'm ugly? You certainly don't look right. Something is definitely wrong with this picture.*

Nina made a point to make the long drive for Jule's first birthday party with her baby. She had always been close to Doug growing up. She really liked Rabbit, and despite her love for her cousin, she had become concerned. She could see Doug falling short and went out of her way to call Rabbit and check on her. She knew that Rabbit wouldn't stick around forever and wanted to make sure that their kids could continue to grow up together. Rabbit had been by her side when nobody else had the time or patience.

It was almost two hours' drive each way, to the birthday party. Nina didn't mind because the rhythm of the car ensured her baby slept the whole way. As she unloaded her car, she made a mental note to use the name Cat while they were visiting here. She didn't want to confuse or disrespect the host family. She understood things were complicated but that didn't affect her desire to show respect and support for Doug's girlfriend.

When Nina and her baby knocked on the front door, she heard laughing as footsteps approached the door. As the door swung open, they were immediately greeted with festive enthusiasm. Doug sat solemnly in the corner of the living room, fighting to maintain the attention of his daughter. Jule seemed more interested in being social with the many people filling the living room. Cat emerged from the hall, thanking them for making the long trip, before disappearing into the kitchen.

Cat's new step siblings were in attendance with their baby. As he was placed into his stationary walker, his mother leaned down and discreetly suggested that Jule be placed in her walker as well. Doug hated being addressed directly by anyone in Cat's family. It made him feel attacked. Rather than cause a commotion in the middle of his daughter's birthday party, he silently agreed by handing the toddler to the standing adult. The happy Auntie bounced away with the gleeful birthday girl in search of the appropriate mom.

Nina noticed the exchanged and moved across the room to where her cousin sat. She demanded his attention and he responded by standing up and giving her a hug. It made him feel better to see her there. He felt outnumbered and isolated. She knew right away that she had made the right decision to come.

"I need to go back out to the car and get his stationary walker." Nina stated while pulling the recently awoken baby out of his car seat. "You can hang out with Big Doug while I go get your stuff!" She handed the blinking baby to her still standing cousin. "I will be right back." Then she turned, moved through crowded living room and exited the front door, leaving it cracked just slightly.

The happy Auntie found Cat in the kitchen. "Where's her walker?" She inquired. "I want to put all the babies together in their walkers." She added. "It's going to make a great photo!"

Cat looked up from the cookbook on the counter before her. "Everything is in the small bedroom." She tweaked her daughter's nose and smiled. "This is all for you. You know that birthday girl?" The happy Auntie laughed, bouncing the little girl as she walked away in search of the elusive walker.

Nina returned to the living room with her son's walker. Doug had moved from the far corner of the living room. Now hovering over the spread at the dining room table, he was amusing himself with trying to feed his little cousin. She intervened with disapproval. "He's not supposed to eat that yet!" She removed him from Doug's grasp and seated him in a brightly colored stationary walker. "We have to be careful and introduce one new thing at a time, just in case he's allergic to something!" Nina scolded Doug before moving the walker into the middle of the living room.

The two babies faced each other with interest. Both were trapped in stationary walkers equipped with a wide range of plastic toys. They briefly eyed each other's toys before settling on toys within their own reach. Then the happy Auntie placed Jule on the floor next to them. Seated in her walker, she was not stationary. She began walking around the other two walkers, bumping into them and laughing. The happy Auntie laughed at the bumper cars and disappeared in search of her camera.

In the kitchen, Cat resigned herself to allow the other new parents to attend to the three bumper walkers in the living room. She knew she couldn't be in two places at one time. Her step-mother and little sister had done most of the food prep in the morning while Cat and Jule had decorated. She appreciated that they supported her efforts in trying keep her daughter's diet healthy. Stepmother had even helped her find a recipe that provided a healthier alternative to the customary birthday cake. Now she was attempting to bake an applesauce cake sweetened with fruit juice, in the middle of a chaotic birthday party. *My baby doesn't need to get used to eating a bunch of crap at such a young age.*

Cat was distinctly aware of Doug's discomfort. He made it obvious to her, as he hovered in the dining room and glared into the kitchen. She could feel his eyes on the back of her head. She tried to pretend like she didn't notice him standing nearby and instead focused on the task at hand. *Why do I always make more mistakes when you're around? Why don't you just go away? Go talk to Nina.* She wanted desperately to feel like she wasn't screwing things up. *I just want a good day. I want to feel like I'm not a failure. Just look at my beautiful daughter. If*

I have no other purpose in this universe than to raise her, then I sure as hell better do it right.

When the birthday cake was finally done and brought out to the table, Jule was intimidated. Seated at the end of the table in a highchair, all the people were standing around her. She began to get nervous and fussy. Then everyone standing around singing proved to be more stimulus than she was able to process. The birthday girl started to cry. Cat knelt down next to the child's seat and tried to calm her down.

Once docile, the toddler seemed more interested in playing with it than eating it, Rabbit struggled to help her understand. "This is for you honey! It's your birthday!" The little girl blinked at her mother and whimpered. The mother smiled at the confused toddler. "This is your birthday cake!" Cat tried to show her that it was okay to put her fingers in it, and to eat it.

It took some coaxing. People began sitting down in the living room and talking among themselves again. Once the crowd dispersed a little, Jule relaxed and bravely put a finger into the cake. Then, two fingers, then a whole hand. Her eyes widened as she received praise and sweet cake. Cat began cutting pieces from the other end of the cake and placing small serving plates on the table for distribution. Some of the adults scoffed at the cake while others congratulated her on the culinary accomplishment. It tasted nothing like birthday cake and was denser than carrot cake or zucchini bread. Doug remained silent.

After the cake fiasco, the two young parents seated themselves on the floor with a cleaned up and sleepy Jule. They took turns helping their daughter open her birthday gifts. They seemed like a happy little family, sitting together on the floor with Jule between them. Extended family had come from both sides and provided a large pile of gifts to work through. With each gift, the toddler became less interested in the commotion. The other toddlers in the house were wearing thin and mothers began retreating to opposite corners to soothe and feed their restless babes.

Cat was glad when the birthday party was all over. As soon as people began leaving, Doug volunteered to retreat to the small bedroom to put Jule down for a nap. The house had been busy with noise and movement for hours. The stimulus was overwhelming for both Cat and Doug, and clearly had been hard for their daughter. Once in the bedroom, he laid her down with a bottle and began quietly strumming his guitar. Once she fell asleep, the bottle fell from her mouth, rolling down next to her. He paused playing to place the bottle upright on the windowsill beside them, then continued softly playing his guitar.

Chapter 22
Cat Steps In

Returning to Sacramento with all of the bounty of the birthday, Rabbit tried to be thankful. *I should be satisfied. I should be happy.* When they got home to their midtown apartment, Doug helped unload the car silently. He made a point to say 'Thank you' to Stepmother before she drove away. He entered the apartment closing the door behind him and turning the lock. The sound of the lock turning made Rabbit shiver. *We managed to have a good weekend with very little arguments. Doug was actually nice to me. I did it right!* Still, something kept her feeling uneasy and apprehensive.

"I'm going to take a shower." He said to her, in an almost monotone voice. She watched him walk through the living room, his direction straight ahead. He never looked at her. Something about him was rigid and cold. He didn't bother closing the bedroom door. Nor did he bother closing the bathroom door.

Jule still sat asleep in her car seat. Rabbit gathered a fresh bottle, set of diapers and bedclothes before rousing the little girl. The sleepy Jule fussed while she was saved from her cold wet diaper. She fussed while she was dressed in a long soft nightgown. She fussed while Rabbit tried to lay down with her on the couch. Rabbit grabbed a lap blanket from the back of the couch and tucked it over Jule. Lying in the crux between Rabbit's arm and her belly, Jule grasped the bottle and looked up at her mother's face.

Rabbit smiled. "It's been a long day honey. But its sleepy time now." She kissed her daughter's forehead and then closed her eyes. Jule watched her mother's eyes close, struggled against the comfortable warmth of the blanket, and quickly lost the battle. Soon both mother and child were asleep on the couch. Doug emerged from the shower to find the pallet of blankets on the bedroom floor empty. Naked, he walked silently through the bedroom, glancing into the living room.

Rabbit lay on the couch listening to the sound of her daughter's breathing in her arms. She gently removed the bottle and placed it on the floor next to the couch. Her reach was a little short and the bottle fell over on the carpet. She started to try and correct the error, but Jule began to fuss. Repositioning herself and closing her eyes once more, the toddler calmed. She heard Doug in the bedroom and tried to remain still. *Please just go to bed without me. I just want my baby tonight.*

Doug paused in the doorway. Disapproval emanated from the bedroom as Rabbit lay frozen on the couch. She exhaled as she heard him close the door to the bedroom. Focusing on the rhythm of Jule's breathing, sleep overtook her. A few hours later, Rabbit was woken up by a wet toddler crying in her ear.

Rabbit got up from the couch, moving Jule onto the floor. She pulled a clean diaper and dressings from the diaper bag. Once the toddler had been refreshed with a clean dry diaper, she made it clear that she was not ready to be awake. Rabbit picked up the half full bottle from the floor. She picked up Jule and headed for the bedroom. *The door is open. Didn't he close the door?*

She entered the bedroom and placed Jule in her crib with the bottle. Jule eagerly held onto the bottle and began nursing. Rabbit looked down at the floor. *He's not here. He didn't even wait until morning to leave.* She went into the bathroom and performed the ritual diaper rinsing in the toilet before dropping the whole pile of wets into the hamper. *I wonder how long he'll be gone this time.* She washed her hands with warm water and soap before leaving the bathroom.

Jule had already fallen back to sleep in the crib. Rabbit took the now empty bottle from her daughter and headed for the kitchen. *I wonder what time it is.* She made a point to stop and lock the deadbolt on the front door before delivering the bottle to the kitchen sink. She turned on the faucet, removed the ring that held the nipple on the bottle, and began rinsing it out. She glanced over at their little alarm clock on the counter. The little white tiles flipped over to show 2:28. *Really? And I'm not supposed to need to leave. Where in the hell is he going at two in the morning? The bars aren't even open?*

Rabbit shook her head. *Why do I even care? I'm happier when he's not around. But I want to be happy with him. I want him to be happy with us.* She shook out the bottle and nipple in the sink before laying them on a towel. She returned to the couch and pulled the lap blanket over her head before falling back asleep.

As spring progressed, Rabbit began venturing out on her bicycle. Thanks to Dad, the bike was fully equipped with a child passenger seat. He has also purchased a helmet for Rabbit and an especially small helmet for her daughter. In order to keep Jule's helmet firmly in place, she had to wear several layers of hats. This made her tiny head heavy straining her neck. Rabbit placed pillows around her daughter's shoulders for support, firmly affixing her in place with tight straps.

At first Rabbit had been very nervous. *What if the straps break? What if Jule falls out while I am riding?* Timidly, she rode slowly in the bike lanes of the quieter streets. She stopped frequently to check on her little passenger. She went on short rides at first. Keeping a hold on the toddler while trying to lock up the bike anywhere posed a bit of a challenge. With each ride, she had the opportunity to think too much about anything except the moment. The exercise got her blood flowing and put her in a better mood.

After a couple of these short rides, Rabbit decided to analyze the bicycle baby conundrum. *It seems a shame to have such a great form of transportation and not be able to use it for errands. There has got to be a better way. If I could take her out of the seat and put her in a stroller she couldn't run away.* She tried strapping the umbrella stroller to the bike. She could find no balanced way to place it on the bike. It would either end up falling into the spokes and causing an accident, or it'd be right in the baby's face. *That won't do. Next?*

It only took a bit of experimenting before Rabbit began to get frustrated. She abandoned the project when she heard the sound of her once sleeping child throwing toys out of the crib. She returned the lock to her bike, snapping it shut. She spun the lock dial and let it hang down. It clanked against the pole where her bike leaned silently. She heard something else through the echo of metal against metal. *How can that be?*

Rabbit looked past her bike into the small courtyard garden. Landscaped with ivy, hostas, and bulb flowers. She'd been enchanted by the landscaping at first but had come to be suspicious of it. She loved the daffodils in February. They brought back bittersweet memories. Rabbit chose to relish the sweet parts. Tulips and irises popped up after the daffodils began to shrivel and fade. The year-round green of the hostas made it feel tropical. *Is there something in the ivy? No. Of course not. But there is something about that ivy.*

The whisper reached out. Just out of reach Rabbit was entering her apartment. Again, a cool shiver down her spine. *What in the hell? I'm losing my mind. Doug is right. I am just crazy.* Rabbit turned to double check and make sure she had locked the deadbolt. She didn't want any surprises. Jule had run out of toys to throw and had moved onto the blankets. When Rabbit reached the bedroom, nothing was left in the crib except a toddler.

"Well. I guess you had something to say, didn't you?" She tried to smile at the child but only frustration showed. Jule cried reaching out her arms to be rescued. "I wish you would use your words. The screaming hurts my head." The little girl kept crying. "Please just stop! I don't want to pick you up just so you can scream in my ear!"

The pleas were not heard. Rabbit began to cry. Colors

and sounds mixed together and soon she was dizzy with sadness. Cat stepped in and picked the screaming child up from the crib. Jule pulled at her mother's hair. "That hurts Mommy, please stop." She responded, pulling the child's hands away from her hair. "I understand that you are upset. I will do my best to help you, but you need to not hurt me okay. I'm already hurting a lot, okay?"

Cat's face was red and wet with tears. She focused on metering her breathing as she placed the seething child on the floor. She sat down and began removing clothing from the revolting toddler. Silent, she did not speak to the child as she moved her arms and legs. The child continued to scream when she was stripped down to just her diaper and wrap. She continued to struggle as Cat pulled the soiled diaper off the child. Jule didn't care whether feces got spread all over the bedspread. She didn't pay attention to whether the screaming hurt her mother's ears. All she knew was that she was uncomfortable and had been uncomfortable for what felt like forever.

Cat picked up the struggling child. Outstretched so as not to get feces on herself or anything else, she carried the child into the bathroom. She placed the child into the bathtub and turned on the water. The toddler stopped crying. The sound of the water rushing out of the faucet was louder than her and she held her breath. When she began crying again it was different. Cat could tell the little girl was scared.

Cat's frustration melted. "Oh honey, it's okay! The water is not going to hurt you!" She used a washcloth to wipe the mess off of Jule's legs and bottom. Jule whimpered a little and stopped crying. "See! It's okay!"

Jule tried to climb out of the bathtub. "Mom-mom-mom" Her mother was not done and blocked her escaped while continuing to try and clean her daughter. "Done-done-done"

Cat chuckled. "Almost honey." She turned the water off. Jule stamped at the water as it retreated down the drain. "It sure hasn't taken you long to get good on your feet!" She picked up the cleaner toddler with a towel and wrapped her snugly. She hugged the bundled child and repeated her earlier complaint. "I love you honey. I know you get upset. But you need to not hurt your Mommy."

Jule leaned her head against her mother's chest. She pulled on her mother's long hair, this time more gently. "Mom-mom-mom"

On her next bike adventure, Cat wore the empty baby backpack when riding her bike. Although Jule was getting a little big for her to carry for long periods of time in the baby backpack, it seemed to be the best option she had for grocery shopping. When she got to the grocery store, she pulled up into the bike rack. The bike rack kept the bike balanced. She got off the bike and took off the backpack, standing it up on the ground in front of her. She removed Jule from the bike seat and immediately placed her in the backpack. She removed the child's helmet, and then her own, running the bike chain through them both.

Once the bike and helmets were locked up, Cat

squatted down onto the ground to put the baby backpack on. She stood up, shifting a little until the pack set comfortably. She double checked that she had easy access to her wallet and then continued into the store. *This is so much easier than having to put her in and take her out of the cart. I don't have to keep her from turning around or trying to climb out.*

Grocery shopping was a spectator sport for a child in a backpack. Jule was irritated that she couldn't reach anything. She wasn't uncomfortable and made her irritation clear, kicking at her mother's back as they strolled through the aisles. Cat responded by gently pushing back on her daughter's feet and singing to the child. Untroubled by the odd looks she got from other customers, she focused forward and on the task at hand. The rhythm of their movement enhanced the effect and soon the disgruntled toddler was asleep.

Cat emerged from the grocery store with three bags. *Paper in plastic. A little easier to carry. I know they looked at me funny, but I don't care.* She pulled the cart up next to the bike rack. She opened the two folding baskets on the back of her bike. *One fits perfectly in each basket!* She put the third bag in the front basket, tying the two plastic handles together. *To keep it from spilling.* Then she repeated this on the two back bags.

Cat unlocked the bike and retrieved their helmets from the chain. She put her own helmet on her head before removing the backpack. She placed it on the ground. Jule was still sound asleep, her head sagging down. She tried to put the awkward helmet on the sleepy little head and the child fussed. "I'm sorry honey. I know you hate this part, but we have to do it to be safe." She whispered at her child as she fumbled with the chin strap. She tried to not let Jule's fussiness impact her mood. *Of course, she is fussy. She was asleep and now I am messing with her. If I am loving and calm, she will just go back to sleep.*

Cat removed the sleepy Jule from the backpack and strapped her into the passenger seat. She straddled the bike and pulled it out of the rack with a hard bump. The bike leaned, heavy from the weight of the load. Taking special care to stay balanced and clear of obstacles, she made her way out of the parking lot. She decided on the less populated route. *This is almost too much weight to carry at once!* Within a block's distance, she found the right point of balance and had established a slow steady pace. *I definitely don't want to have to deal with traffic right now.*

When Cat arrived home, she found that Jule had gone back to sleep. She leaned the bike against the pole. Heavy with the weight of the groceries, it was not stable enough for her to keep it balanced while removing the sleeping Jule. With one hand holding onto the handlebars, she used her other hand to pull the groceries out of baskets. One by one, she placed them on the ground. *Now the bike isn't as heavy!*

Cat shifted the bike a bit, taking special care to ensure it was balanced enough for her to let go of the frame. Then she began to unstrap her daughter from the passenger seat. She left the bike with groceries alone as she carried the sleeping babe. Holding Jule firmly with her left arm, she rifled in her right pocket for her keys. Placing the key in the lock, she turned the knob and swung the door wide open. She left the apartment door open as she walked in with her daughter.

Cat went directly into the bedroom, placed Jule in the crib, and tried to remove the helmet without waking the child. Quietly shushing the child, she unstrapped the helmet, and pulled it off her head. She set it in the corner of the crib and began softly singing as she peeled the extra hats off her daughter's head. Tiny eyes gently fluttered as Cat brushed her cheek with the back of her fingers. Melodic words of love and comfort put the baby back to sleep.

Cat stood quietly observing her sleeping child. Breathing in the moment, she smiled to herself. *I made you. You really are amazing. The miracle of life has got to be proof there is some kind of god. Just the fact that you exist in the first place blows my mind.* Silence hung in the air with only tiny echoes of air moving through their passageways. Suddenly Cat remembered that the door was still open.

Cat was distinctly aware of being vulnerable with her back turned to the open door. She had lost bicycles before, from not locking them. She darted from the bedroom, into the living room where she could see her bike and the groceries waiting through the open door. Still uneasy, she moved quickly to attend them. She locked up the bike and then realized she was still wearing her helmet and the baby backpack. She grabbed one bag of groceries and headed back to the open door. She placed the grocery bag just inside the door in the living room. She removed her helmet and placed it next to the groceries.

Cat she sat down on the ledge and pulled her arms out of the baby backpack. *It really is just like my old frame pack. Hard to put on. Hard to take off. Easy to wear.* She leaned it against the wall of the living room before getting back up for the last two bags of groceries. She placed the two bags next to the first and returned to the stoop at the front door. *It really is lovely out here. I wonder why I get so spooked sometimes. It really doesn't make any sense.*

Chapter 23
Back To Work

After overcoming her initial fear of wrecking with her baby on the back, Cat rode her bicycle more frequently. She felt uncomfortable in her body and presumed that getting in better shape would make her feel better about herself. *It really is beautiful here in the spring. I love riding. It gives me something to do with Jule that doesn't cost money and gets me out of the house. Bonus, I could actually lose some weight!* She rode her bike all over town with Jule in the bike seat. Bravely venturing out, she attempted to interact socially without Doug's presence. She was tired of waiting for him and tired of feeling isolated.

Cat knew she wasn't entirely alone. She had Jule and they were a team. She enjoyed sharing the world with her daughter. As they cruised around the capital city, Cat talk to her daughter about their surroundings. She tried to use their outings as opportunities to teach Jule about colors, shapes, and sounds. As fulfilling as their partnership was, she wanted something more. She wanted to be able to talk to other adults. She knew she needed more social interaction.

They made their way toward Old Town and the pier. Sometimes other hippie parents would take their kids to the park by the pier. Cat had seen them before and had been too timid to approach. Now, she was determined to make friends with other parents. *I need women to talk to. I'm not trying to cheat on Doug. I just need the social support of other people who are dealing with parenting stuff! I think that's reasonable. Doug doesn't want to share his friends with me, so I will simply go find my own.*

Capital Park was the place to go to find drugs, do drugs, or just hook up with people in the transient party scene. It was not the place to go hang out with a kid. Cat had walked there with Jule a couple of times. Once the summer of Jerry's death had faded, so did the people that were left behind. Riding the bike through the park, she decided to keep moving. She rode past the rose garden and the old capital building. Continuing south, she headed toward the river.

Old Town seemed to be a different sort of scene. This seemed to be a step or two up the ladder. People that hung out here had homes. Most had some form of income. Some of them had children as well. Bike racks by the pier made it easier for her to lock up & dismount with Jule. The two roamed the business district, looking in the windows. They picnicked by the big trains. It was fun for a little while. *This would all be a lot more fun if I had money. I really need a job.*

Doug came home sometimes. Sometimes he didn't. Cat spent most of her time alone with her daughter. Doug was not working as consistently as necessary to provide the income they needed. Sometimes when he was leaving, he would imply that he was going to work. He didn't want to hear the nagging. It gave him an excuse to leave for hours. Often, there was no actual work to be had, or he simply flaked out on his boss. Work didn't really interest him. He found other things to do, visiting friends, playing music and getting high.

When Doug did return home, his girlfriend always asked for money and demanded to know where he had been and why he had been gone so long. It was a real drag to him, so he looked for reasons to keep from going home. Eventually, he had to return home, to bathe and rest and see his daughter. The novelty of his daughter did not outweigh the stress of his girlfriend. So, he often left more quickly than he intended.

Cat wanted to believe that Doug was being honest with her, and yet, deep down she knew that he was lying. She tried to get more from him when he was around because she never knew how long he would be gone. They took turns attacking each other and recoiling in defense. As the arguments got worse, Cat's emotional seizures spun out of control. She would get really upset and cry a lot. He would say she was crazy and blame their problems on her 'mental instability.'

Bills began to stack up and Doug was not forthcoming with the money they needed. It became apparent that they were getting too far behind. Cat reminded him how much money she needed to pay the utilities. She inquired about where they stood with the rent and he was impatient with her.

"We're behind, but I'll take care of it." Doug snapped. "I don't want to talk about it." He began to grow taller.

Cat failed to shrink and stood her ground. "The landlord is your boss. What the hell? I thought it was a reasonable expectation that you should be able to manage the rent!"

Doug raged back at her that he'd lost his job. "I told you I didn't want to talk about it!" Jule began to cry, pulling on Cat's legs to be picked up. "I'm sick of carrying all the weight. I shouldn't have to be the one to do everything!"

"Well." She started to respond, picking up the frightened child. *Do everything huh? I don't know what you spend your days doing but it sure feels like I am doing everything here by myself with the kid.* "I guess I will have to go back to work then. You can take a turn with spending the days with Jule, and I will see about taking care of the rent."

At first Doug gruffly agreed, emphasizing that it was 'about damn time she carried some weight.' Cat insisted that if he wanted her to get a job, that he would have to stick around to babysit. He didn't see the point in sticking around if she didn't have a job yet. "Well, what if I get called for an interview? I have to be able to say yes, and go right in. I could lose out on a good work opportunity, waiting around for you to come home."

Doug hung around while Cat went through the phone book. He played with Jule silently while his girlfriend called employment agencies and made appointments. He tried to pretend not to notice how gleeful she seemed to be about leaving him there with the child. Within a week, she had secured warehouse work. She was excited to share, "I start Monday!" The news was received with lukewarm enthusiasm.

Cat was nervous when getting ready to leave Doug at home with Jule for her first shift. It would be an hour and half each way on public transit. That added to the length of the day and she had gotten used to always being with Jule. She was excited about the prospect of having a job but knew she would miss her daughter.

By the time she returned home from work on Friday evening, Doug had quite enough and was ready to bolt out the door. Cat was exhausted from working on a tedious assembly line all day. She was hoping that she would come home to find Doug had made some kind of dinner. Instead, she found him sitting on the front stoop playing his guitar. "What took you so long?" He demanded as she approached the front walk.

Cat started to respond with the bus route and times but trailed off when she realized it was a rhetorical question. "Why do you care? All you had to do was take care of the kid and the house, I was busy working. Remember?"

Doug grumbled something incomprehensible, then stood up. "The baby is asleep. I've gotta go. I'm late to band practice." He put down his guitar to grab his jacket from off the living room floor. Then he picked up his guitar and began heading out of the courtyard.

"I have to work again next week." She reminded the back of his head. "Don't forget, you have to come back, so I can go to work."

Doug did not respond and continued out of sight. He did not return that night. He did not return on Saturday. By Sunday Cat was getting nervous. If she didn't have childcare, she couldn't go to work. She had only been there one week. True, she didn't really like the job, she did like the opportunity to make money, and being gone all day certainly made her appreciate the weekend with Jule a lot more. She called Nina to try and figure out childcare alternatives. In the end, she decided that all the alternatives were even more complicated, so if he didn't come back, she would simply call in.

Doug returned to their apartment on Monday afternoon, proclaiming that he had taken care of the back rent. He added, "Now you don't have to go back to that warehouse job."

"What if I wanted to go back to work?" Cat responded indignantly. "I'm glad you took care of the rent, but did it every occur to you that I might actually want to work?"

"I don't care." Doug responded. "If you want to get a job during the day, then you are going to have to find a babysitter. It's too inconvenient for me to deal with it. I can't get anything done when I am stuck here taking care of a baby."

Cat was insulted. *Why is it babysitting for you to take care of your own daughter anyway?* "You could just take her with you. That's what I do. We have a stroller."

"This is bullshit. You're her mother. It's your job to take care of her." Doug walked away from the argument, closing the bedroom door behind him.

Jule stared with wide eyes from her walker. Cat sat on the couch trying not to cry. Jule toddled to the couch, pulling the plastic walker along. "Mom-mom-mom"

Cat kissed her daughter on the forehead. "I love you sweetheart." She fidgeted with the plastic toys affixed to the walker tray. "Daddy loves you too. He's just a little mixed up."

Doug emerged from the bedroom in a fresh change of clothes repeating, "The rent is taken care of." He placed a twenty-dollar bill on the counter. "Here's a little for groceries." He started for the front door with his guitar in his hand.

"Where are you going now?" Cat inquired.

"You said we still have utilities to pay for, right?" He responded defensively. "So, I have to go find more money." He stepped off the stoop, then paused to look back. "You just stay right here and take care of my daughter." Then, he disappeared down the walk and out of the courtyard.

Disgruntled with his girlfriend's behavior, Doug temporarily made more of an effort to focus on work. The gradual deterioration of his ability to take work seriously was overshadowed by his growing discomfort being in a relationship. He took refuge in street corners and his guitar. It wasn't a real job, but playing guitar is all he really felt passionate about.

Six months passed in limbo. Fighting and making up, trying and giving up, their love affair was painful and exhausting. Doug's employment was inconsistent, and he continued to come home irregularly. Some of his friends were nice to Cat. She tried hard to be a good parent, and a supportive partner. *But I'm terrible at being the woman he wants. I hate myself. No wonder he hates me. Look at me.* Cat looked in the mirror and saw only ugliness.

When Thanksgiving arrived again, Cat decided this time she would take Jule and go visit her family without Doug. He didn't argue about it or question. He barely seemed to care about saying goodbye. During her visit, she spent a lot of time crying. She was miserable and didn't know what to do. Talking with Stepmother and Little Sister, they told her "you shouldn't go back if you are so unhappy." Cat was afraid of being a failure and insisted that she had to try harder. She talked with Dad while he drove them back to Sacramento.

Finally, Cat gave up entirely. "I can't be this person anymore." She announced to Jule, who was playing with toys on the living room floor. "I can't be two people. I just need to be one person. And I deserve to be a happy person." The toddler looked up from her toys to see her mother unhappy again. "Mommy?" She got up and hugged her mother's leg. A tear formed in the corner of the eye. Time froze. A storm brewed inside her. In the humid dusk alley, a lone silhouette looks up at the sky. The shadow of a young man smiles and opens an umbrella.

Pane by pane, the brilliance of her shining Jule filled Cat with a warm summer rain. She sat down on floor, wrapping her arms around the little girl. She leaned down as little legs stretched up, and little arms stretched out, to greet her mother's loving embrace. "I love you so much honey." Tears poured down her cheeks, unseen from prying eyes. "I love you too Mommy," the little girl replied. Petting her hair, the crying parent held her daughter, rocking back and forth as she sang a medley of Steve Goodman songs.

Together parent and child danced and laughed, tickled and wrestled, played and rested for a couple of hours until Jule began to get sleepy. "Hungry Mommy." Cat kissed her daughter's forehead, placing her daughter in the center of the living room floor. She gathered up the toys that had been spread all over the floor and placed them in a neat pile next to Jule. She stood up, talking to the child as she walked into the kitchen.

"Okay honey. I will make food for you. But you have to play nicely with your toys in the living room while Mommy is in the kitchen. Okay?" With no intention of waiting for a response, Cat went directly to the fridge. *Applesauce? Check.* She opened the jar and examined the contents before placing it on the counter. *Will have to get more. Or find something else she'll eat.* She looked back in the fridge. There were a few pieces of fruit. *Some carrots. Half a gallon of milk. Half a loaf of bread.* She grabbed the bread and closed the fridge. "How about special sandwiches?!"

Again, she didn't wait for a response. Cat deftly spread the peanut butter thin across four slices of bread. Placing the slices together on the counter to form two sandwiches, she cut the crust neatly off. Next, she cut the sandwiches diagonally, rotating, repeating, and finishing with a plate full of peanut butter diamonds. She arranged the diamonds in a circle, placing a small bowl of applesauce in the center of the circle. "Perfect!" She tossed the silverware into the sink and carried the plate into the living room.

Sitting on the floor eating sandwiches and applesauce for dinner, Cat showed Jule how to dip the sandwiches in the applesauce. "Do you want to go back and visit Grammy and Grampy again? It was fun, wasn't it?" The toddler smiled and clapped her hands with a mouth full of peanut butter and applesauce. After she swallowed her food, she laughed. "I'm silly Mommy." The young mother replied that the little girl was silly and sleepy. She began cleaning up the toys as her daughter finished eating. After dinner, she got her daughter ready for bed.

Cat had gotten used to sleeping with her daughter. Jule had long since outgrown her first cradle. That stopped being safe once the baby could sit up. Now it was set up in the corner of the bedroom full of stuffed animals. The larger crib served more as a containment bed for naps. *She's slept in bed with me almost every day of her life so far. It shouldn't matter whether we're in Midtown or the old ranch house. As long as we're together, everything will be fine.* She snugly tucked her daughter into blankets. "Now you are a burrito!" Her daughter giggled as Cat laid down next to the burrito baby girl. Pulling her own blanket over the both of them, she laid her head down on the pillow next to her daughter.

Lying in bed next to Jule as she fell asleep, Cat petted her daughter's hair. "Dream about every day being a happy day at Grammy & Grampy's house." The toddler fell asleep nestled against her mother's belly. The young mother lay restless, silently crying herself to sleep. The silhouette closed the umbrella. Following the distant glow of a barrel fire, he disappeared into the darkness.

Chapter 24
Uncomfortable Christmas

Just one week after returning from visiting the Bay Area, Cat called Dad, "Please can I come back home with you? I can't take it here anymore." She couldn't take the fighting. She felt so alone. He assured his daughter that her and Jule were welcome to stay as long as they needed. She was thankful he did not ask questions.

When Dad arrived, Cat was waiting in the doorway. He moved in full stride approaching the apartment. He expected to find her there waiting with everything neatly packed and ready. Instead, he found a young woman in the middle of an emotional crisis, being trailed by an equally emotional toddler. Some of their things were packed. Others were just thrown in bags, or haphazardly packed. He bypassed her emotions by focusing on the practical task at hand. "What's going and what's staying?"

Cat pointed out everything in the living room she had separated. Some of Jules stuff had been dragged into the living room. Cat had not seen Doug for at least 18 hours. *I really hope he doesn't get here before we leave. I don't want to deal with the stress. I just want to run away!* She was thankful of her father's take charge attitude. *He probably doesn't like doing this. I wonder if he's disappointed with me.* She suddenly remembered the look on her mother's face of total disapproval. "If you don't face up to whatever you are running from, you will always be running." She shuddered. *I am doing the right thing for Jule. I am doing the right thing for me.*

Father and child worked together the best they could, with the toddler underfoot. Before long, she was relieved to discover that they were reaching max *capacity*. "Anything else is not as important. It will just have to stay. Except that painting." She stopped to point out the large masterpiece she had spent nine months working on. *He brought you that canvas. You should be glad to leave it behind. But I spent so much time on that painting! Look at how good it is!* "This one I really want to come back for. This is one of my best paintings so far, and I don't want to just walk away from it."

"Well, there's not room for it. If you wanted to bring it, you should have spoken up sooner." Dad responded as he carried the car seat out the apartment door. He stopped just before reaching the doorway. Doug stepped through the threshold. Everything froze. She perceived his words, heard them, felt them, almost saw them, as his anger permeated the room.

"What the hell is going on here?" Dad was quick to respond with a 'she's leaving your ass' as he pushed his way past Doug's toxic energy. Without touching, the two men moved past each other. Doug made way for Cat's father to leave with the car seat. Cat picked up the toddler and headed for the door. "So that's it? You're just going to leave? Well, you can't take my daughter." She paused for a moment in the doorway, balancing her daughter on her hip.

"What are you going to do when you go to work? You can't take her to work with you? Do you even know what she eats these days? What are you going to do when she needs to be potty trained? What are you going to do when she gets sick? You can't stay out late partying with a kid. You can't go to band practice with a kid. Do you even know what games she likes to play?" She stopped herself and turned to leave. After stepping through the doorway, she looked into the apartment. "I'm leaving because I am not happy. I don't have to explain myself. And I don't have to stop taking care of my daughter to do it."

As Cat walked towards the truck, she heard him holler after her. "Go ahead and leave. And don't come back. I don't ever want to see you again!" Standing at the curb, she leaned into the cab to fix Jule's seat belt. She got in the truck, put on her seat belt, closed the door, and rolled down the window. She could hear a faint "Fuck you!" on the wind as they drove away. She tried not to cry as she looked down at a confused young girl.

Cat's family was very supportive. Everyone was quick to offer their personal perspective. Words of encouragement and advice flowed as abundantly as the days moved quickly. They hinted at how this was just the beginning. Dad mentioned that Cat would need to look for work.

Step-mother was quick to offer to babysit as necessary, adding, "You don't need to worry about that right now. It's the holidays. Just relax and enjoy being with family. We can tackle that together in January. Don't worry Firecat. You're not alone here. You have help now." She delighted in spending time with her grandchildren, and this would be the perfect opportunity to get plenty of Granny time in.

Christmas was getting closer every day and Doug began calling less than a week after Cat's departure from their Midtown apartment. First, he called wanting to know whether he would get to see Jule for Christmas. His tone was demanding, and Cat did not respond well. *This is why I left! He can't talk to me that way! I deserve better. He does have a right to see his kid. I wish he actually wanted to spend more time with her! She deserves to have a daddy.* She did not hang up the phone, but kept her tone cold, and responded with short answers.

Doug called back a couple days later. He repeated his request to spend time with his daughter for Christmas. This time his voice had lost its sharp edge. His smooth tone soothed her nerves, and she relaxed a bit. He asked how Jule was doing and Cat filled him in on the latest 'firsts' that he had missed. He listened and remained calm and smooth on the phone. She assured him that something could be worked out but didn't offer any specifics. Feeling uncomfortable and not sure what to say, she said that she had to get off the phone. He assured her that he would call back soon.

The next time Doug called, he continued to present a smooth calm demeanor that kept Cat relaxed. This time he wanted to know whether he would get to spend any length of time with them both. She got anxious. *He actually wants to spend time with me? Maybe he will change? Be careful. It's a trap! Shut up! Maybe now that he's had a chance to miss me, he realizes how much he really loves me? Be careful. You can't trust him!*

Cat wanted to be hopeful, and still felt apprehensive.

Doug had been on his very best behavior each time he spoke on the phone with Cat. *Still, the first time he called, he was pretty demanding. But he's been nice since then. Of course, he has! He knows how to get what he wants! No. Shut up! He loves me. It's just hard for him. You don't know what he's going through. Whose side are you on sister? Can't you hear it in his voice? He's a different person now.*

Doug asked if he could talk to Jule and Cat obliged. The young toddler didn't understand the concept of the phone receiver. She tried to put it in her mouth. "Jule honey. It's Daddy. Can you hear me?" She pulled it out of her mouth, holding it three inches from her face. She examined it as he continued. "Jule honey. Do you want to see Daddy for Christmas?" She put the receiver back in her mouth. "Firecat. What is she doing? Does she know it's me?"

Cat chuckled as she removed the phone receiver from her daughter's slimy grip. Jule began crying. Cat wiped the receiver with the bottom her blouse before returning it to her ear. "Your daughter doth protest." She told him, laughing gently into the phone. She stopped short. *I have to watch it. He will trick me. He will be nice for a little while and then things will go back to the way they were.*

"Did she even understand that I was talking to her?" Doug's voice came through the receiver like static. Jule fussed, searching for something to ease her teething discomfort. Cat searched for something nearby to subdue the fussy child. *Everything is in the other room. This is a sign. Get off the phone.*

"Hold on. The baby is fussing, and I gotta go in the other

room to get the stuff to make her stop screaming. Can I call you back?" Doug responded that he could wait. She carefully put the phone receiver down on the kitchen counter. The long curly cord hung in the air like something out of a Dr Seuss book, connecting the phone to the wall. She picked up her daughter and carried the unhappy child into the small bedroom.

After changing a diaper, changing clothes, and completely distracting her daughter, there was peace in the bedroom. *Shit. I wonder if he's still waiting on the phone. I better hurry up.* She made sure that the little one was settled with toys before sneaking off to the kitchen. She picked up the phone receiver that lay idly on the counter. "Sorry that took so long. You still there?" She held her breath for a moment. *Wait! What am I wishing for?*

The sweet sound of Doug's guitar bristled through the receiver with just enough static to reduce the effect of the gesture. *He's doing it again.* "It's okay. I was just sitting here practicing my guitar." *Of course, you were.* "How's my little girl. Is she doing okay?" Cat held the phone receiver on one shoulder while she emptied the dishwasher. She made the appropriate listening noises until he pushed her to interact more. "Are you even listening to me?"

"Yes. Yes. I am listening. You were asking about Jule. She's doing fine. She likes it here with all the family. You asked me about Christmas. We are doing something here. But I am sure that we can figure something out so that we can bring her there for a day or two." She closed the dishwasher door and took a deep breath, holding the phone to her ear with her hand. Standing up straight, she looked out the window as she spoke. "Wait. Do you still have the apartment? Where is 'there'? Who are you staying with? I want to know where she is staying before I agree to a weekend visit." *How do I know he will give her back?* She went prickly. *What if he steals her? My heart would break!*

"No." He responded. "I'm staying with my cousin again. We might go over to my mom's house for a little while on Christmas Day, but Nina's driving. So, we can leave early if we want to. She won't mind." Doug knew that Cat wasn't comfortable with staying for too long at his mom's place. She would tend to drink a little much and forget to keep her conversation age appropriate. He knew that Cat was protective of their little girl. He knew he could use that to his advantage.

"You know, Nina invited both you and Jule. You are more than welcome to come and spend Christmas with us. Then you can make sure that she is okay while she's here." Cat's heart began to race. *Maybe he really does care about me? I love him so much. I really want to believe he loves me too. Maybe we can work this out. Maybe this can be good.* "I miss you both. I'd really like to see you too."

Cat finally broke her silence. "Well. I don't know. I will have to talk to my dad about his schedule, see when he is available to give me a ride." She didn't want to get excited. More importantly, she didn't want him to know that she was getting excited. *If he's just faking it, I can beat him at his own game.* "For now though, I have to get off the phone." Holding the phone in her right hand,

Cat leaned on the counter with her left arm. Balanced on one leg, she pivoted at the waist like a mercury bird. *This conversation is making me uncomfortable, and I need to pee.* "Call me in a couple days. Give me a chance to figure it out."

"We're less than a week from Christmas." Doug reminded her. "Call me back tomorrow. You can reach me here at Nina's." Worried she would keep him from spending time with his daughter, he tried his very best to control the situation. Unfortunately, there was only so much he could do from where he was standing. *He needs them to be close in order to really make an impact.*

Cat talked to her stepmother about the situation. She explained that she didn't like the way he treated her. She didn't like that he had been gone so much. She didn't like feeling trapped. She didn't like being depressed all the time. Stepmother listened, offering a shoulder to cry on. She also reminded her that she'd be glad to babysit Jule so that Cat could go job hunting. "First I have to get through the holidays." Stepmother agreed and didn't push her. As an afterthought, Cat added, "Thank you though. After the holidays, I will take you up on that offer."

The next day Cat called Doug back in the morning. She was still apprehensive about going, as well as not going. *If I spend the night with Doug, things may go well, or they may be terrible. If I don't go along, I can't be there to make sure he doesn't kidnap her or leave her with a dangerously drunk family member. I need to be there to protect Jule from the violence that always emerges at his family gatherings.* She didn't want him to have power over her, and yet, she really didn't want to be without him.

Doug was persistent and after a half hour of chatting on the phone Cat had caved in and agreed to the details of a visit. Spending time together would make things more confusing. *Why does this have to be so hard? Why can't I just hate him? It would be so much easier. But I do love him. And just maybe he still loves me.* She became more anxious with each day as the weekend approached.

Cat's thoughts wandered between excitement and concern as her stepmother drove her and Jule to Sacramento. Doug showed genuine care when they arrived. Stepmother said very little. She reminded Cat to call if she needed anything and was on her way. Doug offered to carry the car seat protecting the sleeping Jule. Cat walked behind him carrying her backpack, purse, and diaper bag. He paused when he arrived at the front door. He waited until she was almost upon him and opened the door, holding it for her. She thanked him as she passed. He followed her, closing the front door gently behind them. She paused in the entryway, unsure how to proceed. Walking around her, he motioned for her to follow him.

Once they got in the bedroom, he said in a hushed voice, "The baby is asleep, and my cousin has had a really tough time getting him to sleep. So, we have to be quiet." He gently set the car seat on the bed. Reaching in to unbuckle Jule, he moved carefully, trying not to wake her. Cat placed her bags on the floor at the foot of the bed. She started to move towards Doug, as if to take the sleeping child. Smiling, he quietly protested. Cautiously, he attempted to lay down on the bed with his daughter, without waking her.

Jule began to fuss a little. Cat sat down on the bed next to them with the diaper bag. Doug talked to his daughter in a hushed voice. He grabbed her hand and placed in on his nose, while he tried to keep her from making noise. Cat moved swiftly to change her diaper and prepare a bottle. By the time Jule had tired of the daddy antics, there was a bottle ready. She happily accepted the bottle and was immediately quiet. Doug continued to lie next to her, helping hold the bottle.

Cat put away the diaper bag. *Crisis averted.* She took off her shoes and extra layers. She laid down on the edge of the bed with Jule as a barrier between the two estranged lovers. They lay on the top of the blankets for a while. Cat began to doze off. A half empty bottle rolled down Jule's limp hand hitting Cat in the chin. The odor from the contents of the bottle made her nose twitch. She opened her eyes, picked up the bottle, and twisted around to place it on the side table. Readjusting her position on the pillow, she shivered. *It's cold in here.*

Doug laid watching the two guests. A baby doll of a girl, his little princess looked so innocent and fragile when she was sleeping. The woman, mother, lover lying opposite him looked so worn out. When she shivered, he spoke quietly. "You know, you could get under the blankets if you want. It would be warmer that way." He gently lifted the sleeping Jule while he pulled the comforter back. Cat got off the bed to pull her side of the comforter back. Both parents climbed under the blanket silently. Jule remained between them through the night.

In the morning, he got up leaving the guests sleeping. Next Jule woke up, which automatically meant that Cat was promptly awakened. She laid in bed trying to snuggle Jule back to sleep, while the girl climbed all over her mother. "I just want to sleep a little longer." The girl giggled and squirmed away from the mothers loving arms, only to jump on her back. "Oh God Please! I just want another half an hour." As if in response, Doug entered the room with a cup of coffee for her.

Doug scooped up the squirming toddler. "Come on kiddo. Why don't we let mommy sleep? You want some breakfast?" Without waiting for a response, he left the room with her. Cat was astonished. *I am not even going to question this. I am just going to enjoy it.* She rolled over and went back to sleep. When she woke again, her coffee was cold. She sat up and took a sip. *Delicious. He knows exactly how I like my coffee.* She drank about half the cup before leaving the bedroom.

Cat felt awkward being there. She wanted to just go back to bed but knew that wasn't an option. Nina stood in the kitchen preparing something. The two babies played in a brightly colored playpen located in between the kitchen and the living room. Doug and Nina's husband sat in the living room, playing video games. *Everything is fine. Everything is normal here. What was I expecting?* Nina was the first to notice Cat had emerged. "Well good afternoon sleepy head!"

The visit went well. Doug showed his most gentlemanly behavior toward Cat while they were there. He even gave her a soft angora sweater as a Christmas gift. *I don't recall him ever getting me a nice gift before! Is it because I left? Is this just a trick?* The emotional roller coaster had not yet ended. They only stayed a couple of days. When Dad arrived to pick up his daughter and granddaughter, Doug kept his head down and said very little. After bags, gifts, and child had been loaded up into the car, Doug made a point to kiss Cat goodbye.

Driving back, Dad asked only basic questions. How did it go? Did Jule have a good time? He made listening noises as Cat responded with basic answers. It went fine. He was fine. She was fine. Then silence. Then he turned on the radio. Jule was always quick to fall asleep once on the road. Cat leaned her head against the window, tucked her hands into her lap, and closed her eyes.

Chapter 25
Winter Visitation

After their Christmas visit, Doug continued to call Cat at her father's house. By the new year, he was making plans to come visit them in Walnut Creek. When Cat was apprehensive, he insisted that he should be allowed to visit with his daughter. *I can't argue with that. He has a right to see his kid. I want him to want to see his kid. I want him to want to see me. Shut up. Don't go there.* Cat could not disagree. It was a reasonable request. Doug provided the details of when he would arrive, and she assured him that Jule would be 'delighted to see her daddy.'

The following Saturday, Nina gave him a ride, dropping him off in the morning. He gave her a hug before she got back into her little Rodeo. She started the engine and rolled down the windows. "I'll be back tomorrow at 7. Be ready to go because the traffic will be terrible." He waved goodbye as she pulled out of the driveway.

As the Rodeo disappeared Doug knew his way out was moving farther away. Past the olive trees, past the orange trees, past the bus stop, past the neighborhood of almost matching ranch houses, past the shopping centers, lay the highway, the path to freedom. Of all the places to spend the weekend, he had chosen to spend the weekend sitting in the jaws of the lion. Cat's father was very protective of his daughter. This was his house, his territory, and he was pissed off at Doug. Doug made a conscious decision that the best way to maintain his safety and wellbeing was to be as nice as possible.

Cat brought an energetic Jule into the front yard. "Daddy!" She ran up to Doug. He knelt down to hug the girl. Tiny arms wrapped around his neck as he picked her up. Doug took a deep breath. Jule rambled details of her day so far. "Mommy made oatmeal for breakfast. It had apples..." Doug took another deep breath and made a point to smile and nod.

Full of energy, little arms let go, and big arms bent down to place the bright Jule back on the ground. Long legs bent down to her eye level as Doug sat down on the ground in the front yard. The animated girl remained standing, smiling broadly as she talked to her father. "Do you like my outfit Daddy? It has cherries." She danced around for a moment and then sat down on his lap. She began pointing at the little cherries and counting, "...Three. Four. Five. I have lots of cherries! Daddy do you like cherries?"

Doug took another deep breath. He forced a smile and nodded. "Yes honey. I like cherries. But they're not in season right now." Doug looked down at the little human sitting on his lap. He was proud to have made such a smart little person. It felt overwhelming to have the child demanding so much personal space and attention. Still, it was less threatening than what lie before him upon entering the house. He'd been in the house before. He was a welcomed guest when they celebrated Jule's first birthday. They treated him like family, but now they saw him as the enemy. It was too much pressure. Doug found it much more convenient to hang out in the front yard as long as possible. "...And I colored with crayons. You can color with crayons too. Daddy. Do you want to make a picture?"

Cat knew that Doug would be apprehensive. He always felt uncomfortable around her family. Now that they had seen the emotional toll it had taken on her, they too were apprehensive. She talked with Stepmother and Dad, each separately, at great length prior to the first visit. All adults agreed that a parent should have a right to visit with their child. It was also agreed that if there was any chance there might be any questionable behavior, it was best that the visit was monitored.

The most practical option was to have Doug visit Jule at their house. The grandparents were focused on safety and security, while the mother was most concerned about a potential for kidnapping. "I know he would never ever hurt her. I'm just afraid he might steal her." Cat was nervous, but she also knew that Jule wanted to see her Daddy. She tried hard not to talk down about Doug around their daughter because she didn't want to include her experience as a partner in Jule's perspective of her Daddy. Talking with her parents helped to ease some of her discomfort. When she had called him, to tell him it was okay, he'd already had a ride set up for the visit and promptly agreed to the terms.

Now that Doug was here in the yard, Cat was afraid to go back in the house. *He can't steal her. Where's he gonna to take her? His ride left 45 minutes ago.* She sat in a folding chair on the front porch. A large paperback self-help book lay across her lap. *He doesn't have a car.* She rubbed her legs, trying to keep them from falling asleep. *He doesn't even have a driver's license. He's not going to leave.* Her stomach grumbled. *If you're hungry then that means you are going to need to feed her soon. Go make sandwiches. Now. While she is occupied and not throwing a fit.*

Cat left the young girl and the visitor sitting in the front yard. She entered the house on a mission, with the intention of getting back outside as quickly as possible. The house felt empty. *Dad isn't home, Stepmother and Little Sister are probably lying in bed watching a movie. It always feels empty when people are hidden away in the bedrooms.* She went straight to the kitchen, effortlessly throwing together four peanut butter and jelly sandwiches, halving them, and arranging them on a tray. Next, she took two oranges out of the fridge, cutting them each into six wedges. Next, she cut each wedge in half to make a little pyramid. She arranged the orange triangles on the tray around the centerpiece of sandwiches. Pleased with herself. She started to take the tray outside. *No. We can eat in here. Its cold out there.*

Cat opened the front door, and stood balancing in the threshold, unsure whether to proceed or retreat. She decided on neither. "It's cold out there. Y'all need to come inside and eat. Are you hungry Julie?" Jule was headed for the door before Cat could finish her sentence. "Doug? Peanut butter sandwiches? I know it's your favorite. How can you resist?" He started to grimace as he was getting up off the ground. He forced a smile as he brushed off his jeans before walking casually toward the front door.

Doug was sweet to Cat all weekend. He complimented

her abilities with Jule. *He thinks I'm a good mom.* When she questioned his ulterior motives, Doug told her that he 'had missed her and Jule both.' She soaked it up, desperately needing to feel loved and validated. She was also guarded, fearing that he was only 'on his best behavior' because they were at her dad's house.

At night, they lay just as they had at Nina's for Christmas. Jule lay sleeping in between the two uncomfortable adults. Cat pretended to sleep while Doug whispered to her. He mentioned that it was a lot harder for him to 'take care of her' when she was 'so far away' and promised to do his best to 'help' when he could. The sweet talk confused the young woman. She needed to feel like she mattered to him. She whispered something almost inaudible about marriage and he silently recoiled.

Doug continued to visit. His intermittent visits got progressively longer each time he arrived. He never brought much money, or groceries to contribute, but he continued to exhibit his very best behavior. He followed Cat's directions and suggestions regarding the daily care of their daughter. Without band practice across town, or local buddies to go hang out with, his sole focus was caring for his daughter and getting along with her mother. The added attention and thoughtful disposition gave Cat hope that their relationship might be salvageable.

Doug ensured Cat did not have time to forget him. The gap between her departure and their Christmas visit had been relatively short. He had begun visiting them in Walnut Creek soon thereafter. The breaks between visits only proved to be more sporadic and unpredictable than his attendance in their apartment had been. Despite her new environment, his inconsistency continued to overshadow her behavior patterns. Her sleeping patterns, eating patterns, outing patterns, and most importantly, her emotional well-being were being dragged along a roller coaster and her family could see it. They were concerned that it affected her so deeply, it changed the way she participated in the daily rituals of caring for herself and Jule.

In Doug's absence, Cat had begun trying to develop a consistent structure of activities for her daughter. Since she always had Jule by her side, the only way to get things done was to find a way to include her child. Accomplishing self-care and housekeeping tasks like getting dressed and bathing, making food and eating, and completing household chores had to be made into a game. If it wasn't fun, then Jule wasn't interested. She tried to adapt these daily rituals to their new environment when she left Sacramento.

When Doug came to visit, Cat was slow to move through the daily rituals, taking extra time to try and drag him through the routine. She assigned some tasks to him, critiqued his performance, and sometimes she even took over midstream. She sensed his frustration and did not understand it. *I'm trying to show him. This is how it needs to be done. Why won't he just follow directions?* He sensed her frustration and resented her for it.

While Doug was visiting, Cat refrained from talking with him about child support or whether he had gotten another job. *He doesn't really seem like he wants to be here. I don't want to scare him away.* Still, by the end of each visit, she was almost glad to see him go. *Finally, our life can go back to normal! I shouldn't have to discuss with someone for an hour and a half whether we should go to the park that's just four blocks away. I should just be able to get the baby ready, put her in the stroller, and go for a walk! Why do we have to argue about what to eat? Just make what the baby will eat and go from there! I shouldn't have to defend my decision to not give the kid candy. She isn't even two yet. Not giving her candy should be a no-brainer. He contradicts me in front of her, and then she won't listen to me! Parenting is so much less stressful when I can make all the decisions myself! I don't want to have to consult someone else, just to make breakfast!*

After visiting, Doug continued to call every few days. He always asked to talk on the phone with Jule. The little girl began to understand that it was her Daddy on the phone. He pumped her up for the next visit by suggesting all the things they could do together. Her attention span was short, but not too short to believe his promises of exciting outings and special treats. When Cat got back on the phone, she would gently scold him. "Don't get her hopes up! She'll be so disappointed when it doesn't happen." He'd dismiss the remarks, suggesting that she was 'too young to remember' and assuring Cat that 'everything would be okay.'

It only took a couple of days of Doug being gone, and Cat had already begun to miss him. She missed the smell of his body when they were sleeping. She missed the way he called her 'Babe.' Most of all, she missed feeling like she didn't have to do everything alone. *It's too much. I can't even take a shower without her. I can never be myself. I'm always just Mommy. I want to be me too.* She remembered how he sweet talked her, opened doors for her, and complimented her on how good she was at caring for their child. She misinterpreted this as adoration. *Maybe he really does love me? Maybe we can have a life together? Am I stupid for getting my hopes up?*

When Doug returned to Sacramento, Cat got depressed. She slept more, laid in bed longer, and cried a lot more. Jule tried to get her mom out of bed. Often, she failed and ended up playing on the floor next to her sleeping mother. Once Cat got up and around, they moved through some tasks with more efficiency. Without having to wait for Doug, she went for more walks with Jule. They went to the park more frequently.

Mealtime was harder when Doug was absent. Jule would refuse to eat. The inconsistency in their daily habits put her on edge. She would get more anxious, eat less, and demand repetitive activities. Trying to make up for other inconsistencies, Jule clung to patterns she could count on. Frustrated, Cat fought with her daughter trying to get her to simply eat small amounts of food that she's previously 'loved.'

In mid-February Doug called to announce he'd rearranged his schedule to accommodate a whole week of visiting. Before his arrival, Dad sat his daughter down to discuss the matter. "He seems to be conducting himself appropriately." She nodded, listening. "And I know he's Jule's father, and that he's important to you." *This all sounds good. But if everything was good, you wouldn't be sitting me down for a talk. What's the catch?* She nodded again, to show him she was listening. Dad paused. He really didn't like Doug, but he also knew that she got incredibly depressed when Doug left, and he couldn't bear to keep watching it. The young man would either need to get it together or stop pulling her chain.

"Doug has a right to see his daughter." He paused, trying to think of the right way to get the point across. "But if he is going to be here so much, he really needs to be contributing." Cat held her breath. "So, either he needs to start bringing money with him, or he should just stay here and get a job." *Does this mean he can stay? Are you really going to let him stay?* She nodded again, expecting him to continue. Dad looked at her expectantly, waiting for a response. The silence grew and she carefully responded.

"So. I can suggest that he simply stay?" Cat took a deep breath before continuing. "But he has to get a job." Dad confirmed that was what he meant. She agreed that it was a reasonable request. "I will talk to him about it." She refrained from sharing all her hopes and fears. Sounds of Jule awakening from a nap saved her from having to continue further. Dad seemed relieved, unsure he had much more to say without sharing his opinion about the man.

By the time Doug arrived for the week, the couple had once again become cozy. Cat regarded him lovingly, and he enjoyed the physical attention. Jule had become more temperamental though. The young child needed consistent daily patterns. Her tantrums challenged Doug's patience. He went to visit expecting it to be like a holiday every day. Cat seemed determined to make sure that he knew it was no holiday, by assigning him mundane tasks. He reminded himself that this is what was necessary for him to spend time with his daughter. He dragged his feet through the days and tried to cram as much sex into the evenings as possible before returning to Sacramento.

Laying in Doug's arms, Cat talked with him every night after Jule went to sleep. By the end of the week Doug appeared to agree to the terms that Cat had presented. He spent the week playing house with Cat and Jule, following orders and grinning through each day. When the end of the week arrived, he tried to hide his feeling of urgency. She woke up early and his things were already packed neatly away and ready to go. He was sitting up quietly tuning his guitar.

"Good morning sweetheart." He sweetly asked, "Will you make coffee and breakfast for us?" He put the guitar down gently against the wall behind him. "I will keep an eye on Jule and take care of her when she wakes up." He smiled down at his daughter before glancing back to her mother. Cat sleepily obliged, throwing on her robe before leaving the bedroom.

Cat started coffee and began surveying the options for breakfast. By the time she had prepared two cups of coffee to take back to the bedroom, Doug was entering the dining room with their daughter on his hip. He put the little girl in the highchair setting at the end of the dining room table. "What have you got for the princess today?" He asked, smiling at Jule as he received one of the coffee cups.

"Well, would the princess like eggs and toast?" Cat responded, before taking a sip of her coffee.

Jule looked up at Doug waiting for a response. He smiled at her. "You want eggs, don't you?"

Then Jule responded without looking at her mother. She slammed her fists down on the table and responded enthusiastically, "Yes Mommy Eggs!"

While Cat stood in the kitchen making breakfast, Doug stood in the doorway sipping his coffee. Sensing her anxiety, he reminded Cat that he already had his ride back set up to coincide with band practice. He stressed that he wanted to come back soon, urging her to be patient with him.

After their breakfast, Doug played guitar for his daughter while she nursed a bottle. Eyelids fluttering, she fell asleep with her daddy in view. It bothered Cat to know that when she woke up, he would have once again disappeared. By ten o'clock Jule had fallen back asleep. Cat opened the window while Doug tucked the sleeping child into the blankets laying on the floor. He picked up his guitar and knapsack and quietly left the room. Cat turned off the light before gently closing the bedroom door.

When his cousin Nina arrived, Cat was apprehensive and unable to hold back her fears. Tears welled up as she tried her best to keep a smile for Nina. After putting his guitar and knapsack into the trunk of the Rodeo, Doug approached Cat, standing at the edge of the driveway. "I do have a life in Sacramento. I can't just walk away from it overnight." Doug pleaded with Cat gently.

"Please understand, I am just going back to tie up loose ends and gather my stuff." He kissed her once gently on the forehead. "And then I will come back to you and Jule." Then he kissed her deeply to seal his word.

Doug sat in the back of Nina's car, watching her toddler sleep in his car seat. Drool stained a bib adorned with baby zoo animals. His little fingers twitched. Nina faced forward and refrained from asking her cousin any questions. She had learned to value the quiet since having a child. Doug closed his eyes and leaned against the closed window. *What have I signed myself up for? How am I going to make this work? She's talking about marriage.* He shuddered silently and zipped up his hoodie. *I just want to get back to Sacramento.*

Before Cat left, Doug had been apprehensive about going home. When he did come home, he was hit hard with her emotional storm. She was unpredictable and he never knew what he would be walking into when he arrived. The more frequently he came home to her manic or depressive moods, the less he wanted to go home. Still, she had been easier to please, easier to manage. Now, against the backdrop of a supportive and loving environment, with a seemingly endless supply of resources, Doug's shortcomings would be obvious in contrast. He intentionally conducted himself humbly, trying to fade into the background.

Doug had managed to maintain just as consistent a foothold with Cat and Jule from a distance as he had when they shared an apartment. He almost liked the long-distance relationship better because then she was nicer to him. He wasn't expected to 'be home' every night, but rather was free to roam and do as he please. He could plan his time with his daughter. Each visit had an ending date that he could look forward to. Savoring the potential freedom to come at the end of the visit made it easier for him to grin and bear the unpleasantries. Now, his freedom was once again being threatened and he didn't like not feeling in control of the situation.

Cat watched as the Rodeo backed out of the long gravel driveway. She waved as the little SUV disappeared over the eastern hill. Something deep inside her knew that Doug didn't want to come back. "But he will." She told the empty driveway. Tears flowed freely now, with no one to bear witness. *Jule is asleep. The window is open. You can hear her if she wakes up. You don't have to rush back in. But that means she can hear me too.* She sniffled and wiped her face with her dress hem. She whispered, afraid of waking her child. "He will come back. I know he will."

Chapter 26
One More Try

Before she left Midtown, Cat's emotional patterns had been dramatically affected by Doug's inconsistent and unpredictable attendance in her daily life. During his recent visits in Walnut Creek, he had been quiet, affectionate and outwardly sympathetic. Now he was headed back to Sacramento again. Cat sat on the front sidewalk with her back against the brick retaining wall, reflecting on the previous week. *Really, he was pretty wonderful this week.*

Cat remained on the front porch for a while, taking in the cool sunshine. Peering out onto the driveway, she examined the small clumps of green poking its way through the gravel. Tiny yellow flowers sat nestled in small beds of bright green. From a distance they looked like soft like moss. Her legs began to tingle, and she tried to get up. Shaky and unstable, she leaned against the brick. *I just have to walk it off.* She stomped her feet a couple of times sending shock waves into her feet.

Once she felt more stable, Cat stepped off the sidewalk onto the little brick path that led to the long gravel driveway. She walked slowly up the driveway, paying careful attention to the tiny bits of foliage thriving in the gravel. She attempted to kneel down for a closer look, but the sharp gravel dug into her knee and she recoiled. She stumbled backward but managed to keep herself from falling down. After regaining her balance, she squatted down in a second attempt to observe the tiny details of the stems and leaves.

Still unable to see the details as clearly as she would like, Cat pulled one of the little bundles up from its root. The nerves in her fingers itched. What appeared to be soft from a distance felt prickly when touched gently. If she pushed too hard it condensed itself, much like she would expect from moss. She stood up with the little bundle of green and yellow. Bringing it closer to her face, she saw fine details of white as well. The bright sun refracted in her eyes and she retreated to the house for a clearer view.

In the dining room, Cat was able to hold the flowers at the right distance from her face to be able to see them. *Still blurry. I am going to need to get glasses again. Someday. I want to be able to see the detail.* She heard the unmistakable sound of a confused toddler coming from the little bedroom. Walking down the hall, she began talking to Jule. *If she can hear my voice, it will help. She will know she is not alone.*

"Jule honey, it's okay. Mommy's coming." Cat opened the bedroom door, shedding light from the hallway on her daughter. "Cover your eyes honey. I'm going to turn on the light." She banished the darkness with a flip of the switch. "I love you Julie! I brought you flowers!"

As soon as they had arrived from Sacramento, Cat had organized their stuff in the little bedroom in baskets, bins, and cardboard boxes. In the middle of the room, she set up her bed with a pallet of blankets. On the east wall, she placed Jule's crib, with the toys and baby clothes organized in laundry baskets underneath the crib. The grandparents had even given them an old television to set up in the bedroom. It wasn't hooked up to cable, but PBS came in clearly. As far as Cat was concerned, television was bad for kids, but she made an exception for Sesame Street.

Cat sat glanced around the room. Jule had not been asleep in the crib but had been left on the floor bed. *It's okay. Everything in this room is child safe now.* She sat down on the floor next to the blinking toddler. Jule climbed on her mother's lap as her eyes adjusted to the light. Her wet clothes stunk, and Cat grimaced. "Oh honey, you are all wet. Instead of climbing on me, why don't we just take care of that problem right away?" She placed the little flower on the floor next to them before steadying Jule in front of her. The toddler protested as her mother stripped her down to her diaper. Once she was naked, her mother laid her down on the blanket.

"Here. I brought you flowers!" Cat said, as she handed Jule the little bundle. "Careful, don't put it in your mouth!" She warned as she prepared a fresh diaper. "You can smell it and you can look at it. It's pretty. Do you see?"

"Pretty flower?" Jule asked, with hesitation.

"Yes honey. It's a pretty flower. Do you like it?" Cat responded. "Okay. You have a clean diaper now. What do you want to wear now?" She added the wet clothes and diaper to a basket. *Full again. Time to do more laundry. This is so much easier with a washer and dryer in the house!*

Jule got up, dropping the flower on the blanket. "I know Mommy. I get dressed."

Cat had included her daughter in the organization process to help her feel more settled in their new home.

Jule was smart and learned quickly. She knew where to go to find exactly what she wanted. This time, she wanted the dress up clothes. She crawled under the crib, pushing out a flowery suitcase. "Mommy help." She puffed, as she emerged.

Cat helped her daughter open the suitcase. She relaxed a little as she watched Jule climb into the suitcase. Sitting in the nest of brightly colored fabric, she picked through her dress up clothes. She commented on different items as they pulled things on and off again. Once she finally decided on a 'princess dress' Jule climbed out of the suitcase, leaving the messy nest quickly forgotten. "Rella Mommy. Rella now, kay?" She pulled at her mother's hand, trying to coax her up and out of the bedroom.

Cat was not fond of the idea of letting Jule watch television, but the grandparents already gotten Jule hooked on Disney movies. *At least they are family friendly. And movies have no commercials, so I don't have to worry about her getting programmed to demand cheaply manufactured toys from me.* She remembered how much Saturday morning cartoons had been jam packed with toy and junk food commercials when she was a kid. *And that is why I don't want my kid watching television. Hell, I am not even that interested. I can't stand the commercialism.* Letting Jule watch Disney movies kept the toddler occupied for longer periods of time. It gave her a nice break, but she felt bad about putting her kid in front of a digital babysitter.

Jule insisted on watching Cinderella over and over again. She memorized every song, while Cat memorized the dialogue. Jule clung to this habit when Doug was gone, savoring the predictable patterns. She knew when the mice would show up. She knew when good things would happen, when bad things would happen, and that everything would end up okay in the end. Cat didn't understand why on earth the little girl would want to watch the same thing over and over again. She tried suggesting alternatives. Jule only accepted the suggestions when Doug was present.

When Doug returned to Sacramento, he waited a few days to call again. On the phone, the turbulent couple told each other how much they missed one another. They shared details about their respective days. His stories centered around personal accomplishments, or family gossip. Her stories focused on challenges she was having with Jule, or new things the baby had learned. "Everything is better when you're around to help." Cat told Doug.

Doug responded that he wanted to take care of them both. "But I still have a lot I need to work out here before I can just leave." He was determined not to give up on playing music just because he had a kid to take care of. "The band is trying to figure out a schedule that I can keep up with. It's not going to be easy to commute 100 miles each way without a car or a driver's license."

Cat sat silent on the line. *Is he just making excuses? Does he really want to come and be with us?* When she had brought up her father's suggestion, she had tried to convey the importance of being present. She had explained that her father just wanted to make sure he wasn't a freeloader. He wanted to make sure that Doug was pulling his own weight. Beyond that, Dad really was trying hard not to intervene. He understood and respected that Doug should be able to be present in his child's life. She had not put any emphasis on Doug's obligation to Cat. She didn't want to push it too far, for fear of scaring him away entirely.

Doug was hesitant to agree at first. "Are you sure? Your dad doesn't like me." He didn't want to live with Cat's family. He did want to see his daughter more. Certainly, the sex was worth coming back for. But to live there? That was pushing his comfort zone a bit too far. Cat insisted that her family liked him just fine, but that they were 'just concerned' for her well-being.

Now, it sounded to Cat like Doug was trying to back out. She suggested that he could continue just visiting and look for a job while he was in the area. Then, once he actually had a job, he could stay. Perhaps that would make the transition easier?

Doug reminded Cat that if he was there all week, he would have to disappear on the weekends. "I can't just bail on my band. They will re-arrange band practice for me, but I still have to show up for practice and gigs."

Cat's attempt to 'ease the transition' proved to be an effort in vain. On Doug's very next visit to the Bay Area, he landed a job. It was about 10 miles away, which would have been okay, had he not been given closing shifts. At 10:30 pm there were no buses running. At first, Dad let Cat borrow Big Red to go pick him up. Within a week or two of him having the job, he stopped contacting her for rides home. Indicating he had made friends with a co-worker who could give him a ride home from work. He began coming home later and later. Doug and Cat began to argue more frequently.

Within a month of Doug coming to stay with them, the couple began arguing again. By the end of the first month, he began intermittently not coming home until the following day. His words would become twisted, she would raise her voice, and then he would leave. Cat cried a lot, while absently listing to her little Jule all the reasons she was such an intolerant girlfriend. Upon Doug's return, he would tell her how important their relationship was to him and Cat would apologize for losing her temper and blowing things out of proportion. She would start to talk about marriage, and how she wanted a guarantee that he wasn't just going to leave again. He would get uncomfortable with the conversation, and redirect it towards something more immediate, like dinner, or chores.

In the few months that had passed since Cat had called her Dad to save her from the clutches of her miserable life in Sacramento, she had gotten comfortably resettled into the house she had grown up in. She had arranged the little bedroom to accommodate Jule and herself, but the room was not comfortable for the three of them. It was too small and contributed to Doug's feeling of being trapped. His situational discomfort did not motivate him to succeed, but rather the opposite.

It didn't take long for him to get fired, or perhaps he quit. Ultimately, it only took six weeks' time, before he was no longer employed. Again, he was vague with his explanation, diverting the conversation when Cat asked for details. She wasn't sure what to believe. She tried to rationalize. *I can't be a hypocrite. My mood swings are as manic as his. I don't know what he's going through. I certainly couldn't keep up with the schedule he keeps.* She tried to be understanding.

Doug returned to Sacramento after he lost the job. He insisted that he was only going for a couple of days, to catch up with the band. He did not call her while he was gone but arrived back a few days later. He began disappearing for a few days at a time, without explanation or contact, as he had done before she left. He always arrived with tales about the mishaps and follies that he had run into. He got her hopes up with plans for money making schemes before disappearing again. When he returned empty handed, there was another story to explain why it wasn't his fault that he had failed.

Cat was becoming disenchanted with his stories. She tried to be compassionate, but Doug made it more and more difficult. *I may be crazy, but at least I am here making sure Jule eats every day.* Her depression tried to blame her for their relationship problems. *You know he wouldn't keep leaving if you weren't so crazy. Shut up! I may be crazy, but he is too.* She thought about their different kinds of crazy. *I am functional. I get things done. I want to do better. I am trying.*

Cat remembered sitting behind a dumpster in Berkeley. The memory of sitting on the cardboard, rocking, crying, and hallucinating was so vivid. She felt like she was there in the moment, and tears poured down her face. The memory seemed so real, and yet she was distinctly aware that it was only a memory. *Just a few years ago, I was doing so much worse. I really have made progress.* She looked across the living room at her little girl. Jule was dancing and singing along with the mice on the screen.

"I'm going to keep getting better. Things are only going to improve." Cat announced to the universe. She got up to dance with her daughter. The two laughed and sang. When the song was over, Cat picked up Jule, carrying her to the couch. "Here. Come sit with Mommy so we can watch the movie together." The little girl agreed, snuggling up with her mother. Both mother and daughter fell asleep on the couch watching Cinderella, as they had done so many times before. They awoke to the sound of other people moving through the living room. Cat's bladder reinforced the importance of waking up.

Lying alone in bed that night, Cat rehashed the pros and cons of her relationship with Doug. She wanted to love him. She wanted to believe that they were on the same page. She wanted to believe in herself and feel better more often. Analyzing her progress helped her to reinforce her self-worth. It also brought to her attention the apparent lack of progress that Doug had shown. She was alarmed to notice a disturbing difference between them. While hers alternated between a nervous happy and hopelessly depressed, Doug's moods seemed to be developing very different personalities. Cat realized that she was frightened by his different versions of self. *I want him to love me. So why am I scared of him? Sometimes he is kind and thoughtful. We have so much in common, we can practically read each other's minds. But then he turns into a scary person. What is happening?*

Doug returned to the house that Cat grew up in, with his usual stories of failure and folly. This time, Cat was more skeptical. He seemed to anticipate this challenge and came prepared. This time, he brought gifts, and enough food stamps to buy Jule snacks for a whole week. Cat showed appreciation for his thoughtfulness. After the child had gone to bed for the night, the couple sat on the front porch talking. "But if you really love me, then why won't you marry me?" Cat pleaded with tears in her eyes. "You keep leaving. And you are missing so much. Jule is growing and learning new things every day and you miss it because you're not here!"

Doug was steadfast. He was not going to agree to marriage. He could barely stand being around this woman for more than a week without needing a break. The idea of committing himself to a lifetime of misery with her was more than he could stand. He held his tongue, instead offering affection. "Of course, I love you." He consoled, petting Cat's hair, and kissing her forehead. "I just don't believe in the institution of marriage. Why do we need a piece of paper to prove it?" He picked her up and carried her to the front door. When they reached the door, he kissed her as he stood her on her feet.

Doug opened the door, motioning for Cat to enter. Silently, he closed the door behind her and took her hand. Leading her through the living room, and down the hall, he motioned for her to go to bed. "We both have had a long day." He pointed to the bathroom. I'm just going to the bathroom. I promise I'll be there shortly." He entered the bathroom and closed the door. She went into the bedroom and laid down to wait for him.

Jule lay sleeping in her crib. The couple laid together on the pallet of blankets on the floor. In the darkness Cat felt passion stirring in the man beside her. *I should roll over and kiss him now. He wants me. Why am I scared? Something is wrong.* She kept her eyes shut tight, pretending to be asleep. Hands moved along her body, and she felt the movement of his hands and genitals against her. She made no sounds or motion to participate. *I feel like my body is being used by a stranger. Something is terribly wrong with this.* Eventually, he found satisfaction and rolled over to go to sleep. Silently tears rolled down her face as she too fell asleep.

Fed up with his inability to keep a job and disenchanted by the strange metamorphosis that Doug had been experiencing, Cat finally stood her ground. "You can't just get a job when you feel like it and leave the job when you feel like it. You told me that you wanted to have this child, but you act like a child. I can't afford to take care of two children." She told him he had to leave. "You said you wanted this. But you act like it's a choice that you can choose or not choose at any given time. But you can't. I can't. And I won't. This time, you have to leave. This time, it has to be for good."

Cat assured Doug that she would never keep their daughter from him, but that the relationship between them was really over. She could not deal with the emotional roller coaster of their relationship. Their argument was loud but not long. Doug stormed out of the bedroom spewing profanities as he left the house.

SHADOWS OF FIRE
Part Two

Chapter 27
Shadows

Cat cried a lot after Doug left her father's house, but she made a conscious effort not to own his failures. She continued to cry daily for months. She wanted to feel better. She wanted to *be* better. She was glad to be in the safety of Dad's home. She was glad that she had her sister and her stepmother to help her. Still, the emotions of failure haunted her. Cat questioned her self-worth. A younger self played back in her head like a broken record. *Nobody wants to be with me because I'm crazy. There must be something wrong with me or I wouldn't be alone.*

Cat's family stood by her side. They assured her that she was smart and beautiful. They assured her that she would grow past this point, and so would Jule. Best of all, they joyfully took Jule out to the park, shopping, and the movies with some regularity. This gave Cat breaks from parenting and with them came new opportunities for self-care.

Depression was exhausting. Despite her lack of energy or motivation, with a great deal of support and encouragement from her family, she began taking steps to improve her life. She was really tired of feeling terrible all the time. She needed to feel like she was in control of her feelings, her well-being, and most of all her future.

As promised, Stepmother and Little Sister volunteered to babysit while Cat was looking for work and taking care of herself. To aid in the process, Dad started letting her use

Big Red. She was hesitant at first, terrified that she might get into an accident and lose what little approval she had from her father.

Dad sensed her hesitancy. "You can use it anytime you want. You have to pay for the gas and the maintenance." He explained, "I put you on the insurance. This way, when you do get a car of your own, you will have already been insured for a while." He explained to her about insurance rates, and emphasized that this would ultimately help her, with her short-term goals of becoming more financially independent, but that it would also reduce the cost of her future auto insurance.

When job hunting, Cat began by looking for any position that would accept entry-level applicants and provide on-the-job training. Although her family urged her to go for 'anything she could get,' she refrained from applying at fast food restaurants. She aimed for retail jobs, but never got a call back. Anxiety bubbled in her stomach as she perused the want ads. Her fears from job hunting as a teenager resurfaced, when she got funny looks turning in applications.

Nobody is going to hire me because they will just look at my name and think it's a joke. When I was a kid, I swore I would change my name as soon as I was old enough to do so. Now, I just wish other people would get over it. I don't want to have to explain the history and validity of my name every time I meet someone new. I have gotten used to my name. I think I may have even grown into it. Now I don't think I really want to change it. Still, I wonder if I had a normal name, would people take me more seriously? Trying to prove the validity of my existence is so exhausting. I thought that as an adult people would stop acting like children. I wonder if they ever do. Are people that terrible? Or is something that obviously wrong with me?

Cat was getting ready for a job interview. She felt awkward getting dressed up. Her parents reminded her that she needed to 'dress for success' if she wanted to be taken seriously. It felt like putting on a costume, putting on lipstick and doing her hair. She looked in the mirror. *This isn't me! They are going to know I'm faking it.* She groaned. *I feel a lot more comfortable in jeans and a sweatshirt.*

Cat went to her parents' room where Jule was hanging out with her Grandma. "This is awful. I don't feel right at all." She waved her hands at the dress she was wearing. "I don't feel comfortable. They are going to be able to tell I am uncomfortable."

"Pretty Mommy!" Jule exclaimed, climbing over her Grandma to get a better look at her mother.

"Yes. Your mother is very pretty." Stepmother responded to Jule, chuckling. "Of course, they will expect you to be nervous. Everyone is nervous in a job interview." She climbed out of the bed. "But we can make this just a little better." She rifled through her closet and pulled out a soft, black cardigan. "Here, put this on over the dress." She handed the sweater to Cat before grabbing a jewelry box off of her dresser. She opened it up and pulled out a simple pearl necklace. "Now add this and your outfit will be perfect for an interview!"

Cat put on the sweater, then added the necklace. "Better?" She asked hesitantly. Jule clapped in approval. "Okay then," Cat added, "I guess I'm off then." She turned to leave the bedroom. "You be good for Grandma! I will be back!"

As Cat left the bedroom and walked through the kitchen, she could hear her stepmother wishing her good luck and Jule chiming in. When she returned a couple hours later, she was pleased to announce she had been hired. She thanked her family for their support and assistance. When she tried to return the necklace and sweater, Stepmother suggested that she keep them. Dad reminded her that she would need more nice clothes for work anyway.

The new job was an evening position working at a dating service, trying to set appointments. It was not a good job, but Dad reminded her that "it's better than nothing. You have to start somewhere." Since she was working evenings, the family could all work together to take care of her daughter. Cat started to make friends with her co-workers and gain a little self-confidence working. Still, something nagged at her and continued to drag her down rabbit holes of depression.

Jule lay sleeping in the crib. Cat sat by the light of a small lamp on the floor. Legs crossed, she sat furiously writing in a notebook. Trying to gain some control of her life meant that she had to figure out a way to tame the depression and anxiety. As her hand moved across the page, Cat allowed all of her pain, frustration, and dreams of a happier life pour onto the pages. Tears rolled down her face, dropping stains onto the paper below. She held back the impulse to sob, intent on not waking her sleeping child.

The walls that wrapped around the room showed no signs of life. Stained periwinkle curtains blocked out the setting sun. Stacked boxes, overflowing laundry baskets, a cardboard box full of toys, all sat frozen. Cat's gaze moved slowly around the room. *I am in the twilight zone. Everything is so still, so dead, it could be any time. I could walk out the door and be anywhere. This is like a prison cell. Only padded, with a little human that constantly needs attention.*

The shadows of the moon speckled the dusty wooden floor. The window to the roof remained open, always ready for a late-night visitor. The lonely shadow lay silently weeping. He prayed to the moon above to send some kind of a sign. Trapped, in his loneliness, the silhouette wished for a tangible presence. Reaching out, he grabbed at the moonlight, as if to tear pieces off. "Please. Do something. Please."

Cat looked across the room. The simple lines of the honey crib framed pieces of Jule. A vertical puzzle of baby girl reflected back into the young mother's eyes. Tears made colors run together, and she felt a great desire to paint. Her eyes moved back to the line of boxes, zeroing in on the banana box. *All my paint stuff is right there. But it would make too much noise. She would wake up. Then I wouldn't be able to paint anyway.* She looked down at the pen, lying on the red spiral notebook. *I just can't write anymore right now. It hurts too much!* The tears got thicker, and her nose began to run.

Cat began to realize that too many nights were passing by exactly the same way. *This is not a habit I want to develop. I need to do something more with my evenings than be depressed. I need to be able to function. I want to be able to move past this depression!* She remembered taking the bus across town to her counseling appointments after school. *I was so stupid then. I really didn't understand that I truly needed help. I need help. I really need help. I need help right now.* She took a deep breathe, wiped her tears, and took another deep breath.

Cat laid down on her side. The pallet of blankets helped her to feel more at home. *For years, I have not felt comfortable in regular beds. Whether in my room, someone's living room, a field, a rooftop, I can always make a pallet and feel at home. I can feel safe. I can do this for myself.* Cushioning her head with one pillow, she placed a second pillow between her knees. Pulling the blankets tight up to her chin, she breathed deeply. *I deserve to be happy. I deserve to be happy. I just want to be happy.* A tight ball of dark fire twisted inside her gut. Little hands grabbed at her heart strings and pulled hard. Her heart skipped a beat. Her chest got tight, and she began to panic.

The faint whisper of a campfire lingered. Cat cradled her knees as her breath quickened. She heard the echo of a boy yelling at her. She couldn't hear the words. Covering her ears, she squeezed her eyelids. *I am done with that. I kicked him out. I am not going to be treated like garbage by another man. Never. I am done with men. Go Away!!* The oily light flickered, casting shadows of blue and yellow into the darkness.

Setting on the far end of a circle, the echo of fire wept in smoky rage. "When is she going to see me? I am done waiting. I could have defended her against that asshole. I can show her she is beautiful. Why does she keep doing this when I have been here all along waiting?" He picked up a glittering black rock. He hurled it violently into the flames. Tiny rockets erupted from the flames showering the meadow in brilliant reds and oranges. "Can you hear me now?!"

Walls moved slowly in ribbons. Shadows expanded and contracted, moving fluidly around the room. Dipping behind ribbons, they emerged gracefully from their dance with the crib. Cat focused on the sound of Jule breathing as she lay sleeping. She forced her eyes along the outline of the crib, framing the east wall as the only point of solid reality. *I can pull myself out of this. I don't know what this is. Maybe a flashback? I've talked enough people through bad trips to be able to get myself through this.* She took a deep breath. Gray filtered rainbows filled her lungs as she closed her eyes.

Pain shot through her eyelids. Fireworks exploded in dark reds and oranges. *I will not open my eyes. Breathe in. Breathe out. You can do this.* Cat struggled to gain control of her breathing. Pain shot through her head, down her shoulders and arms. Hot flashes of burning sadness spread across her chest. *Maybe you're having a heart attack? You've been praying for death for years.*

Maybe now you win the prize. The sound of maniacal laughter echoed faintly in the distance and the young woman began to question her sanity. *No. I am not crazy. I can get through this. I know how to do this. I've got this.* Tears streamed down her face. Her eyes opened just enough to see the shadow of a boy wipe her tears away. Curling into a ball, she squeezed her eyelids closed and pulled the top blanket up to her chin again.

Fire's smoky feet danced around the circle. A storm cloud of pain and rage, he screamed. "Stop pacifying me! Stop it! Why can't you see me? I am not a panic attack. I am real! I am here dammit!" A light mist of raindrops swept through the circle. Fire collapsed to his knees weeping. "Why? I don't understand." Blue pig tails wrapped in red plaid sat cross legged on the ground beside him. She stroked his head, coaxing him to take refuge in her comfort. Wrapping his empty arms around her, he succumbed to her offer. As he wept deeply in her lap, the rain got thicker, and the meadow was cradled in a smoky fog.

Chapter 28
Strong and Beautiful

Cat woke haunted by echoes of lucid dreaming. *Who is the girl with blue pig tails?* She rubbed her eyes and the memory faded. She turned to pull the curtain open halfway. "Just enough to let the sunlight in." She didn't have any more energy than normal, but Cat felt a determination to better herself. "Today is a new day. I can make it a good day." She folded her top blanket and sat on top of her pillow. Sounds of life transmitted from the waking Jule. Cat's ears received an electrical tap, causing her gaze to shift towards the crib.

I felt terrible when I went to sleep. I feel better now. I know I can do this. I'm here to raise my little girl. I have to be able to keep my head straight to do that. Deft hands gathered tiny clothes, cloth underpants, plastic pants, and finally, the sleepy child. *If it's in my head, I should be able to control it.* Jule fussed briefly, emitting high pitched cranky whining noises. Upon recognizing her mother's touch, and smell, the little girl quickly shifted to using short words. "Potty Mommy. Icky. Potty." Cat returned the communication with soft tones and kisses on the forehead as she carried Jule to the bathroom.

Mother stripped the sleepy wet child of the stinging clothes. Squatting next to her daughter in front of the toilet, Cat dropped the little toilet training insert into the toilet seat. She turned to the little girl rubbing her eyes and picked her up at the waist. "Ow. Mommy your too hard." Cat placed her daughter on the training seat, apologizing. *I barely touched her. What did I do? I can't even get through ten minutes without screwing up.* The sound of the toddler emptying her bladder into the toilet echoed in the bathroom.

Cat stood up, dropping the wet nightclothes into the bathroom hamper. Hands moved without guidance from the faucet to the soap. Washing, rinsing, plugging the sink. Echoes of running water were louder than the toddler urinating. Hands turn off the faucet. "Mommy mommy mommy." Cat suddenly looked up and saw the mirror. *That's not me. Who is that? What the hell am I doing here?* "Mommy! I'm done, Mommy!" *Oh Shit!* She turned to the left and bent down to pick up her Jule.

"Of course, you are dear! What a good girl you are!" She kissed her daughter's forehead and lifted her onto the counter next to the sink. "Now stand here still like a good girl." Jule complied, familiar with the morning routine. Cat picked up a washcloth, dipped it into the half-full sink, and began wiping down her daughter's bottom and legs. "Remember, you have to wash all of you." She dipped the cloth in the sink again before wiping down the inside of Jules legs.

Leaning with her hands on her mother's shoulders, Jule dipped her left foot into the sink. Giggling, she lifted her foot back onto the counter and repeated the ritual with her right foot. After each foot had been dipped, Cat reached for a towel. "Okay kiddo. You're clean enough for now. You can take a bath later." She wrapped a rainbow towel around the toddler and carried her into the bedroom.

I can do this. I can do this. It's just one foot in front of the other. I can do this. Cat sat down on the floor with the little clothes and her daughter. Jule responded accordingly. "I don't want to wear that!" The young mother breathed deeply. *You can do this. Just let her play.* She leaned over and grabbed a laundry basket full of clothes. She dumped the contents into a pile between them. Jule's eyes widened.

"Okay then." The mother responded to her daughter's surprise. "What do you want to wear then?" The little girl giggled, pulling one of her mother's shirts off the top of the pile. "I don't think that will fit you. Do you think I should wear it?" The little girl smiled, shook her head, and put it back in the pile. The two played the game for about a half hour before Jule finally conceded to getting dressed.

Getting through breakfast was equally as joyful and tedious. *As long as I can just relax and enjoy the process, I will be fine. She's not worried about getting anywhere on time. She's not worried about whether you go to work on time. She has no idea all the stresses of being a grown up. And she shouldn't have to know those things. Just relax and let her be a kid.* Cat gave herself time outs and little reminders to breathe and relax several times throughout the day.

The afternoon rolled in, right on schedule. Cat prepared herself for the evening shift. Handing her child off the Stepmother, she headed out the door stuffing her hesitation neatly in her purse. Wedged in tightly between cigarettes and a wallet, hesitation began self-medicating. Waiting, slowly sipping, hesitation steeped itself in misery while she pushed herself through another evening of calls and hang-ups. It was nice to have a job, but she was not planning on sticking around for this one any longer than necessary.

Driving Big Red home from the dating agency, Cat considered her options. Talking through various scenarios, she practiced talking with her family about it. By the time she arrived home, hesitation was drunk with anxiety. Turning the key off and removing it from the steering column, Cat looked at the key in her hand. "I have the key. Its right here in my hand." She swung her purse onto her left shoulder and felt a distinct pull of sadness. She dismissed the urge to tear up and looked again at her hand. "Okay. I still the key." She opened the door, climbed out, and stood for a moment with the door open. She looked down once more at her hand. "Yes. Okay. I still have the key." Pushing the button on the door, she locked the truck and closed its steel door hard. Steel echoes reverberated through the open air between the neighborhood houses.

Cat looked around, embarrassed. *I hope nobody heard that. Geez.* She saw empty yards, privacy fences, and a quiet street. *Nobody cares. What is your problem?* She ran her fingers through her hair and headed up the brick path to the front porch. Moving quickly to the door, anxiety crawled up the young woman's arm, tickling the back of her neck. She scratched the back of her neck and felt a twinge. *Why is this yard so creepy at night? It always has been!*

Cat opened the door and stepped through the threshold

to find her father sitting at the dining room table. Sorting mail and drinking a beer, Dad looked perfectly satisfied with his current task. The garbage can and recycling bin sat next to him on the floor. She closed the door behind her, and he looked up from his handiwork. "Evening. How was work?"

Walking into the dining room, Cat sat down along the east side of the table. She dropped her purse down onto the table as she took her regular seat. "I hate my job." Dad paused from dismantling the junk mail to grimace at the comment. "I know. I know. Don't leave until you have another job to replace it." She made circles on the table with her finger as she spoke. "I have been looking. I haven't found anything yet. But this job really sucks." She got up and headed towards the kitchen. "Nobody wants to pay a bunch of money to a dating agency. It's really invasive to even be calling them."

Dad nodded. "Yes. I agree. However, at least you have a job." He returned to dismantling the junk mail. Paper with colored ink couldn't be recycled and got tossed in the trash can. Dad's fingers removed the plastic from the window envelopes, dropping the plastic into the trash, and the paper envelope pieces into the recycling bin. "Do you have any idea what you want to do next? What kind of job are you looking for? You don't really have any skills."

Cat felt her father's words under her skin, sending stinging waves from her shoulders across the front of her chest. A hot dark pain pulsed in the center of her chest. *I can do this. I can do this. I can do this.* She took a deep breath as she poured a glass of water. She drank deeply emptying half the glass before placing it on the counter. She turned to pause in the doorway. She glanced to her left to notice her childhood timeline marked along the doorway with ages and dates.

"I don't know exactly what I am looking for Dad." She paused to force another deep breath. *You can do this. You can do this.* "I don't think I am going to be good at anything until I find myself." He blinked at her soundlessly waiting for her to continue. Her legs began to cramp, and she seated herself in the nearest chair. She rubbed her legs while she continued. "I am looking for another job, but in the meantime, I think I need to get back into counseling."

Dad supported the idea. He reminded his daughter that she was in the presence of family, and that they would be more than willing to watch Jule while Cat went to counseling sessions. She had been worried that he would judge her for needing help. Dad was relieved to see his daughter taking the steps necessary for self-improvement. He saw her struggling so often and was powerless to do anything about it. She was an adult and would have to learn some things the hard way. Still, he was comforted that she felt safe enough to share her intentions with him.

Cat stopped rubbing her legs to wander through the refrigerator. She stood with the fridge door open, picking at leftovers. Her father suggested that she go ahead and fix a plate. "No. I'm not really that hungry." She grabbed a meatball out of a tray of sauce, loosely covered with saran wrap. Popping the meatball in her mouth, she closed the refrigerator door. She rinsed her hands off at the kitchen sink and then headed out of the kitchen. She said goodnight to her father as she walked down the dark hall. Quietly, she turned the doorknob, careful not to make a sound as she entered the room where her Jule lay sleeping.

When Cat started counseling sessions, she temporarily abandoned job hunting. *I hate my job, but there is only so much I can do at once. I want to be successful, so I need to not overload myself. Maybe after I have been in counseling for a while, I will feel better about myself. If I am feeling better, then job hunting will be easier, and I will get a better job. In the meantime, I need to work on myself.* The first evening visiting the counseling center, she was very nervous. The staff were friendly, and the counselor was so calm, that Cat immediately began to relax when she sat down on the over-sized plush chair in the counseling office.

The first visit was really just introductions. The second visit they dove right in. Cat indicated that she wanted to start first by focusing primarily on addressing her anxiety being around other people. "If I always get anxious around new people, I am never going to be able to get a better job or make any new friends."

Most sessions, Cat spent the bulk of the hour talking through her tears. Sometimes, when she felt like she really needed some extra support, Cat would call up her counselor and ask, "Can you schedule me for a double session? I don't think one hour is going to be enough this week." Spending two hours in the room, they would manage to work through a lot of pain.

When Cat returned home after counseling, she was exhausted. She fell asleep quickly and slept hard. In the sessions she rehashed memories of being alone as a child. Sobbing, she described in detail the way she used to abuse herself. Trying to break down all the little pieces of self-hate that she had built up, she released pain that she had long forgotten even existed. She shared memories of being teased and learned that many of her inner demons were just voices repeating the same things the kids used to say to her when she was a child.

"I hated being alone. We moved into the Walnut Creek house when I was in the middle of fourth grade. I was not good at making friends. The kids in the neighborhood teased me about my name. They teased me for not knowing how to ride a bicycle. They teased me for being weird and different. A couple of girls in the neighborhood were nice to me. We did start to develop friendships, but they didn't know what to do with my emotional roller coaster. They didn't know how to respond to my depression." Cat concluded that, she must have created her own loneliness by isolating herself from other people.

"Spending afternoons alone at home, I spent hours yelling at myself for being ugly. I knew there must be something terribly wrong with me 'because otherwise I wouldn't be alone.' I believed that I was alone because people didn't want to be around me. My mother had left me. Dad was always gone. My dad's girlfriend made it clear she didn't want me either. All the kids playing outside with each other were too mean for me to be able to handle being around them. I wanted to play with the boys, but they didn't want to play with me. I didn't like being a girl. I wasn't pretty enough. I wasn't graceful enough. I didn't like myself at all."

"I felt so much pain inside. I wanted to be able to control it. Attempting to control my pain, I inflicted pain on myself. Hitting my head against the wall in the hall over and over. I tried to knock myself out. I only succeeded in giving myself a bad headache. Deciding that the wall was too soft to be effective, I moved to the bathroom. Hitting my head against the bathtub, I prayed for a concussion. I would tell myself, 'Perhaps if I am knocked out when Dad comes home, he will find me? Perhaps if I have to go the hospital, he will discover that he misses me, and will actually want to spend more time with me? Would anyone really miss me if I was gone?'

Cat's counselor listened, nodding her head. Tears stained the young woman's cheeks and blurred her vision. The image of the room swam around her head. *Breathe in. Breathe out. You can do this. This is a safe space.* The counselor listened and took notes. She asked leading questions, but really let Cat lead with whatever was on her mind.

Eyes scanned slowly around the room, meticulously examining the details. Time seemed to have stopped, or perhaps was moving very slowly. Frame by frame Cat felt each breath enter her lungs and exit again. Frame by frame, she took in the details of her surroundings. Desperately trying to regain her vision, she reminded herself to breathe.

North and South walls were painted in a yellowish sort of eggshell. The East and West walls had been prepared with a rancid chocolate. Floor to ceiling, navy blue curtains covered Southern bay windows, allowing only enough light to keep the room feeling thick and musty. The smell of campfire smoke entered her nostrils. Cat winced. *Keep going you've got this. Just breathe in and breathe out and focus on what you know is real.*

The Northern Wall was bare except a few small photographs strategically placed across the wall. Each photograph was a point of view picture taken by somebody on a body of water. Each was in black and white neatly framed with a black metal frame and a thin sheet of glass. Below the photographs, the counselor sat perched in a padded chair next to a small table adorned with a conservative lamp.

The Eastern side of the room contained a door and one large, framed picture. Cat gazed at the picture for a moment, examining the simple print of a flower in three colors. *Breathe in. Breathe out.* She felt a strong tug at the side of her head, urging her to look towards the other end of the room.

The Western end of the room was the darkest. Cat glanced briefly at the small bookshelf and box of toys. Something painful was trying to demand her attention. She averted her eyes looking again towards her counselor expectantly. The simple lamp gave the counselor a soft yellow aura reminding Cat she was, in fact, safe.

As the counselor paused, Cat took a moment to catch her breath and steady her vision. The counselor handed the young woman a box of tissues. "See how strong and beautiful you are. You can cry and remember the pain.

And still you have made it this far. Because you are a strong beautiful woman." Cat thanked her for her support as she filled the wastebasket with tissues.

Along the western wall, hiding behind a book on sexuality and human psychology, a secret passageway sat waiting. Musty smoke drifted down the alley, revealing only the shadow of a boy crouched down, leaning against the brick wall. "I don't feel strong. I feel weak and tired. I'm tired of feeling weak. This is not helping. You just don't get it." He pulled at his hair, weeping empty echoes.

Cat continued to drudge on, every day, with a regular routine. She tried to remind herself each morning that this was not a drudgery. *This is my life. Dedicating myself to the care and upbringing of my child is my life's purpose now.* She told herself the same story every morning and cried herself to sleep most evenings. Still, she continued to go to counseling every week.

It took several months of counseling sessions to get through the memories of being suicidal as a child. Cat had felt guilty for years. She believed that she must be selfish. "Dad always made sure I had clothes, food, and school supplies. He took me to the doctor for my checkups, scheduled regular dental appointments, and got me braces when the dentist recommended doing so." *He always made sure I had what I needed. I have no reason to complain.* "It could have been a lot worse. I could have been abused. I could have gone without."

The counselor pointed out that neglect is a form of

abuse. "You have every right to be upset. Have you ever told your father how you feel?" The young woman nodded her head slowly indicating that she had not. Looking at the ground, she dared not look up. "Perhaps you should invite your father to come and sit in on one of our sessions? Maybe you will feel safer telling him how you feel then?"

Dealing with suicidal thoughts as an adult, Cat recognized it was unhealthy and unsafe. She was glad to have the support of her counselor. *I want to be healthy!* She was nervous about the idea of telling Dad about all the feelings she had regarding her childhood. When Cat asked Dad to come with her for counseling, he agreed without hesitation. Sitting in session with the support of her counselor, she let all of her feelings roll out of her face with her tears. She admitted how lonely she had been. She shared with him her history of self-abuse. She told him about all the times she had tried to commit suicide. He sat quietly listening. Finally, when he did talk, he responded, "I'm sorry. I didn't know."

Counseling was helping Cat. Making friends at work was helping too. The support she was receiving at home was helping. She started to have good days. Some days were more difficult than others, but she actually started to laugh again. She could tangibly recognize how the changes she was making in her life, were making a positive impact. She hated her job, and finally developed enough confidence to return to job hunting.

Cat landed another telemarketing job that was during the day. She only stayed for about a week. They were reselling telephone services. It was a big scam and she felt like they were being encouraged to trick people just to get them to sign up. She felt strongly that what she was being told to do was immoral. She decided that she would never again force herself to try and sell something that she couldn't stand behind.

Chapter 29
Pushing Too Hard

Discouraged by unemployment, and her lack of education, Cat decided she needed more than a job. *I need training. I need a program that will help me get a job worth keeping.* Sitting at the kitchen table, she positioned herself with a notebook and pen, the telephone, and the phone book. She opened the book flipping to the employment section. After making a few calls, she had secured an appointment with what she thought was an employment training program.

Two days later, Cat arrived early in the morning for her appointment. Standing around outside with other people dressed sharply, she quietly observed their demeanor and listened to their chatter. At nine o'clock the doors opened, and the waiting crowd was greeted by a man in a suit and a blue striped tie. He herded the strangers down a narrow hall into a large room lined on one side with tinted windows facing the parking lot.

The room was filled with round tables, each hosting 4 or 5 chairs. At the front of the room, there was a podium. The well-dressed strangers began scattering, choosing seats next to people who seemed familiar. *These fluorescent lights make me feel like I am sitting under a microscope. Everyone is staring at me. Do they know that I don't belong here?* She scanned the room, searching for an empty table but they had all been eliminated. Walking around the edge of the room, she approached a quiet table and motioned towards an empty chair at the otherwise occupied table. A woman looked up smiling meekly over large glasses. "It's all yours honey."

The man with the striped tie approached the podium and tested the podium microphone. Returning to a desk in the front corner of the room, he grabbed a stack of paper folders and began distributing them among the tables. Waiting quietly for her set of papers, Cat held her breath. *Who are these people? What am I doing here? I don't belong here surrounded by suits. If they knew anything about me, I'd be eaten alive. They are like vultures waiting to prey. I can feel it in my bones!* A chill ran down her spine and she shivered under the bright lights. *This is a new life. I need to be brave and open to new experiences if I am going to be successful. I have to stop expecting the worst. They are just human beings who need to live, just like me.*

Cat saw the blue striped tie approach her table. She silently accepted a thin white folder, placing it on the table in front of her. A voice broke the quiet mumbling of the room. "Good morning ladies and gentlemen. And welcome to..." Looking up at the front of the room, Cat focused on the man speaking from the podium. His words echoed in the background, but she wasn't really paying attention. *Gray slacks and sport jacket, and a white mock turtle. Who does he think he is? Don Johnson? He looks like a salesman not a teacher.* She looked down and noticed that other people were going through their folders following the speaker's directions. She fumbled to try and catch up.

The morning dragged on as Cat shifted in her seat and half-heartedly tried to pay attention. Her butt was numb, and her legs kept tingling and cramping. Her feet twitched and she winced, hoping nobody would notice. "And so, with our program, we can guarantee that you will become leaders in your careers. On Thursday, I look forward to seeing your shining faces walking through my door again. Remember to complete your registration paperwork before you return. And we don't want anyone to miss this great opportunity, so if you can't pay in full on Thursday, see Miss Judy to sign up for the payment plan." A mouse of a woman waved from the front corner desk, smiling wide and pointing to her name tag.

When Cat returned home that afternoon, she was disappointed. *It was a sales pitch. They aren't going to help me. What a bullshit scam! Preying on the desperate! Nothing in this morning's presentation addressed job placement. They didn't actually help anyone get jobs. Why are people expected to pay for a program when they don't have a job? It wasn't an interview at all. It was a great big sales pitch! Nobody ever asked me anything about myself, what I had to offer, or what I wanted to learn.* She decided that she would not be returning on Thursday and threw the folder in the garbage. She entered the bedroom where her daughter lay sleeping in the crib. "I love you little Jule."

The next day, Cat returned to the kitchen table. Again, she prepared herself with paper, pen, the telephone, and the phone book. This time, she opened the phone book to the very front government pages. *I must be missing something. If I start from the beginning and scour this book, I am sure to find something or someone that can help me.* Starting with the State Department of Education, she began calling people and telling her story. "Can you help me? Or can you point me in the right direction" Dialing up social workers, educational consultants, and anyone listed as being even vaguely associated with vocational services, she left phone messages on many answering machines.

Each time, Cat explained that she was a 22-year-old single mother. She had a GED. She had very little work experience. She needed a program that would help her get on her feet. She kept dialing and leaving messages. For two days she diligently worked her way through the government pages. In between caring for Jule, she made calls and took notes. When she reached the end of the government pages, she was exhausted. After another night of crying herself to sleep, she decided she had worked hard and deserved a day off.

"My birthday is coming soon. The weather is beautiful." Cat announced to Jule, playing quietly on the floor as she pulled the curtains wide open. "Let's let some light in, shall we?" She looked down at her daughter and smiled. *I have a lovely daughter who wants to go have fun. So, let's go have some fun!* She sat down on the floor next to the little girl. "What are you playing honey?"

Jule handed a blue plastic shape to her mother. "It's a star, Mommy." She picked up a green plastic cube. Cut outs interrupted the green mesh cage. "Where's it go? Can you do it?" She offered the shape cube to her mother. Cat smiled down at her shining Jule. *She is so smart. I made that. I did that.* A warm fullness rushed through her chest. She closed her eyes, felt the sun shining through the window on her face, and smiled. She opened her eyes, outstretched her hands, and picked up her daughter. Little arms and hands struggled not to drop the toy while the brimming mother hugged her child.

Cat pulled back, settling Jule on her hip. "Do you want to go to the park? If you want to go to the park, we have to eat lunch first." She crouched down to place her daughter back on the blanketed floor. Jule made sounds of excitement, occasionally protesting when her mother wanted to put away a toy, she suddenly found interesting. Mother hustled to clean up the bedroom and pack the diaper bag for a trip to the park. Cat wandered into the kitchen to gather snacks with Jule trailing behind like a little duckling.

Cat walked through the narrow kitchen to the dark pantry. Turning on the pantry light, she thumbed through various boxes. Without turning her head, she called out, "Do you want cheese crackers with peanut butter or plain crackers with cheese?" Cat turned to see her daughter at her knees. "Oh! There you are! Go get your backpack so you can carry your own snacks!" *The earlier she starts to learn how to take care of herself, the better off she'll be later.* Animated by this task, Jule turned and ran back into the bedroom.

The little girl returned promptly, reciting all her favorite snacks. "...And I want strawberries. And grapes. And crackers. And fruit snacks. And cookies. And Capri Suns." She handed her mother a small backpack emblazoned with stars and a unicorn with a rainbow mane. "It's my magic bag and I love it!" She unzipped the zipper, beaming at her mother. "See! I did it!" Loving eyes smiled at the little girl and accepted the satchel.

"Okay. You want to fill your magic bag with snacks, and we can do that. But remember," Cat pulled snack packs out of boxes, discreetly placing them into the backpack, as she reminded her daughter, "we have to eat lunch first." Jule began to protest, insisting that she could eat snacks at the park. *Oh no we're not. This is not going to happen.* Cat placed the half-full pack onto an empty shoulder level pantry shelf and ushered her daughter back through the kitchen to the dining room. "You can sit in your seat while I get your food. You will survive this. I promise you."

The brightly colored booster seat had developed a meaningful relationship with the chair it had been strapped to, for the better part of the last year. Setting Jule down into the seat did not calm the protests, but it did provide the opportunity to strap down the noisy toddler. She pushed the chair towards the table so Jule could begin banging on the table as she protested. *She'll stop as soon as she has some food in front of her.* Despite the whining and crying, Cat talked to her daughter calmly as she returned to the kitchen and prepared lunch.

"I know you are angry that we are not going to the park right away." Cat continued as she fumbled through the fridge. "But if you use up all your energy throwing a temper tantrum, you won't have any energy left to have fun at the park." She returned to the dining room with a bowl of grapes. Jule began dismantling the bunch of grapes as soon as her mother walked away. Cat noted the silence and smiled to herself. She stood in the kitchen, listening to her internal DJ as she made cream cheese and ham sandwiches. Cut neatly into triangles, she arranged them on a plate surrounded by sliced apples. She carried the plate out to the table and returned to the kitchen for two cups of water.

Sitting in the dining room with Jule, all was calm. By the end of the meal, it was clear that the little girl had indeed become sleepy. *I knew it.* Cat cleared away the small lunch mess and loaded up the stroller with all the necessary gear for the park adventure. *She will fall asleep in the stroller before we even get there. But I could use the exercise.* She took Jule to the bathroom so they could each go potty and wash their hands before heading out.

The midday July sun was hot and bright. Cat crossed the street to walk in the shade of the trees. She was sweating by the time they reached the top of the hill. She crossed the street to turn right onto the sidewalk. No shady options presented themselves and she bent down to adjust the stroller shade. *Asleep already. I knew it.* She adjusted the shade to protect Jule from the direct sunlight as she slept. *No point in going directly to the park if she's asleep.* She continued walking shifting her direction to the neighborhood market a few blocks down.

The corner market was a place of comfort for Cat. She had been coming to this market since her Dad had first moved them here. It had gone through several changes as ownership had changed hands. Still, it was a monument to many who had grown up in the neighborhood. *I remember buying Blow Pops for a nickel here! And hanging out in the middle of the night in front of the store, smoking cigarettes and talking. So many memories.* As she approached the market, she noted differences that indicated yet another change of ownership had occurred since her last visit.

Navigating the stroller in the tiny aisles was not going to be an option, so Cat peeked under the hood of the stroller. *Still sleeping.* She quietly parked the stroller just inside the front door. Cat turned to look at the clerk behind the counter and made a quiet motion putting her finger to her pursed lips before proceeding to locate a cold beverage. She perused the tiny market, checking on her daughter frequently. After gathering some tea biscuits, gummy fruit slices, and lemonade, she headed to the register. She quietly requested a pack of Camels and paid for the whole pile before taking the stroller back outside.

Picnic tables with benches provided partial shade in front of the little market. The faded blue stroller was parked next to the bench. Cat sat with her back against the wall, legs stretching the length of the bench. To her left, she monitored the still sleeping Jule. She quietly sipped her lemonade, leaning on the table to her right as she tapped her cigarette into the black plastic ashtray on the table. She had managed to quit while she was pregnant, but the stress of the last year had been too much to handle and she had returned to the habit. Now, she made sure to sit downwind from the stroller, trying to protect her daughter from the harmful smoke.

After chain smoking a couple of cigarettes, Cat packed up her stuff. *Only one block to go. I bet she will wake up as soon as we get to the park.* She unlocked the wheels on the stroller and returned to pushing up the street into the sun. *Pushing. Up the hill. I always feel like I am pushing up a hill.*

Cat had been pushing hard. She felt an unspoken pressure from her family to produce results. Every daily plan now had to include some effort to make money. If she didn't have a job interview, she had to be visibly searching the newspaper, making lists, making phone calls, and ultimately leaving the house "in search". Despite her own need for pocket money, the pressure she felt from her family provided the motivation that nothing else could. She felt ashamed of her failures and inadequacies.

Jule twisted in the stroller. Cat looked over, placing her left hand on the little back. "You decided to join the living? And just in time! Look where we are!" Cat rubbed her daughters back gently as the toddler stretched and sat up. Little fists rubbed little eyes. Mother smiled at daughter, twisting to reach her right arm around her body. Mother's arms delivered loving hands to lift the little girl out of the stroller. As soon as her little feet hit the ground the child was moving.

Cat sat half-relaxing and half-ready to move quickly, if necessary. Closely monitoring the little girl's movement, she let Jule explore the playground independently. Jule left her mother on the bench in thought, while she followed the trail of a small white butterfly. Landing briefly on wildflowers growing in the sand, it floated on the gentle breeze that teased its way through the play structure. Escaping the confines of the structure, it adventured towards a sea of flowers just over the next ridge of cement.

Time passed slowly. Frame by frame, Cat savored the moment. *How many of these moments will I get before she doesn't like me anymore? If I am always gone working, when will I have time to take her to the park?* She allowed the enthusiastic toddler to cajole her into the sand. Sitting in the shade under wooden planks, the two sheltered in the shade together, wrists buried in the sand. The little girl babbled broken pieces of a story. Words floated across the highway of thoughts, causing traffic shenanigans in Cat's mind. Princess dropped a castle in the middle of rush hour. Hands spun the wheel to the right, landing on a soft embankment of damp sand next to eleven-inch dandelions.

The late afternoon sun shone hot and orange. Sweaty, dirty, and passed out, the Jule lay faded in the stroller. *Sunglasses are not made dark enough for California summer.* Sweat dripped, collected, and soaked all the parts that reminded Cat how uncomfortable it was to be a woman. *Tits are proof. If there is a God, he's a pervert. Fantastic for everyone else in the world except the person who has to deal with them. They're heavy, hot, itchy, and they get in the way.*

Cat embraced the warm shade of the olive and oak, parking the stroller quietly. Glancing at the driveway, she determined that nobody else was home and began searching for keys. Slow, controlled movements made little sound as hands pulled keys from the magical bag of everything. Despite the law of key rings, no scratching of metal against metal echoed while hands moved towards the doorknob. A slow turn of the wrist elicited a click-click-click. The door swung open with an audible creak. Cat held her breath and looked down at the stroller.

Frame by frame, time moved backwards as hand and keys moved back into the magic bag. Cat exhaled and looked again at her sleeping child in the stroller by the front door. *I know what I have to do. I have to take a shower. I really have to take a shower. And if I move quickly enough, I can do it before she wakes up!* Cat took a deep breath. Time stopped. Frame by frame, she moved deftly through the house. First, stretching only two steps to silently place the magic bag into an armchair. Frame by frame, the young woman deftly lifted the stroller wherein the sleeping child lay. Silently. Fluidly. And perfectly balanced.

The stroller traveled over the threshold, landing softly on the honey floor. Virtually levitating, the stroller followed a path through the living room, down the hall, and into the bedroom. Cat paused for a moment. *Don't even try to move her. Just leave her in the stroller. What if she wakes up and knocks the stroller over? She's not going to wake up. Unless you don't hurry.* She stopped watching Jule sleep and began rooting through a pile of clean laundry. *You better hurry before she does wake up! I just need clean clothes to put on. Wear a towel. Who cares? Just get in the shower while you still can!*

Cat was thankful to get a chance to take a shower

without having to ask for someone to keep an eye on Jule. *I couldn't have anyway. Nobody else is home. Fantastic!* The warm afternoon had covered her skin with a sticky itchy film of dead skin, sunshine, and salt water. The cool water poured over her head, cascading down her shoulders, forming rivulets between her breasts. She shivered and adjusted the faucet. The water warmed and Cat removed the shower head from its wall mount. Taking care to leave no part untouched, she rinsed her body thoroughly before placing the shower head back on the mount. Reaching for the shampoo, her momentary lapse of pleasure was interrupted by the sound of a toddler realizing they were alone in a dark room.

Chapter 30
Demon Princess

Cat gave up on shampoo. Redirecting its destination, the hand veered from soap shelf to faucet handle. The frustrated young women held her breathe briefly, savoring a faint glimpse of silence. The wailing resumed. *Did you really think you were going to get away with that? You get no time. No time. Remember. You sold your soul for a baby. Shut up!* She exhaled as she stepped out of the shower.

"I was just in the shower honey!" She called out as she dangled her head upside down. "You don't have to worry." Cat shouted through the closed bathroom door, as she wrapped a towel around a long-wet mane. "Calm down honey! Mommy's coming!" She bellowed as she wrapped a second towel around her body and turned the old brass doorknob.

Jule was standing on the other side of the door, red nose and eyes staring wide. "Why'd you close the door on me?" The little girl moved forward to wrap little limbs around the toweled mother as she tried to leave the bathroom. "Honey. I love you. But I need to get dressed." She encouraged the child to dismount and allow her passage, but the toddler protested. "You closed the door on me!" The last word echoed as the shrill voice dragged the 'eee' across the hall as they moved. Cat, dragged her anchored leg with an urgency, closing the bedroom door quickly behind them.

"You have to let go of my leg so I can get dressed

honey." Cat pleaded with the child. "And furthermore, I did not close the bathroom door on you. You were asleep. I simply went into the bathroom to take a shower." Clearly dissatisfied with the response, Jule reached for the bedroom door.

"But Mom! I need to potty!" Cat, opened the door, swooping up the little girl and rushing back into the bathroom. She mumbled frustrations, while trying to be supportive of her daughter. Her parents had seemed to think she was pushing the potty too early, but Jule had shown interest in ditching the diaper early on. Cat knew that she'd never be able to get her daughter into Preschool until she was potty trained. *She is so smart! And so bored! She needs other kids to play with. She needs to be someplace where she is learning something more than what I have to offer.*

Cat pulled the snaps open on the little girl's jumper and pulled her disposable underpants off. She lifted her daughter onto the training seat. Jule began to cry again. "What's wrong honey? I thought you wanted to potty?" The woman knelt on the cold bathroom floor, one hand still clutching the corners of the damp towel.

"I had to go potty!" Jule cried, as she sat on the training toilet. "But you closed the door on me!"

Cat looked down to see that the little girl had soiled her disposable pants. Tears streamed down the little girls face in shame. "Oh honey! It's okay! You tried. I was just in the shower."

"No! Mommy. You closed the door on me!" Embarrassed by her bodily functions, the toddler blamed her mother for the mistake. "You closed the door on me! I needed to go potty!" Suddenly amused by the fierceness of the child, she fought to hold back a chuckle.

"Yes dear. I closed the door. Because I had to get clean." She placed the pants in the trash can and stood up. Stretching her legs, she tried to regain feeling. *Clearly, I should not have been squatting down so long. Now here come the pins and needles. Mother fucker. Lovely. Now smile for the camera. The children are watching.* She straightened out her towel, re-tucking the end in snugly to free her hands. Standing at the sink, she washed her hands with soap and water as she talked down to the grumpy child.

"I know you don't like it, but sometimes I need to bathe." Cat dried her hands on the towel affixed to her torso. "I'm glad that you tried to hold it for the potty. I'm not mad that you didn't make it. Just try one more time now, and then you can take a bath too!" She bent down, gathering dirty clothes from the bathroom floor. Jule continued to protest, but the noises faded away with the sound of water running in the bathtub. "You just sit there on the potty for a second while the bathtub fills up. I will be right back!"

Cat darted into the bedroom, leaving the bathroom door wide open. She rifled with the clean clothes in the basket, grabbing pajamas and a fresh pull-up before returning to the bathroom. Jule looked up at the toweled woman. "Up!" She demanded, raising her arms in the air. "I'm all done Mommy!" Cat pushed the bathroom door closed with her foot as she leaned in to pick up the little girl. Jule squirmed in her arms, loosening the towel.

As she bent down to put her daughter in the filling tub, the towel fell, landing a dog-eared corner directly in the bath water. *Of course.* "But I don't want to!" The girl continued complaining. Ignoring the protests, Cat added bubbles to the running water. She began pulling toys out of a plastic basket that sat silently in the corner next to the tub. Sounds of protest quickly transformed into sounds of glee as the bubbles began to multiply. Cat reached over and turned off the faucet.

"Okay. Now you have bubbles. You have toys. You have everything you need." She held her breathe for a moment. *Please just be happy. Please. I just need the evening to go okay. We only have a few hours before I can go to bed and forget the world. Even if just for a little while.* "Are we okay now honey?" She exhaled, waiting for her daughter to respond.

"Look at the bubbles Mommy!" The little girl gurgled. "I like bubbles!" Tiny fingers grasped a big blue boat, pushing it down into the water until it disappeared out of sight.

"Yes honey. I know you like bubbles." She smiled at the child covered in bubbles. Tiny patches of bubbles had landed on her head, dripping down to nestle along the crook of her ear. "You're okay now, right?" *You better be okay. My legs are killing me. I need to stand up. I need to not be crouching next to this tub right now.* She grabbed the towel, sitting at her feet, and began wrapping it back around her body as she stood up. *Oh ya! That's cold!* Remembering that the towel had gotten wet, she grimaced.

"Well. If you're okay." She hesitated, examining the scene with the child in the bathtub. *You know it doesn't take much for the kid to drown. That's plenty of water. Shut up. She'll be fine. It's just for a second.* "Mommy's gonna go in the bedroom really quick, okay honey? I just need to get some clothes on. She darted across the hall, clutching the damp towel. *Through the archway of the door, to the right. Laundry basket. Doesn't matter what it is.* Hands identified an olive-green pullover sundress. *It's see through. You need another layer. Shut up. It's just for a minute.*

Cat darted back across the hall, shedding the damp towel in the bedroom doorway as she moved. Ten seconds passed slowly as she moved from doorway to doorway. In one long stride she crossed the hall. One more and she reached the tub. Terrified by the silence, she peered into the bathtub to discover a happy toddler playing quietly with her favorite blue boat. The woman exhaled. Jule looked up at her mother. "Mommy this is the biggest boat. It's the best." She smiled wide, displaying a weaning beard of bubbles dripping down her chin. "I'm a pirate and this is my ship! You want to be a pirate too Mommy?"

Cat observed adoringly, "I see that you have managed to get bubbles all over the place!" She knelt down, hesitated, and got back up. *Stool. Stool. Where is the stool? If I were a stool, where would I be?* She looked under the sink, behind the toilet, and in the tiny cupboard behind the door. "Hold on honey. I'll be right back." She started back out the door.

"Mom mom mom. Water's cold! I'm done." Jule

proclaimed as Cat rifled through the hall closet.

"Okay honey." Hands attempted to close the closet door. They landed softly with a bump, about an inch away from closet. She pushed again without success. A third try was enough for her to decide to give up and attend to the crying child. Standing in the doorway of the bathroom, eyes moved from the foot stool in her right hand to the toddler standing in the bathtub. *I guess I don't need this anymore.* The closet door opened. The enveloping darkness of coats consumed the foot stool before the door eased shut. Left behind in the moment, unnoticed by the urgency at hand.

"Be careful honey. I don't want you to slip and fall." The woman cautioned as she rinsed a washcloth with warm water in the sink.

"I'm fine." Jule responded with a nod of her head. "I'm okay Mommy." Hands on her hips, the toddler was unaware how silly she looked with bubbles oozing down her little body. Cat chuckled as she instructed her daughter to hold still. "Be nice!" Jule called out when she thought her mother was being too rough. Cat responded with soft soothing sounds as she wiped the bubble bath off the verbose child.

Bubbles wiped off the small body with a warm wet washcloth, bubbles sliding slowly down the drain, bubbles in her head, and she couldn't explain what she was feeling. Autopilot kicked in as Cat toweled off the little girl. Looking slightly over Jule's shoulder to the left, she talked to the child while drying her off. She waited to allow her eyes to reach the child's body until she was pulling a soft nightgown over the little blond head.

"I'm hungry." Jule stated plainly as Cat pulled the new disposable underpants onto the toddler. "I want to eat. I want to each peaches Mommy."

Cat picked up the little girl and carried her into the bedroom. "I don't think we have any peaches." She turned around to reach the light switch with her left hand before closing the bedroom door behind them. Once the door was firmly closed, she put her daughter down on the floor. "Please play with your toys for just a little bit while I finish getting dressed, okay?"

"No! I want to eat peaches now! Mom-mom-mom." The sound of wailing echoed through Cat's head hurtling small throwing knives at targets placed randomly throughout the front yard. A boy sat in the shadows, tied to the base of the olive tree. He could smell the oil of tiki torches burning nearby but refused to open his eyes and locate them. It didn't matter. He couldn't move. He didn't want to see this. He didn't want to be here. He had given up. He felt the wind of knives move past him as he prayed one would land in his heart. Cat looked down at the child. "I want peaches now!"

"You are just going to have to wait a minute while I put more clothes on." Cat added and removed and added more layers until she satisfied her need to be properly covered, and still comfortably dressed. The child wailed. Tears streamed down her face. The woman's head echoed with thoughts of sadness and anticipation that felt strangely foreign, and yet somehow distantly related. Pulses of pain moved from the nape of her neck, snaking a sharp path through the frontal cortex, landing with piercing heat on her forehead. She placed her hand on her forehead, inhaled, and then moved her fingers through her hair.

"Please. Stop. Crying." The haggard mother begged the little shining demon. "Mommy is moving as fast as I can. Please stop screaming." She knelt down, picked up the child, and reached for the door. "Now, I told you honey. I don't think we have any peaches..." And the wailing resumed, this time with kicking. Cat held the toddler tight against her hip, her right arm like a vice. "Listen kid. You're not going to starve. We will get you some food."

Little fingers reached out in anger for dirty blond hair, tangled from the shower. Cat had not yet had an opportunity to brush her hair. She hadn't even had a chance to shampoo it! Jules little fingers hooked neatly into her half-dreaded tangles, yanking her neck sideways. "Ouch! That hurts Mommy!" The muscles in her arms tightened. *I will not drop my kid. I will not drop my kid. I will not kill my kid. I will not kill my kid.* Tears streamed down Cat's face as she tried to maintain composure. "You have to be nice to me! I'm the one who feeds you!"

"But I Want Peaches!" Insisted the toddler, as she flailed her arms and legs. The young woman carried the screaming demon down an echoing hall of pine in a steel cage. Cold and sharp, feelings eradicated, a fetid mist floated timidly two steps behind, inviting a dark left turn down a path toward painful and gratuitous satisfaction. "Stop it Mommy! You're hurting me!" She loosened her grip, exhaled, freed her hair from the torturous hands of the toddler, and placed her into her booster seat. "Peaches! Peaches Mommy! And cookies!"

The demon continued to hammer out orders as the young woman numbly moved the straps together, snapped the buckle, and placed the food tray atop the booster seat.

Cat left Jule sitting, strapped securely adjacent the dining room table. Wordlessly she walked into the kitchen. Placing both hands on the edge of the counter, she bowed her head and closed her eyes. *Please gods keep me from killing this kid. I love her. I love her. I can't do this alone. Why did he have to be such an asshole? He said he wanted a kid. You don't just get to change your mind.*

A train barreled through a tunnel between her ears causing a loud bellowing noise to drown out all other thought. Screeching brakes triggered spasms of pain that shot from the front of her head into the back, and down her neck, nestled into a hot ball between her shoulders. The sound of someone opening the front door caused her to stand up straight. She inhaled, exhaled, wiped her face with her blouse, and ran her hands down her front in an attempt to convince herself that everything was just fine.

Stepmother moved through the living room landing in the dining room. Placing a handful of shopping bags on the dining room table, she addressed the suddenly distracted child. Jule's face lit up when she saw her Grammy. "Did you bring me cookies?" Stepmother smiled and shook her head.

"No. I bought shoes." The older woman pulled a box out of one of the shopping bags. "See! They're sandals. For my feet." She held them out for the toddler to see. "You wouldn't eat sandals, would you?"

Jule giggled in response. "You're funny Grammy." Cat sighed with relief as the screaming demon was once again transformed into a bubbling brook. Searching through the pantry she tried to find something quick and easy. *Peaches! One last can! Success!* Emptying the serving size can of peaches into a little bowl, she placed the empty can in the sink.

Cat emerged from the kitchen triumphant. "Guess what honey? I was wrong! We did have peaches. One last can. Just for you!" She placed the bowl on the serving tray in front of Jule and sat down at the table next to her. Breathing carefully, she was extra conscious not to show her stepmother any signs that she hadn't been in control of the situation the whole time. She looked across the table of shopping bags at her stepmother. "That's a lot of shoes."

Stepmother got up from the table, grabbing the bags. "Yes. Well, I had better put all this stuff away." She smiled at the mother and daughter as she turned to head through the kitchen into the master bedroom. She paused by the telephone. "Did you know there's a message on the answering machine?"

"But I want cookies!" The shouting returned. The small bowl flew over the side of serving tray, landing sideways on the table next to them. It continued rolling towards the edge of the table, depositing a small lump of peaches. A trail of syrup and juice formed, uncovering the mysteries of the true level of the old house. Cat closed her eyes and bowed her head as she reached out to catch the rolling bowl.

"I hadn't noticed. I will check it after I am done dealing with the demon princess here." Stepmother nodded acknowledgment without slowing her pace out of dodge. The screaming ricocheted along the inside of her skull. Fireworks exploded behind her eyelids. She opened her eyes and saw herself picking up the screaming child, chair and all, and hurtling it across the room. *No. You know better. That won't make her stop crying. She'll only scream louder.*

Cat closed her eyes again, breathing deeply. She scooped the peaches into the bowl and got up from the table. The loud hollow echoes faded into darkness, as a hot dark stench seeped into her chest. Stumbling through the muggy darkness, she found the sink. In a test of faith, she plunged her left hand into a dark hole and discovered a cold metal surface that she hoped was the sink. Following with her right hand, she let go of the bowl, and was pleased when the test was not followed by the sound of anything breaking. *Only silence. The screaming has stopped.*

Cat hesitated, exhaled, and opened her eyes. Out of the corner of her eye, she saw a little boy. Standing quietly, just out of sight, he waited for someone. *Where did you come from?* She blinked. Jule sat in her booster seat, bent over, her cheek neatly glued to the tray with a small puddle of high fructose corn syrup. Cat grabbed a washcloth, rinsed it with warm water, and approached the sleeping demon.

After awakening and subsequently cleaning the child, Jule returned to the rally for peaches. Sitting in their little bedroom, Cat tried to reason with the sleepy child. Jule yelled at her mother, pulling her hair. Cat yelled at her child, shaking her fiercely. The two screamed, cried, and eventually fell asleep in each other's arms. When Cat later awoke with a full bladder, she was slow and careful to remove herself from the dim room without waking Jule.

Chapter 31
At Risk

Cat left the door open a crack, so that light from the hallway peeked in on Jule. *I can't close the door again. With my luck, she will wake up alone and freak out. Then I will have another demon child on my hands. Once a day is more than enough.* She left the bathroom door cracked as well, just in case. After using the bathroom, she glanced into the bedroom. *Yup. Still asleep. I'm sure she'll wake up soon. I better hurry if I want any quiet time to myself.*

Cat tiptoed into the kitchen. She was glad to find that if anyone else was up in the house, they were tucked away in their bedrooms. *I really don't want to have to face my family. I'm not in the mood to get a lecture about why I shouldn't yell at my kid. I know they could hear us. I'm so ashamed. I know I shouldn't yell at my kid. She doesn't know better. I'm supposed to be the grown-up. I should be doing better, but it's really hard.* Her head pounded as she poured a cold cup of coffee into a cup and put it in the microwave. While the coffee was heating up, she pulled a bottle of Tylenol off the shelf and opened it up. *It says take two, so that means I need three. My head hurts so much I can't see straight.*

The microwave beeped and Cat pulled out the hot cup. She added sugar and enough milk to cool it down. Then she swallowed all three pills with a gulp of the warm coffee. The memory of vomiting up handfuls of lithium popped in her head and she choked. *Gawds no. Not now. I don't want to think about that now.* Tears welled up. She turned on the faucet and filled a glass halfway with water. She drank the half glass quickly and put the glass in the sink.

Cat turned the faucet back on and rinsed her hands. She wiped them across her face and tried to gain her composure. *There's no time for that right now. Save it for counseling. You have to keep your brave face on in this house.* She picked up the coffee cup and turned to leave the kitchen. Passing by the answering machine, she noticed the blinking light. *That's right. I'm supposed to check the messages.* She grabbed a pen and pad from the countertop under the phone.

There was only one message on the answering machine. She listened to the message, in disbelief. *It was actually for me!* The voice on the machine introduced themselves as an administrator that helped at-risk youth find jobs. Her head was pounding, and she had to listen to the message a few times to write down all the information. *Well, at least one good thing happened today! I will call them back first thing tomorrow morning!*

The next morning, after feeding Jule and getting her settled down to an episode of Sesame Street, Cat returned her phone message from the prior day. Nervous and excited, she dialed the number on the notepad. A man picked up the phone after just two rings. She introduced herself and thanked him for calling. Someone from an agency had gotten her phone message and forwarded her information to him. He asked her what exactly she was looking for.

Cat talked with the administrator for a while about what

she could do and what she wanted to accomplish. He explained to her that he helped place 'at-risk youth' in jobs. To qualify, she had to be between the ages of eighteen and twenty-two. She got nervous. Her birthday was next week, and she would be turning 23.

"Well, let's hurry up and get you started before your birthday then!" The administrator responded. "I think I have the perfect job for you. Training starts Monday. Do you think you can make it into the office today to complete the necessary paperwork?"

Cat agreed right away. "Absolutely! But" she paused before continuing, "I'm not sure if I can find a babysitter with such short notice." She didn't know what her stepmother had planned for the day and didn't want to take the chance of losing the opportunity. "Would this be a job interview? Or just paperwork? If it's just paperwork, is it okay if I have my daughter with me?"

"Well, I can't hire you sight unseen. Typically, there is somewhat of an interview." The administrator responded. "However, given our timeline, and the circumstances, I believe we can make this work." He assured Cat that part of what qualified her as 'at-risk' was her status as a single mother. "If you have to bring your daughter, then I will be delighted to meet her."

Cat wrote down the address and confirmed her afternoon appointment time with the administrator before hanging up the phone. She refilled her coffee cup and checked on Jule in the living room. *Still just fine.* Jule was singing and dancing with the Muppets on the screen. "Mom's gonna step out into the back yard, okay honey?"

"Okay Mommy." The little girl responded. "I'm watching Elmo!"

"Okay Julie. You know where I will be. If you need me before I come back in, just come to the back door and I will see you, okay?" Cat reminded her daughter before stepping onto the back porch.

Cat sat down on the back porch so that she could see the back door from an angle. The partial privacy was just enough to make her feel better about lighting a cigarette. *I don't want her to see me smoking.* She was excited. She was nervous. She wasn't sure, but thought perhaps, maybe even happy? *Everything will be okay. I can do this. I can.*

Cat sipped her coffee while she smoked. After finishing her coffee, she lit another smoke and got up. Pacing the back yard, she finished the second smoke before going back into the house. Opening up the back door, she called out to her daughter. "Jule honey, you doing okay?"

"Yes Mommy!" Jule responded from the living room. Cat entered the living room to see that the program had changed. "This is my favorite Mommy! It's Between the Lions!"

Cat sat down to see what it was all about. She was not familiar with the show and wanted to know whether it was appropriate. Within five minutes of watching the show with Jule, she was already impressed. It was all about books and reading! *Makes me think of that Prince song my mom always liked. "Don't let your children watch television until they know how to read, or else all they'll know how to do is cuss fight and breed."* Well, if *this show is going to help her learn how to read, then I'm all for it!*

"Well honey. I think this is my new favorite show too!" Cat told her jubilant daughter. "Are you hungry? Do you want a snack?"

"Juice Mommy!" Jule responded, and then added, "Pleeeease."

"Of course, Julie." Cat got up and went to the kitchen. She returned and handed her daughter a juice pouch with a tiny yellow straw poking out. "Thank you for your good manners. It makes Mommy feel good."

Monday morning, Cat had to get ready and get out the door before Jule was ready for her to leave. Jule was outraged that they would not be participating in their normal morning routine. She was used to her mom always being around and she made it clear that she was unhappy about her mother's change in behavior.

Stepmother was up and ready. "Don't worry Firecat. She will be fine. She will get over it." She addressed the crying child throwing a temper tantrum at the dining room table. "Don't worry Julie. We are going to have a great day together! But we have to let Mommy go to work!"

She waved at Cat to hurry out the door. "Go on. It's fine. The sooner you leave, the sooner I can get her to settle down about it."

Cat was extraordinarily thankful as she drove up the street in the truck. With the administrator's help, she was able to get a job working as a participant in the program on a three-month temporary assignment. It would be like a probationary period. Then, assuming all went well, she could apply for a permanent position with the agency. It was another phone center, but this time it was an in-bound center, so she wouldn't have to call anyone.

Cat spent the first two weeks in training. It was Monday through Friday, forty hours per week. She had never had a full-time job and was surprised at how exhausted she was by the end of the week. *And this is just training! I wonder if it will be harder or easier once I am actually on the phone center floor.*

The two weeks of training flew by. Cat felt confident that she understood the database system they would be using. She had never used a database system like this before, but it seems supremely simple, and she wondered why they needed two weeks of training. *I could have started taking calls after just one week of this training, but if they want to pay me to sit here through another week of training, so be it.* She was surprised at how many people in the training class had a hard time learning the system.

Working in another phone center was less challenging that starting something entirely new. However, Cat would no longer have to call people and harass them. Plus, she would be selling tickets to live events. *People will be calling for something that they want. So, I don't have to talk them into buying something they don't want!* As an active phone representative, she quickly learned that just because it was inbound, didn't guarantee the customers would be any nicer to her than at the dating agency.

Cat thought she was prepared. She understood the database well enough. Still, she wasn't quick enough with her calls and had a hard time when customers wanted to pick and choose their assigned seating. She got easily frustrated when customers were rude to her. It took some time and practice. Her performance continually improved and when her temp assignment ended, they were happy to move her into a permanent position.

The phone center had to always be populated, so phone reps had to sign up in advance for their breaks. She got two ten-minute breaks and one-half hour lunch with each 8-hour shift. Hanging out for ten minutes in the break room was a lonely experience. Soon she realized that the break room was empty because everyone was downstairs smoking. Making her way downstairs, she got a chance to actually talk with her new co-workers while they too were smoking. *Reminds me of high school, hanging out on the steps at the University.*

Cat was thrilled about her progress. She didn't love her job, but she could handle it. Being able to take care of her own finances nurtured her confidence. She started to look for childcare for her daughter. Working full time was going to be too much for her stepmother to take care of Jule all the time. Plus, she was a rambunctious toddler. She wanted to play with other kids. Cat visited a few different childcare centers and found one near the house. *That way, if for some reason I need my parents to pick her up for me, it will be easier on them.*

The childcare center was a wonderful place. The staff took great care of the kids, and Jule thrived. She got along with the other kids, and the teachers loved her.

She was so smart! At two and a half years old, she was already having in-depth conversations with the teachers. She did well with toilet training. She listened and cooperated and was fully engaged in her learning experience. It would take a large portion of her paychecks to cover the cost, but Cat felt it was worth it. *My baby girl is doing wonderful because of her time at the center. I get to go to work like a real adult. When I have time off, I can actually do things with Jule and I don't have to ask my father to buy things that we need. I can just go get them myself!*

Dad had been letting Cat use Big Red for the better part of a year. He decided to give her the truck. It had almost three hundred thousand miles on the motor and it gave him a good excuse to buy himself a newer car. He told his daughter, "You use it all the time now. So, it really seems more yours than mine at this point."

Cat was appreciative. She had grown to really enjoy driving Big Red. She didn't feel bad about her father simply 'giving her the truck.' *I've spent almost $2000 on repairs and new tires, so I figure I've pretty well paid for the truck by this point anyway.* She told her father "thank you for helping me so much."

Chapter 32
Perfume

At twenty-three years old, Cat had a regular full-time job, her own vehicle, and her daughter was in school. She knew that she had made a lot of progress. She knew that her father was proud of the changes she had made. Stepmother was very supportive. Still, she missed her own mother. She savored memories from when she was younger and had gotten along better with her mother. *I will write her a letter! I want Mom to know that I've cleaned up my life. I want her to know that I'm not on drugs, or in an abusive relationship. I want her to be proud of me for trying so hard to be a good parent.*

Cat wrote a long letter about some of the progress she had been making in counseling. She shared with her mother some of the insight she had been gaining. She remembered how much her mother had enjoyed exchanging letters with other people and looked forward to a response. She did not wait to receive a response before writing and mailing a second letter. She mailed the third letter and received her first response in the mailbox the following day.

Mother did not respond the way Cat had hoped. Within the envelope she found a long response to the first letter. Instead of commending her daughter for the progress, or even recognizing that she was accomplishing important life goals, she put her daughter down. Cat decided not to compose another letter right away. Her feelings were hurt. *Maybe she hadn't gotten the other letters when she wrote this. Maybe when she reads the other letters, she will understand better.* Her hopes were not fulfilled. The second response letter was more painful than the first. When the third letter arrived from her mother, she almost didn't want to open it.

When Cat finally opened the third letter from her mother, she gave up. Mom had decided that Cat had turned into a 'young Republican Nazi' and didn't want to have anything to do with her. She feared that Cat would 'turn her into the police' and 'have her little brother taken away.' The last letter Cat received disowned her. Tears ran down her cheeks as she read the words, 'Do not attempt to contact me again.' She did not write or receive a fourth letter.

Cat cried a lot in counseling over the loss of her mother. She had been so important to Cat when she was younger. "I just want her to meet Jule." She explained to her counselor, "If she could meet her granddaughter, she would be able to see that I am doing good, that I am not a bad person."

Falling into a regular pattern of adulthood sort of happened without Cat realizing it. In some ways, she was acting with intention. She wanted to be a good parent. She wanted to be happy, to feel secure. She knew that children thrive on consistency. They learn about the world through repetition. She felt compelled to do her very best to provide everything she could for her daughter. Still, she wasn't trying to be *an adult* as much as she was trying to be a responsible parent.

Cat took care of her daughter. She took her to school. She went to work. Developing friendships with co-workers on breaks and during lunch, she began to heal from her relationship with Doug. Success in the workplace propelled her through each day at a lightening pace. At the end of each day, she picked up Jule from day care. Since the whole family was now on the same schedule, evenings were spent having dinner with Dad, Stepmother, and Little Sister.

Each night, Cat retired to the small bedroom that she had crammed with all their belongings. Cat was haunted with memories of so many nights she had spent in that room over the years. The bad decisions she had made in the past hung in the shadows like ghosts. She couldn't really make them out, but she knew there was something there. She knew that she had to work really hard to provide a good life for her daughter, to protect her from the pain of abandonment. Trying to compensate for the absence of a father, Cat tried to be her "whole" parent, not just a mother.

Cat hadn't kept up with the friendships she developed at the dating service, nor had she gotten in touch with Carrie or Katie. Still, she missed being social. She expressed an interest in going out for 'my' time. Her parents had agreed to babysit Jule in the evening, so that Cat could 'go out.' After the family dinner routine, she got all dolled up. Trying to make herself pretty, she did her hair and put on makeup. She was not satisfied with her reflection. *It doesn't look like me.* She tried to ignore the fact that she didn't recognize the person in the mirror and instead focused on making her reflection match what she thought "attractive" might look like to someone else.

Leaving Jule at home with her family, Cat headed out in truck. Driving around, she looked for places she might feel comfortable going out by herself. The first evening out, she drove to Berkeley. Parking next to People's Park, she walked down to Telegraph Avenue. Looking down and avoiding the gaze of people that she recognized from her past, she was relieved when they didn't see her. Walking the four blocks between Dwight and the UC Berkeley Campus, she peered into store fronts. Looking for people that she would actually want to see, she visited places that had been meeting points for her younger self.

So many places had changed, but the people appeared to be just as destitute as they had always been. Cat no longer viewed them as novelty 'street corner poets.' Revisiting her past on Telegraph only reinforced the compulsion for her to move on. Getting a coffee at the Cafe' Med, she sat on the balcony, watching the door and sketching as she drank her coffee. Half hoping that Mike would walk in the door at any time, she wondered what he would think of her as a parent. *Have I grown up to be what he had imagined?* When she reached the bottom of the glass, she packed up her things and returned to driving the truck around.

Next time she got an evening out, Cat tried finding a place to go, that was closer to home. She had heard of a couple of different night spots in Concord. Driving around for a while, she passed by places that looked popular. There were several vehicles in the parking lots.

Driving past them, she contemplated stopping and going in. Eventually, she settled on taking herself out to a restaurant where she could get a coffee.

Sitting, drinking coffee, she observed people as they entered in groups. Writing and sketching in her notebook, she wondered what she needed to do, to be like that. *I appreciate the support that my family provides, but without a social network, without friends, I still feel alone.* Listening to people laughing with each other made her sad. *Something is wrong with me.* Old tapes played back in her head. *Something must be really wrong with me, or I wouldn't be alone.* Not yet strong enough to erase the old tapes looping in her head, she finished her cup of coffee, left money on the table, and resigned herself to returning to her child and their little bedroom world.

Crying herself to sleep at night, Cat continued to question herself. She was going through the motions. She was trying to be a strong person. Still, she felt weak. She felt fake. *I feel like something is terribly wrong with me.* She couldn't seem to identify the source of her misery. The idea of trying to make new friends was an intimidating prospect. She wanted people to be close to her, and yet she was always terrified that as people got to know her, they would just think she was crazy.

The next couple of evenings that Cat attempted to 'go out,' she tried to plan ahead. She spent time looking up where there would be live music. She brought enough money for her to pay a cover and buy a couple of drinks. She drove directly to the nightclub where a band was scheduled to be performing. When she arrived, Cat sat in her truck. Smoking with the window down, she listened to the radio. Talking to herself, she tried to motivate. *After this cigarette, I will get out of the truck and walk to the front door of the club.* But it didn't work. She kept putting it off, playing with the radio, and checking her reflection in the rear-view mirror. Terrified of walking into a crowd of people she didn't know, she was paralyzed. After spending about an hour sitting in the parking lot, she turned the truck back on and drove home.

Days flowed into weeks, and before she knew it, Cat had been working as a telephone representative for a whole year. Promotions and other internal positions were posted in the break room for everyone to see. Usually only the phone reps were hired fresh. Most other positions, they tried to fill internally, giving experienced telephone representatives the opportunity to advance. Cat was urged by her supervisor to watch the board for postings.

When the position of Assistant Teamleader opened up and was posted in the break room, several of her co-workers encouraged her to apply. If she got the position, it would continue to provide a regular schedule, plus there would be benefits. *That would help a lot.* She felt like she had been at her Dad's house too long. *I want to have a place of my own. The support of family has been wonderful, but I really need to be on my own, to have my own space, my own living room, my own kitchen.*

Cat was nervous about applying for the new job and even more nervous when she was scheduled for an interview. The process terrified her. She was afraid of rejection. She brought her fears up in counseling. Her counselor helped her talk through the anxiety, suggesting that she 'approach the interview as a chance to show her initiative at work.' When the day of her interview arrived, Cat was still incredibly nervous. Her anxiety was blatantly obvious in the interview. Once the interview was over, she stopped being nervous. *Thank God it's over. Now I can go back to what I know.* She returned to the phone center and the task of attending to the queue.

A couple of days later, Cat was offered the position of Assistant Teamleader! She was astounded. *I succeeded! I applied, interviewed, and I really got the job! Now I can start looking for my own place!* Cat was scheduled to transition into the new position the following week. She met with the Human Resources Rep and filled out the appropriate paperwork for her benefits. Her co-workers showed that they were proud of her. The gal whom she would be working underneath was really nice. Her encouragement helped Cat to feel valued. She went home and gloated to her family. Dad didn't seem all that impressed.

Disappointed by her father's lack of enthusiasm, Cat tried to dismiss her feelings of frustration. *I want him to be proud of me. I'm still living in a tiny room in his house with my daughter. He still sees me as a dependent child. But I am not a child. I have to prove myself if he is ever going to believe in me.* The rest of her family showed a little enthusiasm, but the conversation didn't last long. *I am still pleased with myself, and that should be enough.* She wanted to feel good about herself. She recognized that building her self-confidence seemed to be directly tied to her ability to accomplish the goals that she had set for herself.

Despite her best efforts, her father's response did cause Cat to question herself. *What exactly am I trying to accomplish? I know that I want to be a good parent. I know that I want to be a solid provider, a stone foundation for the life that I share with my growing daughter. I know that I still feel lonely, and I want people to love me for who I am.* She looked in the mirror and she still didn't feel love for herself. But she was trying. She decided that it was an issue of mind over matter. She mattered, and she would have to dig into the depths of her mind and convince herself that this was true.

With Cat's new position at work, she actively began creating a new routine. Every morning when she was in the bathroom getting ready for work, she looked in the mirror and talked to herself. "You are strong. You are beautiful. You matter." She spoke to her reflection. *If I repeat this practice every day, perhaps I will begin to believe the words.* She began changing all her passwords at work to "strong", so that she would reinforce the concept several times per day.

With the new job, she did get a regular schedule. As a Telephone Representative, her schedule had fluctuated somewhat from week to week. As an Assistant Teamleader, she had Fridays and Saturdays off. This worked out alright for her. Jule was in school Monday through Friday and spent Sundays with the family. That meant that every week Cat would have a day for herself while her daughter was in school. Fridays she could spend running errands, or working on projects, or just spend time doing things for herself. Saturdays she got to spend doing things with her daughter, just the two of them together.

Dad pointed out that while Cat was working hard, she was still 'being irresponsible with her money.' After bills were paid, she was still spending money on 'things she didn't need.' Cat was taken aback. *I really enjoy being able to do things with my daughter.* Always the practical one, Dad reminded her that she would be happier when she was able to have her own place. If she was ever going to reach that goal, she needed to practice more responsible spending and saving. *Why can't he just be happy for me?* She avoided speaking with him further about money or what she was doing with her extra time.

Cat began to develop friendships at work that extended past the workplace. She started hanging out with her new friends after work. A younger gal, Melissa, began working in the phone center. She lived with her Dad. She had masculine qualities to her personality, and Cat got along with her well. Melissa seemed to really enjoy hanging out with her and Jule. Sometimes, after work she would pick up Jule from school and go spend the evening with Melissa, instead of with her family.

Melissa was an intriguing young woman. She loved working on cars. She kept auto parts and tools in her closet the way other girls kept extra pairs of shoes. She took pride in the fact that she had managed to convince her high school to let her play football. Being the only girl on the Junior Varsity team, she had made the newspaper. She had won the respect of her teammates and played a good game. Melissa's Dad seemed proud of his daughter's individuality. Cat was always polite to him, and although she didn't exactly feel comfortable opening up to him, she didn't feel like she needed to pretend either. Better still, he seemed absolutely thrilled to see Jule every time they arrived.

Cat found herself attracted to Melissa's personality. She was careful not to flirt with Melissa, and terrified of ruining a good thing, she didn't dare mention to Melissa that she was attracted to women. She never made a move or sound that might give her secret away. She really enjoyed and appreciated their friendship and more than anything, Cat didn't want Melissa to be uncomfortable around her.

Through Melissa, Cat and her daughter began being social with other people as well. Melissa introduced her to new people and Cat slowly started feeling a little more confident being social. Mostly they were social with other guys. Similar to her, Melissa seemed more comfortable being social with the men. She liked being around feminine girls but didn't seek out relationships with them. This similarity was interesting to both of them, and they discussed with each other, how uncommon it was for them to bond with other females. As their bond grew stronger, they carefully expressed to one another how much they appreciated each other's friendship.

Things went well for a several months, until Melissa's boyfriend returned from service. Cat thought it was strange that Melissa had not mentioned him much until right before he returned. Then, it seemed like all of a sudden, he was all she talked about. Melissa became absorbed. Spending all her non-working hours with her boyfriend, she backed off from spending time with Cat.

When Christmas came, Melissa bought Cat a bottle of expensive perfume. *Nobody has ever done something like that for me before.* Cat was surprised and a little embarrassed. *I didn't buy her an expensive present!* She started wearing the scent frequently. It made her happy because it reminded her that someone really appreciated her.

Melissa missed hanging out with Cat. The year passed quickly for Cat as she focused primarily on parenting, working and saving money. A few times, Melissa tried to invite Cat to join her and her boyfriend when the two of them had already made plans. *This feels awkward. I don't want to intrude.* While it seemed that Melissa was trying to include her, and her boyfriend didn't seem put off by her presence, Cat felt uncomfortable. *I feel like a third wheel.*

Melissa decided that she would make it work. Of course, she liked hanging out with her boyfriend, but she didn't want to just be romantic all the time. She wanted to be social too. She insisted that they 'had to hang out' on New Year's Eve. Cat's parents agreed to babysit, so Cat didn't have a reason to back out. Melissa found a blind date for Cat, and insisted it was 'going to be great!'

Melissa was enthusiastic. "I miss hanging out with you! If this goes well, and y'all get along, then the four of us can makes plans and go out together as a group!" She added, "And nobody will be lonely!"

When New Year's Eve arrived, Cat got especially dolled up. She wore a classic little black dress and gold hoop earrings. She painted her face and coated thick red lipstick on her lips. She felt like she was in drag. *It doesn't look like me. But I do look good!* She finished off the outfit with a spritz of the perfume Melissa had given her for Christmas. When she arrived at Melissa's apartment, her friend was overjoyed to see her and greeted her with a big hug.

The evening was enjoyable enough, but Cat drank entirely too much. Conducting herself in a manner that was irresponsible and not at all nurturing, she fell back into behavior patterns that were easy. She had fun, sort-of, but really, was uncomfortable. It became clear she did not have much in common with her date. He was in the military with Melissa's boyfriend and their personalities were not a good match. Still, Cat tried to make the best of it.

When Cat returned home the next morning, her head pounded, and stomach twisted with a bad hangover. Spending the better part of the day recovering, she took it easy in the little bedroom. Her daughter watched Sesame Street at the foot of the bed while Cat napped off and on. Jule made sure to get her mother's attention whenever she needed anything. Lying in bed, Cat questioned whether she was making progress or not. She was confused by her inability to connect to the people she found physically attractive and her attraction to people with whom she did not want to be romantic.

Chapter 33
Rejection

There was a manager at work that Cat was always interested in talking with. The woman seemed confident and self-assured. Cat suspected she was gay and found out after a while that she did, in fact have a female partner with whom she shared a home. She was a little older than Cat. *She is beautiful and friendly.* Cat began flirting with her casually, making jokes to ensure that nobody took her seriously.

Cat wanted so badly to be recognized by someone who was not straight. She wanted to know where she could meet other women and she was terrified of asking. So, she stayed safe by keeping it casual, in the workplace. She never actually came out and said that she was gay. She never made advances to try and be social outside the workplace with the woman. Instead, she asked questions about where she and her partner went out.

Cat never actually tried to go to those places. She wanted to be seen, and still, she was terrified to be seen. As the new year progressed Cat began refocusing on self-improvement. *I want to lose weight. I want to feel good about myself. I need to save more money.* Between her social habits and her work schedule, the amount of time that she spent sharing meals with the family had dramatically decreased. She began eating alone with her daughter more often. Cat struggled, trying hard to get her daughter to eat.

When it was just the two of them, Jule didn't seem all that

interested in food and she began to get worried about her daughter's health. The child was so much smaller than her classmates. Cat was scared that it was because she wasn't eating enough. Additionally, Cat was trying to stretch dollars. *Dad said I need to save money. And if I ever want to get us our own place, then I have to save a lot. So, I have to stop buying lunch.*

Cat didn't like being hungry all the time. She didn't want to spend so much money on food. Also, she was starting to hurt at work. She had to push herself harder to succeed at everything. So, she began taking diet pills. They gave Cat extra energy. She rationalized, to avoid feelings of failure. *This isn't the same as messing with powders, the way I did when I was younger. First of all, this is legal. Furthermore, this enables me to budget money. I don't need to buy as many groceries with a smaller appetite.* She prepared food for her daughter and she tried her best to get Jule to eat. Then, Cat would eat whatever was left over, after her daughter refused to eat anymore.

Doing this for a couple of months began to take its toll on Cat's sanity. Her emotional roller coaster became more vigorous. She was having a challenging time handling stress. Cat's co-workers began expressing their concern for her. *I'm losing weight though!* She liked that she was getting thinner, so she continued to rationalize the behavior patterns. When she got down to one hundred twenty-five pounds, Cat went out and bought herself some new clothes.

Cat tried making friends at work with a couple of guys who struck her as feminine. One fellow was of particular interest to her. She recognized his name from somewhere. She couldn't place exactly where. After a while she figured it out. *This was the one and only guy I danced with at a middle school dance.* When they began talking, they each had their own unique memory of the event, which contrasted each other drastically. He had thought she had been "a real bitch to him at school when she saw him after the dance."

Cat's friends had told her that "he had asked many girls to dance with him," and therefore she reacted to the event as if she had been the butt of some kind of joke. *Just a number, a tally in his hat.* She had shown him the cold shoulder thereafter. In reality, both of them had struggled with making friends in their own unique ways.

The two old schoolmates began talking on breaks, and after sticking her neck out, Cat managed to get him to make social plans with her outside of work. They went to a movie. They went out to lunch. They even made plans to go to a carnival together. As she talked with him, she had contradicting feelings. There was something about him that felt gay to her. She found him attractive. He was not attracted to her, relating to her as a platonic friend. She pushed the limit a little, trying to flirt with him and this pushed him away. After that, they stopped hanging out.

Another fellow who was also an Assistant Teamleader struck her in a similar a manner. They also seemed to have some things in common. She found something about him attractive and wanted to get to know him better. This took a lot of effort. Again, she risked the possibility of rejection, trying to make plans with him. Again, she read him as gay, and he related to her as a platonic friend. Hanging out with him, she was able to forget about her femaleness and just be a person. After hanging out a couple of times, she made advances towards him. He abruptly stopped being available for social plans with her.

These two failures led her to question herself again. Cat looked in the mirror and saw a thin young woman. It was a was pretty enough reflection. *But it's not me. I don't understand.* She tried to see herself in the mirror, and when she failed to be happy with the image before her, she returned to the mantra, "I am strong. I am beautiful. I matter." Continuing to pour herself into her work, she pushed too hard.

Returning to her Dad's house with Jule in the evenings was beginning to feel like defeat. She laid on the pallet of blankets at night drifting in and out of consciousness. Cat was unhappy about so much. She tried to remember a time when she had been happy.

> As an adolescent, living alone with Dad and his girlfriend, I looked forward to visits with my Mama. The visits were sporadic. Mama's addiction and life stresses put her in a state she didn't want me to see. Gaping holes filled in the gaps between visits. This made every visit an extra special treat. Mama made sure to put her best foot forward whenever I was visiting. I got to experience the very best of her, and subsequently put her on a pedestal. Shining and golden, I viewed her as some kind of guru. I could say

anything, ask her anything. She seemed to have some kind of mystical answer to just about everything.

I enjoyed the talks we had in Mama's studio. I remember bringing in a plate of peanut butter and jelly sandwiches. Settling down in an armchair, I'd hold the plate on top of my lap and ask Mama if she'd like a sandwich. Mama always stayed focused on her painting. Without showing any visible changes in her physical attention, her voice would address me and then I'd know it was okay to start talking. While I watched Mama's hand dart back and forth between easel and palette, our conversations provided me the opportunity to talk about things that I couldn't talk about at home with Dad.

I told her how awkward I felt in my body. I've never been happy about my shape, and it especially bothered me as I developed and grew. I told her that I didn't like my body. "Nothing feels right." She knew I felt uneasy, and she wanted me to feel good about myself. She stressed the importance of loving oneself. I remember her telling me "Your body is your temple. It is a beautiful thing to be a woman, a blessing from the goddess." She strove to instill a healthy self-esteem in me. Where did it go wrong?

It was nice to get the attention, and I always looked forward to our talks. But it hurt. My legs would go numb. I remember leaving my body, floating above *the scene. Like fresh air, the freedom from my body brought a sense of relief.*

I saw a little girl wringing her hands and pulling on her own hair. She didn't look very happy. Observing the scene from above, I recognized that my mother loved me very much. Feeling a sense of duty to stay I lingered in a fog of thoughts. I knew I needed to live up to her expectations because she loved me so much. I wanted to be accepted.

Cat began experiencing pains in her hands and wrists. All the typing at work was beginning to take its toll. Writing was becoming harder for her as well. Still, she pressed on. Just a few months of diet pills had dragged her body and mind through the ringer, and she was crashing hard. Her Teamleader and work-friends were truly concerned and decided it was time for an intervention. They convinced her to stop taking the pills and insisted she throw what she had left. She was warned that if they ever caught her taking them again, she was going to 'get her ass kicked.'

Replacing the diet pills with ibuprofen, she continued the habit of frequently popping pills instead of eating properly. One of her co-workers noticed her taking pills and gave her a hard time. "I thought you said you were done with diet pills?" She responded defensively that they were not diet pills, but painkillers, showing them the bottle.

Cat's Teamleader was alerted and came around to her

desk. She was concerned with the frequency with which Cat was taking the pills. She was nearly in tears because her hands hurt so much. *I want to be strong. I have to be strong, and push through the pain. This is just a little thing, and I can overcome it.* Cat saw her hand and wrist pain as an example of weakness. She was ashamed of her weaknesses and wanted to be perceived as strong and capable. Cat's Teamleader insisted, "No. This is not okay." She reported Cat to Human Resources. Dragging her into a meeting with HR, Cat was forced to complete a work injury report.

When asked how long it had been going on, she couldn't provide an exact date. They were not happy with her. "You are supposed to report this sort of thing right away!" *I feel like a failure. But it hurts so bad, I just can't hide it anymore!* Sending her to one of their Workers Compensation doctors, it was determined that Cat had Tendinitis in both of her hands and wrists. The doctor told her that she would need to attend physical therapy three days per week, during work hours. Leaving the phone center for her appointments, she drove across town and underwent the prescribed therapy for six months. She had to wear braces all the time at first. As she healed, the amount of time she needed to wear the braces decreased. Eventually, after about six months of therapy, Cat finally reached her goal of being pain-free.

As the year progressed, and Cat's social life devolved into a series of failed attempts at connection. She began running away. Picking her daughter up from school on Thursday afternoon, she'd discreetly inform the school that Jule would not be attending the following day. Then, as she buckled the little girl into her car seat, she would excitedly say, "Guess what? We're going on an adventure!" and take her for an overnight road trip. With all the extra things they would need already packed in the back of the truck, it was easy to play hooky from the "real world." Cat looked over at the toddler asleep in her car seat. "I love you little girl."

Some weekends Cat and Jule would travel north, sometimes they'd go south. Camping in the back of the truck, they enjoyed the short adventures. The young mother made the most out of every moment spent with her daughter and the little girl seemed to flourish in the sunlight of her mother's love. Several times, Cat drove up to Mendocino and visited the redwoods that had brought her peace in the past.

Jule never fussed about riding in the truck with her mother. Staring out the window, she'd soon fall asleep from the rhythm of the wheels on the road. Cat would have to wake her up when they'd stop somewhere for dinner. Enjoying her time with her daughter, she treated it like a date with a good friend. *This is a very special time I get to spend. She is only going to be small for a little while.*

Cat's thoughts strayed to memories of her own childhood. She remembered her mother being sad when she wasn't little anymore. *She wanted me to adore her, and I just wanted to go do something else. But for now, it's just the two of us. I wonder what it would be like to share this experience with a second parent.* She dismissed the thought quickly. *I love laughing with her and playing with her. I'm not sure I want to have to share this with anyone else!* After dinner, she would continue driving, singing along with the radio and talking to Jule as she fell asleep in her car seat.

Eventually, Cat reached a place where she could pull over under a tree and park without being bothered overnight. The back of the truck was like a home away from home. Arranged like a little bedroom, there was an air mattress, several blankets, a milk crate full of clothes and pull-ups for Jule, another milk crate full of snacks and non-perishable foods, and a bag of art supplies and various personal items for herself. She had tools, rags, jugs of water, and jumper cables. She even carried a portable training toilet.

Crawling into the back of the truck, Cat readied the bed for the two of them. Returning to the cab of the truck, she'd carefully remove Jule from the car seat, and slip into the back of the truck, snuggling Jule in her arms. When morning broke, the little girl would wake up amazed at being in a new place. The two shared their morning routine in the back of the truck, with breakfast snacks and getting dressed. Then, Cat would drive to whatever Saturday destination she had planned.

Saturdays consisted of exploring a beach, or hiking in the woods, or playing at the river. Jule would start to fade as the afternoon waned and Cat would begin packing things up. Driving back to Walnut Creek, her daughter would again fall asleep to the rhythm of the road and the sound of her mother singing with the radio.

After spending two days playing hooky from the daily grind, Cat never looked forward to returning to pattern of the workweek. *I just want to run away and live like this forever.* She remembered being younger and promising herself that if she ever had children, she would want to do so alone. The idea of fighting with someone over child rearing decisions seemed like a potential burden in her mind. *I don't need or want someone second guessing my decisions.* The bonding between Cat and her daughter felt more important than any other kind of love relationship. *Still... Wouldn't it be great? A school bus converted into a house, parked somewhere in the woods... A bunch of hippies sitting around the fire pit making dinner, while their children were running around playing in the dirt together. I wouldn't be alone, and we would have family.*

She tried to eradicate the daydream of alternative living, but it remained hovering in the background of her mind. Cat focused on the road. *Submitting to the societal structure of child rearing feels like a spiral path into misery. But I want to be a good parent.* She looked over at her daughter sleeping in the car seat. *There has got to be some happy medium, some kind of compromise. At least we have the weekends.*

Every time she went to visit her godmother by the river or old friends in Mendocino, she spent hours walking through the woods and relaxing in the slow pace of rural community. Exploring the prospects of moving away from the city, she picked up local newspapers on their weekend trips. She desperately wanted to find a way to get out of the city. Dependency on the urban economic structure made her feel trapped. She felt like the city had rejected her and she had come to the conclusion that the feeling was mutual.

Chapter 34
Sweet Acceptance

Cat continued to make occasional trips to Berkeley. Something inside her hoped that she might accidentally run into her mother, or possibly would see someone who may have seen or heard from her. She knew that Mama wouldn't speak to her. *But I really want her to meet her granddaughter.* She thought that if Mama met Jule, then she would surely fall in love with her grandchild. *I want her to see that I'm doing well and take me back. I want my mother to love me again.* Searching for news of her, Cat kept her eyes open for anyone that also knew her mother.

Sitting on the Avenue behind a table covered with jewelry, Tam sat twisting wire with pliers. Unlike others along the street, Tam recognized her right away. Clearly glad to see her, he put down his handiwork and emerged to offer a big hug. Cat remembered Tam as "the guy with the school bus". He'd parked his bus in the driveway at the Oasis. He had treated her like a teenager when she was only 12 and gotten in trouble with Mama for getting her drunk. Now, he casually flirted with the young woman, commenting on how beautifully she'd grown up. Tam invited her to come sit behind the table. Pulling the stroller behind the table, Jule was given full stage for attention.

Sitting at the jewelry table, Cat reminisced about a world from which she had removed herself. Tam talked to her daughter and she was well received by everyone who came by the stand. The longer Cat sat and visited with Tam the more old faces would appear. Different people would walk by or arrive by bicycle. Each person stayed for a couple of minutes visiting. Each reinforced their pleasure at seeing her as a healthy beautiful woman. It felt good to be remembered and perceived positively. Driving home, her daughter fell asleep in her car seat and she was left alone with her thoughts.

Completely confused, Cat tried to understand why she was so unhappy? *I could feel the acceptance from people. They were happy to see me, telling me how beautiful a woman I am. So why do I feel so terrible in my body? I want so badly to feel good. Why can I not seem to absorb this positive reinforcement that is so freely given? Maybe it's not that at all. Maybe I am just misinterpreting my unhappiness. Maybe I'm just disappointed because nobody had news of my mother. I must just be missing my mom.*

Cat tried to picture her mother sitting in her studio, painting and sharing tea and toast with her. Instead, the memory of her angry mother shouting at her, before she left Lawton popped in her head. *"You are a hateful manipulative person. You destroy everything you touch. And you are going to keep failing as long as you keep running."* She blinked, as tears began to stream down her face. "No." Cat whispered to herself. "I am not running. I am moving forward." She tried to wipe the painful memory away as she focused on driving back to Walnut Creek.

On the days when Cat was scheduled for a later shift, she began going out to Berkeley in the morning for breakfast, after taking Jule to school. She'd stop by the stand when Tam was setting up and offer a helping hand. Already dressed in her work clothes, Cat blushed as she received comments about being a sexy businesswoman. They made her feel a little uncomfortable. Still, she liked the attention. Cat got to meet Tam's girlfriend, Allie. The three would all sit and have coffee together at the stand for a little while before Cat politely excused herself to go to work.

As her visits became more frequent, she began developing a friendship with Allie. Cat flirted with her and Allie responded warmly. The two women openly joked with Tam, that Cat "only came to visit his beautiful girlfriend." All three of them interacted comfortably and naturally. Cat learned that Tam and Allie were actually staying in Contra Costa County as well. After several failed attempts to coordinate schedules, she began occasionally visiting them at home in the evenings.

Tam and Allie shared a relationship that was somewhat 'open.' The three adults openly discussed the natural attraction that Cat and Allie were experiencing, and Tam did not feel threatened by it. He was supportive. He began calling Cat on the phone, to invite her. "Allie wants to spend time with you. You should come over for tea. I think she is too embarrassed to call you herself. I won't tell her you're coming over. It will be a surprise!" Allie was always glad when Cat showed up to visit.

When the two women were intimate, they communicated in a way that felt natural. Mutually enjoying the beauty and divinity of one another, their sexuality was fluid and seemed to break the rules of gender expectations. Driving home Cat was glowing. *When we are that close, I feel like I can really absorb the moment. I could really feel the beauty that Allie sees in me. It doesn't make me feel any more or any less like a woman. I just feel loved.* Cat grinned and sang along with the radio as she drove home. For just a little while, she felt happiness in every part of her body. *I want to feel this good all the time.*

Between working, weekend trips, and social time, Cat spent less and less time at home with her family. The independence was uplifting. She began to feel a little hopeful of what her future might bring. *I am okay. At least, I know I am going to be okay. I feel like I am control of my life.* She was thin, sexy, and independent. She was finally developing a network of friends with whom she could be herself. She was taking care of her daughter, providing a consistent schedule while including Jule in her social life.

Katie left her abusive husband and moved into a place in West Berkeley with a new boyfriend. Together they shared an apartment that was positioned just a few blocks away from the old Oasis household. She held onto fond memories of spending time with Cat at the Oasis. *Her mother had been so crazy cool! It's too bad they had to move away. It would be so cool if they still lived right around the corner!* She didn't worry too much though. Her bond with Cat was so strong. Despite long periods of absence, their lives always seemed to reconnect at just the right time. Now, while her boyfriend was at work all day, she got a little stir crazy taking care of his little girl. *I always wanted to be a mommy. Now I'm getting my chance! I shouldn't complain, but still, it sure would be nice to be able to spend time with an adult! Share conversation without the expectation of being served!*

Katie soon got her wish. Cat bumped into her at the Flea Market one Saturday afternoon. Two strollers sat facing each other in the sunshine, carrying grumpy, hungry toddlers. The two women bubbled at the serendipity and exchanged phone numbers. Cat immediately began visiting Katie on her days off. Katie was overjoyed at the opportunity to get know Cat's darling daughter. Cat told her, "I chose you, to be Jule's Godmother." Katie beamed, and then grimaced briefly. "You know, that's probably not very helpful, choosing a dying woman to be god mother for your daughter. I'll probably be dead before she's grown." An uncomfortable silence fell briefly between them and Katie got up to check on the kids. She peaked in on the girls playing in the bedroom.

Katie returned to the living room and lit another cigarette. "They're fine. Off in their own little world." Cat forced a smile. "Well, you are not dying anytime soon. I won't allow it." She reached for her coffee and shifted in her seat. "And I'm not going anywhere anyway. I don't think you could get rid of me if you wanted to." The two women smoked cigarettes and drank coffee in the living room until the little girls emerged from the bedroom asking about lunch. "I will make sandwiches soon." Katie responded, "Now go back to the room and play. We will let you know when lunch is ready."

Katie and Cat's conversation migrated to the kitchen.

They talked about the stresses of dealing with toddlers who have more energy that their parents. As Katie cut the crusts of peanut butter and jelly sandwiches, Cat stacked them on a plate. After lunch, Cat drove the four of them around town. They ran errands together and shared the burden of corralling demanding toddlers through the grocery store together. While Katie complained a lot about the miseries associated with her love life, she truly relished the time she got to spend parenting. *I really do love being a mommy.*

Katie really liked the afternoons she spent with Cat. It was like co-parenting without the burden of being in a relationship. *Why can't it be this nice when my boyfriend is around?* Some days she was sicker than others, but Cat still came around. And Katie still tried her best to be a good mommy. So focused on the parenting, Katie didn't notice Cat falling in love with her.

It took less than a year for Katie's relationship to turn sour. *Why do I keep ending up with these assholes? I'm really going to miss being a mommy. This was great, but I just can't stay. I have to take care of myself.* Katie moved out of the hot little apartment and left the little girl behind with her father. *Yet another man that I had thought would be different, and then he wasn't.* She moved north to Sonoma County, to stay with her mother.

Katie's mom lived in a tiny place, a short walk's distance from a cute little beach on the Russian River. When Cat came to visit, she brought her daughter and Katie got more toddler time. Every visit was the same. Katie took control and played mommy, insisting that her best friend relax. "Let me take care of everything. I miss being a mommy, and you work too hard." Cat sat back and relaxed while Katie busied herself with the task of catering to meet whatever needs Jule presented.

The three of them would spend the afternoon together enjoying the beach. Jule spent time playing in the sun and sand and water. Picnics were always an adventure for the little girl. Meanwhile, Katie and Cat got to spend quality time with each other. They talked about the past, and what they thought the future might hold. Katie shied away from dreaming too much about her own future, as she knew her time was limited. So, they focused on imagining Jule's future. "What will the world be like for her when she is our age?" After a couple of hours playing at the river, Jule would get fussy and tired. Packing everything back up, they'd walk back to the little house.

Once the little girl was settled into a bed, Katie would suggest she do the cooking for Cat. Katie's mother would step in and insist they just relax and enjoy their visit, while she cooked for all of them. She enjoyed Jule as well and made comments about how it was fun to pretend to be a grandma.

Katie's mom tried to create a romantic atmosphere. Sometimes she was subtle, but this time she was fairly obvious about it. Katie called her mother out for it, trying to discourage the effort. "Mom. Just stop it. I am not gay like you. I love Firecat. Of course, I love her. She is my best friend. But I like men." Her mother frowned and shook her head, saying "penis" as almost a whisper."

Katie responded in retort. "That's right Mom, penis. P-E-N-I-S. I like all of it. Sorry to disappoint you." Cat sat silently, trying not to pay too much attention. Katie saw that the exchange made her friend uncomfortable and changed the subject. "Mom, why don't you play grandma? Jule is asleep anyway. We are going down to the corner store."

Katie grabbed Cat by the arm. "Come on. Let's take a walk." Cat threw on her shoes and stuffed her smokes in her pocket. Heading down the hill, Katie suggested they get a couple of beers. Drinking at her mother's house was not going to happen. Her mom was a sober alcoholic. They might not get along, but she knew better than to break the 'no alcohol at the house' rule. They held hands browsing through the corner market, giggling and chattering like they were 15 again.

Picking out a couple of tall bottles of beer they approached the cashier. He looked at them, and smiled, greeting Katie as a regular. "You ladies better hurry up! We are about to close, and I got plans tonight!" Cat insisted on paying for the beers, while the cashier put them neatly in their own brown paper sacks. He warned the two women to "stay out of trouble" as they left and then locked the door behind them.

Katie led her friend to a picnic bench nearby and motioned for them to sit down. Cat inquired about the local police and drinking on public. "They don't care. As long as we aren't being too loud or causing trouble, they won't give us trouble. Besides, they know me." Katie smiled. "A little flirting goes a long way. Love a man in a uniform." She opened up her beer and motioned for Cat to do the same. "We gotta finish these before we go back home. I would catch holy hell from my mother if I brought them home."

Smoking cigarettes and talking, they took about a half

hour to finish their 20-ounce bottles. They talked for a while longer and then headed back up the hill. Cat remarked that the hill seemed a little steeper walking up than it did coming down. Katie returned, "Ya? You should try it in the rain!" When they reached her mother's place, they sat outside and talked for a while longer, smoking another cigarette before heading inside. Once inside the room was dark and quiet. Cat didn't want to wake up her daughter, and Katie was tired, so they got ready for bed. Katie nestled into bed with her best friend and the little Jule lying between them. *Why can't I find a boyfriend that makes me happy like this?*

Living with her mom was meant to be a temporary arrangement while Katie was waiting for housing in San Francisco. She had gotten signed up on a waiting for a special subsidized housing project dedicated to terminally ill residents. It was taking longer than she would have liked and the weekdays seem to drag by. Getting to see her best friend on the weekends definitely eased the discomfort. Katie loved her mother, but it was clear that they did not live together well.

One weekend toward the end of Katie's stay, her mother was having a conversation with Cat. Katie's mom was casually referring to one of her friends as a transgender man. Katie rolled her eyes in disapproval. This was someone her mother had been spending time with and clearly Katie didn't get along with them. Cat was confused. "What's a transgender man?" The terminology used was not clear and she had to ask for clarification. Katie explained transgender men were women who were in the process of getting a sex change to male.

Why would a man hating lesbian want to become a man? She didn't understand. "I'm sure Cat doesn't want to hear about your weird friends Mom. She came to visit me, you know."

Full of too much coffee, Cat chattered on. "I have met so many lesbians who express revulsion towards men. The seeming hatred in the gay community has turned me off from trying to associate with any of them. Their prejudice feels no different than the prejudice against gays that straight people show." Normally, she didn't feel secure opening up, but for some reason she liked Katie's mom. "But I guess I'm bisexual. I mean, I don't really think about peoples' gender as much as I do their personality. I mean I usually get along with men better. Still, women are really attractive," she glanced at Katie, "but they are intimidating too."

Katie smacked her on the arm. "Shut up! We're not intimidating, we're awesome!"

Cat snapped back, grinning, "See what I mean?"

Katie's mom chuckled. "You two really should be a couple."

Katie snapped at her mom, "Don't start with that again!" Her mother admitted defeat and busied herself sweeping the kitchen floor. Cat gulped down the last of her coffee and put the empty cup on the counter. Thanking them both for another fantastic weekend, she said that she needed to head back to Walnut Creek and get ready for another work week.

Driving back home, Cat tried to recall memories of

talking with her mother about her grandfather getting a sex change. She knew they had talked about it, but it seemed so long ago. It was hard to remember. The idea of going through surgeries to permanently alter her body was terrifying. The idea of creating an even broader gap of prejudice between herself and people that she might potentially meet terrified her. *You probably have to be independently wealthy to be able to afford that kind of surgery.* The details of the process were never really discussed as Katie was quick to dismiss the conversation. Katie's voice echoed in her head, *"I'm sure Cat doesn't want to hear about your weird friends Mom. She came to visit me, you know."*

Cat was half curious. Still, she had gone to visit Katie, not her mother. The last thing she wanted to do was make her best friend uncomfortable. Cat wondered whether she might be able to talk with Katie's mother more about this during a later visit. But that never happened. Later that week, Katie called her best friend on the phone. "Guess what? My name came up! I am moving to San Francisco! Now I will be close enough to take BART to come visit you instead!" She was excited to finally be moving into her own place. Cat quickly forgot about talking with Katie's mother.

Chapter 35
Work In Progress

Cat had been working at the same place for over two years. She knew she made enough money to be on her own. Butting heads against her parents, it became clear that they would get along better if they were not living together. She decided that it was time. She really needed to move out. She needed her own space. She began working out the numbers, trying to figure out how much she could afford and how she would make it work. Soon she was looking for places within her price range.

It took a couple months, but by the end of the summer, Cat was signing papers and getting her own set of keys to a cute little duplex in Martinez. She had been half hoping to find a way to leave the Bay Area. However, the reality was hard to deny. A long-distance move was out of the question. She would have to stay where she had a job until she could save up quite a bit more money.

Cat was in love with the idea of having her own place. The duplex apartment wasn't ideal, placed directly across from a noxious refinery. *The price is right though. And it has a backyard with a privacy fence!* Barely six hundred square feet, the basement duplex provided just enough space for the two of them. The landlord lived upstairs, but his entrance was on the opposite side of the building, so she wouldn't have to see him often.

With the move, Cat also had to shop for a new childcare center. Jule had outgrown the old center and was ready for preschool. After touring a couple of places in Martinez, she found an excellent center. They had a garden and accelerated program for the children who showed exceptional talent in academics. The teachers there were pleased to have her daughter join their classes. She was glad to have found a place that was close to their new home. The dependency on her family had been severed. She was now taking care of everything.

Cat began bringing boxes over to the new home before the utilities were turned on. As soon as the electricity and gas were turned on, she brought Jule to their new home. She gave Jule the bedroom and settled herself into the small den outside of the bedroom. She bought Jule a brand-new toddler bed. She would not be in a crib and could get up and out of bed without assistance. The girl was ecstatic!

Organizing the bedroom was fun for both of them. Once that was done, Jule was excited to play independently in her new room while her mother worked on unpacking and organizing her own space in the den. Then Cat moved onto the kitchen with glee. She was excited to have her own kitchen and took great joy in organizing her cabinets.

The small backyard was mostly dirt, with small patches of grass. A large shade tree sat in the center of the yard, sheltering an old picnic table. In the late summer sun, Cat sat on the picnic table smoking while her daughter played in dirt with plastic dinosaurs. She tried to enjoy the warm summer breeze, while ignoring the foul stench it carried. Putting her cigarette out, she tilted her head up and closed her eyes. *Everything is going to be fine. We have reached our destination.*

Cat suddenly snapped her eyes wide open. She felt like someone was behind her. She looked down at her daughter, still contently getting filthy as she played. *You know there isn't anyone else here. You're just being weird.* She stood up on the picnic table, reached out her arms toward the tree, and pulled herself up. Climbing into the crux of the tree, she called out to Jule to look up.

The little girl looked up and laughed. "You're silly Mommy."

Cat smiled back at her daughter making silly faces, so she laughed again. She looked around the yard. *I can see everything from here and there is no one else here. See. You're just being weird.* She climbed back down out of the tree, lowering herself onto the picnic table before returning to the ground.

"Alright honey. You and your dinosaurs got pretty dirty! How about a bath?" Cat stooped down, to help gather the toys. Jule began to protest. "That's fine. You can carry all the dinosaurs if you want. I was just trying to help." The little girl realized she couldn't carry them all at the same time and handed her mother one dinosaur, then a second, before getting up. "Okay now, let's go inside and get cleaned up!"

"I can give my dinosaurs a bath?" Jule inquired, as they made their way through the kitchen door.

Cat chuckled. "Yes honey. They are all dirty. I definitely think that you need to give them a bath." She led her daughter into the bathroom and turned on the water in the tub before returning her attention to her daughter. Stripping her of her dirty clothes, she suggested that Jule use the toilet before getting into the bath. Once the tub was half full of bubbles, the child was happy to climb in and get to work on the task of bathing her toys. "Okay honey. I'm going to leave the door open so I can hear you. You just let me know when you are done, okay?"

Jule nodded, face covered with soap bubbles. "Okay Mommy."

Cat returned to the kitchen. She stepped back out the door, sat down on the stoop and lit up another cigarette. The setting sun filtered through the great tree, casting shadows across the yard. A chill ran down her spine and she peered out into the yard. "Who's out there?" Silence responded delivering a cold feeling of loneliness. *There is nobody there. What is wrong with you? Can't you even go for one whole day being happy with your life? Why do you always have to sabotage things? We have everything we need here. Don't ruin it.*

Cat put out the cigarette, and got up, stepping back into the kitchen. *It's a beautiful evening. You have a privacy fence. You don't need to shut the world out, just the flies.* She left the door open, closing only the screen behind here.

As soon as Cat got her phone turned on in the new place, she called her friends and updated them on her new phone number and address. With the landlord above, she would not have a housewarming party. Instead, she began inviting individual friends over for dinner on different evenings. It felt liberating to have her own space and was pleased to play hostess. She invited Tam and Allie for dinner one evening. She tried to invite Carrie, but her old friend seemed a little too busy. Then she called Katie who was pleased to come out for a visit to see the new place.

When Katie arrived, Cat was the happiest that she had been in a long time. Cat felt a warm feeling watching Katie play with Jule. She stayed for a few days, playing housewife while Cat was at work. When Cat got home with Jule after work, they took turns caring for the little girl while the other made dinner. Then, sitting altogether, they enjoyed dinner family style. After her daughter was asleep in bed, the two friends would stay up late drinking and talking. Eventually Cat would insist that they retire to bed, indicating that she 'had to work in the morning.' After a few days of this, Katie went back home to her place in the city.

At first, Cat was enthralled with her new surroundings. After only a few quiet nights in their new place, a feeling of loneliness began to return. Cat loved her daughter and the independence she had with her. Still, she longed for adult interaction. She wanted desperately to feel loved and needed as more than a parent.

Cat had gradually reconnected with a couple childhood friends. She had developed a couple of new friendships as well. Most of her friends were all on different schedules, in different places in their lives, and not connected to each other. The need to provide a consistent structured schedule and environment for her daughter kept her from being social as often as she needed.

To fill in the void, Cat spent long hours talking with Katie on the phone in the evenings. After Jule was in bed in her room, Cat paced the kitchen floor chatting on the phone with Katie. They talked about all kinds of things. They played Battleship over the phone. They each had a set, and it didn't require being in the same room. They laughed about the scenario.

Cat tried to talk her into coming back to visit them in Martinez. Katie was hesitant, battling her own health issues, she had appointments that kept her close to home. Occasionally, she'd come back to visit, and briefly, Cat would feel truly happy. When Katie returned home on the subway, Cat would curl up in bed alone and shut her eyes. *She is never going to love me the way I love her. What is wrong with me? You should be happy. You have everything you need.*

Pulling up the blankets, Cat rolls over to face the wall. Shadows fall on the baseboard from the soft living room light. Something about the darkness had always frightened her. She had often slept with the light on. It wasn't the dark necessarily that frightened her, but something beyond the darkness, a shadow that followed her, just out of sight. Falling into sleep, she let herself forget about her fears and just relax.

Cat had been in counseling for a couple of years. Her counselor noted all the progress that Firecat had made. She had gotten full time employment, received a promotion, and was successfully raising her daughter on her own without child support or roommates. The counselor suggested that since her patient was doing much better, it may be time to move from individual counseling to a group. The counselor suggested that Cat might find her anxieties to be less overwhelming if she was meeting with others who experienced similar feelings.

Soon after, Cat stopped seeing a counselor and instead, began attending a single mother's support group. She only went for a few weeks before she began intentionally missing the scheduled meetings. It seemed to her that these women spent the whole time bitching about how terrible men were. *This isn't emotional support. It's just emotional vomit.* The experience did not feel productive to her.

Cat didn't want to focus on the negative of other people's mistakes. She wanted to become stronger within herself. A couple more inconsistent visits, and she was struck by a distinct feeling of being in the wrong place. *I know I am supposed to feel connected to these women. Our common experiences are supposed to help us feel supported by each other. Then why is it that the person I relate to the most in this long sob story is her ex-husband. Geez. I would leave her too.*

Cat felt ashamed of her internal dialogue. Silently, she listened and only spoke up when she was pressured to 'take a turn.' She knew that the women's group was meant to be a safe place and she felt like she was violating the sanctity of their safety by being there. *It doesn't make sense. But I don't feel comfortable here either.* Before long, she simply stopped attending.

Cat continued to lose weight, fitting into pants that had been Dad's years before. She began wearing the men's suit pants with nice sweaters to work. In the office, it was perceived as professional attire. At home, alone in the bathroom, she played with bandages and scarves. Experimenting with different ways of binding her breasts, she tried to imagine what she would look like as a guy.

She played dress up, trying to make herself look the way she imagined she might look if she were male. Toying with the idea of actually going out in public that way, she always ended up taking the binding off before anyone actually saw her. *What if somebody saw me. What would they say?*

Between pushing through her work schedule and filling her weekends with road trips and visits, another year had passed. Cat's birthday was rapidly approaching, and she had been promoted again at work. Now she was a Teamleader with her own team of phone representatives to monitor and supervise. More responsibility and a mentorship from one of the managers had succeeded in rounding off some of her gritty edges.

Cat learned better how to present her ideas for growth and improvement without offending her professional peers. She learned how to speak in a politically correct manner. Her professional posture was beginning to reflect less of her street experiences, and more of her responsible 'adult' habits. Her success in the workplace had its drawbacks. The harder she pushed the worse her mood swings got. She began to once again feel like she was living on a roller coaster. Experiencing extreme mood swings began to affect her ability to function properly at work. In an effort to maintain control of her physical and mental health, she decided it was time to actually go to a doctor. With her employer sponsored medical insurance, she embarked on a new kind of roller coaster ride.

The doctor explained that finding the right medicine for anxiety and depression was like an experiment. "Mental health is not an exact science. There isn't really a test I can just give you to determine what medication is going to help." The doctor explained to Cat. "Different people have different reactions to medications, so we just have to rely on the 'trial and error' method until we get it right."

Cat accepted the prescription given to her. She made sure to always take the medicine as prescribed but was unhappy with the results. The new pills seemed to be making things worse, so she went back, and he gave her a different prescription. Again, side effects propelled her along a difficult roller coaster. She returned once more to the doctor.

"I can't take this anymore!" Cat cried to the doctor. "I'm exhausted and depressed all the time now. I keep falling asleep at work, even after I slept all night. I am going to end up getting fired from my job if something doesn't change." She pleaded with the doctor. "I know that we have to just keep trying, but until we get it right, how am I supposed to function?"

The doctor gave Cat a letter recommending that she take a temporary medical leave of absence while they attempted to get her medication and mood swings under control. He also issued her a referral to a Psychiatrist.

"A Psychiatrist will be better equipped to help you find the correct medication." The doctor suggested. "Once you and the Psychiatrist agree that you are stable enough, you will be able to go back to work." He informed her that the Psychiatrist's office would be calling her to set up her first appointment. Before she left, he added. "Now bring this letter to your work. The Family Medical Leave Act will protect you with the letter." She accepted the letter, nodding solemnly. Keenly aware of his patient's uneasiness, he added, "Don't worry. Everything is going to be fine."

Cat brought doctor's note to the Human Resources department. She was embarrassed and ashamed. *I always knew there was something wrong with me, and now I have a doctor's note to prove it.* The ladies in the HR department were polite and gentle with Cat. Having grown fond of her off-the-wall personality, they told her that they looked forward to her coming back to work.

"But don't feel like you have to rush." They added. "FMLA Leave is for healing, so take your time. We don't want you to come back until you are ready." They pulled out a stack of paperwork and dropped it on the desk in front of Cat. She blinked, confused. "These are the forms that you need to complete and mail to the Unemployment Department. So that you can continue to receive an income while on medical leave." They made a couple of copies of the doctor's note for her, so that she could include one with the application, and keep one for her records. They filed the original letter away and then urged her to 'go on home and get some rest.'

Once home, Cat completed the forms she had received at work. Stuffing an envelope with the forms and copy of the doctor's note, she dropped it off directly at the unemployment office on her way to pick Jule up from school.

The following day, Cat received a call from the Psychiatrist's office. They conducted a screening over the phone and then scheduled her for her first appointment the following week. She continued to get up at the same time and get Jule ready for school. She took her daughter to school and picked her up at the same time as if she was at work. She tried to hide her illness from her daughter, but Jule was too perceptive.

The Psychiatrist prescribed Cat all manner of pills that she didn't like taking. She felt like she was just hopping off one roller coaster to embark on another. Like a roller coaster, she felt nauseous and exhausted from the ride. Returning home after dropping Jule off at school, she laid down on the couch and cried. Sobbing and shaking she allowed it to all flow out of her. *It's okay to be sad sometimes. Nobody here can see me. I am safe here. Eventually I will run out of tears and then I can go back to living.*

Without a regular work schedule, Cat found she had acquired a much-needed vacation from the daily grind she had been subjecting herself to. She knew that when it was too rainy, Tam and Allie didn't bother trying to set up their jewelry stand in Berkeley. Instead, they stayed home in the warmth and worked on producing more inventory. She decided that she was tired of being lonely, and spending the rainy weekdays visiting Allie was much better for her than laying on the couch crying by herself. Visiting Allie while Jule was at school, Cat found a happy place inside herself. Something about spending time with Allie filled her up the way spending time with Katie did. *Only when Katie leaves, I am sad. After visiting with Allie, I feel like I am walking on clouds. Spending time with her feels natural.* Cat could be herself around Allie, without having to think about what that meant.

Upon Cat's arrival, Tam greeted her with open arms and no questions. Allie was always pleased with the visits. Mutually, they lavished in the comfort that they afforded each other. Both women were going through their own hardships and they licked one another's wounds with unconditional love and acceptance.

For a few weeks, there were some days when Cat didn't even bother to take Jule to school because she was too depressed to get dressed or leave the house. She was overly conscious about her daughter seeing her in that state. She cried too much. Dishes piled up. Laundry piled up. Everything seemed to be falling apart. Soon, it became clear she would not be able to maintain financially for long on disability. She returned to the psychiatrist to review the medication regiment and told him that 'it would just have to do'. The doctor issued a return-to-work letter and urged her to continue to follow up on her appointments.

Cat couldn't take it any longer. *It doesn't matter if I feel like hell. I have to put on the happy face. I have to make this work. My daughter is depending on me and I don't have any other choice.* She dragged her game face out of a box underneath her bed and went back to work.

A combination of Buspar and Effexor were meant to keep Cat from crying or having panic attacks at work. One Ritalin in the morning was meant keep her from falling asleep. One Ambien at night helped her to go to sleep. Cat pushed through each day with a rhythmic structure dictated by her daughter's needs, her medication schedule, her work schedule, and the overarching schedule of when bills were due. Moving into autopilot, she stopped feeling lonely and just settled into exhausted. It didn't matter if she had a social life. There wasn't any time for that anymore.

Cat had achieved her goals. She was now an independent, self-sufficient, single parent. She went to her doctor's appointments. She went to the grocery store. She went to work. She went home. Auto-pilot took over and she was not present except when engaged with her daughter. The shadow that had been following her seemed to disappear. The pills took over and Cat went numb. There was no shadow. There was no darkness. There was only gray and the light of the little Jule beside her.

I have no reason to complain. I have no reason to worry. This is my life, and I am in control. Holding back tears she could not feel, Cat wrapped her arms around her little girl. "I love you little Julie."

Jule accepted the embrace, letting her mother pick her up and dance her around the room. "I love you too Mommy."

Epilogue

In March of 1999, the winds of change blew Will and Mama back to the Bay Area. With them came a sadness that Mama was not ready to face. Will knew that he had failed her and found himself struggling to offer comfort. They had shared few words since the social worker had taken away their son. Will knew her heart was breaking and felt powerless to help. In an effort to cheer up his lady, he drove them to her favorite restaurant in North Berkeley.

Sitting across the table from each other the couple silently hid behind their respective menus. Will raked his mind, searching for the right words. *She feels like she lost her daughter, and now I've lost our son. What could I possibly say or do to make this right for her?* He took a deep breath before asking her, "Do you know what you're having?"

Mama put down the menu, carefully placing it on the edge of the table. "I'll have the same thing I always do." She smiled gingerly. "I do love the salad here."

Will put his menu down on top of hers signaling the server to approach their table. "The lady will have the Harvest Salad with chicken and apples, a side of balsamic and oil, and a pot of hot black tea." He waited for the server to stop writing before continuing their order. "I will have the meatloaf dinner with the garden salad." He handed the server their menus, concluding with, "and two glasses of water please."

The server nodded and scurried away to retrieve their

glasses of water. She returned, placing the glasses of water at their table. "Anything else I can get for you right now?"

"No thank you." Mama responded, smiling courteously up at the young woman. "We're fine."

The server left the couple to attend to other guests. Mama and Will sat silently enjoying the warmth of the restaurant. Soon the server returned with a tray. She placed the pot of tea on the table in front of Mama. Then she placed the teacup next to the pot, cautioning her patron 'to wait a bit for it to steep and cool.' Mama nodded in understanding and the server left them alone again.

Will took a deep breath. "You know, we could call Firecat." Mama looked scornfully at her partner and he apologized. "I'm sorry honey, I just know that you miss her."

"And what would I say to her?" Mama asked. "I have no good news and nothing to offer her."

Will started to respond but held back his words. Silently, he reached across the table squeezing Mama's hand. She squeezed back in response. Sharing the moment, their eyes recognized each other's pain. Time stood still until the server returned with their dinner.

Mama smiled wide revealing an awkward grin. "This really is my favorite restaurant, and this is my favorite meal." She looked at Will, who had already begun clearing his plate. "Thank you, sweetheart. I know you mean well." She picked up her knife and began cutting up the chicken and apples into tiny pieces. "I just wish I had more teeth to chew it!" She laughed at herself before placing a strategically portioned bite into her mouth.

"I love you." Will responded between mouthfuls. "I just want you to be happy."

The couple took their time finishing their meal. Will put forty dollars on the table and got up from his chair. He took Mama's coat off the back of her chair. She got up and put her arms in the sleeves of her coat as he held it for her. Then he handed Mama her walking stick and offered his arm to her. With the walking stick in her left hand, and right arm linked in his, the two walked out of the restaurant together.

Greeting the chilly March evening, they walked up the block to where their home was parked. Will opened the passenger door for his lady. She stepped up into the passenger seat of the RV, placing her walking stick between her legs. Will closed the door and walked around the front of the RV to the driver's side. He opened the door, climbed in, and started the engine.

Will pulled into traffic, heading south. *What can I do? All I can do is my best.* He looked over at his lady to see her face go white. "Honey?"

Mama put her hand over her heart. "Oh my!" Pain shot through her chest and the world began to dim. Mama's hands suddenly fell limp in her lap and her head slumped against the window.

CPSIA information can be obtained
at www.ICGtesting.com
Printed in the USA
BVHW081053230621
610212BV00002B/46